The Family

The Family

Shimazaki Toson

Translated and with an introduction by
Cecilia Segawa Seigle

UNIVERSITY OF TOKYO PRESS

UNESCO COLLECTION OF REPRESENTATIVE WORKS:
JAPANESE SERIES

This book has been accepted in the Japanese Series of the
Translation Collection of the United Nations Educational,
Scientific and Cultural Organization (UNESCO)

Translated from the Japanese original
IE by Shimazaki Toson
© Shimazaki Osuke
Published in English in Japan by arrangement with Orion Press

ISBN 4-13-087022-X
ISBN 0-86008-165-6

Third paperback printing, 1989

Acknowledgments

I am greatly indebted to Professors Hiroshi Miyaji and E. Dale Saunders, both of the University of Pennsylvania, for their invaluable advice and for the many hours they devoted to supervising the translation. No words of gratitude can adequately express my deep appreciation to both of them.

My thanks also go to Dr. Adele Rickett, Dr. Barbara Ruch and Professor Adolph Klarmann for their reading of the manuscript and their valuable suggestions for its improvement.

I wish to express my deep thanks to Kawazoe Kunimoto, of Waseda University, and Senuma Shigeki, of Nihon University, for their help. Professor Senuma provided me with the galley proofs of volume XVIII of *Toson Zenshu* (The Complete Works of Shimazaki Toson), published in eighteen volumes by Chikuma Shobo between 1966 and 1971. This volume would not otherwise have been available to me. Furthermore, I have depended heavily on Toson's biographies written by both of these scholars. My thanks also go to Mr. Shimazaki Kusuo, of Magome, for information he supplied orally concerning Toson; to Mrs. Takase Teru, of Kiso-Fukushima, and Mrs. Furuhata Toshie, of Tsumago, for their assistance; and to Mr. Takahashi Kazuo, of Chikuma Shobo, for his letter.

My deepest thanks go, above all, to my husband, Dr. Daniel Seigle, without whose understanding, encouragement, patience, and assistance I could not have completed this work.

Japanese names are written in the Japanese style: surname first and given name last. I have followed the Japanese custom of using pen names in referring to literary figures, e.g., Shimazaki Toson rather than Shimazaki Haruki, and Tayama Katai rather than Tayama Rokuya. Chinese-style pen names such as Toson are often used independently as in the Japanese custom. The translation is based on the text as it appears in volume IV of *Toson Zenshu*.

Philadelphia, 1971

v

Translator's Introduction

Toson's Biography

Shimazaki Haruki (Toson) was born on March 25, 1872 in Magome, Misaka Village, Nishi-Chikuma-gun, Nagano Prefecture. He was the fourth son and youngest of seven children born to Shimazaki Masaki (1831–86) and Shimazaki Nui (1837–96). Toson lived in Magome for the first eight years of his life, and nostalgia for his childhood remained with him ever after, as did his basically provincial taste and lifestyle, even though he lived in Tokyo a good part of his life.

As is repeatedly recorded in his writings, Toson's father saw in him an innate love of learning and often said, "Haruki is my son, my spiritual heir." When Toson was nine, he and his older brother Tomoya were sent to study in Tokyo. They stayed with their sister Takase Sonoko and entered Taimei, one of the most modern elementary schools in Japan at the time.

Sonoko and her husband, Takase Kaoru, returned to their home in Kiso-Fukushima the year after Toson went to Tokyo, and he was relocated in the household of an old acquaintance. A year later he moved to the household of Yoshimura Tadamichi, the man Toson called *onjin* (benefactor) throughout his life. Yoshimura had come to Tokyo from Kiso with his wife and her mother to seek his fortune. A boy, Shigeru, was born while Toson was staying with the family, and the two were brought up as brothers.

After he graduated from elementary school at the age of fourteen, he briefly attended two preparatory schools. In September 1887, he entered Meiji Gakuin, a Presbyterian school run by American and Scottish churches, for his college education. He was fifteen at the time, one of the youngest students in the school.

Less than a year later he was baptized at the district Presbyterian church by the minister, Kimura Kumaji. Christianity was the only religion Toson ever embraced, though briefly. Although religion interested him in his later years, he remained critical of it.

In his first years at Meiji Gakuin, Toson was somewhat of a dandy, ambitious, and dreamed of becoming a politician. Being a top student, his foreign instructors liked him very much and always directed the most difficult questions his way. He began to change after the second year; for some reason he ceased caring for fashionable clothes and lost all desire to be well thought of by his professors. Still, in his own way, he was absorbing all he wanted to learn. He translated Morley's *English Men of Letters,* a collection of critical biographies of eighteenth-century poets and writers. He read Byron, Burns, Shakespeare, Matthew Arnold, Wordsworth, and Milton in the original, and Dante and Goethe in English translation. He graduated in 1891 near the bottom of the class with no plans for the future and decided to help out at Katsushin's emporium of imported goods in Yokohama, which his benefactor, Yoshimura, managed. Nevertheless, he was more interested in reading the English translation of Taine's *History of English Literature,* which he concealed under his desk at the store.

Early in 1892, Toson began helping Iwamoto Yoshiharu (1863–1943) translate articles for Iwamoto's *Jogaku Zasshi* (Magazine for Female Instruction). This was Toson's first venture into creative writing, and the world of literature unfolded before him.

In September of the same year, Toson took a teaching position at Meiji Jogakko, a modern girls' school where Iwamoto was dean. He used Taine's *History* as a basis for his lectures. He was twenty, younger than most of his students in the junior college division, and soon he fell desperately in love with one of his students, Sato Sukeko (1871–95), who was a year older than he and already betrothed. In less than five months Toson resigned from the school, unable to cope with his unrequited love which was doomed because of Toson's poverty and Sukeko's betrothal. He borrowed money and began wandering aimlessly. For ten months he traveled along the Tokaido Highway to the Kyoto area and Shikoku. This self-appointed exile was styled after the wanderings of the poet Basho (1644–96), and he wrote poems, essays, and plays in verse, which were published in *Bungakkai* (Literary World) magazine.

A frequent contributor to *Jogaku Zasshi* and *Bungakkai* was Kitamura Tokoku (1868–94), who gave young Toson lifelong fuel for his creative drive and inspiration. Their friendship lasted only two years, as Kitamura committed suicide in 1894, but Toson's affection and respect for his friend grew with the years, and he continued to discover new meaning in Tokoku's brief leadership as the guiding light for young Meiji writers. Tokoku's spirit of individualism, respect for humanity, and idealistic fight for a new morality greatly influenced Toson, who learned from Tokoku to value, examine, and develop one's self as much as possible. All his life Toson searched for his identity as an individual.

Returning from his wanderings, Toson was forced to resume a teaching position at Meiji Jogakko in April 1894, for the care of his mother was suddenly thrust upon him. His eldest brother, Hideo, had been involved in a questionable business deal and was imprisoned. In August 1895, Sato Sukeko, who had married, died during pregnancy. Toson was heartbroken and resigned from his position immediately.

From September 1896 to July 1897 he taught at Tohoku Gakuin in Sendai, where he felt that his life "dawned" and that his "winter days" were over; the words began to flow from his pen. He published his first poetic anthology, *Wakana-shu* (A Collection of Young Leaves), in August 1897. His poems were written in simple, everyday language; "his words are nothing when standing alone; yet when combined, they result in an astonishing freshness and originality."[1] The charm of his passionate, lyrical, or pathetic poems captured the imagination of younger Meiji writers and poets. Back in Tokyo, Toson wrote the novel *Utatane* (A Cat Nap) in 1897, an important work because it was his first effort in colloquial Japanese.

In April 1898, he entered the Tokyo Conservatory piano department. This rather unusual move was prompted by his interest in the sound of words in poetry, and lasted only a year. In the summer of 1898, he visited the Takase house in Kiso-Fukushima, Nagano Prefecture, where he completed a collection of poems, *Natsukusa* (Summer Grasses). *The Family* opens with a description of the first days of his visit to the Takase house.

---

[1] Yano Mineto, "Toson to Ariake" (Toson and Ariake), *Geirinkanpo* (Essays on Art), XIX (Jan. 1948), p. 36.

In April 1899, Toson accepted an invitation from his former teacher and minister, Kimura Kumaji, to teach English and Japanese at Komoro School, a small secondary institution founded and directed by Kimura and located in the obscure town of Komoro in the foothills of Mount Asama. He returned to Tokyo in the same month to marry Hata Fuyuko, the daughter of Hata Keiji, a wholesale merchant of fish nets in Hakodate, Hokkaido. The marriage had been arranged by his friend Iwamoto. Toson was twenty-seven and Fuyuko twenty-two when they moved into their first house where they began an extremely frugal life together.

In May 1900, their first daughter, Midori, was born. Toson became a good friend of the artist Miyake Katsumi (1874–1954), who had gone to Komoro in 1899 to teach and paint landscapes of the area. Miyake often carried an easel and sketchbook as the two strolled together, and Toson also carried an easel, which he used as a desk for writing down his observations. He accumulated a number of word sketches over the years, and later incorporated much of this material into stories and novels. He published essays entitled *Chikumagawa no Suketchi* (Sketches of the Chikuma River) in 1912.

In 1901, *Rakubai-shu* (The Collection of Fallen Plums), a fourth collection of poems, appeared; this was to be his last venture in poetry. Toson's transition from poetry to the novel was not an abrupt one; he had always written prose in one form or another. During his *Bungakkai* days, he wrote long poems with dramatic plots as he groped for an outlet for his creative drive other than short lyrical poems. Gradually he began to feel that the novel was the most appropriate form for expressing his ideas.

In November 1902, he published *Kyu Shujin* (The Former Master) and *Wara Zori* (The Straw Shoes) in two different magazines. The response of the literary world was favorable, and Toson wrote several more novellas marked by strong local color. *Suisai Gaka* (The Watercolorist), published in 1904, was the most successful, and it gained unexpected publicity from protests made by the artist Maruyama Banka (1867–1942). The story was based on a letter written by Toson's wife to her former boyfriend and on Toson's love for the pianist Tachibana Itoe (1873–1939), both of which are described in chapters V and VI of *The Family*. Toson had used both episodes in connection with a character resembling Maruyama, who taught art at Komoro, and who later charged that Toson's impropriety resulted in considerable distress to his family. Many Japanese critics have considered Toson to be a writer of limited imagination. His self-taught ability to observe things enabled him to reproduce reality in his works, but it resulted more than once in protests from those after whom his fictional characters were obviously modeled.

Toson's first novel, an important step in his recognition as a novelist, was *Hakai* (The Broken Commandment), published in March 1906. As described in Chapter X of *The Family*, the work was begun in Komoro during the spring of 1904. When the idea for the novel had become fairly well formulated in July 1904, he went to see his father-in-law, Hata Keiji, in Hakodate to request 400 yen for publishing a private edition of the novel. Hata agreed to lend him the money, so Toson resigned from the school to concentrate on writing. He still required additional help to meet living expenses and approached Kozu Takeshi, a wealthy young landlord in Nagano Prefecture, for help; Kozu agreed to give him assistance. Toson's appeal to Kozu and his decision to leave Komoro in order to concentrate on writing in Tokyo are faithfully described in *The Family*. Kozu sent Toson money, food, and other material gifts for years, as Toson's numerous thank-you notes attest.

Toson left Komoro with his pregnant wife and three daughters in April 1905 and moved into a new house in Minami Toshima-gun in Tokyo. The next eleven months were a veritable battle for him, and his struggle to produce his first novel was difficult and took its own toll. He lost his three daughters, one after another, within a year. Although their deaths were caused by meningitis and intestinal catarrh, Toson, in fact, regarded them as sacrifices; the last ten chapters of *The Family* were entitled "Sacrifices" in the original publication. Most likely, the children had been deprived of the necessary means to maintain adequate physical resistance to the fatal diseases because of the tightly budgeted life Toson subjected his family to in order to continue his writing. In the end there was artistic, if not financial, success. *Hakai* won acclaim from both the literary world and the public as the first modern Japanese novel comparable to those of Europe.

THE SHIMAZAKI(Koizumi)*FAMILY*

MASAKI = NUI
(1831–1886)   (1837–1896)
(Koizumi Tadahiro)

THE TAKASE
(Hashimoto)
FAMILY

KAORU=SONOKO
(1856–1914) (1856–1920)
(Tatsuo)   (Otane)

TAZU
(1878–1932)
(Osen)

CHIKAO=MISAO or
(1875–1910) SETSUKO
(Shota)   (1879–1955)
           (Toyose)

HIDEO=KOMAE or
(1858–1924) MATSUE
(Minoru)   (1861–1929)
           (Okura)

SAIMARU=ISA
TETSUZO (1887–)
(1882–) (Oshun)

SAIMARU
SHIHO
(1911–)

SHIMAZAKI
TOSHIKI
(1912–)

SHUJI
(1894–1894)

TSUTAKO
(1898–1909)
(Otsuru)

HIROSUKE=ASA
(1860–1928) (1871–1918)
(Morihiko)

HISAKO
(1890–)
(Onobu)

KOMAKO
(1893–)
(Okinu)

SHIGEKI
(1907–1927)

SHOJIRO
(1913–)

TSUGI
(Died in
infancy)

YO

TOMOYA
(1869–1911)
(Sozo)

HARUKI=FUYUKO
(1872–1943) (1878–1910)
(Sankichi) (Oyuki)

MIDORI
(1900–1906)
(Ofusa)

TAKAKO
(1902–1906)
(Okiku)

NUIKO
(1904–1905)
(Oshige)

KUSUO
(1905–)
(Taneo)

KEIJI
(1907–1944)
(Shinkichi)

OSUKE
(1908–)
(Ginzo)

RYUKO
(1910–)

In October 1906, Toson moved to Asakusa-ku near the Sumida River, where he lived until he left for France in 1913. Here he wrote *Haru* (Spring), and between 1908 and 1909 he wrote sixteen short stories, which were later published as *Toson-shu* (A Collection of Toson Stories). He wrote *The Family* from 1910 to 1911.

Members of the Shimazaki and Takase families described in The Family

The novel *The Family* covers a period of twelve years, from 1898 to 1910, and deals with the disintegration of the Koizumi and Hashimoto families. In reality, the former is the Shimazaki family, formerly of Magome, that moved to Tokyo in 1893, and the latter is the Takase family, of Kiso-Fukushima, Nagano Prefecture, into which Toson's elder sister Sonoko married. The genealogical chart of the two families will clarify the relationship between them. The names appearing in parentheses are fictionalized ones occurring in *The Family*.

The Shimazaki Family

The Shimazaki Family originated from the prominent Miura clan of the peninsula of the same name during the Kamakura period (1185–1333).

SHIMAZAKI KENMOTSU   In 1513, a descendant of the Miura family, Shimazaki Kenmotsu Shigetsuna, moved to the Kiso Valley and became a vassal of the Kiso clan, a branch of the Minamoto. He lived in Tsumago, and the eldest of his four sons established the Magome branch of the Shimazaki family, to which Toson's family traced its origin. The second son inherited his father's house in Tsumago. These were the two branches of the Shimazakis of Kiso.

SHIMAZAKI MASAKI (Koizumi Tadahiro)   Toson's father was the seventeenth head of the Magome Shimazakis. Although the family's prestige in the community remained unchanged, the repeal of the post station system by 1870 and the construction of a railroad that bypassed Magome and left the family outside modernizing currents resulting in a change in its fortunes. The Shimazaki family was still held in esteem by the villagers and Masaki remained the head of the village until 1873, but his possessions rapidly dwindled because of his son Hideo's mismanagement, and with them went his mental faculties. After several years of insanity, Masaki died in 1886.

SHIMAZAKI HIDEO (Koizumi Minoru)   In 1875, Toson's oldest brother succeeded as head of the family. Hideo was an honest and sincere man but extremely gullible and visionary. He conceived four ambitious enterprises and failed in each one. Hideo went to prison in May 1894, after assuming the entire responsibility for the second enterprise, and was released three years later. His third failure was the invention and manufacture of carriages to be moved by manpower instead of horses; the business venture is described in Chapter III of *The Family*. Hideo lost what he had salvaged of the family's and much of his friends' capital. The fourth adventure ended in his being imprisoned for two years while the guilty parties went free. As a result of this final blow, his younger brothers Hirosuke and Toson advised him to leave the country;[2] he went to Taiwan in 1906. This meeting is described in Chapter XIV of *The Family*.

SHIMAZAKI ISA (Oshun) and TSUTAKO (Otsuru)   Hideo and Komae (Okura) had three children. When the oldest, Isa, was about eleven, Toson encouraged her to take art lessons. She studied with Noguchi Shohin (1847–1917), a woman Chinese-style painter. Isa was married to Saimaru Tetsuzo in 1909 and became well known as Saimaru Shoen, specializing in the southern Sung style of painting.

The second daughter, Tsutako, died on April 2, 1909 at the age of eleven, after being pushed off a second-floor staircase by a classmate at school.

SHIMAZAKI HIROSUKE (Koizumi Morihiko)   Toson's sec-

[2]Letter 474, *TZ*, XVII, p. 244, written much later (Dec. 9, 1916), refers to this meeting.

ond oldest brother was stoic and spartan in conviction and lifestyle. Adopted as a child by his mother's family, the Tsumago Shimazakis, he later married his cousin. Like all other Shimazaki-Takase heads, Hirosuke neglected his home, but not for the same reason as the others. He lived away from home and devoted much of his life to public causes. From the age of twenty, he was involved in the so-called Forestry Incident, which is frequently mentioned in *The Family* but not explained.

The incident refers to a series of disputes, lasting several decades, between the government and inhabitants of the Kiso Valley, over the ownership and use of the rich forest stands in the Kiso area. Toson's father had been involved in the struggle, as was Hirosuke who exerted his own efforts until 1905, at which time final reparations were made by the government to the Kiso Valley inhabitants. Another incident concerning hydroelectric power development of Kiso River occurred, and Hirosuke opened new negotiations with the government. The dispute ended in 1926 with the granting of indemnities to Kiso villages.

During the entire period in which Hirosuke worked for the public interest, he lived in dire poverty away from his family. Even after the Kiso River incident, he refused to accept a proffered remuneration.

SHIMAZAKI HISAKO (Onobu) and KOMAKO (Okinu)   Hirosuke and Asa had four children, two girls and two boys. Only the older two, Hisako and Komako appear in *The Family*. After finishing the eighth grade in Tsumago, Hisako went to Tokyo to live with Toson's family and entered Joshi Gakuin. Unable to cope with advanced class work, she was at first plagued with constant headaches, to which Toson refers in *The Family*. She withdrew and went to another school. Her cousin Isa came to help look after the household during the summer of 1906 when Toson's wife made a trip to her home in Hokkaido. Komako followed her sister to Tokyo and entered Miwata Jogakko.

SHIMAZAKI TOMOYA (Sozo)   Toson's third brother was born to Toson's mother, Nui, and Inabaya, a Buddhist ascetic in

[3]Saimaru, p. 42.

Magome, in Masaki's absence.[3] The knowledge of his birth seems to have contributed to Tomoya's unhappy and cynical "black sheep" personality. Tomoya went to Tokyo with Toson and entered Taimei School, but when he flunked and Toson skipped one grade, he refused to be in the same class and quit school. He began to work as an apprentice at a paper wholesaler, but left the job as described in *The Family,* having struck the chief clerk on the head with an abacus. About 1891, he reappeared in Magome, but only caused trouble for his mother and Hideo's wife. It is said that he made advances to his sister-in-law, and again disappeared after Hideo reproached him.[4] When Hideo's family moved to Tokyo in 1893, he landed upon them again. Venereal disease had left him, paralyzed, and during the last three or four years of his life he lost his sight. Tomoya is said to have been the best writer of *waka,* traditional Japanese poetry, in the Shimazaki family.[5]

SHIMAZAKI FUYUKO (Oyuki)   Toson's wife was the second of six daughters of Hata Keiji of Hakodate, Hokkaido.

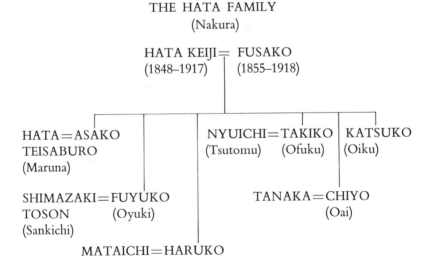

THE HATA FAMILY
(Nakura)

HATA KEIJI= FUSAKO
(1848–1917) (1855–1918)

HATA=ASAKO   NYUICHI=TAKIKO KATSUKO
TEISABURO   (Tsutomu) (Ofuku) (Oiku)
(Maruna)

SHIMAZAKI=FUYUKO   TANAKA=CHIYO
TOSON   (Oyuki)   (Oai)
(Sankichi)

MATAICHI=HARUKO

The head of the Hata family was a wealthy wholesaler of fishing

[4]Saimaru, p. 43.
[5]Senuma, *Hyoden,* p. 67.

net, a self-made, practical man. Fuyuko graduated in 1896 from Meiji Jogakko. Although Toson was unhappy about his wife's lack of understanding of his work and came to distrust all women because of her,[6] the couple grew close toward the end of her life.

The Takase Family

The Takase family came from the Kikuchi clan of Kyushu, which moved to Kiso-Fukushima around 1614. Yasumichi (d. 1813), known as Kitsuo, or "Old Man Orange," is called Chikuo ("Old Man Bamboo") in *The Family*. Toson says he was the founder of the Takase apothecary, but the history of the family business goes back to the late seventeenth century.

TAKASE KAORU (Hashimoto Tatsuo)   Takase Kaoru was the tenth head of the family. He married Toson's sister Sonoko in 1874. Around 1879, Kaoru's philandering caused the hereditary managers of the apothecary to depose him as the family head and send him to Tokyo. There Kaoru opened another apothecary, but he was not happy with the family trade and became a schoolmaster. By the time Toson came to Tokyo in 1881 to live with Kaoru's family, he had already obtained another position. Nothing lasted very long since Kaoru was spoiled and easily tempted by feminine charm. He returned to Kiso in 1882 and taught at an elementary school in a nearby town until he was permitted to return home to follow the family trade.

As Toson says in *The Family*, the time he visited the Takase family in the opening scene was probably the best for Kaoru. The family trade was prosperous, and Kaoru enjoyed social prestige. He soon came to be associated with the management of the Kiso Bank in his hometown, evidently embezzled bank money, and in order to cover the expense, invested heavily in one of Shimazaki Hideo's enterprises. When Hideo's venture collapsed, Kaoru fled with his geisha mistress, leaving his family with no resources.

[6]In *The Family* he expresses trust, then disappointment, in his wife: "His desire to learn about women came also from what Toson does not mention: his mother's adultery. Senuma, *Hyoden*, p. 74; *Zadankai Meiji Bungaku-shi* (Colloquium: A History of Meiji Literature) ed. by Yanagida Izumi *et al.* (Tokyo, 1961), p. 244.

TAKASE SONOKO (Otane)   Sonoko, Toson's eldest sister, was probably the most unfortunate of all Toson's relatives, a "true representative of the Japanese woman of the old days."[7] As Toson repeatedly mentions, Sonoko, of all the children, most resembled her father in looks and disposition. In 1873, she was betrothed to a young man she disliked, and slashed her own throat in an attempt at suicide. The Takase family was impressed by her courage and arranged her marriage with Kaoru, the family heir.

She was constantly plagued by her husband's philandering, and repression and frustration gradually led to mental disorder. Some scholars, and even her relatives, attribute her insanity to the venereal disease she contracted from her husband and from which she suffered throughout her life, but it is more likely that she inherited schizophrenic tendencies from her father. Toson had special affection for Sonoko. Similar to his love and respect for his father, his feeling toward her seems to have increased with age. He depicts Otane in *The Family* with a mixture of detachment and pity.

TAKASE CHIKAO (Hashimoto Shota)   Sonoko's son did not have much formal education, and little is known about his early life. About 1903, when the Takase family went into bankruptcy, he struggled to save the apothecary with the managers Shimojo Junsaku (Kasuke in *The Family*) and Yasuda Bunkichi (Kosaku). Chikao soon left the business to Bunkichi and in 1905 went to Tokyo with his wife, whom he had married in 1900. His whereabouts from 1905 to 1909 is not clear, except for what is mentioned in *The Family*: the trip to Sakhalin and his illness in Aomori. In April 1909 he was living in rented quarters by the Sumida River near Toson's house. Chikao tried his hand at many enterprises but invariably failed in all of them. He went to Nagoya as a stockbroker in 1910 and died of tuberculosis the same year.

TAKASE TAZU (Osen)   Chikao's younger sister was gentle and sweet, and her slow mind was not at once detectable in casual

---

[7]Shono Junzo, "Ie no Otane" (Otane in *The Family*), *BDST*, p. 282 and Kimura Sota, "Ie ni Tsuite no Insho to Kanso" (My impressions and Feelings Concerning *The Family*), *TZ*, XVIII, 156.

conversation.[8] She never married, but lived with her mother in Kiso and Tokyo until the latter died.

TAKASE MISAO (Toyose)   Setsuko (her name was changed to Misao when she married Chikao) came from the Suyama family of Niekawa, Nagano Prefecture.

TAKASE BUNKICHI (Kosaku)   The adopted son of the Takase family, Yasuda Bunkichi, married Shimazaki Kin (Oshima), the younger sister of a relative, in 1908. They were divorced two years later.

Toson and Naturalism

The Family is a major work belonging to the middle period of Toson's literary career. It has been designated his best naturalistic work and a masterpiece of Japanese naturalism.[9]

The term "naturalism" poses a problem. It encompasses literature of many different shadings that developed in mid-nineteenth-century Europe, either independently, as in the case of English and Russian naturalism, or under the influence of French naturalism, as in the case of German and Scandinavian naturalism. What naturalism meant in each country and even to individual writers in the same country varied widely. At the same time, the naturalism that developed and declined in Japan in the short span of ten years (1902–12) is so different from the European kind that it should be termed "Japanese naturalism."

[8]Mrs. Furuhata Toshie and Mrs. Takase Teru, private interviews, August 1970.

[9]E.g., Senuma Shigeki, "Shimazaki Toson no Hito to Sakuhin" (Shimazaki Toson, the Man and his Work), *KBKK*, p. 18; Kawazoe Kunimoto, "Shizenshugi no Bungaku" (Japanese Naturalist Literature), *INBS*, XI, 34; Hirotsu Kazuo, "Toson Oboegaki" (Memorandum on Toson), *TK*, p. 167; Masamune Hakucho, "Shizenshugi Seisuishi" (The Rise and Fall of Naturalism), *Masamune Hakucho Zenshu*, XII, 319; Yamasaki Takeshi, *Toson no Ayumeru Michi* (The Road Toson Took) (Tokyo, 1949), p. 148; Ino Kenji, "Shimazaki Toson" (Tokyo, 1954), p. 60; Yamamuro, *op. cit.*, *NBZ*, X, p. 404.

Naturalism was first introduced to Japan by Zola's novels in the 1890s. In studying naturalism, Japanese writers imitated the salient features in Zola's novels instead of assimilating the theories he developed in his essays. Consequently, the concept of naturalism that most Japanese writers identified with during the late nineteenth century dealt with the miseries of life such as Zola described: hereditary vice, drunkenness, deformity, disease, and all forms of animal instinct, as long as they were described truthfully.

Besides European—in particular French—naturalism, Christianity and its concept of self as the created versus God as the creator greatly affected Toson's particular type of naturalism. In contrast to the Japanese view in which nature, human beings, and deities exist as part of a whole, Christianity brought many young poets and writers to a new consciousness of self, of the individual as distinct from nature and the divine, hence to a new respect for individuality. Such poets as Kitamura Tokoku, and Ishikawa Takuboku (1886–1912), with their Christian background, espoused romanticism and the emancipation of emotions. As a result, the naturalist writing in Japan did not constitute a literature of social consciousness as in Europe, but rather the deeply introverted study of self, a faithful record of everyday life and its deepest emotions. Japanese naturalism reflected the gloomy, unhappy, and harassed lives of the writers. Toson's *The Family* fits this definition perfectly.

Toson himself had neither publicly nor privately considered himself a naturalist. Although he respected Zola as a writer, he could not accept Zola's portrayal of the animal side in human beings as seen in Zola's novels.[10] Further, he had developed his view of literature independently, not by adopting what was popular in the late Meiji among many Japanese writers.

Toson's literary naturalism developed largely through his encounters with and observations of environment first, and then human nature. It developed out of a mixture of influences from his reading and his own trials and errors.

I will not engage here in a lengthy discussion of the gradual de-

---

[10]"Furoberu to Mopassan" (Flaubert and Maupassant), *Nsn*, *TZ*, VI, 208; "Mopassan" (Maupassant), *Sn*, *TZ*, VI, 19; "Shizen-ha to Hishizen-ha" (Naturalists and Non-Naturalists), *TZ*, VI, 514.

velopment of the style peculiar to Toson.[11] In the early days of his career, neither the style of modern prose nor the technique of novel writing had been established in Japan. Toson learned much from the translations of Russian Literature by Futabatei Shimei as well as his own readings of English, French, and German literature in English. What we find in *The Family* is the product of many years of study, toil, and rigorous self-discipline, the embodiment of some of his literary theories that had been formulated over many years.

The Writing of The Family

In *The Family* (1910–11) Toson demonstrates considerably greater maturity, objectivity, and writing skill than in his two previous novels. He is technically successful in this work because he exercises tight control over his material.

Approach

In 1930, twenty years after the publication of *The Family,* Toson explained his attitude toward and use of the material he employed in writing this novel:

"When I wrote *The Family,* I constructed it block by block with sentences as if I were building a house. I excluded all that occurred out-of-doors, and tried to limit events to those inside the house. I described the house from the kitchen, from the entrance vestibule, and from the garden. I wrote about the river only after walking into a room where I could hear its sound. Thus I tried to build *The Family*. It was not easy to be consistent in using this technique in writing two volumes of some twenty years of family history."

Toson is trying to refute the criticism he received at the time of publication that the social and historical background of the period

[11]See Cecilia Segawa Seigle, "An Integral Translation with an Introduction of *Ie* (The Family) by Shimazaki Toson (1872–1943)," Ph.D. diss.(University of Pennsylvania, 1971).

was not depicted at all.[12] In *The Family* he does not touch on the Restoration and its impact. Nor does he mention any of the sociological, economic, or political developments that deeply affected the old rural families in Meiji times. During the period immediately before and after the Russo-Japanese War (1904–05), the nation was confronted with numerous serious problems, but Toson purposely excluded all social phenomena outside the Koizumi and Hashimoto households. In doing so, he even rejected a number of potentially dramatic events such as Sankichi's wedding ceremony, the finding of Osen after she strayed off into the night, the death of Ofusa, Minoru's imprisonment, Oyuki's trip to the north, and Tatsuo's elopement; these are mentioned but not described.

By being strictly selective with his material, Toson established a definite line of demarcation between the outside world and the family centering around Sankichi. Thus he succeeded in achieving a tight unity of subject matter and was able to fit twelve long years into twenty chapters. As Toson said, "It was not easy to be consistent in using this technique." One obvious danger was that he might fall into monotonous and repetitious descriptions of similar events in similar settings. For example, Sankichi visits Morihiko at the inn several times, and Shota and Toyose, together and individually, visit Sankichi several times, but a careful reading will reveal each visit to be different, each telling more about the protagonists' personalities and the effects of family disintegration on them. The first two chapters describe in detail the Hashimoto family in happy and prosperous days. Descriptions of the old family's sense of dignity and pride, and its anxiety about the marriage and future of its heir, Shota, set the tone. The activity taking place in the larger financial world is not described, but the effects of financial reversal on family members are related. The author does not waste time depicting the Koizumi family's past prosperity, which is described only through the reminiscences of Okura. Thus the past glory and the present abject state of the family are subtly contrasted. This confining of

---

[12]E.g., Soma Gyofu, "Toson-shi no Ie to Shusei-shi no Kabi" (Toson's The Family and Shusei's Mildew), *TK*, p. 108.

description to events within the family creates a sense of darkness and oppressiveness.

Themes

The Family encompasses a great quantity of material. It reviews Toson's life to 1910, looks back to his works already written, and looks forward to themes he later developed. From this standpoint, *The Family* holds the key to many of Toson's works, but the main theme of *The Family* is the oppressive, restrictive power the traditional family system exerts over its members, stifling individual development and fulfillment.

The Japanese word *The Family* implies more than either "family" or "house." It connotes not only the large, dark, heavy-roofed Japanese house and its immediate occupants, but also the family in an inclusive sense, embracing both ancestors and relatives. It is the weight of all these components that one carries when one is responsible for the family.

In *The Family* the authority of the family head is emphasized again and again. Koizumi Minoru drags the family through his disgracing bankruptcy and prison sentence, yet he loses none of the dignity and authority accorded the master of the house. His mere presence commands obedience. This also applies to Hashimoto Tatsuo, even though he has deserted the family, leaving it in financial shambles to elope with a geisha. The family heir is brought up with utmost care, and a sense of family responsibility is instilled in him at a young age. Shota is constantly reminded of his future duties as provider for his employees and family members, and is forced to abandon his studies in Tokyo in order to succeed to the hereditary trade he so dislikes.

The reverence for ancestors, the emphasis upon class in the arrangement of marriage, the persistent attempts to recover the family fortune as a duty to the ancestors...all are part of the code of ethics governing the family complex. As Sankichi says, "Wherever we go, we carry our family on our back "; but of all the family members, Sankichi is the only one who looks critically at such tyranny and questions the wisdom and value of the family obligations that deprive one of spiritual and financial freedom.

The direct cause for Toson's writing of *The Family* was the ever-present monetary problem. Ten years of struggle as teacher, poet, and writer had left him with no financial reserves. Whatever reward his work earned had been largely consumed by his impoverished family and relatives. Thus in spite of his fame as poet and novelist, he was as hard-pressed for money as ever.

Toson had a pessimistic vision: while the weak feasted on the food provided by the toil of the strong, the weak, the ones who had nothing to contribute, were the ones who benefited most in the end draining the strong of their strength. The prime example in *The Family* is Sozo, the invalid, who is the strongest of all precisely because of his inability to work and his detached take-me-or-leave-me attitude. Toson shows Sankichi's bitterness toward Sozo's ingratitude and arrogance to be just as strong as his resentment of Minoru's pomposity and authoritarianism. But Sankichi, because of his sense of responsibility, is incapable of ignoring his brothers in need. Toson was a kind and generous man by nature, and money itself was not the cause of his resentment. He was used to poverty, but he despised what poverty did to people. While still in Meiji Gakuin, he wrote: "The evil of poverty lies in its power to restrict people. If there were no such restriction, poverty would be the same as wealth. This restriction causes a man to wither."[13]

Toson purposely avoids showing social forces at work against his family partly because he discerned the cause for the family's fall in the self-destructive personalities of the Shimazakis and Takases. He shows how the various family members are unable to relinquish obsolete values and rigid modes of thought and behavior. Toson holds that any family of long lineage inevitably produces characteristics that make degeneration and financial disintegration a certitude. He presents two kinds of degeneration. One involves certain acquired, psychological characteristics...impracticality, pride, gullibility...traits that militated against an ability to cope with the changing realities of life. The other is moral degeneration; to Toson,

---

[13]Shimazaki Toson, "Hinku"(Poverty), *Fusetzu*, III (June 1966), 31.

one important manifestation of bad blood was moral weakness. In describing the less attractive side of his characters, Toson is so thorough that none of them is particularly appealing. Each character in his own way confirms the weakness of the family system, and the author emphasizes that these characters' flaws, combined with their lack of adaptability to the new era, were the true cause of the family's downfall.

Style

While Toson was not as successful stylistically as he was thematically, some passages of *The Family* are strikingly beautiful. Yet the major portion of *The Family's* style leaves much to be desired. It is a strange mixture of directness and indirectness, conciseness and prolixity. There are those who condemn Toson for being ambiguous and pretentious;[14] others praise him for his fresh, simple prose.[15]

There have been few writers whose style has received so much criticism and at the same time so much praise. Such diversity of critical opinion makes it difficult to evaluate the novel strictly on its literary merits, but the complexity in analyzing Toson's style comes from one factor.

During the years that Toson made studies of naturalists' works and observed nature around Komoro, writing sketches and sharpening his power of perception, he developed a theory on the novel. He insisted that the writer must be able to see things accurately and capture the essence of things.[16] This was the creed that Toson developed from reading French writers and that he strove to follow for the rest of his life:

[14]E.g., Iwano Homei, "Shosetsuka to Shite no Shimazaki Toson-shi" (Shimazaki Toson as a Novelist), Iwano Homei-shu *MBZ*, LXXI, 371–79.

[15]Mayama Seika, "Suisai Gaka" (The Watercolorist), *Chuo Koron*, November 1908, p. 79. Ara Masahito, "Toson no Miryoku" (The Charm of Toson's Works), *Kaishaku to Kansho*, March 1958, pp. 3–5; Katsumoto Seiichiro, "Shimazaki Toson-ron" (An Essay on Shimazaki Toson), *TZ*, XVIII, 345; Nanbu Shutaro, "Kugatsu no Sosaku" (Fiction in the September Issue), *TZ*, XVIII, 270; Senuma Shigeki, *KBKK*, pp. 61, 78, 82, 146, 186.

[16]"Shasei," pp. 33–34; "Shinsaku no Kozui" (The Flood of New Works), *Nsn*, *TZ*, VI, 211–12; "Kawagishi no Ie Yori" (From the House on the River Bank), *TZ*, VI, 544.

"Who would be a better writer? The one who describes every-thing he knows even though he knows very little, or the one who reveals sparingly only the essence of what he knows thoroughly?"[17]

What he meant by "capturing the essence" was to find the most con-cise way in which to express the nature of the matter. The writer must learn to observe details of things, describe them accurately, and eventually be able to present the essential aspect of the whole. *The Family* demonstrates Toson's various successes and failures in practicing his theory. Sometimes he was masterful. Most vivid is the depiction in Chapter XVI of the night Osen strays from home, when each person shows a special reaction to this minor catastrophe. Shota ordinarily shows little affection toward his sister, but on this occasion his concern for her takes the form of anger toward his wife. Toyose feels responsible for the mishap and reacts just as emotionally as her husband. Though Otane is worried and mentally ill, she shows in the worst situations—as at the side of dying Shota in Chapter XX—surprising good sense and strength. The characterizations are accom-plished in a few lines. Toson is particularly effective in his descrip-tions of nature, presented as they are in a brief, simple manner.

His constant effort to seek the essence of the matter with the most economical use of language could result in obscurity, for he some-times misjudged what was objectively the minimal essential informa-tion needed in a novel; for instance, the relationship between Sone Chiyo and Sankichi is extremely puzzling. And obscurity often stemmed not from Toson's misjudgment of what was essential in-formation but from his personality. "You can describe it," he said, "if you look at it well, and if you describe it, you will learn to ob-serve."[18] But honestly and openly transmitting what he observed and knew, in simple and direct expressions, was not easy for him.

It was also hard for him to reveal certain facts concerning his life. He was a product of the mountains in Nagano Prefecture and had a personality considered typical of a man from that region: phleg-

---

[17]"*Haru* Shippitsu-chu no Danwa," p. 509
[18]"Miru Koto to Kaku Koto" (Observing and Writing), *Nsn, TZ,* VI, 143. His habit of observation later became something he could not escape from. He called it "gokusei no jigoku," (hell of ultimate objectivity), *Umi-e,* p. 29.

matic, reserved, deliberate, taciturn, persevering, and tenacious.[19] The result was a mass of contradictions.

Ambiguity was created by what he wanted to write about but could not as a man of integrity and reserve, such as guarded details of family secrets.

Toson believed that one should not say everything. In his characteristically modest, passive way, he could not see eye to eye with anyone whose writing theory was to expose all. To Toson, a true artist does not give out every bit of information in his possession. It was important for him that an artist be considerate and humane, that he be a friend of humanity. A true artist should not exploit every unseemly personal secret in life, whether it concerns himself or others. Thus Toson's expressions sometimes carry a tone of decorous ambiguity, or even extreme vagueness, as when he avoids plain-spoken terms concerning sexual matters.

There are times when, because of his conviction to give only essentials, Toson exercised poetic judgment. An example occurs in Chapter X, where Sankichi visits his friend Makino one cold winter day:

"A friend had promised to go with Sankichi, but the temperature dropped so sharply that she gave up the idea."

The point is his experience, crystallized by the day's coldness that made his friend give up the trip; who the person was is unimportant. This was the kind of essence of an experience that brought him a sense of reality. More than he realized, Toson was involved with the Japanese tradition of poetic realism, in which a specific and concrete image plays an important role. His method of reliving an experience is not typically and traditionally Japanese, but what his eyes caught and what he chose to present as an essence of the matter belong to the Japanese poetic tradition.

Toson's effort to capture the essence resulted in occasional disjointedness of style. The Japanese reader, accustomed to brief Japanese poetry and prose writing of the haiku tradition in which poetic

[19]Ichimura Hiroshi, "Hakobe wa Moezu" (The Chickweed Has Not Sprouted), Fusetsu, I (December 1963), 41–42; Ito K., *Shimazaki Toson Kenkyu,* p. 59.

descriptions are concentrated in a few concrete images, demanding that the reader supply what is missing between the lines, is not disturbed by the sudden shifts. In *The Family* Toson often does not clearly indicate his shifts in thought.

> "Through an open sliding panel in the skylight, one could see a patch of clear blue sky.
>
> An old peasant in work pants came up from the well behind the house, bearing a bucket of cool water to the sink. Otane had to remember to feed him too.
>
> Otane had lived in Tokyo . . . ."

The Western reader, accustomed to logically developed prose, may receive jolting effects from such passages.

The disjointedness in *The Family* is also noted in larger segments. This is characteristic of many novels written specifically for serialization in magazines and newspapers. The disjointedness of passages such as the following results from lack of editing of the original serialization:

> "Sankichi was now at a point in life when this man could make him think of his father, who had died insane, with greater understanding. (End of installment.)
>
> For some time, Tatsuo, head of the Hashimoto family, had been in high spirits. His office was. . . ."

The Family was only the second serialized novel Toson wrote, and he still had difficulty producing the daily installments. He filled out some sections with trivia that he slashed in revising for the book edition, but since he did nothing to provide transitions, such deletions interrupt continuity and lend a disjointedness to the novel. Space has been inserted between most such passages in this translation to cushion the disjointedness.

Such stylistic deficiencies may obscure the basic merits of *The Family*. But unlike works by other naturalist writers, which were read mostly only in literary circles, *The Family* appealed widely and won broad public support for Toson;[20] situations described in *The Family*

[20]Ito Sei, *Shosetsu no Ninshiki* (Awareness in the Novel), *Ito Sei Zenshu* (The Complete Works of Ito Sei), XIII, 250.

were instantly recognized by ordinary people, to whom its drama
was familiar. Toson had many admirers, but only a few admit the
extent of his direct influence upon novel writing.[21] Unlike his
demonstrable influence on poetry, his impact on prose is more subtle.
Many stylistic traits he initiated have become absorbed into modern
writing and seem normal to the reader today. Ikuta Choko (1882–
1936) stated in 1911:

> "No one imitated Toson's new expressions as they were; how-
> ever, many writers were stimulated by them. After everything is
> said and done, Toson influenced modern writers more than any-
> one else. I think this is so because of his ardent search for a new
> style."[22]

The preceding brief evaluation of the literary merits of *The Family*
has been presented for two reasons. First, the uninitiated reader will
not immediately discern the value of this work and thus not appreciate its position in the history of early modern Japanese literature.
Second, although many Japanese scholars have acclaimed *The Family*
as a masterpiece of Japanese naturalism, they have engaged in little
critical analysis of it.

In his critical biography of Toson, William Naff makes this significant observation:

> "Toson was not a philosopher, nor was he a pedant. He built no
> systems and, in spite of his desperate effort for literary honesty and
> objectivity, he achieved something less than scholarly objectivity.
> . . . His education which he continued throughout his life
> brought about a broadening of the scope of his sensibilities rather
> than an accumulation of scholarly objectivity. If these distinctions
> are kept in mind, his writings are of the highest importance for
> those hoping to understand late Meiji and Taisho Japan; if they

[21]Minakami Takitaro (1887–1940) says, in "Shimazaki Toson Sensei no Koto"
(Things about Shimazaki Toson), *TZ*, XVIII, 418: "Our wholesome, youthful passion was nurtured by the Master's (Toson's) poetry, and a method of solid description
worthy of reading was learned from the Master's novels." He also quotes Kubota
Mantaro (1889–1963) who has often said that his novel was influenced by Toson more
than by anyone else, and who sometimes—mostly when he was drunk—proudly
stated: "I am imitating Toson."

[22]Ikuta Choko, "Toson-shi no Shosetsu" (Toson's Novel), *TZ*, XVIII, 177.

are not in mind, the reader will find himself taking Toson to task for failing to accomplish that which he had never attempted to do."[23]

Toson was not a literary giant, not at least of the stature of the Western writers he so admired, such as Shakespeare, Goethe, Flaubert, and Tolstoy. Nor was he the intellectual equal of such contemporaries as Natsume Soseki and Mori Ogai. He had a strikingly limited imagination and used only actual events and real people in his novels. Writing did not come easily to him, and what he put on paper was always the result of constant self-discipline.

Toson is nontheless a unique and important writer. First of all, he was a literary pathfinder, the father of early modern poetry and a mentor for the major romantic poets of modern times. His first novel, *Hakai*, ranks as the first socially conscious modern novel, and it provided an unprecedented stimulus to Meiji literary circles. His second novel, *Haru*, along with Tayama Katai's *Futon*, was blamed by certain critics for leading the modern Japanese novel toward the *watakushi shosetsu* (first person) type.[24]

Toson, faced with the conflict between his desires and the realities around him, felt an imperative need to write down his past history rather than to write about social problems. *The Family*, written at the peak of the naturalist movement, has been called an outstanding example of Japanese naturalism. With his next work, *Shinsei*, he shocked the reading public with revelations of his private life, just at the time that *watakushi shosetsu* writing was becoming popular. After Tayama Katai's *Futon* and Toson's *Haru* came out, most writers turned to structuring their writings in the autobiographical mold. And it gradually took on a special introverted brooding and intimate tone—a true confession of one's innermost feeling and thinking. This form was labeled *watakushi shosetsu* just about the time *Shinsei* came out. Whether directly influenced by *Shinsei* or not, many contemporary writers turned to the confession style of writing after the appearance of Toson's work, and persisted in working in this particular

[23]William Edward Naff, "Shimazaki Toson: A Critical Biography," Ph.D. diss. (University of Washington, 1965), p. 242.

[24]Nakamura Mitsuo, Fuzoku Shosetsu-ron (Discussion on the Novel of Customs and Manners), (Tokyo, 1950), pp. 45, 54, and 75; Hirano, p. 47.

genre for years to come. Toson turned to the historical novel *Yoake-mae* during the late 1920s. *Yoakemae* provides a panoramic view of the entire country, of an entire epoch, seen through the eyes of rustic mountaineers, and most critics recognize it as the greatest historical novel of modern Japan.[25]

Second, Toson is unique in his understanding of European philosophers. This enabled him to arrive at an appreciation of Western literature deeper than that of most of his contemporaries. He was struck by Western philosophy with its humanistic and positive attitude toward life. He was fully aware of the dangers of superficial imitation;[26] thus, while other Japanese naturalists were loudly and not very originally proclaiming the ugly realities of life,[27] Toson quietly went about studying and writing in his own fashion. The importance of observation, which he had learned from Ruskin, and the accuracy of description, which came from reading the French masters, ultimately led him to strive for simplification in both his art and his life. He sincerely believed that life and art were inseparable, that no single phase of existence should be neglected.

Third, Toson is important for his contribution to modern Japanese prose writing. In later years, again and again he would recall the difficulties that beset all Meiji writers in their struggle to create a new colloquial style.[28] He himself emphasized the importance of keeping language simple and alive by using everyday words.

The Family, as a major novel from the middle period of Toson's life, provides basic material both for understanding the man and the writer and for grasping the full import of the author's other works. It is a pivotal work in a lengthy literary career.

Thematically, *The Family* outdistances the efforts of other natural-

[25]Yoshida, II, 768; Hisamatsu, *Nihon Bungaku-shi*, (A History of Japanese Literature). V, 527.

[26]"Kino, Ototoi," p. 87.

[27]Tayama Katai (1871–1930), Iwano Homei (1873–1920), Kunikida Doppo (1871–1908), Tokuda Shusei (1871–1943), Chikamatsu Shuko, Masamune Hakucho (1879–1962), Nagai Kafu (1879–1959), all turned to exposing the misery and ugliness of life based on their experiences.

[28]"Kokugo Mondai Oboegaki" (Notes on the Problems of the Japanese Language), *TZ*, XIII, 483; *"Chikumagawa no Suketchi* Okugaki," (Postscript for *The Sketches of the Chikuma River) TZ* V, 590–91; "Genbun Ichi no Niryuha" (Two Schools of Unification of Literary and Colloquial Languages), *TZ*, VI, 487–89.

ist writers. Other authors dealt with the problems of the family, but Toson examined them in much greater depth. Where other writers saw only individual unhappiness in the family situation, Toson perceived the fatal flaws in the entire system. He saw how the system deprived one of individual freedom. He scorned the virtuous custom of mutual help within the family, which drained away the money of those few who were able to work. He concluded that a long, illustrious family lineage produced nothing more than impractical misfits in a changing society, and he felt that many members of his family were doomed to moral decay. Neither he nor his nephew was able to establish the modern family they desired. All this he describes in *The Family*, and such themes bring out the less attractive side of a system hitherto considered the cornerstone of the nation. Toson viewed the family system as antimodern, opposed to the individual and to progress, standing against all the things for which modern man strove.

However objectively Toson pointed up the weaknesses of the system, he was not concerned with social reform. He purposefully excluded all events except those involving the immediate family. The novel would perhaps have been more significant if it presented more clearly the relationship between outside events and the disintegration of the family. Then it would have been a tragedy with the family system functioning as a social force, instead of with individuals passively submitting to the dictates of tradition and heredity. It might then have placed the Japanese family in proper perspective. Nevertheless, the approach Toson took in *The Family* is effective in establishing a harmony of form and content.

It was inevitable that Toson should restrict his subject matter. Even though as a naturalist writer he dealt with his material objectively, he was a poet and an introvert. Outside events and their effects on family members interested him less. It is logical that he should regard the deterioration of the family as the result of flaws in individuals, though he was well aware that such flaws were produced by the family system and perpetuated by that system. *The Family* is unique in that it shows the delicate balance between Toson's introversion and his social consciousness, a position he reached only after *Hakai*, a socially oriented novel, and *Haru*, an inward-looking one.

The Family is not a stylistic masterpiece, but it shows Toson's literary theory in practice. In his attempt to keep to essentials, his prose sometimes lacks clarity, and the obliqueness in *The Family* stems in part from his personality, for he was taxed with both a desire to speak out and an inability to do so.

The Family shows an undeniable structural deficiency in the handling of segmentation. Toson himself had no illusions about the significance of the works he and his contemporaries were creating. He knew that better writers would follow and that he was merely providing a foundation on which they might build. In the postscript to *The Family*, written in 1937, he claims that late Meiji Japan was caught up in a whirlpool of revolution, overwhelmed by the influx of Western ideas. He knew that his views of nature and life would be forced to change:

> ". . . in those days we were impatient to open new fields, and everyone placed progress above all else, leaving lesser matters for later. 'Try anything new,' we used to say. Thus it was inevitable that our views of nature and of life should be forced to change. We knew that we should have to await a new generation before we could study nature and life in depth. Yet Meiji writers started out with high ideals and considerable foresight. Those were the days when even imperfect works of literature were acceptable because of the spirit they embodied; the times were filled with the zest of a modern age."[29]

---

[29]"*Ie* Okugaki," p. 621.

Chapter 1

T he kitchen of the Hashimoto house was full of activity with lunch preparations. Ordinarily, six male employees, from head clerk to office boy, had to be fed; but now there were Tokyo guests too. Including the family, thirteen had to be served. It was not easy for Otane, mistress of the house, to cook three times a day for such a large number but she had gradually become accustomed to feeding so many, and managed quite well with the help of her daughter and a maid.

The spacious *irori** room had polished cupboards and a spotless wooden floor. The prepared food was carried from the kitchen and served at the *irori*, where a fire burned even in summer and over which hung a soot-covered bamboo pothanger suspended from the ceiling. Soft shafts of light from a skylight entered the old-fashioned, imposing structure, and through an open panel in the skylight a patch of clear blue sky could be seen.

An old peasant in work pants came to the sink with a bucket of cool water from the well behind the house. Otane had to remember to feed him too.

Otane once lived in Tokyo, where her daughter, Osen, was born; but she had spent most of her life in the country, so her speech was a mixture of standard Tokyo and regional dialects.

"Oharu!" she called to the maid. "What's happened to Shota?"

"The young master? He went to the Yamases'," replied the seventeen-year-old girl, who blushed for no apparent reason.

"He always seems to be visiting at his friend's," Otane mused, then turned to her daughter. "Your brother stays so long when he goes to the Yamases'. He probably won't be home for lunch, so put his tray aside."

Osen did as her mother instructed. She was in her late teens and

* An open hearth sunk in the floor.

taller than her mother, but a childhood disease had impaired the normal development of her mind, and she could not stand to be away from Otane for long. Even the simplest work Otane gave Osen was preceded by kind, detailed instructions. For her daughter's sake, Otane treated her young maid as Osen's companion rather than as a servant. She had the girls' hair done at the same time and let them sleep in the same room.

According to Hashimoto family custom, seating at the individual tray-tables was arranged in order of seniority, beginning with the master and guests. As she worked, Osen, by nature a sweet girl, was solicitous of the younger maid.

Speaking to her daughter, working beside Oharu, as though to a child, Otane said, "Now, Osen, lunch is ready. Go tell the guests." The girl went to the rear of the house to make the announcement.

The Tokyo visitors had come to spend the summer at the Hashimoto house. Sankichi was Otane's youngest brother. Naoki, an acquaintance's son, was in junior high school and looked up to Sankichi as to an elder brother. This first visit to his parents' hometown was the city-bred Naoki's first real trip.

"The guests seem fascinated by the *irori*. We'll eat here," Otane said to her husband, Tatsuo, as he sat down. Sankichi and Naoki sat at tray-tables beside Tatsuo.

"Where is Shota?" Tatsuo asked, apparently unhappy about his son's absence.

"He's visiting the Yamases and will probably have lunch there again," Otane replied.

There were a great many flies.

With Oharu serving, the family and guests began to eat. The loyal head clerk, his son Kasuke, the apprentice clerk Kosaku, and other apprentice clerks passed behind the master and mistress to take their regular seats. They were far from ordinary store employees; their relationship to the Hashimoto family was like that of feudal servants in the home of their master. Some of their families had worked for the Hashimotos for two or three generations; thus the affairs of the Hashimoto family were the most important part of Kasuke's life. Even the old peasant, who had been working in the back yard, joined them. He had wiped his feet with a towel and now sat rigidly formal on the wooden floor.

"Come, help yourself," Tatsuo urged kindly. The old man bowed several times, then raised his bowl of rice to his head to show his appreciation; only then did he begin to eat along with the rest.

"Sankichi," said Otane, "doesn't this country cooking remind you of your childhood? There are a lot of things I want to make for you and Naoki. When you were small, you loved pickled taro stalks —remember? I'll make them for you soon." Such homey chatter put both host and guests in a good mood, and laughter resounded as they ate.

When Otane came into the Hashimoto family as a bride, Sankichi was still very young and lived in his native village. Their parents were alive then, even their grandmother was in good health, and the large old buildings of their estate had not yet been destroyed by fire. Gradually, Otane's younger brothers had migrated to Tokyo, and now only she remained in the country.

"Oharu, you probably haven't heard this yet." Excited at seeing her brother again, Otane was talkative. "When Sankichi first went to Tokyo to study, Mr. Hashimoto and I had already been there for some time, and the three of us lived together for about a year. Sankichi still had a runny nose then, but look at him now—grown up to be quite a gentleman and coming to see us!"

Chasing away the flies with her fan, Oharu looked at the diners' faces and smiled.

It had long been a Hashimoto family custom for each member, including the master, to clear his own tray-table at the end of a meal, in a manner similar to the ritualistic precision of the tea ceremony. Those who had finished eating wiped their bowls and chopsticks and covered them with a napkin before leaving.

The Hashimoto house stood on a hill at the edge of town, near an old turnpike. After lunch Naoki descended the winding stone steps along the steep cliff to visit relatives on the other side of the valley.

"Sankichi, come and see," Otane said as she gave him a tour of the house. "This room was built specially when I married into the family." Once used as a storage room, it now contained a chest of drawers, a mirror stand, and other items. On a sliding door was a poem artistically written by someone in the family of Otane's late mother-in-law.

"When I first came here," Otane explained, "Grandmother Hashimoto thought it inconvenient that I had no dressing room, so she had this one built. She was very considerate."

Sankichi grinned. "You were quite young then."

"Of course." Otane smiled back. "I married when I was younger than Osen is now."

The grinding sound of a chemist's mortar came from beyond the wall. Through a half-open door they could see part of the center room, where clerks and apprentices were diligently mixing medicinal herbs for the apothecary that had been the Hashimoto family business for generations. From time to time there were bursts of laughter.

"Kasuke must be amusing them again," Otane observed as she led Sankichi through the dark entrance to the rear apartments and into the *irori* room. Passing the side of the shop where a large shingle hung, they came to two guest rooms facing the courtyard.

"Pleasant rooms," said Sankichi, looking around. "No one is better at carpentry than country workmen."

"You and Naoki may have these two rooms," his sister said. "Do whatever you want—read, take a nap, anything."

"Coming from sweltering Tokyo, I don't feel as if this is summer weather."

"We don't use these rooms unless we have guests or there's a horse fair or something special in town. I'll let Shota sleep here with you and Naoki too."

"I can hear the sound of the Kiso River!" Sankichi exclaimed after listening intently.

After a while the two went to the front garden, where they inspected the mulberry patch and a chicken coop Shota had built, then circled around to the back entrance. Behind the house was a slope with terraced vegetable gardens, and at its top they could see the tilled land belonging to the family.

They mounted the stone steps and saw under the shadowy grape arbor a clear stream emerging from a spring. The high wall of the godown shone dazzling white in the sun, and the fragrance of lilies hung in the air.

Standing under the summer-pear espalier, Otane looked over her shoulder at Sankichi. "These days I get up early and walk as far as the upper vegetable gardens. Quite a change from the old days. I don't stay in bed anymore. I've gotten very strong."

"Was something the matter with you?" asked Sankichi, concerned.

"I was always in and out of bed. Something chronic."

"What do you mean by 'something chronic'?"

Otane fumbled for an answer, then began to walk on as if she had suddenly remembered something. "Let's stop talking about sickness. I want you to see the garden I've been working on—the vegetables have done well this year."

Midway up the slope they came to a garden of well-tended lilies, peas, and other plants, passed under a dark green pumpkin trellis, and stepped into the garden where the old peasant was working. Along the stone wall ran a pleasant path with flowers, from which they could look down on the town in the valley.

Gazing into the valley, Otane said, "I haven't been to town many times since the day I came to this house. . . . I'm always tied to the place. When I need something, there are errand boys and the maid to go shopping, and Kasuke and the other clerks go out on errands for me too. I don't usually leave the house. Women are supposed to be this way, you know."

She pointed out the house of Naoki's relatives, where he had gone visiting. They could see the rocks placed on the shingled roofs as weights against heavy winds and snow, a necessary precaution against the gusty mountain winds of Kiso.

Osen caught up with them and announced, "Mother, Mr. Sawada is here." The three went down to the house together.

As they passed the storehouse, Otane moved close to Osen and said, "It seems to me you were talking about Uncle Sankichi every day before he arrived. Are you happy now that he's finally here?" Not knowing how to express her joy, all the simple girl could do was utter a heartfelt "Yes! Oh yes!"

They entered the back parlor through the garden, and Otane introduced the old man there to Sankichi. Sawada, Naoki's uncle, was an exceedingly nervous person whose fastidiousness verged on neurosis, but when he was calm, his speech and manner were gentlemanly. He first thanked Sankichi for his kindness in accompanying Naoki from Tokyo.

Otane said, "Sankichi, Mr. Sawada admires the principles of the National Learning school and Shintoism just the way Father did. He often visited Mr. Sawada to exchange poems and talk."

Her remarks brought back memories. "Quite true," Sawada affirmed. "Your father used to have his kimono front full of all kinds of books when he walked about. . . . "

Meeting this old, almost forgotten friend of his father stirred Sankichi, for the slightly built man, though as dignified as a feudal warrior, trembled with age and melancholy. Sankichi was at a point in life when this man could make him think of his father, who had died insane, with greater understanding.

For some time, Tatsuo, head of the Hashimoto family, had been in high spirits. His office was in front of the old central pillar of the house; seated next to the head clerks and apprentices, he conducted the daily business from eight in the morning until sunset, dealing with the many matters that required his attention: ordering raw pharmaceuticals from distant provinces; purchasing aloe wood, musk, ginseng, bear's gall, and gold leaf; and shipping the orders out. Printing wrapping paper and preparing for the autumn sales trip also required his supervision; and besides keeping all the accounts, he even found time for menial tasks like wrapping medicine and stamping parcels to keep up his employees' morale.

As a leading citizen, he was often called upon to deal with local problems and to participate in various civic matters. But he avoided party politics as much as possible and devoted most of his time to the family business. Tatsuo's energy and industriousness astonished Sankichi, even though he was accustomed to the rush of Tokyo.

On the third day of the visit, Naoki again went to call on his relatives. Tatsuo took the afternoon off and stayed in the back parlor, the family gathering place separated from the bedroom of Osen and Oharu by a paper door. Seated before the tea shelf, Otane called to Osen, who was absorbed in folding envelopes for medicine at a little desk in her room. The girl appeared with a smile on her oval face.

"Take a rest, Osen. We'll all have tea," said Otane, and Osen sidled up close to her mother. Nothing made her happier than winning her mother's approval.

Sankichi came in and sat down.

Otane said to her husband, "Just look at Sankichi, dear. He's the image of father the way he's sitting there. His hands especially. They're just like father's, much more so than any of my other brothers."

"So Father had ugly hands too?" Sankichi laughed, looking at his hands.

Otane smiled. "Father would say: 'Sankichi's the one who really likes to study. He's the only one I'll let succeed me in my work. I'll make him my only spiritual heir!' That's just what he used to say."

Sankichi glanced at his sister. "If that strict father of ours saw me now, writing romantic poems, he'd give me a whack with an old broken bow."

"But your work is so convenient. You can take it with you wherever you go," said Otane.

Tatsuo sat with his legs crossed, jiggling his knees nervously, as was his habit. "More and more young people are writing these days. Literature is fine, but it hardly brings a regular income, does it?"

"I'd say you writers do it for the fun of it," Otane put in. Sankichi made no reply.

"Shota likes what you and your friends have written. He reads everything," she continued. "I suppose all young people enjoy the same sorts of things. I encourage him to read as much as possible because I know very well that youngsters shouldn't cling to old-fashioned ideas like ours. But, Sankichi, I don't think I'm at all behind you young people. Anyway, since I think reading is good for him, I let him read new books like yours."

"I'm afraid he can't learn much from my books," replied Sankichi. Otane and her husband looked at each other and smiled uncomfortably.

"Tell Shota tea is ready." Otane sent Osen to fetch her brother from the guest room.

Shota was three years Sankichi's junior, but he was taller. Standing side by side, they looked more like brothers than nephew and uncle.

As Shota entered the room, Tatsuo suddenly became stern and silent. The son appeared dissatisfied and irritable, but he inspected the room silently with a clear, youthful glance.

A broad scroll with the calligraphy of an ancestor named Chikuo hung on the wall in the old alcove. Chikuo was the founder of the Hashimotos' apothecary business, and to this day his favorite chestnut rice was respectfully placed at his grave on the anniversary of his death. His spirit seemed to live on in his calligraphy, hovering over his descendants.

Shota was not interested in the atmosphere in the room. It seemed restrictive, stifling, and gloomily monotonous, and he was unable to stay in his parents' company for very long. After gulping down the tea his mother offered, he abruptly left the room.

Tatsuo sighed. "Sankichi, I've been meaning to ask you ever since you came and haven't had the chance . . . it's about that watch you have. . . ."

"This one?" Sankichi took out a silver watch from his sash and placed it on the large table. "It's a very old one. See, it's got engraving on the back."

"Actually. . ." Tatsuo hesitated a moment. "When I sent Shota to school in Tokyo, I saw to it that he had a gold watch. I thought carrying a gold watch, he might not be looked on as some ordinary poor student. But one summer, he came home wearing a different one. I asked what happened to the gold watch, and he told me a friend had talked him into letting him borrow it and he had his friend's silver watch. And now the same watch turns up in your sash."

Sankichi began to laugh. "Actually it belonged to Sozo. He gave it to me not long ago. Shota probably borrowed it just to have something to show." Sozo was Sankichi's brother, immediately his senior.

Tatsuo and Otane exchanged glances again.

"Strange . . . I thought it very curious," mumbled Tatsuo.

"Sankichi seems to be more honest than Shota," Otane said.

The transformation of a gold watch into a silver one did not surprise Sankichi in the least. A young man selling or pawning his watch seemed understandable enough even to him, who had just been labeled "honest." Apparently Tatsuo thought differently.

Otane lit her long pipe and again began to talk about her son. "I wonder what sort of a man he is going to be. He's a peculiar boy on the whole and even I don't understand him sometimes. He is so reckless in everything he does."

"You mean Shota?" said Sankichi, smoking a cigarette. "But he's still very young. I find him pleasant to talk to. But sometimes, I don't know why—he gives me a scary feeling, and I find that intriguing."

"As a matter of fact, I do too," Tatsuo agreed.

"Anyway, he's got to behave with more discretion. He's the family heir," said Otane, looking at Sankichi. "Tatsuo's been very worried about him lately. Thank heaven, business is much better. Medicine sales have doubled since a few years ago, and if only we can keep them up, we'll be pretty well off financially. We have no other worries. Only Shota. . . ." Suddenly she lowered her voice. "He's been seeing a girl."

"Nothing unusual about that," said Sankichi, defending Shota.

"You always talk like that," Otane scolded. "You mustn't side with young people all the time."

"Is she from this town?"

"Yes, she is, and neither of us likes it."

Osen was bored. She got up and sat down several times as the others talked. When she thought she had grasped some of what her parents were saying, she smiled to herself and suddenly came close to her mother.

"Osen, do you understand what we're talking about?" Otane asked tenderly.

"Yes, I do," she replied, looking alternately at her mother and her father.

"Do you really," laughed Tatsuo.

Otane explained. "When talk gets the least bit involved, she doesn't understand. But at least this helps her remain innocent."

"She's grown up to be quite a nice girl," observed Sankichi.

"She's a woman already," Otane said. "I've explained what that means . . . physically, that it happens to everyone. She understands.

It's a pity she can't marry, but there's nothing we can do about that. Eventually we'd like to build a separate house for her and let her live there in peace. It would be best for her."

"Better find her a husband," Sankichi suggested playfully.

"The things you say!" Osen giggled and ran to her room.

Oharu came in and announced that the bath was ready, and Tatsuo went to unwind from the fatigue of several days' hard work.

"Osen, let's have our hair done." Otane called back her daughter and beckoned to the hairdresser, who had been waiting by the *irori*. She brought an old-fashioned mirror stand and the comb box into Osen's room.

"Excuse us for a while, Sankichi," Otane said, seating herself before the mirror. "You know, I like flowers so much, and I took special care of them this year. Look, don't you think the summer chrysanthemums are beautiful?"

Sankichi stepped into the garden, and as he picked his way among the large rocks, suddenly he became aware of the hairdresser standing behind Otane; he watched her with curiosity. She was communicating with Otane by various hand signs. Otane smiled at her brother and explained. "She's a deaf-mute, but very intelligent. She can express anything with her hands. She was just saying she heard we have guests from Tokyo."

Otane, though homebound, was able to learn from the hairdresser all the events of the town that only women would take an interest in. The deaf-mute observed various goings-on that escaped the notice of most people, and she would pass on the news by the cumbersome sign language. Now, again she gossiped about town affairs, holding out her thumb, indicating a man, and her little finger, signifying a woman, and then putting both index fingers to her forehead to show the horns of jealousy.

Toward evening, Tatsuo and Sankichi took their tobacco sets to the veranda where they could enjoy the cool breeze. Kasuke joined them, and Osen and Oharu brought dinner trays-tables from the kitchen. Otane placed one in front of Kasuke. "We have Sankichi visiting us, and Mr. Hashimoto has taken the afternoon off. So why don't you have a drink with them? We have nothing special, just sake and little fish."

As usual, the head clerk ran his hand over his bald pate in response.

"Let me pour you some sake," said Kasuke, moving closer with deference. He wore a tradesman's apron, but his physique indicated some experience with swordsmanship. With his large, workman's hands he offered wine to his master and the guest.

Gradually the conversation again drifted to Shota. Otane had been going to the kitchen from time to time to oversee the cooking; she returned quickly to share the concern about her son.

"Why don't you let him marry the girl he likes?" Sankichi remarked with a student's simple, direct logic.

"That's quite out of the question," Otane scoffed. "You say the silliest things because you don't really know the situation."

"Besides, sir." Kasuke looked at the guest with his bloodshot eyes. "We don't like the girl's parents. I may be wrong, but they seem to be pushing her behind the scene."

Suddenly fear flashed in Otane's eyes as if something threatened her, but she remained silent.

"Even if they aren't," continued Kasuke, "their social status is different from the Hashimotos'. How could we accept the heir's bride from a family like that?"

Night was beginning to gather. The shadow of the mountain fell on the roof, crept over the garden, then over the white wall of the towering storage building, and finally over the pumpkin and gourd trellis on the stone walls above. The land where Tatsuo's father had once drilled artillery troops was under cultivation now, but it remained family property. From there up to the top of a small hill, the evening sun still cast a bright luminescence.

The old peasant, carrying a hoe on his shoulder, came down from the upper field.

The evening gong echoed across the valley from the temple. On the veranda Tatsuo looked over the family orchard on the slope and filled a sake cup for his guest, another for his industrious head clerk, and one more for his own health.

"May you soon find a fine bride for our young master." Kasuke raised his cup. "We'll all be so happy then. That is best for the family's solidarity."

"The bride is the question," said Otane emphatically.

Tatsuo laughed heartily. "There's no one in this town. That much is sure."

On her fingers Otane counted the young girls among her acquaintances. Many had reached marriageable age, but no one seemed good enough for Shota.

"Now that girl in Iida," Otane said, turning to Kasuke, "why don't you look into her background?"

"I'd be glad to."

Sankichi was curious. "Is there a good candidate in Iida?"

"Not really. Nothing's certain yet. . . . Well, yes, there's someone," Tatsuo answered, recrossing his knees.

"We've heard about her from reliable people," Otane explained to her brother. "This fall Kasuke will be going there on a sales trip, so I've asked him to get more information. Finding a bride is a major project, you know." Before they could think of the union of the young people, they first had to examine the marriageability of the two families.

Osen had returned unnoticed and had been listening to the conversation beside her mother. But by the time Otane realized her presence, she had already slipped out. Otane rose to her feet and casually looked into the next room.

"What are you doing there, Osen?" Her daughter did not answer, and she added consolingly, "What a funny girl you are! Whoever heard of a girl crying hearing about her brother's marriage?"

"What's the matter, Osen?" Sankichi called from the veranda.

Otane looked back at him. "She's terribly sensitive. She's all in tears if Shota teases her the least bit."

Later in the evening Sankichi said that he was tipsy from the little sake he had drunk and retired to the guest room, while Kasuke went to take a bath. Shota had not yet returned from town, and Tatsuo and Otane sat alone in the back parlor.

"Shota's rather close to Sankichi," Otane said. "He seems willing to tell him everything."

"I suppose so. Being about the same age helps."

"I think Sankichi's visit will probably do him a lot of good."

"I think so too."

Suddenly Otane bent over the lamp, pulled her sleeve up to her slender white elbow, and began to search around under her skirt for a flea.

"I felt all itchy. No wonder, I'm terribly bitten up." She lifted the hem of her unlined kimono, searching.

"Does it bother you that much?" Tatsuo laughed.

"I get chills all over if I feel even a single flea." As though she had lost all patience, she hurried to the kitchen with a wry smile on her face.

Sankichi's visit pleased Tatsuo as well as Otane. He had no brother himself, and always considered Otane's brothers as his own. With Sankichi there, many different topics of conversation came up. And the more they talked, the more emotions surfaced in Tatsuo, and his concern for his son only deepened.

Even matters ordinarily forgotten returned to his thoughts. His own father died when he was still young. In those days three men shared the responsibilities that Kasuke had now. They were called apothecaries, and they firmly controlled not only the traditional apothecary matters but also the family finances and social affairs. In his youth Tatsuo, like his own son, rebelled against the family restrictions. He left home full of ambition, and endured endless difficulties before he finally returned to his mountain home by ricksha with his old mother and family. The ancestral trade of generations struck much deeper roots than he could possibly have put down by his own efforts over a couple of decades. His forebears had provided a comfortable "refuge" for their less favored descendants. When he accepted the humdrum routine of the family trade handed over by hereditary managers, Tatsuo realized for the first time the impressive abilities of his ancestors.

Shota was now the very image of himself as a youth, Tatsuo said to himself. But the son was even more of a dreamer than the father and was on the verge of destroying the root of the family. With a heavy heart and musing on his inability to control his own son, he retired earlier than usual. After the rest of the family had gone to bed, Otane lit a lantern and went to check the guest room. Sankichi and Naoki were already asleep side by side, but Shota had not yet returned. She walked to the front garden and unlatched the wicket gate, violating the strict household rules of security for her son.

Chapter 2

The days were hot even in the valley at the edge of the great Kiso forest. Throughout the summer Sankichi tried to arrange his thoughts coherently while shut up in the guest room of the Hashimoto house. To provide some diversion, from time to time Otane brought out various heirloom ceramics, lacquerware, incense burners, and other articles to show him. One day, carrying a large key she took him to the storage building behind the house.

Next to the high, white-walled structures, directly facing the storage building for household goods, was a low-roofed depository for bean paste. Otane stopped to let Sankichi peer into the large vat and told him that the homemade table soy sauce they used every day was fermented there. Then she took him inside another storage building with a tightly closed heavy door covered with metalwork. The loft was shadowy and spacious. A shaft of sunlight from a side window fell on a jumble of bookcases and old furniture. Otane opened another window and pointed out the wedding clothes brought by grandmother, and then a large chest of her own trousseau. She let Sankichi browse through the collection of books by himself.

After she left, Sankichi looked into various bookcases. He recalled the time when he visited his childhood home, before it burned down, and had leafed through his father's library. Now he compared it in his mind with the Hashimoto collection, which was not as extensive as his father's. There were only a few volumes on the Motoori school of Japanese studies,* to which Sankichi's father was devoted, little on the *Man'yōshu*† or the *Kojiki*† and very few

* Motoori Norinaga (1730–1801), one of the four great scholars of Kokugaku, or "National Learning," of the Edo period.
† *The Collection of Ten Thousand Leaves* is an eighth-century collection of ancient poems compiled by Tachibana no Moroe.
† The *Record of Ancient Matters* was completed in A.D. 712 under the auspices of

Japanese and Chinese history books and anthologies. On the other hand, the collection was rich in hand-copied texts on the family specialty of martial arts and the way of the warriors. There were also some Confucian classics and books on Chinese philosophy. A Chinese translation of the Old Testament that someone in the family had acquired was a novelty. But after close examination, Sankichi found only a few volumes in the collection of interest to him. A large wicker trunk stood by the window, its cover off. Several notebooks with labels in Tatsuo's hand lay scattered in it; they were old diaries. Sankichi picked one up.

The name of Naoki's father appeared. It was a record of the period when Sankichi lived with Otane in Tokyo, and as he skimmed through it memories of his boyhood came flooding back. In those days they frequently had sake parties. Naoki's father would sing Kiso folk songs, and Tatsuo would respond with popular tunes of the day in his resonant clear voice. Sankichi remembered that Naoki's father had also kept a very detailed diary. Tatsuo's was not particularly discursive, but it seemed to bear the stylistic influence of Narushima Ryuhoku.* It made frank, even sensual, reference to some of the writer's sexual relationships which Sankichi recognized.

Sankichi walked over to the casement. Outside the window of the silent storehouse the garden trees were wilting in the hot luminous air. He tried to guess who had opened the trunk, wondering if Shota had discovered this hidden nook and started reading the story of his father's dissolute life.

He closed the heavy door behind him and descended the stone steps. Before him, the grape arbor and the roof over the well cast cool shadows. A clear stream trickled down by the tall stone wall. Rockfoils with their heart-shaped leaves covered the whole area.

Osen had chosen this spot to set up a tub and begin her washing. Oharu was drawing water from the well. She seemed difficult to please and was always grimacing in front of the young shop clerks.

the imperial court and is the oldest book extant in Japanese. It is the court's statement about the origins of the imperial clan and the genealogies before the eighth century.
* Narushima Ryuhoku (1837–1884) was a newspaper reporter noted for his *manroku-tai,* or "random style."

She was proud and would not be treated as an ordinary maid. She was feminine and charming now as she talked with Osen. Oharu was also from this region where women were known for their hot passionate blood.

Sankichi stopped to speak to Osen for a moment by the well. Shota happened along to wash his muddy arms; he seemed to have been working on the trees in the garden. Blushing, Oharu followed his orders and poured water over his arms straight from the well bucket, while Osen looked on innocently.

His arms clean, Shota spoke to Sankichi as they strolled back to the house. The maid rushed by them with a bucketful of water. The old peasant bowed to them as he passed. His eyes seemed to convey to Shota a special message: "Young master, you are wrong if you think you're just an ordinary young man. We're depending on you. I'm an old man, still working as much as I can, but I'll soon be counting on your support." While Shota felt a sense of pride, he resented his position that made even these peasants look so entreatingly at him.

His heart harbored a vague but persistent rebelliousness. "Why does the whole family worry about me all the time? Why do they fuss so much about me? I wish they'd leave me alone." The oppressive atmosphere of his family watching his every move had become intolerable.

The Hashimoto house was built in typical country style. From the back entrance one could go through a narrow passage to the front. As they walked through the garden toward the guest room, Sankichi and Shota met Sawada, who had just come to visit the shop.

"Mr. Sawada's still doing odds and ends for us," said Shota. "He folds medicine envelopes."

The eyes of the nervous old man seemed to say: "Master Shota, your grandmother and your mother both came from fine old families. Your father squandered the family fortune because he studied the wrong things. You've got to learn how to handle an abacus. Your responsibility is very great, you know."

Shota wanted to escape from all their eyes. Returning to the guest room, Sankichi opened the sliding doors so that he could see the slope of the mountain across the valley. Shota placed a large lacquered papier-mâché table in the center of the spacious room. These enjoyable chats with Sankichi invariably made him envious of his uncle, who could remain a student as long as he wished; no one worried over what Sankichi did or thought. As for Shota, he had been forced to abandon his studies in Tokyo, about which he had become enthusiastic, and to return home. The old master studied too much and squandered money, so the young master needed no education, the managers insisted. They believed that life in the big city was fraught with evil influences for a young man. Faced with this attitude, Shota often wondered why he should be concerned about what happened to the family.

He had become so accustomed to the sound of the Kiso River in the valley, it made no fresh impression on him. And he was tired of the gloom of the forests. Was he to be cloistered in these mountains all his life? The mere thought was hard to bear. Sometimes, in the middle of a conversation, he cocked his head and listened, and his eyes took on a dreamy look as if he were drawn to the sound of the mountain stream.

Otane came in. "I've made some good herb tea for you," she said hospitably, looking at the two young men. "Shota, pour some for your uncle."

Sankichi used to drink *nebu* tea, made from the leaves of a shrub, as a child.

"Did any of the books in storage look interesting to you?" asked Otane.

"Yes . . . some," replied Sankichi halfheartedly. Otane watched the two talking together for a while and then left the room.

The conversation soon turned to the beauty of Kiso girls. Sankichi asked Shota how he felt about the girl Otane had mentioned. The nephew said simply that he thought she was lovely. Before talking about the girl, Shota really wanted to explain how his love always became degraded.

For some time the two sat in silence.

"There are a lot of young men in this town," Shota said finally, "but those who stay put forever aren't worth knowing. It seems I can talk only to the kind of fellow who works hard and plays hard."

Uncle and nephew continued talking as they drank the fragrant tea and smoked cigarettes. Shota had business aspirations. In Tokyo he concentrated on studying lacquerwork and dyes, and on the side he tried to learn about painting. He was quick to learn and was interested in all forms of knowledge, including literature. He took Sankichi's half-finished poem, which had been left on the desk, and read it in a clear strong voice that resembled his father's.

For Shota the two years in Tokyo, especially the winter vacation he spent with Sankichi in Sendai, were unforgettable. Sankichi was living in a quiet room on the second floor of an inn when Shota visited him, and together, they went to see Sankichi's friends and scenic Matsushima. During his visit, Shota asked to see Sankichi's poems and read them aloud by the poor lamplight of the inn through a long winter night. He could not resist mentioning it.

"Oh, yes," Sankichi recalled. "You came when I was invited to a Christmas party in Iwanuma. I had never seen such a bucolic Christmas in my life. The congregation cooked a special rice dish and other country dishes, and I was treated royally. I stayed at the house of a dry-goods merchant who was an elder of the church; I went to see the Abukuma River the next morning. I found you waiting when I came back to Sendai by train."

"That's right. We could hear the sound of the ocean from that room," cried Shota enthusiastically.

"Sendai was nice. Vineyards, pear orchard . . . I could borrow all the books I wanted. I felt as though my life was starting. Until then, I was nothing—might as well have been dead." Sankichi heaved a sigh. "When I think about it, I wonder how I've managed to get through life till today."

Shota gazed at his uncle's face as Sankichi continued. "The night I arrived in Sendai, I was already a different man. Everything came alive. I wanted to write."

"We've kept your manuscripts from that period."

"It's the future that counts for you and me, Shota. I'm still young too, and I'm going to move ahead."

As the two men talked, Naoki came in from outside holding wild flowers, looking exhausted. He had entered junior high school in April.

"Where have you been, Naoki?" asked Sankichi.

"I took a long walk along the river."

Shota brought out a vase from the alcove, arranged the lilies and pinks the boy had brought back, and placed it on the desk.

Naoki delivered a relative's message. "Sankichi, my cousin Yamawaki says you should come and visit her sometimes. She says you are so awfully reserved." Sankichi was not inclined to call on local acquaintances.

The sound of bells echoed in the valley. Shota's eyes brightened as he looked out at the landscape.

"Oh, the Mount Ontake climbers have arrived," he said as if to himself. Bells suspended from the waists of the climbers tinkled loudly. They had traveled long, looking forward to resting at the nearby inn. With them, the vitality of the outside world seemed to flow into the ravine. Shota had longed to hear the sound of the outside world. He stepped out onto the veranda to listen.

The day of the summer festival was a holiday for the entire Hashimoto household. Red and white artificial out-of-season flowers decorated the gate where the apothecary shingle hung together with the large black fire-fighting tools. The office boys changed into new uniforms and strutted with shiny faces under the festival lanterns.

Otane came into the guest room. "Sankichi, you don't have a *haori*** to wear with your kimono, do you?"

He had changed into a crisp cotton kimono. "I don't need a *haori*. This is enough."

"I'll let you have one of Shota's *haori*. The portable shrine is going to pass by the house soon. You'd better go out with Tatsuo."

"Isn't it odd to watch a festival in borrowed clothes?"

"What's odd about it? You have no choice when you're traveling," said Otane.

"It doesn't really matter to me, but if you think I should wear a coat, I will."

As a visitor during the festival, Naoki had many invitations from various relatives. Shota and the young men of the shop all went to take in the spectacle. The town was vibrating with noise, and the house seemed all the more lonely.

Sankichi called to his sister, who was just going to fetch the coat,

* A short formal coat worn over a kimono.

"I've been plagued with dreams lately. It may be my health. Do you happen to have any saffron you could give me?"

"Of course, I'm sure we have some. I'll get it for you."

"When mother was alive, she used to make me drink saffron. She said it was a female medicine but it was good for me too."

"I know. Men have dizzy spells too," said Otane as she left the room.

She returned shortly with a summer coat bearing the crest of the Hashimoto family, a bag of herbs, and a cup of water. She soaked the red saffron petals in a tea cup specially made for serving tea to the apothecary customers and handed it to Sankichi.

"What sort of dreams do you have?"

Sankichi frowned with pain. "Some of my friends say they dream about landscapes. I've never dreamed about scenery. I always dream about women."

"Don't be silly!" Otane scoffed.

"No, I'm telling you the truth. That's why I asked for this herb."

"Are they women you know?"

"No, I never know who they are. I try and try to think who they are after I wake up, but I'm sure I don't know them. Mostly they are barefoot, and they run after me as though on fire. Last night, for instance, a woman chased me into a place that looked like an apple orchard. I was wedged between two trees and couldn't get out. And she was just about to catch me when suddenly I woke up. I was soaked in sweat."

"A very likely dream for someone like you!" Otane commented, snickering.

Osen came to say that the parade was approaching, and they went out to the street through the gate. From there they could see over the roofs of the village houses and the Kiso River meandering through the center of the town. Sankichi's coat was a little too long for him, but he went down with Tatsuo to the foot of the cliff.

After the procession had passed, Otane sent Osen off with the maid to see the festivities and returned to the house. At the store entrance Kosaku, an apprentice clerk, was leaning against the large apothecary sign and playing a bamboo flute. Shortly he too left, and Otane was alone in the big house.

Suddenly the silence engulfed her. It was as still and empty as a temple hall. She sat down by the *irori* and waited quietly. Not only the local young people but also inhabitants from distant villages came to participate in the festival, and every year the town was overrun with people. The paroxysms of excitement were contagious; everyone was restless. Even on such a special occasion, Otane believed it her duty to stay behind and watch over the house.

Memories of her father, Koizumi Tadahiro, constantly came to her. The Koizumi family estate at the head of the Kiso valley, where she and Sankichi were born, was some twenty-five miles from the Hashimoto house. Otane had spent her girlhood there. Her father was a big man, and he wore extra large custom-made socks. Often when he was tired of reading, she was summoned to massage his shoulders in his study overlooking the peonies in the garden. His admonitions on such occasions were something she would never forget. Even as calligraphy models from which she was to practice handwriting, Tadahiro wrote such moral injunctions as "the beauty of chastity and fidelity," "the virtue of woman's dedication," "love of neighbor," "diligence," "fortitude," "thrift," "sincerity," and "humane deeds."

Brought up by such a father, Otane married into the Hashimoto house and gave birth to Shota. Otane lamented that Shota would not follow her wishes in areas other than those that also worried Tatsuo. Now, again, she brooded about him as she sat by the hearth.

Imitating the rhythmic shouts of the men carrying the shrine, an office boy ran into the garden. His eyes wild with excitement, he took a ladle from the tub, filled during the day by the old peasant, and gulped down water.

When Sankichi returned, Otane served him steamed rice with red beans, which was customary for festivities, and mixed vegetables at the *irori*. Shota came in breathless.

"Mother, give me something to drink. I'm dying of thirst." His eyes twinkled. "We just stripped the decorations off the portable shrine. Took the phoenix off too. Now the real festival is beginning. I'll kick up a storm this year."

"Good heavens, what a commotion!" Otane exclaimed. "Why don't you have some red-bean rice too, Shota?"

"Did you see it, Uncle Sankichi?" Shota looked at him. "How do you like a country festival like this? It's different, isn't it? Our god is especially rambunctious. We're going to charge the shrine right through town and at the end, we'll roll it over to the main shrine grounds and slam it against a tree. Smash it to pieces . . . even the carrying poles. Every year we build a new shrine with unpainted wood, you know. It's a rough affair. There is even a dignified mustached old man who hides behind a mask and comes out to smash the shrine."

After quenching his thirst, Shota was gone again.

The office boy, a towel round his neck, followed after him, shouting the rhythmic calls. As he watched all this, Sankichi felt he could no longer remain quietly at his sister's side.

After dark the town in the valley was transformed into mirthful bedlam. Waves of men and women crowded the narrow streets lined with colorful lanterns to see the festival. They invaded the streets like a rising tide. The movement of the portable shrine, which struck the ground as it was pushed and buffeted, and the roar of the battling youths excited the spectators. Young girls in groups marched from miles away along the bank of the Ōtaki River, singing songs and holding hands so as not to get lost or be trampled in the press of the masses. Some of them took advantage of the crowd and bantered with men they did not know. Shrewd town merchants baited the mobs with hair ornaments, food, drink, and other goods, scheming to make the country people spend their hard-earned money in one night. A dance was started in the large shadowy square at the center of town.

After making the rounds of the festivities, Sankichi, his kimono tucked up and his feet bare, joined the throng gathered at the portable shrine. With the others he pushed it along, cheering and shouting. After a time he returned to the Hashimoto house, wiping the perspiration from his forehead. He washed his feet and went to the cool guest room, where he stretched out on the floor.

"You are back, Sankichi." Otane entered the room, holding a fan. "I think I'll lie down too. Let's talk a little tonight," she said, stretching herself on the floor. She talked of the Koizumi family in Tokyo.

She talked of her hopes for Minoru's success, of the fact that her second brother, Morihiko, had not written her for some time, and of the sickness of her third brother, Sozo. Her talk drifted from one brother to another and finally settled on her son. She anticipated trouble and imagined things about Shota that Sankichi had never even dreamed of.

"After all," she remarked, "he's young. You never know what sort of mistakes he might make. What if he should get the girl pregnant? I'm worried about that." She spoke scornfully of the loose morals in Kiso. The rollicking atmosphere around the shrine posed a threat, she felt, that would lure her precious son into a licentious world. She imagined him strolling somewhere with a girl. She fretted that her mother's love was not enough to protect him from the cheap sweet whispers.

"I've told him a hundred times that his father made so many mistakes about women and not to follow his suit; I always told him to be careful not to have people talk about him. Oh yes, he knows all about Tatsuo and his scandals."

Sankichi listened in silence. Otane sighed.

"My husband's a good man, you know. He's gentle and kind to the employees. And he's been working very hard recently—which helps his reputation in town. But he's no example for Shota. He's done so many inexcusable things he can't justify to his own son. He's repentant now, and he works hard and doesn't complain. I understand his feelings. If only he, and Shota too, wouldn't get involved with women, they'd both be ideal. It's such a shame."

She seemed embarrassed to talk about her husband even to her brother. Conditioned by her father's admonitions, she was reluctant to talk of deep wounds her husband had caused her.

"Being a lady's man is a hereditary sickness in the Hashimoto family," Otane mused. "I can do nothing about it." She spoke no more about her husband.

Down in the valley, the rumbling sounds of the portable shrine resounded like earth tremors deep into the night.

Naoki stayed only about a month. He liked plants and collected rare alpine flora such as the tree orchid, the plantain lily, and the round-leafed orchid, which could be found only deep in the mountains. With these and specimens of other fragrant flowers, he left the Hashimoto house before *bon*, Buddhist All Souls' Day. Sankichi decided to stay until his work was finished.

Bon came in mid-July. Since Tatsuo's father's time, the Hashimotos had made their offerings to the spirits of their ancestors in Shinto, rather than Buddhist, style. Otane intended to combine the second anniversary of her mother's death with this occasion. As she grew older, such matters assumed more and more importance for her.

Otane accompanied Sankichi on the annual visit to the family cemetery, one of her rare outings. Osen set about preparing vegetables for dinner following her mother's instructions. She placed a cutting board on the kitchen floor and began to peel a gourd. The vegetable garden behind the house had produced a number of large gourds that would be sliced into strips and preserved by drying.

"Oharu, your hair looks lovely," said Osen to the maid, who was working at the kitchen sink.

"Do you think so?" Oharu looked back with a pleased smile. "Your hairdo looks good too, Osen."

Osen tittered with delight and started to cut the vegetable into slices. She lined up the knife and sliced several pieces but they were not of even thickness. She laid the knife down then took it up again, but she had no idea how to cut pieces evenly. Some were too thin, some too thick. Her hands began to tremble.

Oharu, totally absorbed in her own thoughts, was oblivious to her predicament. Delighted to be working in a new kimono and a new apron, she was enjoying herself. She had the night off and was looking forward to visiting her aunt.

When the party returned from the cemetery, Otane saw at once that Osen was in difficulty. The girl's finger was bleeding a little.

"I suspected as much," said Otane. "I'll help you, dear. I'm sorry, it was my fault not to leave you sample pieces."

Osen was totally perplexed.

"Look, put something on the cut." Otane fretted. "We even had our hair done today and we were going to enjoy ourselves. How can you have a good time with a cut finger?"

Oharu came over to Osen. Otane looked at her brother and said, "This is why I can't let her out of my sight. Really she's just a child.

On New Year's Day, Shota's friends came over to play cards. Yamase was there too. He's a good friend of Shota, so he invited Osen to play with them. Well, she practically sat on Yamase's knee! But you know she couldn't have been more innocent! She had no idea that what's all right with her brother may not be all right with her brother's friends. She's really very naive."

The evening of *bon* was one of the happiest of the entire year for young people. Everyone in the Hashimoto household was permitted to go and watch the *bon* dance when darkness had fallen. The cool of the summer evening brought relief to complement the pleasure of the festival. It was dark and the stars shone brightly. People naturally headed toward the temple grounds, cool in the evening breeze.

Oharu, who had gone to visit her aunt, was coaxed by friends and had gone to see the dance. Men and women in a large circle were dancing and singing, keeping time with their feet. Many women factory workers from other towns had joined the circle. Some young men, their heads covered with towels, moved back and forth around Oharu, frightening her. She was finally pulled from the crowd by Shota, who saw her plight as he happened by.

In September, Sankichi completed the work he had started at the beginning of summer. A letter came from the old head of the family that had adopted Morihiko, Sankichi's second eldest brother. This branch of the Koizumi clan was located about five miles closer to the Hashimotos than the place where Otane and her brothers were born. The letter said something to the effect that the old man had heard that Sankichi was about to return to Tokyo and suggested that he need not make the usual obligatory visit to the family. He suggested that Sankichi go directly home instead, and closed the letter saying that it would be easier for both that way.

"Easier for both. . .? The old man can be quite blunt." Tatsuo, laughed, passing the letter to Sankichi. Even the simple writing paper and envelope showed the miserliness of the old man.

The day of Sankichi's departure drew near at last. Tatsuo regretted to see him go, for it was difficult to know when he would visit them again. He read aloud some of the poems Sankichi had written in the guest room.

The best present to his relatives in Tokyo, he said, would be the news that the apothecary was doing well.

Sankichi was busy with packing and with the visits by local people when Tatsuo called from the *irori*. "Sankichi, come and see, we finally got the special treat we ordered for you."

"I want you to taste some wasp larvae." said Otane, "And I want you to take some home with you. We're just taking them out of the nest. Look, this is the nest. Isn't it huge?"

The five-layered wasp nest had been separated into sections and placed on the floor. Otane, Osen, and Oharu were extracting the larvae and half-grown wasps from the holes and putting them in separate piles. The insects, much smaller than honeybees, were highly prized delicacies in the region, and as a child Sankichi often went hunting for these nests with the grown-ups

"Mother, the photographer is here," Shota called as he came in. "Change your kimono."

"He is here? Well then, we must hurry. Osen, leave the larvae there, and let's change quickly. Oharu, you'd better get ready too."

Her husband shouted into the shop, "Kasuke, everybody, come and get into the picture!"

As a memento, a family photo was to be taken in the garden facing the back parlor. The head clerk and employees could stand wherever they wished. Tatsuo placed himself in front of the azalea. According to the family legend, it had been planted by the founder of the business, Chikuō.

"The women should be in front," Tatsuo directed, and the three women took places on chairs.

"Uncle Sankichi, come a little more to the center. You're the guest," suggested Shota. Sankichi moved to the boulder surrounded by wild chamomile.

Wisps of white mountain clouds drifted above. The sun was in and out, hindering the photographer's work. Kasuke abruptly looked up at the sky, and as if something had occurred to him, he left his place.

"Where are you going?" asked Otane from her chair.

"You'd better not move," Shota warned. "Here comes a big cloud. When the shadow reaches us, he'll take the picture."

"Well . . . no," mumbled Kasuke, "I just thought I'd . . ."

He crossed to the front of the group and stood beside his master where it was more shadowy. The cloud approached. The apprentice clerk Kosaku and Kasuke's son, Ichitaro, were also in the group.

In the morning of the day of Sankichi's departure, the whole family gathered in the back parlor. Sankichi had changed into a summer suit and was winding his gaiters around his legs as he looked at the fall begonias in the garden. He wore a jacket that was worn out in the back. He explained that the jolting in the horse-drawn carriage on his trip down had been quite severe.

The manuscript Sankichi had completed in the mountains was carefully packed in his suitcase, as if it were a gift from Tatsuo and Otane. His heart was finally free of the dark unhappy memories of his youth, for he had given them literary form in the quiet setting.

That morning, Kasuke and his son crossed the river earlier than usual to send off the guest from Tokyo. After breakfast the family gathered by the *irori* and drank tea before saying goodbye. Otane was truly sorry to see Sankichi go. "It's always so wonderful to see you," she said. "It seems so simple to travel, yet I know it's not all that easy for you."

"Oh no; it's not simple at all," interjected Kasuke. "Mr. Koizumi, how many times have you come back home?"

"Once a long time ago when Grandmother died, and again for mother's funeral. This is the third time."

"He's been gone ever since he left home when he was only eight," Otane said to Kasuke.

"If the old Koizumi house hadn't burned down, you would have returned more often," Tatsuo said frankly.

The driver of the horse-drawn carriage, who had been informed the night before, came into the garden.

"Uncle Sankichi, the carriage is here," shouted Shota as he carried out the luggage.

Still at the *irori*, Otane spoke to her brother. "Well, then, I'll say goodbye here. Give my best to everyone. Apologize to Minoru for my not writing for such a long time. And you take good care of yourself too."

With a few brief words of parting to Osen, Oharu, and the others,

Sankichi left the house. Tatsuo accompanied him down the stone steps to the carriage.

The carriage was waiting at the foot of the cliff. Two or three passengers were already inside. It was scheduled to go only as far as the inn at Yabuhara, where wooden combs, a special regional product, were sold, and travelers going farther had to cross the mountain on foot to board another carriage.

"When I came here with Naoki, we walked from Kukkake. The horseflies were terrible!" Sankichi remarked leaning through an open window of the carriage.

"Oh yes," said Shota, "Flies, gnats, and all, they're famous on the Kiso Road. It's probably because horses are bred all around the area."

In the typical easygoing country way, the carriage showed no signs of departing; Sankichi had ample time to speak with Tatsuo, Kasuke, and the young clerks who gathered around the carriage. After some time no other passengers appeared, the driver blew his whistle briefly and took up the reins. The wheels began to move along the sunny road at the foot of the cliff, and the people with whom Sankichi had spent the last two months gradually receded into the distance.

Chapter 3

Word reached Minoru in Tokyo that his brother San-kichi was returning. Among the many brothers-in-law, Hashimoto Tatsuo and Koizumi Minoru were particularly close to each other. They were about the same age, and both had similar responsibilities as heads of old families and similar prestige as gentry in their hometowns.

Minoru's father, Tadahiro, had been neither samurai nor master of an apothecary, as was Tatsuo's, but the patriarch of a village and an influential landlord. He was a man who spent his entire life in anguish. After brooding for some time over the condition of Japan, he abandoned his home to devote himself to patriotic activities. Thereafter, Minoru was obliged to take over as head of the family at the age of seventeen. The young and dutiful son became a victim of circumstances. When his father died, Minoru was still living in the country, engaged in local affairs as an elected county council-man and prefectural assemblyman; he was highly respected by all. But after moving to Tokyo to run various business enterprises, he met with a series of failures. Starting with an ice-making venture, his schemes soured one after another, each ending in a fiasco, com-pounding the loss.

Eventually one slightly shady deal led him to imprisonment. To this day he had not forgotten the ecstasy he felt on being released, when he inhaled the air of the outside world after so many months. His brothers Sozo and Sankichi were waiting for him at the huge gate of the red brick prison. What thirst for sunshine! What beauti-ful morning dew! Overwhelmed by freedom, Minoru ran through the grass, his feet shod only in white socks. In one long puff he fin-ished the cigarette given him by Sankichi. In the prison, inmates had discussed whether, if paid a thousand yen, any of them would will-ingly return to the black hole for a single day. No one said he would. Now Minoru was undertaking another enterprise in the outside world he had so yearned for.

Naoki's father was also a businessman from the same province. His long friendship with the Koizumi brothers made them as close as blood relatives. Naoki's father's employer, called "Boss" by his employees, was a wholesaler in a commercial district in Tokyo and he supervised his business from behind the scenes. He had become, as a matter of course, Minoru's "boss" too, having made an exceptionally large investment in the business so that Minoru could recover his losses.

In the small garden at the rear of the house, with its latticed doors and the signboard of the Koizumi Company, Minoru was watering some bonsai plants. He had learned a lesson from his failures and made it a rule to wear simple cotton kimonos no matter what the occasion. He had many problems on his mind: the large estate in his home province, the mountains, the lands, the rice fields, the woods— all the properties that had been turned over to others had to be regained for the honor of his ancestors as well as for his own. There were debts upon debts to be paid.

There was also the question of Sankichi's marriage. One new prospect sounded promising. He had to urge Sankichi to accept the proposal and see it through successfully. He was immersed in all these thoughts when his brother returned from his trip.

Sankichi appeared with his sun-tanned face at the entrance.

He had returned to Tokyo with a request from the Hashimotos to find a suitable bride for Shota if he could. The city house now seemed terribly crowded to him. The anteroom near the entrance was occupied by his invalid brother, Sozo. A baby slept in the corner of another room. His niece Oshun was playing on the veranda. The adjacent room, with an oblong brazier, was flanked by the kitchen, where Minoru's wife, Okura, and a young maid moved busily in and out. A narrow alley ran outside the window along one side of the kitchen, and the wall of the house next door could be seen through bamboo curtains.

It was close to dinner time, and Minoru had his tray-table placed by the brazier. He began to drink sake as he listened to Sankichi's brief report on the Hashimoto family.

"This is a gift from your sister in Kiso," said Okura, timidly placing a plate of sautéed wasp larvae before Minoru.

Minoru's authority as head of the family had never diminished. Away from home he was known as a very amicable person, but with his family he was extremely strict. To the present day, he exhibited as little affection for his wife as when they were newly married years ago. At that time the young couple hardly spoke to each other, eating beside the pleasant, spacious *irori* in the presence of his grandmother, who was quick with sarcasm.

"Has Otane been well?" Okura inquired as she set out tray-tables for her brothers-in-law and daughter.

"I've got to relax like this to feel as though I've eaten something," Sozo said sitting cross-legged, facing Sankichi. "Oh, it's been a long time since I've had goodies from the country." Unable to hold chopsticks with his withered right hand, Sozo ate with a fork or a spoon in his thin left hand.

"I see you've got your usual big appetite, Sozo," Sankichi jeered.

"My usual big appetite? Don't be insulting!" snapped Sozo.

"That's putting it mildly," Okura retorted. "For a sick person, he certainly puts away a lot of food."

Sozo did not act with the reserve of an unproductive dependent before his elder brother. Minoru seemed offended by this attitude, and he looked at Sozo disapprovingly, but he remained silent. The two brothers rarely spoke to each other. Minoru was aware of an inner voice constantly cautioning, "Family harmony first! Family harmony first!"

After dinner Sankichi, while sipping tea, began to talk about his trip. Minoru glanced at his daughter.

"Oshun, why don't you show Uncle Sankichi some of your drawings?" Obediently, the young girl brought from the back room painting models and some exercise sheets.

"Thanks to you, she's taking art lessons every Sunday now," Okura beamed.

"I see they start with orchids," Sankichi commented, looking at the model pictures. "The teaching method is quite different from European painting. I'm sure Oshun will become a good artist, since she likes it."

"Japanese painting is more suitable for girls," Sozo said. "She doesn't have to become a professional painter."

Minoru looked at his daughter's drawings with obvious pride. He then said that he was going for a stroll and left the house. He showed no interest in Sankichi's account of his trip, as he shared nothing in common with his younger brother.

After Minoru left, Okura, who had never been able to speak her mind in his presence, joined in the conversation with Sozo and Sankichi. A certain spiritual bond existed among the three, forged by sharing hardships during Minoru's absence. Frail Okura and disabled Sozo had barely survived with Sankichi's help.

"Your hair has turned quite gray," said Sankichi, looking at his sister-in-law's head. Her dyed hair showed gray roots.

"My husband says that I can dye it, but only when he's not looking," laughed Okura. "It's sad to get old so fast when I still feel like a bride."

"Yes indeed!" Sozo remarked, his eyes smiling. "She certainly is still the honeymooner. I can tell."

"Don't make fun of me," rejoined Okura, with a trace of provincial accent. She detested Sozo, but talked with him to be sociable. Massaging his numb right hand out of habit, Sozo said to Sankichi, "While you were gone, we had a big farce. A man with a whole entourage came to see Minoru's business. He was introduced as some wealthy man from Hachiōji, and had such a buildup that Minoru catered to him day and night. They talked business at restaurants, wine and dined, went out on the town, called in geisha . . . Minoru went out of his way to entertain him, but the fellow turned out to be anything but wealthy. He ate and drank to his heart's content and then vanished into thin air. Minoru's so damned gullible, and he has absolutely no excuse, especially since Inagaki was along to advise him. As if that wasn't enough, the fellow who introduced the scoundrel suddenly turned up because he was short of cash. Mind you, even if one felt sorry for him, it was not the time to help him at that point; but Minoru was crazy enough to give him money to get him home. Oh, it's so utterly exasperating!"

"Really we've never been so completely hoodwinked. The very thought of it makes me furious," complained Okura.

"I just watched, because I didn't want to say anything out of spite," Sozo said with the tentative air of an invalid. "I wonder what's going to happen to the Koizumi family if we go on like this."

"How's Minoru's venture coming along?" Sankichi asked.

"They say that the car is still in the experimental stage at the factory," Okura answered. "He's taken on more than he can handle."

"I suppose he has to plan big because he owes so much," said Sozo pensively. "Well, anyway, I hope he'll succeed this time for his own sake. I hope he won't have to go through the jail business again. I'm fed up looking after an empty house for him." Sozo regurgitated bits of food, which he chewed on as he talked.

What was to be done then? Neither Sozo, who was hardly a businessman, nor Okura, who had no knowledge of business, had any suggestions to make. And so Sozo began to enumerate the petty family extravagances: how the house was crowded with furniture, and how such and such a brazier was unnecessary. Okura complained that her maid spent too much time primping these days. "Sankichi, won't you talk to your brother?" she begged. "He pays no attention to me, no matter what I say. He never talks to me about his business."

"It's the same with art objects," Sozo went on, remembering additional gripes. "Look at the alcove in the back room. There's a fake Buncho hanging there. If I were Minoru, I'd hang an original, even if it were only painted by a friend." His eyes showed the discontentment and sadness of one who is sick. "To me this family's just like that Buncho. Everything's phony. It's all a fake."

Sozo began to condemn Minoru mercilessly, and Okura reacted by defending her husband, speaking of his great responsibility.

"Preaching like a priest doesn't help, Sozo," she protested. "Every piece of furniture is a front for business. After all, Minoru didn't start his business with a whole lot of capital. Instead of accusing us of extravagance, you might show a little consideration yourself. You're always complaining you can't eat this and that." Okura looked at Sankichi. "Do you think I'm wrong? Of course sometimes we do order raw fish fillet just for Minoru and not for the rest of us."

"But it's not fair if I don't get my share too," said Sozo showing his true character, as he lit a cigarette with his left hand.

The lattice door opened and a man came in. "I hear Sankichi's back," he called. It was Inagaki, Minoru's business assistant who rented a house nearby.

"I just got home, gulped down my supper, and came right over," said Inagaki, taking out his tobacco pouch. "Since Sankichi's back, I thought I'd drop in to see him. What a day! I went to the factory, then made the rounds of the banks . . ."

"We appreciate all you're doing," Okura said.

"Excuse me for saying so, but I have good reason to work hard," Inagaki answered in high spirits. "If we get even a single car moving, it will mean big money. I don't mean ten or twenty thousand yen. . . Even now I'm wondering how I'm going to spend all the money."

"What a smooth talker you are!" laughed Okura.

"Just keep on dreaming," Sozo chuckled. "By the way, Inagaki, you pulled a big one the other day, didn't you?"

"Eh? You mean the guy from Hachiōji?" Inagaki waved his hand. "Let's not talk about it."

"Well, we've just told the story to Sankichi," Okura said pointedly. "I do hope business will improve."

"There's nothing to worry about. Nothing at all. We have Minoru." Inagaki spoke as though he had full confidence in him, and Okura felt a little better.

Oshun came from her room and sat beside her mother. Oshun's hair was not very thick and was especially thin at the temples. Every morning before she went to school, her mother applied juice of the kazura vine when she combed it.

"Oshun, do you practice painting every night?" Inagaki asked. "I was amazed to see one of your pictures the other day. How do you paint so well?"

"Not to change the subject, but she's awfully funny." Okura looked at her daughter. "She hates to be called a 'country girl.' She's furious if someone says that to her."

Oshun shook her mother. "Mother, please!"

"My daughter too," said Inagaki, unable to resist bringing up the subject. "I may let her take lessons in Western music, the piano may-

be, since Oshun is studying painting. Somehow it's much more refined than the samisen* or Japanese dance."

It was Inagaki's habit to turn the talk invariably to his daughter.

"You've no idea what a doting father he is," Sozo commented
after Inagaki left. "His flattering sometimes makes me sick, but he
means well."

The difference in age between Sozo and Sankichi and between
Sankichi and Shota was exactly the same. The relationship beteen
Sozo and Sankichi began with quarrels, fights over food, and rough
games in the mountains. They were still little boys in elementary
school when Minoru took them to Tokyo to be educated. Morihiko,
the next to the oldest brother, had also come to Tokyo about that
time, as a delegate for the Forestry Incident.

In those days, Morihiko used to run around in a fashionable otter-
skin hat, busily negotiating with the government. Later Sozo left
school and went to work in a wholesale paper house. While he was
there, Sankichi used to bring his laundry, and Sozo would come out
smiling, wearing an apron of rough striped cotton. The two talked
about childish things, leaning against the wall of the shop's storage
house, where baled goods were kept. Having been pampered by the
entire village as a child, Sozo did not fear the head clerk of the large
store. One day the latter made a few unpleasant remarks, and Sozo
in a fury struck him on the head with an abacus. That was his last
day as an apprentice. His drifting began. Not even his brothers knew
much of the shadowy existence he had led after that. When still
young, he contracted a disease from a prostitute in Yokohama and
eventually returned to his family, his legs and arms withered and
almost useless. His mother was still alive then, and she used to tease
him: "Plum blossoms bloomed on Sozo's body."† She had insisted
on taking care of him herself until she died. Now he had no one he
could really talk to except Sankichi.

The day after Sankichi's return, Sozo wanted to tell his brother
how much he had suffered during the summer. First he asked what

* A lute-like three-stringed musical instrument with a small, skin-covered sound box
and a long neck.
† "Plum poison" in Japanese refers to syphilis.

Sankichi wrote during his trip. The younger brother showed him the poetry he wrote while listening to the murmur of the Kiso River. Sozo read a passage aloud. He looked at Sankichi as if to say, "Of all our brothers only you and I can appreciate literature." He then dragged himself with his spindly legs to the corner bookshelf.

An old-fashioned scroll hung in the alcove. It was done by an artist from their hometown, who was a contemporary of their father. It showed a man in Chinese dress feeding a bird. The picture with quiet colors and a serene figure came from the old Koizumi house in the country; it had been well-suited to the atmosphere of the household.

Sozo took out a draft of his own poems, which he had written during Sankichi's absence, and placed it before him.

"The form is a little dated compared to yours, but anyway, I spent the entire summer on them. I'd like to have your criticism. You were lucky to be in a cool place like Kiso. Think of working in a hot, humid room like this. It was ghastly this summer!"

He read his thirty-one-syllable poems to Sankichi. Sankichi was moved less by the poems than by the thought of Sozo toiling to express his thoughts, trembling as he held the tip of the writing brush in his mouth to steady his feeble hand. Though afflicted, Sozo could not bear doing nothing. He had an unusual amount of energy for an invalid. His limbs were desiccated but his torso was as sturdy as the trunk of a giant tree. This man, who ate twice as much as the others even when sick, could find little consolation in anything other than the classic form of poetry. As he read his poems to Sankichi, streams of tears fell from large unblinking eyes filled with a mixture of anger, remorse, and defiance.

"I spent a lot of time thinking while you were away." Sozo took out a towel and, as if he were perspiring, wiped his face. "I've never thought about so many things as I did this summer."

Sankichi felt pity for Sozo as he looked at him. "Even in Kiso," he said, "we had some very hot days. Of course the mornings and evenings were quite cool compared to Tokyo."

"I just can't tell you how hot it was. Besides, there's no ventilation in here. Sometimes I just lay by the window without moving. Then I'd remember father . . . and mother." A small opening had been cut through the lower part of the wall to make it cooler. Sozo's bed was under this window. He continued. "Speaking of father, I browsed through a lot of his writing while you were away. And some of my books may be useful to you. One of these days I'll pass them on. You can take a look."

There was a narrow garden outside the room with a camellia and a few other trees. Sozo's world from morning to night was within this limited space. He used to visit Inagaki often, but now even that had become too troublesome. As no visitors came to see him especially, he was almost completely isolated from the rest of the world.

Noises drifted up from the street. Sozo listened. "Sankichi," he said, "I can talk this way only to you. I don't want to go on living when I'm looked on like a parasite. I've thought about it seriously this summer. I tried not eating for three or four days. But a human being is a strange thing. A man can't die so easily even if he wants to unless his time is up." Sozo spoke casually as though he were talking about eating or drinking.

"Once in a while someone asks if I'm all right," he went on. "They sound very kind, but what they really mean is 'Oh, is he still alive?' You know, my brothers all wish I were dead." He snickered. "Well, I'll eat if they feed me. If they don't, that's all right too."

He's at it again, thought Sankichi. The atmosphere in the family had grown intolerable. He opened the lattice door and stepped out to look at the sky. There was a nearby intersection with the main road, where a large boulevard ran from Hongō to Yushima.

The day the photograph arrived from the Hashimotos, Minoru was away on business. The other members of the family gathered in Sozo's room to look at it. Inagaki's wife was there, she had had a quarrel with her husband and looked unusually downcast. But soon she was drawn to the photograph.

"Really," exclaimed Okura, "Otane's beginning to look just like her father!"

"That's true, she does look like him." Sozo gazed at the picture.

"She isn't really grim like this," said Sankichi, "but here she's father come to life." Even Sankichi could not recognize the smiling face of Otane he had seen every day in Kiso, in the melancholy, austere likeness in the photograph.

"Tatsuo has aged too. Look at him." Okura pointed him out for Inagaki's wife. "He and Otane are the same age."

"So, this is your sister in Kiso," Mrs. Inagaki remarked.

"Shota's head is down too much. Osen looks best of all," judged Okura.

"After all, she's the most innocent," Sozo commented.

Sankichi laughed, explaining that the head clerk had purposely selected the shady spot, but his bald pate was just as shiny. The garden with its many boulders, the white godown wall to one side, the glimpse of a sunny slope in the background—all suggested the tranquil country life even within the limits of a photograph.

"It must be lovely to live in a place like this, especially if you have the money," Inagaki's wife mused. "Well, we'll have to push our husbands to start making some pretty soon."

"I agree. This is no life. Everything is just floating," Okura sighed.

The Koizumi house in the country before the fire was vivid in her memory. Looking at the picture of the Hashimoto family, she could not help reminiscing. Sankichi also recalled those early times as he listened to Okura's words. Just inside the gate were some old camellia trees; the family often extracted camellia oil from the nuts. The special entrance, built for receiving high-ranking guests, was flanked by a room with a wooden floor where his mother and sister-in-law did weaving. From any of the many large rooms the picturesque Mino plain could be seen extending in the distance. Pine trees and peonies grew in front of his father's study. On cold mornings, the family gathered round the *irori* and ate a local favorite, steaming roasted taro-and-buckwheat cakes dipped in grated turnip, blowing on them to cool them. In the evening an open fire burned, making the children's cheeks grow hot, while an old hired man making shoes out of straw told the stories of the will-o'-the-wisp deep in the mountains. The hearth held such pleasant memories.

Okura described how a Koizumi ancestor had founded the mountain villages several hundred years before. In those days the community was a hamlet of only three families: the Koizumis, a family later known as Tonya, and one traditionally called the "keeper of the mountain pass." The Koizumi ancestor had laid out everything in the village, began cultivation of the valley, selected the mountain slope as the site for houses, and built the temple and a chapel for the Buddha of medicine for the protection of the villagers. The major part of the land belonged to the Koizumi family. The patriarch gave parcels to new inhabitants and gradually built up a community. Even after Okura came into the Koizumi family, a villager had only to say, "Sir, won't you give me some lumber? I have to make a hut," and Tadahiro would answer, "Oh, take it, take it." Everything was done in that fashion. On New Years's Day the entire village gathered in front of the Koizumi gate to wish the family a good year, and in return, festive rice cakes and wine were distributed. The family henchmen would work for two or three nights preparing the rice cakes. In reply to the villagers' New Year wishes, the Koizumi gentry customarily responded: "Yes indeed, an auspicious year." Okura, her chest puffed out, mimicked the magnanimous posturing of her father-in-law and husband on such occasions. Her imitation of "Yes indeed" made the brothers guffaw.

Unprompted, Okura told the long story to her brothers-in-law and Mrs. Inagaki. "It was just like giving the all the property away. It's been a custom from way back. It was expected of the Koizumi family. When my husband was very young, they said that things couldn't be settled unless the young head of the Koizumi family ran the village; so he became the mayor. Even then, he gave his own holdings for public use. My father-in-law would run away from home whenever he got upset. The 'keeper of the mountain pass' would bring him back, and this meant more expense. We sold mountains and forests one after another. Finally Minoru realized he couldn't keep it up, and he began to work in the county office. It was just the same after he turned his hand to business. He never once made any profit for himself; he always lost. When business was too demanding he hired all kinds of people. And every time he ended up paying their debts besides his own. I feel so sorry for him when I think about it."

"It's true. He never made any profit for himself," said Sankichi.

Sozo was unusually congenial on this day. Engrossed in Okura's tales, he seemed to forget his own bodily miseries. Although Minoru had served a jail term, the younger brothers felt special respect for him whenever stories of the past were told.

Minoru returned, followed by Inagaki. At the sound of her husband's voice at the door, Inagaki's wife quickly hid herself in the kitchen; soon after, concerned about her daugher, she slipped out the back entrance.

"Has my wife been here?" Inagaki peered in from the veranda.

"Yes . . . she left only a minute ago," Okura answered with a smile.

Sozo said teasingly, "Inagaki, did you throw her out of the house? She came complaining to us."

"Oh no," the neighbor smiled wryly and answered in an impatient tone. "We had a little fight and in a tantrum she broke her *kōgai.** It's foolish, but I guess there are quarrels in every family."

"Only children keep couples together," Okura consoled him, smiling sadly.

After looking at the Kiso photograph, Minoru took Inagaki into the living room. The two discussed business matters and went over the bankbook.

When Inagaki left, Minoru called in Sankichi and broached the subject of his marriage.

Some of Sankichi's friends were engaged to be married, some had just married, and others already had children. A certain Professor Oshima had suggested a possible bride for Sankichi. Minoru had taken it upon himself to pursue the marriage negotiations with the professor.

Sankichi's past was filled with misery. When still young, he was made responsible for the family during Minoru's long imprisonment. Throughout the period he met with countless difficulties. Sometimes his heart was so heavy that death itself seemed insufficient to lift the burden. No sooner had he seen a gleam of hope in his future than his mother, the one who had shared the hard times with him, passed away. These experiences made him a pensive man.

Sankichi had once met the young woman proposed by Professor Oshima six or seven years earlier, when she was about fifteen. Okura knew her better, having spent a summer at the seashore in Bōshu with her. The girl was not accustomed to the level of poverty Sankichi had known. Though he was free of debts he owned no

* An ornamental bodkin for the hair.

property, and had repeatedly declined the marriage offer. But Oshima claimed to know all about the girl's parents, who were content to marry their daughter to a mere student of literature. Minoru also showed his confidence in the marriage and insisted that everything be left to him. So Sankichi put the matter in his hands.

"Oyuki would be just right for Sankichi," Okura said approvingly.

"At any rate, according to Professor Oshima, she's the favorite among her father's daughters," Minoru said. "I haven't met her, but she must be a nice girl if she's the favorite."

"I know her very well," interrupted Okura. "When I went to the Bōshu shore for my beriberi, Oyuki and another girl about her age were there with their schoolteacher. We spent a month together. Of course she was still rather young—almost childish, making a big fuss about collecting shells with her friend. But she's a fine girl, I assure you."

"The professor told me he visited the parents and stayed at their house," Minoru continued. "They probably started talking about this at that time. The father sounds like a character."

He talked some more about the girl's family and chuckled. "So Sankichi has grown up enough to take a bride. . . . How time flies." Minoru, wearing a tradesman's apron, sat cross-legged at a large desk of paulownia wood. Okura moved behind her husband, and with little tinkling noises took out some change from the desk drawer. She soon returned to the kitchen.

"It doesn't seem right for me to marry before Sozo," said Sankichi.

"He's no damned good," Minoru blurted out in provincial dialect. "I've told him time and again, he should realize he's as good as dead. He should keep calm and behave like a sensible person. I say this all the time, but he just doesn't understand."

"I wonder how he's come to this."

"That's what he got for sleeping around."

"He probably ran into a specially low-class woman."

"He owes everything to himself," declared Minoru. "If he realizes that, he'll be a little more contrite. But his attitude is all wrong. In every big family there's always a rotten apple. You find one like him in every home."

Whenever the subject of Sozo came up, Minoru would bite his lip and speak bitterly. He let it be known that Sozo was a selfish and spoiled man with a shameful disease, and a heavy burden to him. Minoru's dislike for Sozo started when he came home sick and dissipated. In Minoru's absence, his mother and wife were keeping house, and Sozo had made improper advances to the young Okura.

"It's his loss if we dislike him," sighed Minoru. "One of these days I'm going to find someone to take care of him and send him away. There's nothing else to do."

Sankichi could no longer continue his studies. He was obliged to find some kind of employment to earn a regular income before he could set up his own household.

One day Minoru called Sankichi into the living room, saying that he had something to show him. Just then, Mrs. Inagaki came in. "I must talk to your brother," she said to Sankichi. "Please let me talk to him first. I won't be long." She walked in, and Minoru saw by the look on her face that something was on her mind. After some hesitation she began. "Of course, it's not for me to question you; it's your business and you are all experienced men. But I wonder when we're going to see some results? I have nothing but my husband's words and I can't feel secure any more."

Minoru coughed several times before he said, "You mean about the vehicle? We have a good engineer working on it. There's nothing to worry about."

"I know. My husband keeps saying he's sorry to worry you about money, but when the time comes and the money rolls in. . . . The truth is, he's so pressed for money, he tells stories to his mother when she comes up from the country, he cries, and he puts on all kinds of acts to get money out of her."

"I've told your husband, if you need money, it's in the bank."

"Thank you very much. I feel better hearing you say so, but somehow . . . unless we can see some light . . . not knowing how long it's going to be before the business starts producing. . . ." Her eyes were still unsure. "If my husband finds out that I came to talk to you, he'll explode. But you know, we women are not like men. We worry a lot about small things."

Not wanting to offend Minoru she did not pursue the subject further. After chatting briefly about Oshun and her daughter, she went off to see Okura.

On Minoru's desk, Sankichi saw impressive betrothal gifts and an itemized list of the presents written on thick formal paper. Minoru opened a package ready for sending and showed it to Sankichi.

"How do you like this? I chose this *obi* material for Professor Oshima to deliver. It's satin brocade."

"I'm sure that it was not necessary for one so fine," said Sankichi.

Minoru looked at him as if to say, "How could we do any less, when I'm your brother? I'd be disgraced."

Sankichi felt embarrassed to have caused his brother this extra expense. He had wanted to make the marriage preparation as simple as possible; certainly there was no need for a show that would cause additional debt. But to Minoru, that was out of the question.

The day approached when Oshun would be graduating from elementary school, and her parents began to talk about selecting a good girl's high school for her. About this time, two openings were offered to Sankichi: one was a teaching position in Kyoto, the other a letter from his old English teacher, inviting him to come teach at his school. Although the school was in a remote mountain area and the salary minimal, Sankichi chose it.

Sankichi set out for his new post before the beginning of the spring term. He had lived with Minoru's family about two years since his return from Sendai. Now he was about to leave the Koizumi household for good.

As he busied himself with packing once more, he resolved to establish his own house on a simple scale.

Chapter 4

Sankichi left for his new post. A month later Minoru received a telegram from Professor Oshima saying that the Nakuras would be coming soon with their daughter. Nakura was the family name of the girl Oshima had recommended.

Minoru called Okura to the living room. "They had promised to come," he said, "but I wasn't sure and I was worried until the telegram arrived. I feel better now." He sent his wife for Inagaki, and the assistant came running.

"Oh, the Nakuras are already on their way?" said Inagaki as he approached Minoru. "Boat, train, and any other kind of transportation. It's not easy to come so far." Laughter filled the house.

A detailed plan was on Minoru's desk: where the wedding was to take place, how many courses were to be served at the reception and for how many guests, how much sake had to be ordered, and how many young geishas were to be engaged for the occasion.

"By the way, about the girls carrying the ceremonial sake ewers," said Minoru, looking up at Inagaki, "I had originally thought of asking your daughter and Oshun, but it's all so much trouble. I've decided to hire a couple of young geishas after all."

"That will be easier," said Okura. "It's hard enough just to teach the girls the difference between the two ewers."

"Yes, I know," replied Inagaki. "In fact we were worried about it. And I think I should be the only one from my family at the ceremony. We'd better keep it simple. Let's make money first, then we can all go to a restaurant. Don't you agree, Mrs. Koizumi?"

"You're so right," smiled Okura. "Even if I wanted to go, I don't have clothes good enough to wear."

"Oh, you shouldn't give up that easily," said Inagaki waving his hand. "If you want to attend the wedding, there are a million ways. My neighbor's daughter, for instance, went to meet a marriage prospect wearing a rented kimono. Look, some borrow kimonos and some make money by renting kimonos. That's how things are today; it's the times."

"Simplicity, simplicity," Minoru said emphatically, as though issuing an order.

Inagaki was taken up with the wedding, and he left to arrange for the reception at the restaurant and then to send a telegram to Sankichi, instructing him to return to Tokyo at once.

"Sozo, I want you to stay with the Inagakis for a while." Obeying Minoru, the invalid, dragging his paralyzed leg, reluctantly left his room and moved in with the neighbors.

On the day of the wedding Minoru rose early, swept the garden thoroughly, and put the house in order. After carefully dusting various pieces of furniture in the living room with a feather duster, he arranged the desk and tea shelf precisely to his liking. He placed cushions around the charcoal brazier and put out a tobacco set, cigarette case, and ashtrays. While the tea steeped, he sat and surveyed the incense-filled room; now he felt he was ready to have the Nakura family come at any time. He found the colors of the peacock feathers in the alcove especially pleasing.

A letter of congratulation from Morihiko said that he was unable to attend the wedding ceremony, unsettled at an inn as he was; he would leave everything to Minoru and wished Sankichi the very best.

"Dear, I've bought some clogs for Oshun. Will you look at them?" said Okura when she returned from shopping with her daughter.

"Let me see them." Minoru examined the high, mat-surfaced, red lacquer clogs with bells attached. "How can I take her to a wedding wearing clogs like these?" he scolded. "This is the kind apprentice geishas wear."

"But she wouldn't listen to me. She kept saying she wanted them."

"What kind of mother are you? These won't do at all. Exchange them for ones without bells and lacquer."

"I thought so too, but. . ." Okura hesitated and forced a smile.

"Let's go and exchange them now," pleaded Oshun, pulling at her mother's sleeve.

Minoru's heart was filled with joy. He prayed that the Koizumis would multiply and prosper. He could hardly wait for the ceremony. Arrangements had been made for the bride, her mother, and her brother to stay at an inn after their long journey. Minoru left the house with Inagaki to meet them at the appointed time.

Osugi, Okura's sister, had recently arrived to help with the chores in exchange for room and board. She and Inagaki's wife dressed Oshun in her finery and tied her *obi* in the formal style. Naoki's grandmother arrived wearing her ceremonial kimono. Congratulations were exchanged. It was almost evening when Sankichi, who had returned from the country, left with these people for the wedding ceremony.

After they were gone, those remaining behind put away the scattered clothes and cleaned the rooms. The lighting in the house was brighter than usual; even the dim entrance was well lit and everything suddenly took on a different appearance.

"Good evening." The Inagaki girl came in and joined her mother. Osugi and Okura were seated at the brazier.

Mrs. Inagaki went to look at the clock in the next room and returned to her daughter's side. "I wonder if they've already gone to the restaurant," she said.

"Oh no, not for a while yet," Okura smiled. "They will have sake at the inn where the Nakuras are staying. They'll move on when they're done with celebrating there."

"They must be drinking right now," said Osugi.

"I understand that Mrs. Nakura and the bride's elder brother came with her," Mrs. Inagaki remarked. "My husband must be talking his head off to the guests from the north. But it's not easy for the mother, if she has to dress the bride and shop for her, all by herself." As she talked, her daughter sat by her, leaning dreamily against her as though imagining what the marriage ceremony was like.

The lights were burning in every room. Okura spoke pensively, as she gazed at the desk lamp with a round shade: "When I was married—it's almost like a tale from long ago—I realized I was leaving my home for good, and as I crossed the threshold, tears gushed out and I couldn't stop them."

"Everyone goes through the same thing," said Inagaki's wife. "There's nothing so sad as that moment."

"I wish I could go through that again," Osugi laughed, moistening her dry lips. "Ah, everything's over for me. I can only get older and older."

"What's the matter with this girl?" said Mrs. Inagaki, looking at her daughter. "She's trembling all over."

"Even I feel shaky," Osugi said as she wrapped her arm around the little girl.

It was a peaceful night. The temple bell at Ueno sounded clear in the still air. The pleasant talk continued as the women waited for the wedding party to return.

At about ten, they all arrived in rickshas, and the house was suddenly filled with people.

"I'm very impressed by Mrs. Nakura. She's an admirable person," Minoru kept saying to Inagaki and Inagaki agreed. The drinking began again, and Sankichi's new wife was introduced to his family and the others.

"Oshun, you have one more aunt now," whispered Inagaki's daughter.

"Yes. Aunt Oyuki."

"Thank you for all you've done in arranging things," said Minoru as he offered a cup of sake to Inagaki.

"No more for me," the assistant declined, waving his hand. "I've never drunk so much as tonight."

"And I've never been so happy," Minoru said repeatedly. "I'm going to drink all night even if I'm the only one drinking."

The day after the wedding, Minoru said casually, "Sankichi, I'm going to ask you to take care of Sozo. I'd like you to take him with you when you go to the country."

Sankichi never dreamed that such a demand would be made of him just as he was starting a new life. Sozo was too much of a burden even for experienced Osugi or Okura, and he wondered if his young bride could cope with him. Yet with all its seeming casualness, Minoru's request had the force of a demand.

Sankichi promised a reply before leaving for the country.

Because of his teaching schedule, Sankichi had only little time to relax after the wedding. But he wanted to at least introduce his wife to Morihiko and Sozo.

A number of trunks arrived from the inn where the Nakuras were staying. "That's a lot of luggage!" exclaimed Inagaki, who happened by and helped the delivery man stack it temporarily.

Sankichi took Oyuki around the corner to Inagaki's house, to meet Sozo, who was still staying there. The sickly brother greeted Oyuki with appreciative eyes as he rubbed his withered hand.

"Now you've met Sozo. It's Morihiko's turn next." They left the Inagaki house to go to see Morihiko.

Oyuki asked, "What does your second brother do?"

Morihiko had spent a long time in Korea. He was interested in the economic development of East Asia, and during his stay he made many contacts in various fields. The family knew that he once tried his hand at foreign trade; but other than that no one had a clear idea of his work. From the day of his return to Japan, he had worked for the people of his province in his capacity as delegate for the Forestry Incident, for which he had worked once before. He regarded himself as a simple citizen who worked for public causes, but it was difficult to define his career in terms of profession.

"Well, suppose you just come with me and meet him," Sankichi simply suggested.

Oshun accompanied the young couple to Morihiko's inn. His second-floor room had a bear skin on the floor, a desk and a go table by the window, and a Chinese trunk in one corner. The orderliness indicated clearly that the occupant was accustomed to living in inns.

"It's nice of you to come," Morihiko said in welcome. "I explained everything to Minoru in my letter. I hope Mrs. Nakura forgave me for not coming to meet her. Let me treat you to a western-style lunch today." He took out a teapot and cups and clapped his hands for the maid.

The mistress of the inn appeared at the door. "Did you call, sir?"

"Yes, I want you to meet my brother's new bride." Morihiko introduced Oyuki and asked for some cake to go with the tea.

"And I'd like some cigarettes," added Sankichi.

"You seem to be smoking a lot," grimaced Morihiko, who neither smoked nor drank. He took his guests to the quiet upstairs room of a western-style restaurant for lunch. There he talked about his wife and children who were waiting for him at home.

Now that Oyuki had been introduced to his brothers, Sankichi thought of letting her meet two of his acquaintances in the hope that they might become friends. Oyuki was interested, and so it was decided that they would visit them.

In the evening, Sankichi first took Oyuki to Sone Chiyo's house. Chiyo was an aunt of one of Oyuki's school friends and lived with her sister's family. According to family custom, a small, oblong ceramic handwarmer was offered to each visitor, including one for a musician friend of Chiyo, who happened to be visiting; the room seemed to have almost too many handwarmers. The house was modestly decorated with few ornaments. Occasionally one could hear a child crying. A fair-skinned girl with long hair, about six years old, came to sit by Chiyo, and bowed to Sankichi and his wife.

"What a pretty little girl!" exclaimed Oyuki. The delicate child twisted shyly and soon left the room to escape the guests.

Chiyo was older than Oyuki, but to Oyuki's eyes she appeared young, melancholy, enigmatic, and preoccupied with her own thoughts and emotions. Though retiring, Chiyo had gone through many experiences.

Since another guest was present, the couple did not stay long. "Well, what do you think of her?" Sankichi asked his wife on the way back to Minoru's house.

"Well." She was at a loss for an answer. She could not form any opinion until she knew Chiyo better.

The couple decided to leave Tokyo the next afternoon, and they were busy with shopping and packing until then. Sankichi went to Minoru and for the time being declined the request to take over the care of Sozo.

"That was a little unreasonable on my part; I was wrong to ask you," nodded Minoru, smiling.

Mrs. Nakura and Oyuki's brother brought twenty yen for Oyuki to buy a new chest of drawers and said that they would not be coming to the station. The couple took their leave and arrived at Ueno Station with their luggage at about three o'clock. The station was crowded.

Sankichi and Oyuki spent the night en route in order to make better connections. Not being in any particular hurry, they took another train the following afternoon, planning to arrive at their destination some time the same day. It was after dark when they reached their new home. Oyuki followed her husband along a dark and unfamiliar road from the station to her new home. One of Sankichi's students, who was also the houseboy, had looked after the house while he was gone to Tokyo and was awaiting their arrival. They entered the house directly from the garden. The boy was sitting by the sunken square *irori*.

"Since tomorrow is Monday, I thought you might come back and waited for you," said the boy after greeting Oyuki. Sankichi explained the delay as he relaxed by the fire.

"So this is our house." Oyuki looked around. She took out some cake and offered it to the boy. She saw the cupboard near the hearth, the dark, soot-covered wall, and the large, coarse dining table.

"They say this used to be a samurai's residence," Sankichi explained. "The original entrance in back is used for storage now. The entrance we just came in was built by the people who lived here before. They left the house in terrible shape. I papered the walls and changed the *tatami* mats to make it a little more livable. And I had the *irori* made over too since I came."

The houseboy brought a lamp from the storage room. Sankichi took it and showed his wife the darkened kitchen. All Oyuki could see was a large, wooden-floored room with a sink, and some obviously cheap, new utensils. Sankichi opened a sooty door on the side, and holding the lamp high, he showed her the charcoal, logs, and kindling stored in the dark.

Then Sankichi led her to an eight-mat room next to the *irori* room. "Suppose you make this your room." Oyuki saw the high ceiling and the alcove patched with brown wallpaper. There was another eight-mat room in the back with books and a desk, and next to it was the houseboy's room. It was a relatively large dwelling but too rustic for Oyuki's taste.

Their luggage was brought by the delivery service from the station. The couple still felt the jostling of the train, and the presence, stares, and whispers of the two passengers, probably a married couple, who had boarded the train along the way and had occupied the seat opposite them. The wife's large eyes and the husband's lifeless ones had embarrassed both of them. They were still shy about traveling together and avoided looking at each other.

The space between the sliding doors grew brighter. Oyuki rose and went to the kitchen to begin work. She stepped out the back door, and the fresh morning air was invigorating. She had never inhaled such cool, clean air.

The surrounding neighborhood, which had been hidden in darkness the night before, now opened before her. She realized that the house she had spent the night in was one of two attached houses with one thatched roof. She could see the distant mountain range between houses and trees that lay just beyond a mulberry patch. The rumbling that had disturbed her sleep came from a water mill.

A narrow stream flowed past the rear of the house. Oyuki, crouching under a silverberry bush, scooped up the cool water with cupped hands. The water came coursing through the grass from a neighboring bamboo grove, surging over the pebbles and stones. She washed her face with the stream water, intrigued by the quaintness of her new experience.

The houseboy came round to the back entrance carrying a bucket. He had to pass between hedges of entwined larchwood branches to the community well to get drinking water.

Now the dilapidation of the house was more clearly visible in the daylight. Used to her own more comfortable home, Oyuki was struck by the barrenness of the starkly empty rooms.

The boy was a considerable help to her. He finished cleaning the back yard while Oyuki was cooking in the strange kitchen. She walked out, bucket in hand, to scrub the veranda, and found the azaleas in full bloom in the back yard. The purple flowers at the base of the mud wall and the white ones at the bottom of the apple tree made an attractive contrast, giving the house a serene air. From the other side of the wall came the sound of someone washing pots. The morning sun reflected brightly on a high white wall in the distance.

Breakfast was ready. Oyuki arranged the dishes she had cooked on the table, and she and her husband sat down with the cheerful houseboy to eat. On this first morning in her own new home, she drank her morning soup from a crude bowl. She could hardly use the black lacquer box of fine chopsticks, a family acquaintance's present, that she had brought in her luggage.

Soon Sankichi and the student had to leave for school. Oyuki prepared a large boxed lunch. A simple cotton kimono was adequate in the country as long as it was clean.

Oyuki's married life began in this manner. In contrast to her previous comfortable life with many servants, she now had to learn to do everything herself. But she had a healthy body and determination to work as hard as she could to help her husband.

When the hoe he had ordered was delivered by the village blacksmith, Sankichi set to work in the back yard as soon as he got back from school. He had rented a section of the mulberry patch from the owner of the house. It was a rough, stony area lying along the hedge; and before he could work it as a vegetable garden, he had to turn the hard soil.

An uncontrollable common weed called "railroad grass," leftover from the previous season, spread along a corner of the hedge. Pulling out the weeds alone exhausted him. Other weeds were also firmly rooted and sprawled over a large area. Green buds were coming out all around.

Sankichi had first begun to watch people working in fields in Kiso; from this he formed some of his thoughts into poems. But it was a novel experience for him to take a hoe in his hands and cultivate even a small piece of land. Unaccustomed to physical labor, he tired easily; his arms and legs did not move as he wished. From time to time he would stretch his back and lean on the heavy mud-covered hoe and inhale the fresh air.

The sunshine was dazzling. He wrapped a towel around his head, and set to work again.

A man passing by peeked over the hedge and chuckled. "I see you're working hard," he called. It was the school janitor, who was a tenant farmer on the side and harvested a considerable crop every year. Sankichi decided to ask for his help with the garden and buy some vegetable seeds from him.

The next day Sankichi went out to the garden again immediately after school. Oyuki and the houseboy came to him through the hedge and the mulberry patch.

"Don't just stand there. How about giving me a hand?"

"I came to help you."

"You two get rid of those rocks. I guess one should really start young for this sort of work. I'm sure I'll never make a farmer," he laughed as he hoed the furrowed ground.

"The towel on your head is real farmer style, but your glasses aren't," said Oyuki, laughing. Sankichi grinned and wiped his perspiring brow with a muddy hand. Boulders constantly appeared in the soil. Oyuki put a towel over her hair, tucked up her kimono hem, and began to pick up rocks alongside the boy. She carried a bamboo basket full of rocks to the stream. She moved the uprooted weeds piled in a corner of the lot. It was no easy task for her to make even a few trips with piles of the tenacious muddy growths. Under the relentless sun the three worked diligently.

After rinsing the hoe in the clear stream, Sankichi, pleasantly fatigued, sat down on the entrance porch to smoke a cigarette. Oyuki came after washing her feet. The region was noted for its hard-working women. A number of them with linen bags hanging round their necks, passed, on their way to the mulberry fields. They bowed to Sankichi. At this outset of her new life, Oyuki realized that a woman could work hard if she tried.

As Oyuki's wedding had taken place but a few days earlier, she still looked like an unmarried girl. Her clothes, a reminder of her affluent home, were hardly suitable for the wife of a poor school teacher. The flaming red of her *obi* was incongruous for one who carried rocks in the field.

Sankichi wanted Oyuki to change her style of dressing. As though educating his young wife, he told her to lower the high back padding of her *obi*, to select subdued colors, and to put away all accessories; and two gold rings were too many. Such admonitions were hard for Oyuki to accept.

"How can I wear a blue *obi* padding at my age?" she said, looking at him sadly. "You tell me to give up these things now, but if I don't wear bright colors while I'm young, when will I ever have the chance again?" Nevertheless, she obeyed her husband. She put aside her ornaments and made up her mind to dress like the wife of a country teacher.

Oyuki placed before her husband a packet containing about a hundred yen. "My father said when he gave me this to use it only for a real emergency." She added that he had strictly ordered her, once she married, never to return home even if she were abandoned by the roadside. Sankichi could sense through her words both the will and the compassion of his father-in-law.

"Fresh seaweed! Fresh seaweed!" some women called from the gate. It was a group of female venders from far-away Niigata. Their dress for the long journey made Oyuki realize with nostalgia how far she was from home. The croaking of the frogs mingling with the sound of the mill came through the sliding doors facing south. From time to time the rumbling noise of a passing horsecart could be heard.

Sankichi's house lay off an old highway running through an ancient town. Oyuki had once been taken through the wooded valley to the school principal's house. From there she could see the windows of the school building where Sankichi taught, beyond the mulberry fields that lay near an old castle site. To reach the school, he sometimes followed the old highway; other times he walked along the back stream, across the new road in front of the railroad station, and then he would wind his way through the mulberry fields and stone walls until he came to the railroad crossing. There he would meet a group of pupils who had walked sometimes four or five miles to reach the acacia-covered school gate. Listening to her husband's explanations, Oyuki learned that their home stood halfway up the slope of a large mountain. He couldn't believe, he said, that they were in the same province as his sister, Otane, separated as they were by many miles. Oyuki was only vaguely even aware of the direction of the Hashimoto house.

The school janitor helped Sankichi plant beans, potatoes, and other vegetables that were easy to grow in the back yard. He bought some scallion shoots from a passing peasant vender and planted them too.

After Oyuki married Sankichi, some things of her past followed her. There was a man who wrote to her under a woman's name that he had hoped she would marry him, and that he was very disappointed, but that he hoped to visit her some time. She showed the letter to Sankichi and told him how annoyed she was by it. Sankichi read it with curiosity but did nothing. At times she fell into a strange silence. If Sankichi criticized her for her housekeeping, her eyes filled with tears, and she sank into a depression that lasted two or three days. Then Sankichi had to give in, realizing he could not win against tears, and he cajoled her into good humor again.

"This chilled bean curd you made is very good. The food is wonderful tonight." Oyuki would then regain her spirits and enjoy the meal with him. Her melancholy never lasted too long, and once she sprang out of her dejection, she again became the usual hard working Oyuki with sparkling eyes. She did not seem to mind her husband's poverty.

The furniture Oyuki brought from home was arranged in her room. Among her things was a leather box bearing a large family crest. It contained her koto plectrums, symbols of more youthful days, and two lovely dolls, a little girl and boy. Her relatives and acquaintances sent gifts and letters wishing her well. Letters came also from the two women Sankichi introduced to her in Tokyo.

"Chiyo's handwriting is just like her, very delicate," remarked Sankichi.

"They all write so well." Oyuki gazed at the letter.

Congratulations also came to Oyuki from Tsutomu, an employee of the Nakura store who was related to her brother-in-law. It was written in the skillful cursive script typical of a young merchant.

The couple's lives began to grow together. Soon, by the time the potatoes budded and the snow peas in the kitchen garden lifted their shell-like shoots, the new dwelling began to take on the air of a home. The middle-aged women in the neighborhood became Oyuki's advisers. One was the next-door neighbor, whose house was separated from hers by a wall. She had a sick husband and many children. These women took turns bringing Oyuki foods of the season and telling her of their household experiences.

Chapter 5

When Tokyo schools recessed for the summer, Oyuki's younger sister Ofuku, her immediate junior, came to Sankichi's house. She had been sent to live at the school dormitory in Tokyo, away from her many sisters. Her mother gave permission for her to come and spend the summer with Oyuki.

Sankichi's school was in the process of being transferred from private control to town administration, and his vacation was half as long as Ofuku's, which ran more than two months. The vegetables in the back yard were thriving and white potato flowers in continuous bloom when Sankichi was finally free of his duties.

He was delighted with the idea of having a younger sister. Between studies he joined his wife, trying to entertain his new in-law.

One afternoon Oyuki brought out a box of photographs of the large Nakura family.

In the airy south room the two sisters sat looking at the pictures. Their eldest sister and her husband, who had been given the Nakura surname, and the sister next in line, who with her husband had established a branch store called Maruna, appeared in the photos; and as they scanned each snapshot, the two girls talked about home. There were pictures of their younger sisters, group pictures of the elder sisters' children, and childhood pictures of Oyuki with her nursemaid. Her pictures showed different stages of her development into a plump young girl. A photo of her Tokyo school days showed her and another girl holding umbrellas; their faces had been torn off.

Oyuki showed her sister pictures of Sankichi too. One showing Sankichi in a turned-down hat was taken when he had just gone to Tokyo. The apron-clad older boy next to him was Sozo, the one in the center with a hat was Hashimoto Shota, this was Tatsuo, that was Minoru, and the one in the back with a scarf around his neck was Morihiko.

"How about this one. Isn't this a snappy one of me?" said San-kichi, pointing to an old picture of himself, taken at Asakusa Park with a childhood friend from home.

"Oh, is this you?" said Ofuku, inspecting it. "It's cute, but you look frightening in the other picture."

They all laughed. The photograph was taken about the time of his graduation from college, and Sankichi's eyes were set in a stare.

Among the pictures Oyuki had were those of girl friends and some men acquaintances. Some were familiar to Sankichi by their names; others were unknown to him.

"Oh, this is Tsutomu, isn't it?" Ofuku took out several photo-graphs of the young man who worked at the Nakura store and gazed at them.

Oyuki called her sister, but there was no answer. The young girl often settled down in a cool spot, such as the wall near the entrance or the storage room, in order to be alone to read and write, but she was nowhere to be seen.

Oyuki called again. Alongside the south room ran a veranda hugged by a hedge, and from it one could glimpse a fenced-in vege-table patch. Through the deep shade of the mulberry trees Oyuki could hear Ofuku answer.

She went around to the back, walking through the thick mulberry grove, and came out into the garden where the snow pea flowers were blooming. Green pods hung from the vines twined around tall sticks.

"I've been looking for you everywhere, Ofuku. So you've been hiding here."

Ofuku looked at her sister through the leaves. "I just stepped out here. I found so many peas I thought I'd pick some for you."

"There are a lot, aren't there," said Oyuki, beginning to pick some. "The letter you promised the other day. . . I wish you'd write it. I'm sending one to mother."

"There's no rush, is there?"

"But since I'm writing . . ."

"Oh well, I suppose I could," Ofuku agreed as she came over to her sister. She emptied the handful of peas she had picked into Oyuki's apron and left the garden. Oyuki remained.

When she returned to the house, pushing her way through the mulberry leaves, Ofuku was still in a back room composing the letter. She put the snow peas on the dining table by the hearth and began to snip off the ends of the pods one by one.

Finally Ofuku brought the letter. "Is this all right?"

"You should write it a little more politely," Oyuki told her.

"But I don't know how to." Ofuku cocked her head, smiling shyly.

She had taken Oyuki's advice, she said in the letter, and decided to marry Tsutomu. She would look forward to her graduation from high school and to the day when her wish would come true. She rewrote the letter and Oyuki enclosed it with her own.

A letter had come several days before from Mrs. Nakura, thanking Oyuki for her care of Ofuku and with it a box of cake. Oyuki immensely enjoyed reading her mother's news from the country. In answer to her mother's, Oyuki expressed her own opinion about Ofuku's marriage.

Oyuki received letters from Tsutomu quite frequently. Another had just arrived and she did not know where to hide it.

One day Sankichi found a letter from Tsutomu to Oyuki among his mail. "Tsutomu writes very often, doesn't he?" he remarked casually as he gave the letter to his wife.

Sankichi had confidence in Oyuki. He showed no particular interest in the contents of the letter, but he was not totally without some idea. He was of course neither young nor naive enough to be surprised. He did not doubt that Oyuki had married him after some romantic episodes, just as he himself had had. She was already twenty-two. It was not strange that such letters should follow her to her new home. He hoped only that she would not be foolish in her judgment, that she would first think of her marriage. And then he had other things to worry about.

It was the season when the vegetables needed much attention. Sankichi would shoulder the hoe and go out to see the progress in the yard. He had already turned over the earth several times along the ridges. He covered the roots of the green onions, which seemed to grow taller every time he made the rounds; then he worked on the potatoes. As he dug, he uncovered large succulent ones. He looked at them with pleasure.

After washing the potatoes in the back stream, he took them up to the kitchen. Oyuki was happily surprised; she boiled them in salt water and served them at the table. The family gathered around to drink tea and enjoy the product of their labor.

That night Sankichi invited Ofuku and the houseboy to his room to play cards. The yellow lamplight reflected on the curious faces of queens and jacks. Ofuku played well and was real competition for her brother-in-law and the young student. After playing for a while, Oyuki left the room complaining of a headache. The lamp by the *irori* gleamed softly. She had been feeling languid lately, and she had missed her monthly period. But she was not too concerned as she lay by the fireplace.

She could hear bursts of gay laughter in the back room. A game seemed to end and a new one begin. When her headache was almost gone, she rolled out the long writing paper on the dining table and answered Tsutomu's letter. She wrote that she was busy with her housekeeping and that her remissness in correspondence did not come from her feelings; she was happy to know that he had accepted Ofuku's hand in marriage. In closing, she wrote, "To my beloved Tsutomu, from a despairing Oyuki."

The next day she wrote Tsutomu's name on the envelope and added the address that he had designated. It was not a communication she wanted to make public. She purposely omitted her name from the back of the envelope and put it on her dresser, intending to mail it later. Then she took her sister off to the hot springs beyond the railroad tracks under the cliff.

The nameless letter on the dresser caught Sankichi's eye. Puzzled, he opened it and read it through. Then, collecting himself, he read it again. It was as if he were driven by an irresistible force. Once the facts came to his awareness, he felt compelled to get at the truth of the matter. He opened the drawers of the dresser, scavenging through her sewing box and even through her hair pieces in the comb box. Then he went to the kitchen. In a corner of the dark entrance stood an empty charcoal bag that was used for wastepaper.

Sankichi took the bag to the back garden and emptied it at the foot of a persimmon tree. Worried about the neighbors and the two women returning, Sankichi looked around often, trembling. Finally some pages of Tsutomu's letters appeared among the trash. In them, he read of the young man's ardent passion, he sensed his youthful, prepossessing, intelligent character. Suspecting the return of Oyuki, Sankichi put the paper in the bag and placed her letter exactly as it had been on the dresser.

The two women came in, parasols in hand. They immediately began to take in the laundry and prepare dinner, while chatting about the view of the apple orchard stretching out in front of the hot springs, of the expanse of green fields, and of the village and mountains beyond the valley.

The family gathered around the table. Oyuki sat across from Sankichi and cheerfully ate her supper. Her gentle eyes were glowing with warmth and happiness. Occasionally Sankichi glanced at her, but he could detect nothing unusual. He did not eat much.

He thought about the problem all night. He had grown so sensitive to hurt that he could recall every word he had read in Oyuki's and Tsutomu's letters. He left the house early and walked aimlessly and did not return until evening.

Oyuki was waiting with his favorite dish of fresh vegetables and called the others to dinner. Snow peas were known as "snow splits" in the area. She had sautéed them in lard and salt especially for her husband. She wanted to see his face light up. Ofuku and the houseboy began eating, but Sankichi, looking pale, did not even taste the food that had been cooked for him.

"You're hardly eating today," Oyuki said in disappointment.

Until late that night, Sankichi leafed through various books at his desk, but he could find no answer in them. Again he brooded throughout the night. He sympathized with the love of Oyuki and Tsutomu, but what to do. Should he write to Mrs. Nakura, or should he consult with Oyuki's close friend?

His confusion was further aggravated by lack of sleep for two nights. In the morning he absently left the house again and after wandering about until evening, returned with the idea of divorce in his mind. If it were possible, he would even go as far as bringing the lovers together.

Flight from home, death—his past came back to him. In those days, at the end of wandering, he had gone back to the family, realizing that he was still young and that there were many things he still wanted to learn in life. Ever since then, he had actively thrown himself into experiencing things. Hardships came soon enough: his brother's imprisonment, the family's bankruptcy, his sister's sickness, his mother's death—he was forced to learn all the things that an ordinary young man did not have to know. His only hope was to build a family of his own. There, he would have a fresh start in life. When he left Tokyo, Inagaki remarked about married life, "It is only the first hundred days that are fun." The "hundred days" had scarcely passed, and Sankichi's marriage was on the verge of foundering. Who would have dreamed it?

Could Oyuki ever return to the Nakura family? It was doubtful. Her father had told her never to come back even if she had to die by the roadside. Her name had been transferred permanently to the official record of the Koizumi family, and would the courts recognize the reasons for divorce? He thought of consulting a lawyer who lived in a nearby town. He continued to think after he got into bed under the mosquito net. The summer night was short.

Sankichi left the house for a walk and took the way to the school principal's house. He entered the formal old gate, went around to the back, and saw a man directing a worker in a rye field on the hill. It was the principal, who, seeing Sankichi, came down. He had hired the school janitor to grow a large amount of vegetables.

He led his former student to the quiet study that looked out onto a flower garden. His long, magnificent beard was almost completely white, and he now needed false teeth, but his spirit was no less vigorous than a young man's.

Sankichi's was a problem he could not discuss with others, but he wanted to ask for the advice of his former teacher, who was like a father. He had also been the teacher of Professor Oshima, who arranged Sankichi's marriage. Sankichi described the situation briefly and asked the principal's opinion about a divorce.

Framed photographs of the principal as a young man and of his first wife hung together on the wall of the quiet study.

"You mustn't even think of divorce," the schoolmaster said after listening. "Think of my case. I married three times, you know. Ah, the first marriage. . . . You can never recapture the happiness of your youth. When I look back on them all, I feel that my first wife was the best. There's nothing worse in life than losing your first wife, and that's my frank opinion."

Sankichi listened to his teacher in silence. The old man made vigorous gestures with his large hands. "Wait until you get older. You're sure to remember what I'm saying. Socrates impresses me about one thing. His wife was a real termagant, you know. But all his life he put up with her. You can't do any better than that. That was probably the noblest quality he had."

The principal began to talk like a preacher. Then he digressed to his past and to pleasant memories of his days in America.

"American women are very sophisticated. They introduce their former boyfriends to husbands and form a new, clean friendship. 'He was my sweetheart,' they say. They're so open. Japanese women should learn something from them."

Another visitor dropped in, and the principal changed the subject. "Well, Koizumi, think it over."

Sankichi took his leave and went out through the gate. But once he set off for home, his anguish returned and weighed heavily on his heart. It pained him even to see the thatched roof of his house.

Oyuki was waiting for him. His heart ached more than ever when he saw the smile on his young wife's face. She was so dependent on him and tried to please him in every way.

He lay down in his room until the lamp was lit.

"Bring me a wet towel," he called, and Oyuki hurried to the sink. He lay sprawled on the mats, and his chest heaved with labored breathing.

"Good heavens, what happened?" Oyuki put the cold towel on her husband's chest.

The next evening Sankichi took out his writing pad and wrote late into the night. The houseboy turned off the lamp in his room, and Ofuku went to bed, but Sankichi continued to write.

"There's something I want to read to you," he told his wife. "I'd like you to stay up until I've finished." Oyuki sat alone by the *irori*, preparing clothes for cleaning. Little summer insects circled the lamp.

When the clicking of Oyuki's scissors stopped, it was almost midnight. Ofuku and the boy were already fast asleep. Puzzled by Sankichi's attitude, Oyuki approached his desk.

"I've written something, and I want you to listen carefully," he said, moving the lamp to the center of the desk. He tried to appear calm, but his eyes betrayed his distress. His voice quavered as he began to read, but he tried to read clearly and intelligibly. Oyuki listened attentively.

> Hesitant though I am to write to you, I have taken up my brush to tell you what is on my mind. I have come to know you, indirectly, by the many good words spoken of you. Although I have never had the pleasure of meeting you, I am going to relate quite candidly the object of my concern. I beg you to remember that this letter does not come with the slightest malice and to read it through objectively to the end.

Oyuki glanced sharply at her husband and listened intently.

> The case in point is your letter to my wife and my wife's answer, which came to my attention by sheer accident. They have shed light on the circumstances connecting the two of you, on one hand; and on the other, they have made my wife's true feelings known to me.

Oyuki blushed to her ears. She covered her face with her hands, as yet unspoiled by housekeeping, and continued to listen, leaning against the desk.

> I myself have experienced many sorrows in life and have some understanding in matters of human emotions. Therefore, if you think I dismiss your tears as banal, as common melodrama, I submit that you judge me wrong.

Sankichi's voice sank, quavering and scarcely audible.

No, such is not the case. I can sympathize with your sorrow, and I take pity on Oyuki's feelings. Thus I cannot consider our union to be destined to last. And so I have come to the decision that I shall release Oyuki from the bonds of marriage, to regard our past as a sad dream, and to do all within my power to bring the two of you together in the union of marriage. I have spent several sleepless nights seeking some method to achieve this goal. One major obstacle is the personality of my father-in-law, whom you know well. Due to him, I fear that my efforts may be fruitless and result in blemishing your name.

The silence in the room remained unbroken.

The bond that unites the three of us—you, Oyuki, and myself —is not to be taken lightly. Many young men today are surely suffering in situations similar to yours. Among newlyweds, some are troubled by questions not unlike mine. The reason I do not hesitate to put aside my shame and infringe propriety by revealing my sorrow and write you as I do is solely because of my wish to help you and Oyuki. She is to be pitied. If you truly feel deeply for her, permit me to be your friend. A new kind of friendship among the three—this is the solution I propose to you. I have come to the decision to welcome you to our home as a friend of the family. You are still young with a long future ahead of you. I am too. Neither of us must interrupt his life because of a temporary sorrow. Perhaps sometime we may have cause to remember this day as we share our thoughts in friendship. Then I shall consider that the greatest of joys. . . .

When Sankichi finished reading the letter, he heaved a sigh of relief, as if a great task were completed. Prostrate on the floor, Oyuki could not raise her head.

"You can't just lie there. Let's mail the letter while they are asleep," he coaxed as he helped his weeping wife to her feet. The mailbox was near the community well. Sankichi thought that going there would provide a short walk with Oyuki.

The couple moved cautiously so as not to waken Ofuku and the houseboy. When they opened the front door, it was as bright as day outside. Phosphorous moonlight fell on the threshold.

A stream ran through the rocks in the bamboo grove, and dropped behind Sankichi's house. Crouching down at the edge of the increased water as it rushed over the waterweeds, Sankichi washed his sleepy face. About eleven o'clock he had a combined breakfast and lunch. He looked around the house as if he had awakened from a nightmare.

While the houseboy was out swimming, Oyuki brought Sankichi a letter, explaining that she could not express herself well aloud. In it she said that she was sorry that the circumstances had caused him such heartache. She did not marry him out of despair. She had her own hopes and was determined to be a good wife when she left her parents' home. And finally, she had written a last letter to Tsutomu, which she would like to send with Sankichi's permission.

"I didn't write the letter to make you give up your friendship. You're wrong if you think I did," protested Sankichi. "He's going to be Ofuku's husband, isn't he? Our future brother-in-law."

Oyuki did not answer.

The younger sister was enjoying a nap in the cool breeze. Leaning against a pillar in the south room, Sankichi decided to ask Oyuki about her past. The couple faced each other; they gazed at faces neither of them had ever really looked at, faces they had only glimpsed from a distance before their wedding.

"What was your relationship with Tsutomu?" Sankichi asked casually.

"What do you mean by that?" said Oyuki, blushing.

"When you were living at your home, I mean. It's better to be frank about it."

Sankichi then discovered that she and Tsutomu were once betrothed, not officially but with their parents' consent. The betrothal was broken when one of the head clerks at the store spread damaging rumors.

What was done was done. The wife now tried to eradicate it all, but the husband could not.

Loneliness welled up in his heart. He wanted to prove to her that he was no less kind to women than any other man. That day Sankichi pampered Oyuki in every possible way while torturing himself.

Tsutomu's answers came at once: one letter was addressed to Sankichi, another to Oyuki. To Oyuki he wrote that he was deeply sorry for having caused her trouble; she was not to blame at all, and he would ask her to intercede for him in his apologies to Sankichi. Oyuki cried as she read the letter.

August came, and Sankichi's household had an unusual guest. Sankichi went to the railroad station and spotted a tall, gray-bearded, simply dressed man among the crowd of travelers. It was Nakura, his father-in-law.

When they reached home, Oyuki rushed to meet him at the gate.

Nakura had given his name and store to the husbands of his two oldest daughters and was living the leisurely life in retirement. He had a strong, impetuous disposition, a practical head, and a forthright mind, and these characteristics all seemed to surface in the deep lines of his forehead. He was a man who rose from nothing to build many houses and factories and his excessive energy did not permit him a sedentary life. He traveled the distance to see what sort of man his favorite daughter had married and what manner of home she was building. Having seen them, he commented with a sigh. "At last, I feel relieved."

He brought a new clock from Tokyo as a gift for the young couple, and it now hung on the pillar of the south room. He took out other packages, explaining this is from Mother, that from an older sister, and the other from another sister.

After making a tour of the soot-covered country house, the old man sat down before a simple serving table in the living room looking out to the garden. He poured sake and sipped it slowly, as he watched the two girls bustling about and listened to the sound of the water mill.

"Don't bother about me, please. I feel much more at home this way," said the old man. He came looking forward to enjoying drinks with Oyuki's cooking, no matter how simple the food.

Sankichi called Oyuki over to the hearth.

"Isn't there anything else you can serve your father?"

"No, that'll be enough."

"There's nothing good to offer him. Shall I send for some canned food?"

"Don't bother. Anyway, he wouldn't eat it if I added something now."

Having been separated from his own father at a young age, he knew very little about fathers. Sankichi was delighted with Nakura's visit. He had never outgrown his awe of the deceased Tadahiro; Oyuki and Ofuku revered their father in the same way.

Nakura stayed for two weeks. When he left Sankichi's house, he took Ofuku with him, for she had to return to school in Tokyo. He left a unique impression behind him, quite different from those Sankichi had known. He realized that other families were designed entirely differently by masterbuilders entirely different from his own father or his sister Otane.

"So what if you did accumulate piles of books like these? They'll be worth the price of trash paper when you come to sell them," remarked the thoroughly practical Nakura; but Sankichi could not help recognizing his extraordinary vigor.

In May of the following year Sankichi and Oyuki became the parents of a daughter, whom they named Ofusa. The houseboy was no longer with them; with no help, Oyuki had to leave her bed by the eighth day and wash the baby's diapers.

Sankichi had never felt the need to travel so keenly as he did during this early summer. The old apple tree in the back yard bore lovely blossoms on the branches near the eaves. Bees were humming pleasantly all around. The things of nature completed a cycle back to the time he was first married.

"My house is an inn. . . . You are the mistress of the inn," Sankichi said.

"What are you, then?"

"I'm a traveler you feed, clothe, and for whom you launder."

"You make me feel terrible."

"On second thought, I'm thankful I can eat three times a day. Aren't you?"

The croaking of frogs in the evening seemed to add to the traveler's melancholy. Sankichi roamed through the house with unbearable yearnings.

He recalled the first days of his marriage. On the way home from Tokyo, the hills, the azaleas, the sunshine—everything had the radiance of hope at the start of his new life. He could still hear the youthful breathing of his wife beside him as he read by the lamp. With all his desire to learn about women, his disappointment in her was correspondingly great. At times he suddenly found himself in the state of mind he had known as a wanderer. While Oyuki worked in the kitchen, he walked around with the baby in his arms, and a desire would surge up, to leave the baby, leave his wife, and to flee the house.

"Nice baby, good baby, sleep. . . ." He sang a slow lullaby to Ofusa and listened to his own voice while Oyuki worked.

In addition to the vegetables grown last year, he now planted eggplant and cucumbers, and pumpkin tendrils climbed the hedge. One evening as he was weeding and sweeping the gate area with a bamboo broom, a traveler approached with a cloth-wrapped bundle on his back.

It was the Hashimoto head clerk, Kasuke, on his annual sales trip. Following the usual itinerary, he had made the rounds of the Niigata area before stopping here. His swarthy forehead and the way he dropped the basket of medicine on the entrance step suggested a rigorous journey. He untied the laces of his straw shoes and entered the house.

"Your sister told me you have a baby now, and your wife probably has no help. I was told to stop and see you but not to stay."

"Don't worry about that. Stay by all means," urged Sankichi. "I'd like to have news of the Hashimotos." He jokingly added that he had made a rule of having a house guest once a year. Oyuki ran in from the kitchen.

The clerk told them that he left the Hashimoto house almost two months before. The long sales trip was a tradition that had successfully propagated the Hashimoto patent medicine; they were known even in this remote town.

When the lamp was lit, Oyuki came with the baby in her arms to join her husband and listen to Kasuke.

"Oh, it's a baby girl, is it? I'll leave some medicine for her. It's a good panacea for children. I'll leave this in place of a gift," said the old man.

"We've heard that a bride came to the Hashimotos'." Oyuki spoke of Shota's wife.

"Her name's Toyose, isn't it?" Sankichi said. "We got a letter from her. She writes beautifully."

"Yes, well, thanks to everyone, we found an ideal bride. A fine girl like her is hard to come by. Mr. Hashimoto and everyone is very happy," said Kasuke, stroking his bald head. It was easy to imagine from his description how lavish Shota's wedding was.

"She must be quite a girl to make Kasuke rave like that," Sankichi said to Oyuki out of the clerk's earshot.

"How lucky Shota is."

Early the next morning Kasuke took his leave. Sankichi's loneliness deepened as he watched the head clerk recede on the dew-covered road.

Sankichi often looked at the distant sky, toward Tokyo; he eagerly awaited letters from his friends. When school was over for the day, he returned home and first of all asked for the mail. There was no friend he could talk to except colleagues he saw every day.

One of the women to whom Sankichi had introduced Oyuki sent a wedding announcement. He also received a letter from Chiyo saying that she was thinking of spending the summer at a nearby mountain resort.

Chapter 6

A train whistle from the direction of the station pierced the mountain air and reached the sliding doors of the south room. It reminded Sankichi of the steamer whistle on Sumida River, and at times it made him feel as if he was near the river in Tokyo. But as he listened more carefully, he realized it could be nothing but the sound of a mountain train. He told Oyuki about this and stood on the veranda listening, all ears, like a man marooned on an island waiting for a ship to come into harbor. Newspapers, letters, parcels of new books—whatever came to him always arrived with this whistle. He remembered Chiyo's letter and wondered if she had already arrived in the mountains.

The resort where she planned to spend the summer was on the same plateau about twelve miles from the town where Sankichi and Oyuki lived. It was a popular summer place.

Students studying in Tokyo began to return to their home towns for the season, and Ofuku again came to stay.

It was a half day at Sankichi's school. He lunched by the *irori* and prepared to go out.

"Where are you going?" asked Oyuki as she waited on him.

"I'm going to see if Chiyo has arrived."

"Do you think she's here already?"

"I don't know. But I'm going anyway and have a look around the resort."

He had introduced Chiyo to Oyuki and hoped to see a friendship develop; he thought she would make a good friend for the family. Chiyo had devoted her life to music, but she was also deeply interested in literature. Chiyo seemed to him one of few people who understood him, and this attracted him.

But Oyuki did not seem happy. When one of Chiyo's family died in a tragic accident, she made the funeral arrangements all by herself.

"You know, she's a very capable person," Sankichi remarked. "This is the third time you've told me the story," Oyuki snapped, as though she had no desire to hear any more about Chiyo. She made no attempt to cultivate friendship with her. Sankichi sometimes sighed, wondering why it was so difficult for two women to become friends.

He laughed at his wife's narrow-mindedness. He himself wanted to know a wide range of people regardless of sex.

"Please remember me to her if you see her," Oyuki said as Sankichi left the house. The day was hot.

Exhausted from trying to find Chiyo's lodgings, Sankichi finally turned his steps homeward. He found the sun-drenched town disturbing. The straggling, newly built villas with their red-painted shutters, the fields of cabbages, the trees along the old turnpike, the vacationers strolling in the shade of the trees, a nursemaid leading a golden-haired child by the hand—all had a disquieting effect on him as he walked.

He recalled his first meeting with Chiyo. She had suddenly appeared at his side in a room crowded with many young men and women, and asked him about a friend who had died. A sheet of music lay on the table, a song by Mendelssohn about the parting of a man and woman entitled "As God Wills." She sang a passage from it in a low, tremulous voice, and her fingers moved mechanically on the table as though tracing the piano keys. This had happened not so long ago. Their friendship grew rapidly. Something indescribable had hastened the development of friendship between them which was unlike that which ordinarily evolved between men.

At this time of year the pumpkin shoots twining around the hedge burst into flower. Walking past the large yellow blooms, Sankichi entered the gate from the road. There an unexpected guest was waiting.

"Naoki!" exclaimed Sankichi, breaking into a big smile.

Naoki came to the door. "I came while you were out."

The boy had grown remarkably since the summer when he traveled with Sankichi over the Kiso Road. His refined polite speech was that of a sophisticated urban youth. To Sankichi, who taught students of Naoki's age every day, the difference was particularly noticeable. He had come to spend the summer with Sankichi with his father's permission.

Not only Sankichi was delighted to have this boy he regarded as his own brother, but also Oyuki, whom Naoki addressed as "sister," was genuinely pleased and welcomed him. And Ofuku, who had nothing to do all day, now had a companion. Suddenly the household came to life.

In less than a day Naoki was a member of the family. He had an innate love of children, in contrast to Ofuku, who was, for a girl, quite indifferent to them. He carried Ofusa around on his back, and Sankichi recalled his own youth when he had served as a houseboy in Naoki's home.

"I used to carry Naoki on my back like that," he told his wife. He had began holding Naoki in his arms from the moment he was born.

"Miss Sone came by to see you a little while ago," Oyuki said as she stretched a washed and starched cloth over a fulling board at the entrance garden. Sankichi, who had just returned, stared at her. He was startled by Chiyo's sudden visit, for she had sent no word of her arrival or where she was staying.

"In fact," Oyuki paused in her work, "she just came to see the town."

"Why didn't you . . . you should have asked her to wait."

"But she wouldn't. She said she was with friends."

"Oh, did she come with others?"

"There were some women waiting by the stream."

Ofuku sat down on the steps at the entrance and spoke out, "Oyuki, her friends must be Christians."

"How do you know?"

"I know from their simple dresses and the way they put up their hair."

"Didn't she say she'd stop by on her way back?" Sankichi asked.

"Yes, she seemed to want to," replied Oyuki with an emphasis. "They told me they would be stopping at the teahouse in front of the station."

"I'll go and see," Sankichi said, and hurried off.

He found Chiyo resting at the teahouse with her two friends. One was a relative, and her dull, dry hair and almost pitifully simple clothes suggested the unhappy life of a widow. The other was a high school girl, plump and taciturn. They all seemed exhausted from walking and were about to have a late lunch. Sankichi wanted to order some food for them.

"Please don't bother. We've brought our lunch," said the older woman, smiling sadly. They took out some rice balls that had been prepared as a picnic snack at their inn. The plump girl ate silently.

Sankichi then took them to the ruins of the Komoro castle. They walked through the mulberry fields, passed over the railroad crossing, and saw a large gate with a framed signboard. The four climbed up the slope along a red-clay cliff basking in the hot sun, and came to a shady stone hedge with tall pines and acacias.

From time to time Chiyo's companions walked ahead, and Chiyo, shielded from the sun by a large parasol, followed with Sankichi.

Wild roses bloomed among the ruins of boulder walls of the ancient castle. Climbing the remains of the stone stairs, they reached the tower area, from where they could see the long slope stretching down to the valley.

Sankichi pointed to the edge of the woods just beyond the village and told Chiyo about a landscape painter who lived at the foot of the long slope.

Chiyo narrowed her eyes as she gazed at the valley below. "I wish I lived in a secluded place like this," she said in a melancholy tone.

The deep valley was partially visible through gaps in the pine grove. At the bottom ran the Chikuma River.

As a bank of rain clouds began to scud over the pine grove toward the mountain, a shower broke suddenly. Sankichi led the visitors to the second floor of a teahouse near the tower site. In the spacious guest room, he ordered tea and fruit, and he and his guests watched the streaming rain. At arm's length from the balustrade of the veranda, mimosa and wisteria groves thrived darkly. The rain dropped from leaf to leaf.

A coolness seeped into Sankichi's heart. Watching Chiyo's hands as she peeled a summer pear, he was disturbed by thoughts of his wife. Chiyo told him that her widowed relative was doing missionary work. She was surrounded by other women who had suffered misfortune but who were determined to live independently. She had been brought up in a family supported by its women, and she was engaged in music, largely a female domain. At times her words were as cold as mountain water trickling down the rocks.

The summer shower passed quickly. Sankichi and his guests left the scenic room and retraced their steps to the castle site.

When they reached the boulder (from which legend held that the image of an oriole would surface after rain), the two women again went ahead and then disappeared behind the protruding stone wall.

Chiyo seemed overwhelmed by the luxuriant foliage. "My doctor told me that I would get better if I went to the mountains, that it would be better for me than the shore. My friends took pity on me and came along. . . . It didn't help after all."

Chiyo, who lived alone, was troubled by some indefinable malady. She was suspicious even of her doctor's advice.

"Since I've been here only a week, they say it's too soon to tell," she continued in the same pessimistic tone.

"What is your illness exactly?" Sankichi asked, lighting a cigarette.

"It's my chronic complaint."

For a while the two walked without speaking. Bright sunlight bathed the grass around the castle.

"You're probably thinking too much about it," laughed Sankichi. They soon caught up with the other two.

When they came to the gate, Chiyo and her friends thanked him for his hospitality. They crossed the weed-covered tracks at the railroad crossing and walked along a sandy road in the shade of a hill. There the three women took leave of Sankichi.

"She hasn't changed a bit," Sankichi muttered to himself as he walked homeward.

Oyuki was taking the fulling board inside when her husband came back.

"Chiyo looks so young," said Oyuki, collecting the dried pieces of cloth.

"You can never tell about a woman's age," commented Sankichi from the porch. "I guess she's about twenty-five or -six."

"She couldn't be! She's too young. . . . She looks no more than twenty-two or -three."

"An unmarried woman stays young."

"Besides, she wears such bright-colored kimonos."

"That's true. She doesn't look too well in them."

"The *obi* she wore was very loud, with large purple and white stripes. She dresses too young, I think."

"She doesn't look good when she's too dressed up. She would be better in a simple kimono. I once saw a formal photograph of her dressed in three layers of heavy crepe de Chine, but from the waist down she looked dreadful. Anyway, she's so whimsical, she's ready to try all sorts of getups. Someone once described her very well: 'She'd say right if someone else said left, and white if the person said black.' "

"But she looks so intelligent. I wish I were half as bright, even for a day. I'm so stupid and ignorant, and I know it," said Oyuki, visibly depressed.

Naoki and Ofuku were whistling bits of songs innocently in another room.

In the evening, Sankichi called in Naoki and Ofuku and chatted with them in the coolness.

"Let's each tell a story," suggested Naoki. "I'll start, then Ofuku, then Sankichi."

"That's counterclockwise," mocked Ofuku.

"Then let Sankichi start, then you."

"I can't. I have nothing to tell."

The young people argued playfully. The idle chatter was soon replaced by a game of cards.

"Come and play with us," said Naoki to Oyuki.

"I think not now." Oyuki stretched out beside her baby.

"Why not?" he asked, disappointed.

"Somehow I don't feel very well tonight," replied Oyuki, watching the baby sucking her little finger.

Carefree laughter filled the room. "What a misfortune! What an ill-starred man I am!" Naoki put on a dramatic air as he counted the cards in his hands. Usually his youthful remarks made Oyuki laugh, but tonight she was in no mood. Suddenly the baby threw herself backward, kicking and whimpering. Oyuki applied talcum powder around the chubby neck of screaming Ofusa. Putting her nipple in the baby's mouth, Oyuki gradually sank into a deep melancholy.

After the regional bon festival, Chiyo again called on the Koizumis. She came alone this time. The sound of the water mill, like everything else, was charming to a city woman. She paused for a while at the gate, looking at the dilapidated house with the pumpkin vines hanging from the hedge.

Oyuki stepped out to see whether her laundry was dry under the persimmon tree and caught sight of the visitor. She called to Chiyo and immediately invited her into the house.

Naoki had gone off, and Sankichi was bored. He was pleased to see Chiyo. But her visit without her companions created an impalpable consternation in the house. It was as if she had slipped unnoticed through the chinks of the door and seated herself in front of Sankichi.

He went to Oyuki and told her to send out for some food and to come talk with them.

"I'm not good enough," she sulked.

"Don't talk that way. You should listen to what other women have to say," he replied and returned to his guest.

From the back room they could see rose moss, Indian cress, and other flowers in the garden. Sankichi placed his tobacco set on the large desk. They began to talk about music and literature; even the life of bees, ants, and spiders came up.

"Out here in the country we have nothing nice to offer you," said Oyuki as she served them the delivered dishes, the child in her arm.

"Oh, is this Ofusa?" Chiyo asked affectionately, taking the baby from Oyuki. She held the child on her lap and put her cheek against her. Ofusa began to scream in fear of the stranger. Chiyo took out a toy she brought as a gift, but the baby wouldn't stop. Oyuki watched briefly and then carried the child off to the kitchen.

Chiyo listened to the crying voice for a while.

"Last night I couldn't sleep," said Chiyo. She had been bothered by the damp fog; it seemed as though her frail body might be swept away unless she found something to cling to.

"May I tell you about my diary?" she said suddenly. "I tried keeping one, but it wasn't very interesting . . . nothing but my complaints. So, I burned it on New Year's eve, and I wrote my will on New Year's Day. Oh, I'm insane. It was a mistake that I was born to this world." Her deep, clear black eyes shone through the tears she could not hold back.

That day she was agitated. Occasionally she laughed as though floating up from a bottomless sorrow, and spoke of men disparagingly.

Oyuki was asked several times to join them, but she withdrew to the kitchen, where she busied herself with Ofuku, taking in the laundry and folding the clothes after dampening them. When Chiyo rose to leave, thanking them for their hospitality, Oyuki spoke to her from the *irori*.

"Oh, must you go so soon? Why don't you stay a little longer?" Oyuki said, but Chiyo answered that her train was due. Sankichi sent Oyuki with her to the station.

When she returned with the child on her back, she discovered under the desk a gift, wrapped and addressed to her from Chiyo.

"How typical of her not to say a word about this," laughed Sankichi.

Oyuki looked at the handkerchiefs under the wrappings. "The train was late," she said, "and we waited at the station quite a while . . . more than half an hour."

"Did you talk about anything special?"

"She said I looked very pale."

Somehow the house seemed empty. There were times when Sankichi and his wife sat at the dining table without exchanging a word, without even looking at each other.

Oyuki's heart ached when she noticed her husband's constant brooding, his constant frowns. Much of what this dour man said totally escaped her. He would fondle and cuddle Ofusa lovingly and say such things as "The child has cheeks just like my mother's." Other times he would blurt out, "Is she really mine?"

"Don't be absurd! If she's not yours, whose is she?" Nothing upset Oyuki more than such irrational remarks.

"Tell me. What did you have in mind when you married me?"

"What did I . . . ? How can you ask such a question? I can't answer that!"

"I wonder if I shouldn't take a long trip. Sometimes I can't shake my wanderlust."

"I don't know how you can feel that way." Oyuki was deeply

hurt. "When you come back from somewhere, you always say there's no place like home. You are so erratic," she protested, unable to believe that her husband was teasing her. He drove her out of her mind.

The hot sun beat down. A thin rope stretched from one lintel to another just as it had the previous summer. Oyuki's kimonos, brought from home and never worn in the rustic town, Sankichi's formal kimono, the one he had worn at the wedding, and even Oyuki's ceremonial undergarments hung on the rope and swayed in the breeze. The *obi*, which Minoru had sent as a betrothal gift, was suspended before her eyes, completely untouched.

"I don't need kimonos or anything else anymore," she sighed.

The child lay on the floor, dressed in a single flannel kimono, a gift from Oyuki's mother.

"Come, dear, let me feed you." Oyuki stretched sluggishly to nurse the child and glanced again at the clothes on the rope.

When she awoke from her nap, half of her face and her hip were exposed to the sunlight. She rose, flushed, her forehead shiny. Her habit was to work harder than usual when she was angry. She put away the aired garments and mopped the house with a wet rag. She prepared a meal for her husband and others, but she didn't sit down to eat with them. Fireflies drawn to the waterweed in the back stream flitted through the mulberry patch and strayed over to the hedge near the south room. Oyuki stood on the veranda and absently looked up at the sky. A neighbor's wife came back from the fields, a sickle attached to her waist, and a man carrying mulberry leaves on his back walked behind her. He bowed to Oyuki as he passed.

A letter came from Oyuki's mother.

Dear Oyuki,

I am writing to ask how everything is going. It's gotten terribly hot, and I wonder how you and the family are getting along. I know I myself have been negligent about writng; but the lack of news from you worries me. We are all well, and life these days is uneventful, so don't worry about us. As for me, I have been busy going the rounds of the sick people hereabouts, and then the house chores and the daily fussing with cleaning the kimonos and starching them take up my time. I haven't even had a chance to take care of the clothes your father wore when he made the trip to your place.

These are some of the reasons for my silence, and I'm really very sorry about it, but then we've not had any letters from you either. I know very well that you have little time, what with a child and no help. But with no letter since your father's return, we think about you and worry about you all the time. Has anything happened? Could it be that you've had a change of heart about your marriage? If so, your attitude toward your husband may have changed, and I fear that you may have become self-centered. I trust you never will. But self-indulgence is a very common thing, and I am not completely sure. Still I am certain that you are not like others and that you will never be selfish. But please write and let us know how things are, whether they're good or bad.

Ofuku's school opens soon. She has probably given you much trouble by staying much too long. Your father and I are very grateful for what you are doing for her.

Incidentally, I have been meaning to send you something, but have put it off until today because of the many chores. I didn't mean to let it go for so long. I have just made a package of some dried salted fish, five dried bonito sticks, some crackers with beans and candy, both rather small amounts, and one apron. They're really not very much, but I'm sending them just the same. The dried fish is homemade; some are in pieces and may not taste good. At this time of year there is nothing else. But one small fish prepared like this still costs forty-five sen at the market. I suppose I shouldn't be talking about the value of a gift. . . .

There are many things I still want to tell you, but I'll stop here for today. Give our love to Ofuku.

Hurriedly,
Mother

P.S.   Last but not least, remember us to Sankichi and give

him our warmest regards. And also, though we have nothing special to send, give your neighbors our best.

Oyuki had not written home for quite some time, and this letter from her mother moved her very much. She laid her cheek on it and sobbed.

"I wonder why you're so unhappy when you're home," Oyuki sighed as she approached her husband with the child in her arms. Near the mud wall in the back yard stood a large plum tree. Ripe purple plums dropped one after another from the heavily burdened branches. Sankichi looked at the child as though annoyed at being interrupted in his thoughts.

"I've never expected to have an especially happy home; from the very beginning I was prepared for a difficult life."

"But you've been brooding every day," she said reproachfully. "I never thought my home would be like this."

"I suppose you wanted to marry a man who would let you run off to the theater or something all the time."

"You're wrong. I don't want to go to the theater or anything of the kind. You always twist things. You like nothing I do. Most of all, you don't talk to me."

"But I'm talking to you right now." Sankichi smiled cynically.

"You call this talking!" Oyuki retorted, and looked at the baby's face. "I wish I were born bright. And I . . . I will be too . . . in my next life."

"What are you going to do if you're reborn smart?"

Oyuki did not answer. "You spend too much time thinking." She gave a chilly smile. "Why don't you go visit Chiyo?"

"That's none of your business!" shouted Sankichi. He wanted to say, "You bring her up with every other word. So what about her? How can you talk to other people with a mind like yours?" But he did not.

"It will do you good to go out a little instead of locking yourself in all the time."

"Whether I go out or stay in is my own business."

The neighborhood children had gathered outside the hedge and were noisily hitting the branches to shake the plums loose.

"Ofusa," moaned Oyuki, hugging the child, "let's go away. Your papa doesn't like us." Dejectedly, she left her husband.

"What a strange thing to say," he mumbled, and returned to his pondering.

After dark Sankichi and Naoki read and talked together by the lamp in the back room.

Suddenly Oyuki had an attack of nausea and rushed to the veranda and vomited.

"What happened, Oyuki?" Naoki hurried to her and rubbed her back.

She sat silently for a few moments. "It's nothing," she said finally. "Thank you, Naoki. I'm all right now."

The vomiting had surprised Naoki, and Sankichi knitted his brows with foreboding. He prepared some salt water and brought it to his wife.

That night Oyuki set up the mosquito net with Ofuku's help and retired earlier than usual. The sisters complained of some mosquitoes that had strayed in, and they rose to look for them by candlelight. Sankichi saw the green light gleaming through the linen net. He read with Naoki until late.

Oyuki stayed awake fanning herself for a long time. Finally, when Sankichi and Naoki were preparing to go to bed, she slipped outside the net to cool off. Sankichi, not seeing Oyuki, looked at the child's bed, but she was not with Ofusa. He wondered where she was and went to look for her. The entrance door was open; the whole neighborhood seemed to have retired. Only the upstairs of the restaurant opposite was still lit up, and the merry sounds of a samisen and women's laughter wafted over in the wind. A gaslight set off the trunk of a solitary willow in stark relief. As he stepped outside, he looked up and saw the Milky Way, like a wisp of white smoke against the dark sky.

"Oyuki!" Sankichi called. She was wandering about the cool air of the evening in her white nightdress. Hearing him, she returned.

"You mustn't catch cold," he said as he called her into the house and closed the door.

The child suddenly fell ill. After the brief summer vacation, Sankichi returned to the routine of walking to school daily with his lunchbox. One day after returning from the school, he found everyone humoring and coaxing Ofusa who clung to her mother crying.

"What's the matter with her?" Oyuki hardly knew what to do.

"She may be teething," Sankichi suggested. "Why don't you try a little of the Hashimoto medicine?"

The couple was worried about Ofusa and nothing else mattered. There was nothing as painful for Sankichi as a baby's cry piercing his brain.

Ofusa screamed constantly, and he would take her in his arms and coddle her as he strolled in the garden, trying to please her with drum, flute, and other toys, but nothing helped.

The baby's fever, so sudden and different from an adult's, made the couple fear the worst. They kept a sleepless vigil, and fortunately, Ofusa finally fell sound asleep. The crisis seemed to have passed. Watching the baby's sleeping face, Sankichi was overcome by exhaustion and dozed off.

He suddenly found himself in a world beyond time and space. Only fear—the fright of an ignorant child, existed there. He was in a sickroom with people who looked like doctors going in and out. The woman in the sickbed was Chiyo. She showed her pale hand to him and said that the origin of her sickness was there. Two small painful punctures appeared on her index finger, with a smudge of blood. A doctor came and passed a U-shaped wire through the perforations while the patient cried out like a child, screaming how cruel he was.

He returned to the edge of consciousness, but he still felt he was by Chiyo's bed, absorbed in attending her. Abruptly he woke up and found himself by his wife's side.

Ofusa's fever that had so frightened the young parents lasted only one night. Soon she was well and laughing once more.

Before long, a jacket was needed in the morning and evening chill, and the summer vacationers began to return to the city. In early September, Ofuku left for school in Tokyo.

The end of Naoki's stay was approaching too. A group of mountain climbers was going to ascend Mount Asama, and he decided to join the party. Sankichi had a half day at school, and when he came out of the school gate, he felt the sudden urge to visit Chiyo. She was so close now but she would probably be returning to Tokyo soon. How was her sickness? His steps led him to the station from the school.

A train for the south pulled in.

Shortly after one o'clock, Sankichi was looking at Mount Asama from the train window, thinking of Naoki climbing there. Dark gray clouds clung to the foot of the mountain.

The highland was enveloped in a thick drizzlelike fog. Chiyo's inn, a remnant of the old Post Station days, was located some distance from the railroad stop. When he arrived, his clothes were drenched.

The rented room was to the rear of the second floor, and several women were gathered there. These widows and spinsters carried with them just as lonely and unfeminine an atmosphere here as they probably did in the city. Chiyo's relative was not present, but the plump high school girl was there. None of them smoked, but addicted to cigarettes as he was, Sankichi found it hard to forego them and took out one.

"Oh, I didn't even give you an ashtray!" Chiyo exclaimed, and called for one from downstairs. The school girl busied herself pouring tea and serving fruit. Sankichi's forehead was bathed in perspiration after the walk from the station.

"Are you really so hot?" said Chiyo. "I was feeling rather cold myself." She pulled her kimono collar together. Her face was pallid.

Unobtrusively her companions slipped from the room. Through an opening in the window, the cold fog drifted into the room. Chiyo talked about her recent visit to Sankichi's house and about the deep impressions the ruins of the tree-covered castle and the view of the Chikuma River made on her. He asked her about her health.

"It hasn't improved particularly," she replied wearily. "After I leave the mountains, I think I'll try the seashore." She began to compare the mountains and the sea and asked him, "If I remember correctly, you prefer the mountains, don't you?"

He persisted, a little annoyed, "What does your doctor say? About your sickness?"

"The doctor? How can you trust what doctors say? As soon as you mention you're ill, they decide it's hysteria."

As usual, she lapsed into her self-analysis. "A friend of mine who began to study music at the same time as I did says there's no one who's quite as hard to understand as I am, even after ten years." She spoke as though taunting herself.

Sankichi remarked detachedly, "You are probably the kind of person with whom no one can become a real friend."

"Then you don't understand me either." She smiled forlornly. "Last night I had a sad dream."

Sankichi's eyes rested on the dejected young woman.

"I dreamed I had died," she said, shuddering. For a while the two were silent.

"I don't feel like going back to Tokyo. I really detest the idea," she sighed.

"You are very lonely, too, aren't you," said Sankichi, lighting another cigarette. A shroud of gloomy fog enveloped the window, but the sun shone through faintly from time to time.

Several books she brought from Tokyo to help pass the time were on the desk. Being a traveler and having nothing else with which she could entertain her guest, she showed them to Sankichi. She had borrowed some books on religion from friends in Tokyo; they were the kind Sankichi used to read. The philosophy they contained had once inspired him too. But after he moved to this area, he gradually lost interest. He picked up a volume just to be polite, but he did not want to talk about books. He had come to see her for a specific purpose: to hear, as he used to from her mouth, her cynical, cutting words tearing men apart. He came wanting to be derided for his stupidity.

Instead, he found her exceptionally tearful and depressed.

She went to the desk near the window. "Sankichi, won't you come and sit here? Please?" She wanted him to sit near her, but he declined.

"I'm perfectly happy where I am," he answered as he lit another cigarette.

A bouquet of dried flowers hung on the pillar. Chiyo stood and smelled the flowers as she narrowed her eyes. Though they were close, Sankichi managed to keep his distance, and Chiyo returned to her seat. In return for his hospitality on her two visits, she seemed to want to reciprocate, but she was at a loss about how to do it. She pared an apple and offered it to him. The conversation shifted from music to her foreign music teacher.

"My teacher says, 'Miss Sone, you must believe in religion. Otherwise, we won't be able to see each other again after we die.' I don't expect to go to Heaven, but I'll be lonely if I don't see anyone."

Soon it was time for Sankichi's train. He asked the proprietor of the inn to order a ricksha.

"I took the train immediately after school."

"You came without telling your wife, I suppose," Chiyo smiled uncomfortably. "Please, when you go home, remember me to her."

The thought of home now troubled him strangely. He feigned a greater indifference than he actually felt when he confessed that she guessed right. He said goodbye to her and hurried through the fog to the station.

Toward evening Sankichi reached his station. At the first glimpse of the thatched roof his feet slowed down. He took the trouble of going by the communal well and stopping at an acquaintance's house. He lingered on, even though he had nothing special to say. He chatted with neighbors about the difficulties the Asama climbers must be having in such bad weather. When the lamps began to twinkle, Sankichi casually turned homeward. Never before had he gone off like this without telling his wife.

Naoki was to stay overnight on the mountain and naturally did not return for dinner; the couple sat at the table and ate without speaking. Oyuki's unhappy face kept Sankichi from mentioning the casual things he could have talked about.

After dinner, Oyuki asked, "Was Chiyo still there?"

Sankichi betrayed himself by his noticeable fluster at the question. "How do I know whether she is or not?" he said with a straight face, but his throat was parched, and he himself felt that the lie was too obvious.

Those were the only words the couple exchanged that evening. Not talking was even more painful than talking. Sankichi lay alone under the mosquito net in the back room and thought about his behavior. He could not sleep with the tacky netting touching his hair.

Sometime after midnight, Oyuki rose under the other mosquito net and called to him, "Are you asleep?" Sankichi kept absolutely silent. Soon he heard Oyuki sob.

"Are you asleep?" she called again, and Sankichi pretended he just awoke from slumber.

"What is it?"

"Please, let me leave you." Oyuki fell prostrate on her bed, sobbing loudly.

"Tell me about it tomorrow. We'll talk about it tomorrow," he answered as though tired, and then fell silent. As he remained immobile, he could hear his own breathing. Trembling in his bed, he feigned sleep but he listened intently. Oyuki emerged weeping from under her netting and began to walk around. The mats squeaked under her feet and the handles on the chest of drawers clanked. The noises struck fear in him, now completely a captive of suspicion. Soon the child under the mosquito net began to cry. Sankichi did not relax until he heard his wife sobbing beside her.

The Asama climbers came back the next morning. Naoki carefully put his treasured mountain plants by the entrance and untied the laces of his straw shoes.

"I was right to borrow your sweater, Sankichi. It was so cold I was shivering all the time," he said. His school uniform was wilted and soaking wet. The boy saw the Asama crater at dawn and then made his way down the mountain on tired feet.

Sankichi let him rest and went out for a walk. Somehow, he had to answer Oyuki.

In the afternoon he returned, his mind filled with the view of the rice fields he had gazed at for a long time, of the grass he sat on, and of the group of travelers who cut across the hill. Naoki had gone to the hot spring to relax, and Oyuki, with the child strapped to her back, was working. For all the unhappiness she exhibited the night before, she did not seem to be living such an intolerable life. Sankichi went to his room and rolled out some paper on the desk.

"Chiyo". . . Sankichi could see before his eyes the pale cheeks of the woman smelling the bouquet of dry flowers. "We are just friends.

We have never been more. We're comrades who have been disappointed in many things." Sankichi could not afford to lose sight of this.

He began to write a final, parting letter to Chiyo. "Someday you may be able to consider my decision sensible," he wrote.

He called Oyuki and showed her the letter of farewell. Then in a rather formal, resolute tone he stated, "I would like to inform you that I have decided to break up this family."

"If you like. But I will not go home," she answered, looking at him sadly.

Why her husband showed her the letter to Chiyo and at the same time announced the disbanding of the family, Oyuki could not understand. "You didn't have to say goodbye, I'm sure," she said.

She gazed at her husband's face, mystified, trying to show her feelings in her eyes. No one asks for a divorce truly wanting it. She then returned to the kitchen.

Back from the bath, Naoki was looking at the back yard from the veranda. The plants he collected at Asama were carefully kept in a corner of the garden. He was pleased with the mementos of his climb that he could take back to Tokyo.

Sankichi found it hard to tell this good-natured youth what he had on his mind. He was afraid he might be laughed at for his rash resolution.

After skirting around, he said at last, "Naoki, I've had some thoughts, and I'm considering a divorce."

Without answering, Naoki heaved a deep sigh. Tears filled his gentle and compassionate eyes.

"I don't know how this sounds to you," Sankichi spoke hesitantly. "But for some reason we can't get along. It may be better if I send Oyuki home."

"But, Sankichi," Naoki blinked, "I feel sorry for her. And more than anything else, it's unfair to Ofusa."

"Yes, Ofusa's the one," he agreed.

For some time the two sat downcast, gazing at the garden in silence.

Oyuki came to tell them dinner was ready. "I feel so useless," said Naoki to Sankichi as he stood up. "I'm completely helpless in a situation like this. And I'm annoyed with myself for only shedding tears."

"Well, let's go and have dinner anyway." Sankichi rose too.

"Please think it over, Sankichi," Naoki entreated as he followed him.

Even as he sat at the dinner table, Naoki was unable to keep back his tears. That night all three went to bed early, but no one was able to fall asleep. Lying next to Sankichi, Naoki began to sob. Oyuki was touched by the boy's compassion and wept as she nursed the child. Sankichi heard the two weeping in the darkness until far into the night.

Before Sankichi spoke of breaking up his family, he had thought of the divorce procedure, the way of returning his wife to her parents, the explanations to the matchmaker, the arrangements for Oyuki's belongings, and his life after the divorce. Obstinate though he was—he did not easily give up an idea once he had reached a decision—the day came when Naoki finally succeeded in persuading Sankichi.

"I appreciate your concern. I promise I'll reconsider," he said to Naoki before going to school. When he returned, a postcard from Chiyo was waiting. It said briefly that she was leaving the resort and asked him to give her regards to Oyuki and Ofusa. Sankichi had mailed his letter to Tokyo, so Chiyo had no way of knowing about it.

Ultimately Sankichi gave in and said he would wait and see about discontinuing the family. Oyuki sighed in relief, and Naoki was delighted that Sankichi accepted his urgings.

"Now I'll tell you about Mount Asama," Naoki said to Oyuki with a bright smile. At last Sankichi too felt like talking about mountain climbing. He recited a local saying: "He is a fool who has not climbed once; he is twice a fool who climbs again." Then pacing around the house, he traced back the memories of the year and half of his marriage.

Naoki left soon after. The morning when he regretfully said his goodbyes, holding his souvenirs of Asama, Sankichi left the house with him, his usual school things wrapped in a piece of cloth and tucked under his arm.

"Goodbye, Naoki," said Oyuki at the gate, holding her baby in her arms.

After leaving Naoki at the station, Sankichi followed the path by the railroad to school. At the end of the day he crossed it again on his way home. This time he took the road in front of the castle gate and came out at the mulberry field near the guard box at the railroad crossing. The watchman was standing there with a green flag in his hand. While Sankichi watched, the afternoon train to Tokyo pulled in, shaking the earth with its thunderous roar.

The plumes of engine smoke crawled in clusters through the mulberry field and then dispersed on the wind. From the crossing he could see the station beyond, the engine emitting white steam, attendants running to and fro, and passengers getting in and out of the train. Soon the piercing whistle sounded.

"Naoki's gone, and Chiyo too," mused Sankichi. He again whispered goodbye, thinking of the boy who left by the morning train.

The locomotive pulled out. Sankichi remained in the mountains.

Chapter 7

A year went by. Sankichi no longer brooded, and he was now ready for work. He tried to fill the void within him by writing.

He now had the simple life he had sought. First he opened his eyes to the world about him on the secluded mountain to learn its meaning.

Almost three years had passed since he and Oyuki established their home. The child was growing up. Having no older people to guide them, bringing up a child was no easy task. They hired a peasant girl of about fifteen as a maid.

Sankichi had made a brief trip to Tokyo on school business, and his family was anxiously awaiting his return.

The neighborhood girls carrying copybooks came for calligraphy lessons from Oyuki after dinner. "Good evening!" they greeted as they came in.

"Come in, come in," Oyuki answered as she sat at the edge of the veranda holding the bare-bottomed child out over the ground.

"My goodness, how chubby Ofusa is getting," remarked one girl. Another asked, laughing, "Are you making wee-wee, Ofusa?"

The baby was half asleep. When Oyuki accomplished her task, she took Ofusa back to her room.

The bed was ready. The maid brought talcum powder wrapped in paper as Oyuki changed the child into her nightdress. She had a diaper rash that had become inflamed and painful. Oyuki sprinkled on the powder, put on the diaper, and wrapped her up as though she were handling a doll.

While Oyuki lay down to put the child to sleep, the girls chatted around the lamp. The maid, having tidied up the kitchen, joined them for the lesson. She had graduated from elementary school, and unlike the girl before her, she did not make mistakes in brushstroke order when writing simple characters.

But she seemed to dislike any form of learning, and while the other girls made effort to perfect their handwriting, she showed no desire for such an accomplishment. When Oyuki finally joined the group, the ignorant maid not only participated in the conversation but also—proud of her ignorance—talked more than anyone else.

She spoke of an incident in town when she was on an errand, carrying Ofusa on her back. Someone remarked, "For a teacher's brat, she's pretty homely. The baby's puffed up and so's the nursemaid. They make a fine pair."

Oyuki and the girls burst out laughing.

"Tomorrow your husband will be back, won't he?" asked one of the girls, and Oyuki talked about his trip.

Sankichi returned with news of Tokyo. He never missed his family and home as much as on the homeward journey.

"Ofusa, I've a present for you," he said, opening his suitcase.

"Papa's got a present for you. I wonder what it is!" Oyuki said to the child while helping unfasten the clasp of the bag. "Good heavens! What a heavy bag. Papa's luggage is always filled with books."

The maid brought tea. Sankichi drank and began to tell Oyuki about the changes that were taking place in the Koizumi family in Tokyo. Minoru's business had brought a disaster: he was saddled with a larger debt than ever; the loan from the bank had been cancelled; his "boss's" family, having invested heavily, was on the verge of bankruptcy, and the family moved into a small house in an alley.

"Remember Okura's sister, Osugi? She died at my brother's," Sankichi said.

"What happened to Sozo?"

"Some family agreed to take care of him, so he moved in with them. I didn't see him. I just left a box of candy for him. Anyway, Minoru's family's changed a lot. But he's pretty calm about it."

"Your sister-in-law must be upset."

As the couple talked, Ofusa toddled over, wanting some tea. Oyuki tried to help her, but the child would not be satisfied unless she held the cup herself. To get her own way, the baby finally began crying loudly.

"You can't drink by yourself yet," said Oyuki as she reluctantly gave her the cup. The child stuck her nose and mouth into the cup, and promptly spilled the contents.

"See! I told you so!" Oyuki took out a handkerchief.

"She's smacking her lips. She thinks she drank it all," laughed Sankichi.

"These days she only imitates me. If I lie down, she pretends to go to sleep, and if I take out the rice server, she mimics putting rice into a bowl."

"Come, sweetie, let Papa hold you. My, you're getting heavy!" said Sankichi as he drew the child onto his lap. Ofusa showed a smile she did not show to anyone but her parents.

"I feel I can't sit around after seeing what happened to Minoru's family," Sankichi said, handing the child back to Oyuki.

"Ofusa," the maid said, laughing, "why don't you show Papa your new trick of looking upside down?"

"Don't. That's not nice," said Sankichi, but the child had already left her mother, and bending forward, peeked at Oyuki through her crotch and shouted "Peek-a-boo!"

"The lady next door said that Ofusa's peek-a-boo trick is a sign another baby's coming soon," the maid said casually. Sankichi and Oyuki looked at each other.

At this time of year the couple felt specially sleepy. After Sankichi came back from his trip, even the maid started getting up later. Sometimes breakfast was not ready by the time he had to leave for school.

The morning light grew brighter through the slits between the sliding doors. As usual the child awoke first and crawled out of bed while her mother was still asleep.

She was playing by her pillow in her nightdress. "You'll catch cold. Come, Ofusa," scolded Oyuki, only half awake. She pulled her into the bed, but the child struggled to get out of her arms.

A rooster crowed near the water mill. The lamp was burning low, dark and red. Oyuki raised her head and tried to wake the maid by the hearth. Again and again she called, but there was no answer.

"It's amazing," Oyuki sighed. Her voice did not arouse the maid, but the child began to cry.

The maid finally mumbled, "Yes, ma'am," then got up at last

and put away her bedding. By the time she opened the kitchen door, the woman next door, an early riser, had already swept her back yard and was on her way to the bamboo grove to throw away the trash mixed with yellow leaves.

"I called you many times, and loudly, but you didn't even answer," Oyuki complained to the maid.

Dark, suffocating smoke crept up the sooty kitchen wall to the beams of the high, thatched roof and billowed back again to the hearth, filling the house for a time. Sankichi was still in a coma-like sleep.

"Wake up, wake up!" Oyuki called. He was tired, and no amount of sleep satisfied him now. Hearing that it was almost time for school, he told his wife to pull off the quilt.

"Shall I? I'll really peel it off," chuckled Oyuki.

He finally woke up and hurriedly got off to school. That day the maid brought a telegram to his office. It was from Minoru, telling him to send money immediately. Sankichi was astonished: the amount requested was not easy for a country teacher to raise.

He returned home, pondering the meaning behind the commanding tone of the telegram, which was overbearing even between brothers. Not knowing the situation in Tokyo, he was all the more concerned. But he assumed that Minoru would never have demanded help in this manner unless he was really desperate. Sankichi sensed ominous clouds spreading over the Koizumi family.

He could not refuse; yet in his present situation he had no savings. Oyuki shared his concern and agreed to provide the money given them by her father for only the most dire emergency. Sankichi went out to send it by telegram.

After her husband left, Oyuki lay down by Ofusa. As the baby grew, she became so lovable that Oyuki found it hard to be apart. At the same time, the child did not give her mother a moment's peace. The new and strange experience of bringing up a baby was filled with difficulties and sometimes Oyuki was pushed to the point of tears. And the inconvenient life with a rough country maid as her companion was generally monotonous.

"Every day, doing the same thing every day . . . ," she sighed with frustration as she lay on the floor. Ofusa resumed her crying.

Oyuki gave the child her nipple, but no milk came. Angry, Ofusa would not quiet down.

Water was boiling in the iron kettle on the hearth when Sankichi returned from the post office. He made some tea and smoked by the fire, thinking about the mountains where autumn colors deepened after each rain, about the rice fields where the crickets sang, and about the lonely woods with the brushwood carts and the grass cutters. Oyuki put the child on the maid's back and came over to him.

"Ofusa, let's go catch grasshoppers," said the maid, leaving the house.

The couple had become accustomed to the country life and now drank tea with pickles instead of with cakes. Oyuki began to smoke.

"Why are you staring at me like that?" she giggled.

"Because you're smoking," Sankichi answered, puffing.

"For some reason, when I'm pregnant I crave smoking."

"Well, in that case I suppose you really are." Sankichi sobered a little. Having children so young, so soon—what would he do if more children came in the future?

Several days later, Sankichi received a letter from Minoru. He acknowledged the money and apologized for his urgent telegram, but he explained nothing about the difficulty he was in. He said only that there was nothing more terrible than debts, and never to borrow money.

In November another urgent telegram came from Minoru. Sankichi felt that he could not oblige every time, but at the same time, he had to do all he could. The entire amount was impossible at this time, but he would send at least part of it. He made up his mind to sell the manuscript he had just finished after three months' work.

"Don't you hear the child crying? If you're just resting, go see what's wrong."

"But I'm tired too. Ofusa, are you going to cry all night again? Come, sweet, be quiet. Mommy can't stand it when you cry so much."

Almost every night the couple was awakened by the child's wails. After Oyuki's milk stopped, Ofusa became extremely peevish, always ready to scream. The fact that she was teething helped little, and she often bit Oyuki's nipple in anger. "Ah, ouch, ouch . . . oh! Why does she bite me so! You naughty little girl, you're hurting me!" Oyuki cried and tweaked Ofusa's nose; the child shrieked at the top of her lungs. Despite the scolding, she still wanted her mother's breast. And whether or not there was milk, she refused to sleep until she had a nipple in her mouth.

Sankichi often paced his room. The child's constant screaming irritated Sankichi more than anything else as he sat at his desk. His study, facing north, was already cold and dark, unlike the sunny south rooms.

The autumn vacation came, a busy season for farmers. Sankichi's school recessed for about a week so that students could help at home.

One day as Sankichi returned from a stroll, Oyuki came running to him with two calling cards. "Mr. Nishi* was here. He said he'd come back later." It was a rare occasion for Sankichi to have his Tokyo friends visit his humble house. Soon he heard a familiar voice at the entrance asking for him. The very sound filled him with delight.

Nishi was a young government official, and Sankichi had known him since before he entered the university; they used to exchange youthful ideas with a third friend, Nakamura.* After such a long interval, Sankichi found Nishi impressive.

Nishi's companion, dressed in a western suit, was introduced as a newspaperman who came from Tokyo to work in the area. He was called B. They began a lively conservation in the back room.

Nishi looked at Sankichi. "I've known B a long time, but I didn't know that he was in Nagano. I called on S at the Nagano Press and happened to find B there."

"Yes, someone sat down right next to me, and it turned out to be Nishi—the last person I expected to see," rejoined the journalist. "Besides, his name has been changed since he got married, and now he sports a mustache. I almost didn't recognize him. In fact, when we heard that a Nishi was coming, S and I expected to see some upstart

---

* Characterized after Yanagida Kunio (1875–1962), poet, government official, and specialist in folklore. He was secretary of the Bureau of Legislation and a close friend of many poets and writers. Nakamura is Tayama Katai.

law-school graduate and we said all sorts of things about him. When he came, it was the Nishi we knew."

Nishi began to laugh. "They were up to no good. I came here because the prefectural government asked me to give a lecture on our cooperative project. But these no good journalists! They were going to write up an article on what I was most likely to say before I came, just to embarrass me. You've got to watch out—newspapers are full of rascals."

Nishi looked around the simple room and flicked the ash from his cigar, as though wondering why Sankichi had withdrawn deep into a hinterland like this. After living for nearly three years in the mountains, Sankichi had become quite countrified.

"B, are you cold? Why don't you go put on your overcoat?" Nishi said to the reporter and shuddered himself. "It's really cold here, isn't it? I never thought it would be this bad."

Hospitably, Oyuki brought tea. Taking out a book he brought to read on his trip, Nishi placed it before Sankichi. "Koizumi, you haven't read this yet, have you? I asked Nakamura if there was anything I could read on the trip, and he let me borrow this. I've read up to where the postcard is. I'll leave it as a gift."

The newspaperman picked up the book. "It's no fun to be swamped by work. I wish I could get away to some quiet place where I could have time to read."

Nishi glanced at his profile.

B sighed. "Koizumi, don't you ever feel that you have some obligation to nature, and that you are forced to work always to pay it back? I'm suffering from that pressure. I'm always driven by this obligation in my mind and I work because I have no choice. Yet, if I work, I suffer. Every day I run around like a rat for the paper. But what will I have to show for it in the end, if I keep on doing the same thing? I sometimes wonder."

"That's because you're a newspaper reporter," Nishi said. "Why don't you quit? You're bound to get that sort of occupational disease when you work for a paper over a period of time."

"But that's not true," B responded emphatically. "There was a time when I had it a little easier. I didn't have to work for a living.

But it was no good just the same. Suppose I quit the newspaper and become a schoolteacher. What difference can that make? I still won't find peace of mind."

"We're all driven on by innate ambition. But even so, aspiration has its value," Nishi smiled.

"I don't know. . . ," the reporter sighed again. "We can't go against nature. To do that, we've no choice but to die. Yet I don't like to obey nature. Why? Because it's cruel . . . it doesn't give me any peace. . . . And so I want to get rid of this inner drive of mine. I want the freedom of mind so I can read whatever I want and sleep whenever I want."

"I sometimes think so too," Nishi seconded the reporter. "There are times when I'm against work, but I don't speak out. Because our host here would rake me over the coals. Koizumi has his own opinion about work. I always knew about it."

"Life is completely merciless," the reporter went on.

"You know," said Nishi, looking at him, "life's pleasure exists only for women, not for men. Even when we read a novel, we don't just read for the enjoyment of it. We read to get something out of it. Man's nature is disgusting, isn't it? Remember Zola's three aims in life? To live, to make love, and to work. A pretty dismal set of principles. And not much fun."

"Don't you get lonely in a country like this, Koizumi?" asked B.

"It's different for a man with a wife," Nishi said playfully, and Sankichi smiled grimly, unamused.

"That's the point," the journalist continued. "Will one be rid of loneliness if one is married? If having a wife meant no loneliness, I wouldn't be a bachelor today. Why should I cook for myself all alone and live in a shabby room above the office?"

Trying to change the subject, Nishi replied, "The whole point about a man working is senseless when you think about it. In the final analysis, the only demand of nature is reproduction."

"If that's so, we are slaves after all," said B. "I wonder if we could not just sing and enjoy life like the birds, without suffering. . . ."

"Yet even birds call their mates. Human beings also are designed so that those who have beautiful voices get the better mates. But the population has gotten so big that reproduction isn't the only human function any more. That's why you can say or do anything today and still go on living."

"I feel that our lives are unreal—as if we were dreaming."

"Who would ever imagine that throughout Japan life is nothing but a mere dream," said Nishi with a theatrical flourish.

Sankichi listened to his guests in silence. The journalist, irked and pained, looked at Nishi, who turned his eyes away. For a while they smoked without a word.

Ofusa peeped in.

"Come over here, Ofusa," Nishi called. The child hid shyly behind her mother. Soon she was brought out by Oyuki and given a piece of cake.

"She's too shy to come out, so she's saying 'thank you' behind mommy," Oyuki explained, smiling.

In the course of the conversation, Nishi glanced at his pocket watch two or three times.

"How long can you stay? Why don't you stay overnight with us?" suggested Sankichi.

"Thanks, but I've got to make the four-thirty train. They're throwing a party for me tonight. Since it's going to be a drinking party, I'm not too happy about it, but. . . . Besides, tomorrow I have to give a speech."

"Well, stay as long as you can."

"Say, that time's wrong." Nishi looked at the clock on the pillar in the next room and compared it with his watch. "It's too slow."

"Yes, it loses time," agreed Sankichi.

Oyuki brought out beer and some snacks she had on hand. "This is rather skimpy, but please help yourselves," she urged. Sankichi passed the dishes, trying to make his friends feel at home.

"I'm sorry to put you to trouble. I still can't drink much, you know," said Nishi. "But since I'm pressed for time, I won't stand on ceremony."

Sankichi poured beer for B too. "Do you intend to stay with the Nagano Press for long?"

"Well, I don't know . . . I may return to Tokyo in a year or so.

There's no one to talk to, and I'm not happy. I have no interest in the region."

Nishi was curious to taste the mushrooms pickled in brine, which were called "cow's forehead" in the region. "When I came over the Usui Pass the day before yesterday, I felt so lonely. Until that point I was unaware of it, but when I came to the tunnel, I suddenly realized I was a traveler. I don't think anyone can go through that tunnel without feeling some loneliness. Don't you agree? What do you feel, Koizumi, when you go through it back and forth on your trips to Tokyo?"

Sankichi accompanied his guests to the station, regretting the briefness of their visit. A peasant warming his hands in his kimono front, a traveling salesman wearing a padded hood, and a gray-haired nursemaid were in the cold, dark building.

Nishi and Sankichi lit cigarettes. The journalist stood with them. "When I met you, Nishi . . . let's see . . . yes, the year you entered the university," he said, "I was the youngest newspaperman around. I think I was twenty, and already I was talking about the world situation and things like that."

"You're supposed to know a lot more now, but I'd say you know less," Nishi laughed lightly.

B guffawed, bending backward and keeping his hands in the pockets of his yellow overcoat. Then he withered, and looking into Nishi's face, he remarked, "You've changed a lot too since those days." Nishi looked back at him in silence; Sankichi paced around his friends.

The three crossed the tracks to the platform for northbound trains. Mount Asama was already white with snow.

"How cold it is!" exclaimed Nishi, trembling. "I may freeze to death in the train."

"Let's walk a bit," Sankichi suggested.

"Yes, let's. We'll be a little warmer if we keep moving," agreed Nishi. Looking around, he added, "This area is pretty much as I imagined."

"The mountain over there that looks slightly grayish purple," said Sankichi, pointing, "is Yatsugatake. Then way over on this side you see the mountain with autumn color. The river at the foot of the cliff is the Chikuma."

"Is the mountain always purplish like that? I thought it would be much drier here."

"It looks different today. There's a lot of humidity. Usually the mountains are much closer."

"The Yatsugatake on the Kōshū border!" the reporter said. "So, that's where it is; my hometown is on the other side of the mountain."

"Oh, are you from Yamanashi prefecture?" Nishi looked at him.

"Yes, I am. So that's where it is. All of a sudden I feel homesick," B said forlornly.

The three men gazed into the distance.

"Koizumi," Nishi called as if he remembered something, "how long do you plan to live in hiding in the mountains? Today you don't have to study so deeply the things you write about, you know."

Sankichi was lost for an answer.

"But being a newspaperman isn't all that wonderful either," continued Nishi.

"You don't have to look down on an editor so much, do you?" smiled B.

Nishi laughed. "There's nothing as futile as working for a paper. What do you learn from the books you read to write your news articles? Nothing stays with you. That would never satisfy me. You should quit soon."

"That's what you say, but I can do nothing else. I'll probably be a news editor the rest of my life. It's my rotten lot," replied the reporter as he strode down the windy platform, his tan shoes squeaking.

The northbound train pulled in, and the young men bade Sankichi goodbye, opened the door, and boarded a second-class car with few passengers.

"Thanks for coming out in this cold weather," said Nishi, putting his head out the window. The conductor raised his hand, and the train began to move. Sankichi stood there a long time.

Yellow sunbeams broke through the clouds. The balmy light now hastened the harvest. The light cut the corners of the roof of the gardener's house and the white wall of the machine shop, and fell upon the mulberry field blighted by the severe frosts and on the mud wall of Sankichi's house. It was the season when every mountain home would wash huge turnips and hang them on the walls for drying. It was an annual chore in mountain homes, and every year, when time came for storing vegetables and preparing pickles, Sankichi was reminded of the long winter ahead.

With the help of her aged mother, who was dressed in a quilted jacket, the next-door neighbor rolled out a straw mat under the large persimmon tree in the back yard. They were preparing to dry turnips. The unwashed vegetables were piled in a mound. Stimulated by these activities, Oyuki wrapped a towel around her hair, tied in her smock with a belt, and began to work with the maid.

From time to time the neighbor came to the broken hedge and spoke to Oyuki, showing shiny blackened teeth* when she smiled. The maid's skin chapped easily, but she plunged her frost-nipped hands into the cold water to wash the muddy turnips.

The local turnip was a tough, short variety that grew only in barren land. Oyuki bought them mixed with some of the Nerima type. Unused to the climate and now pregnant, Oyuki found preparing the vegetables for winter no easy task. It was hard for Sankichi to watch idly, so he took care of the child while Oyuki worked.

Ofusa grew every day and could no longer be handled like a doll. When Sankichi tried to work, she pulled at the hanging scroll, tore up an album, and broke the paper on the sliding doors. Bored with her toys, she crawled up on the desk, mashing a half-eaten persimmon, and stood up and raised her arms in glee. She whimpered if Sankichi's attention wavered from her for a moment. Frustrated, he finally took her to play in the room with the mirror and comb box. She took out a comb from the box and tugged at Sankichi's hair saying, "Hair, hair." She combed his hair in the wrong direction.

"Come on now, let's go to sleep," Sankichi said, putting her on his back. He walked around the room as he read his book.

* The custom of blackening the teeth by women, with a mixture of gallnut powder, began in the Heian period and persisted to a limited degree to the end of the nineteenth century.

By the time the maid came in from the kitchen entrance, Ofusa had put her head against her father's back and fallen asleep. A sleeping mat for the child was prepared by the foot warmer.

"I couldn't possibly do what you women do," said Sankichi, almost dumping the child on the mat.

"We've finished tying the turnips, will you come and hang them up?" the maid asked. She had the habit of speaking in a precocious tone and staring into people's faces.

Sankichi went out to the back entrance. About half the pile, now completely washed and tied, was ready for drying. He brought a ladder from the persimmon tree and propped it against the mud wall. Then he hoisted the bound turnips on his shoulder and struggled up the ladder that Oyuki and the maid steadied as they giggled.

"Forgive my long absence," said the midwife. She had attended Oyuki at Ofusa's birth and now returned to see Oyuki. The greeting amused the hairdresser who was working on her hair.

Sankichi received astonishing news from his brother Morihiko in Tokyo. It was notice of Minoru's second incarceration. Only then could he grasp the significance of the repeated telegrams. The letter bitterly denounced Minoru's lack of consideration for his ancestors' honor and for his brothers. Morihiko was deeply hurt that the eldest brother had forgotten his responsibility and brought nothing but disgrace to the entire family.

Sankichi read the letter twice, three times. He could imagine how Minoru, in his effort to maintain the eminence of the old family, made one ignominious mistake after another. Sankichi's past distress was partly from his involvement in the precipitous fall of the family. He had spent months and years in deep despair, abandoning his youthful dreams.

Minoru's family—Okura, two daughters, and Sozo, who was now in the care of another family—were again thrust upon Morihiko and Sankichi, and Morihiko's letter asked for Sankichi's opinion. He showed it to Oyuki with disgust on his face.

"Good heavens! What on earth did your brother do?" she exclaimed. The couple would now have to be ready for ever greater hardships.

On the day of the winter solstice, it was decided that the household would eat the customary pumpkin and flowers of the butterbur boiled with beanpaste. Oyuki went to the mulberry field near the stream and picked butterbur flowers that had just bloomed. The clouds seemed laden with snow. Sankichi, shivering, returned from school and sat down at the table without taking off his cotton *hakama*.* The child, disobedient as usual, grabbed at her rice bowl, snatched pickles, and wanted to eat with chopsticks by herself. She threw a tantrum when she could not get her way. Oyuki could scarcely taste the pumpkin and the butterbur specially cooked for the occasion.

Feeling a cold coming, Oyuki stopped sewing the New Year's clothes. Now that the year's end was near, the neighborhood girls no longer came, lantern in hand, for calligraphy lessons. While Oyuki sat at the foot warmer, her head pressed against the frame, the maid spent her time idly applying ointment to her chapped hands.

The night was cold. The maid was scarcely the type to volunteer learning a single character more than she had to, but out of consideration for her mistress, she began willy-nilly to recite from the reader. Soon her mind drifted to the pleasant rice fields where she could catch grasshoppers and lie in the grass. She read aloud just so that Oyuki would hear her, but the same passage over and over. Feeling drowsy, she finally fell asleep with her face pressed against the book.

Suddenly Ofusa began to cry and the maid started to read again.

"She knows I have a cold, but she wouldn't help me at all," Oyuki said out loud, and her patience gone, suddenly rose from the foot warmer. She snatched the book from the lazy maid and threw it against the wall.

"Be quiet!" she shouted.

The maid, goggle-eyed, was petrified.

"You don't have to do a thing for me!" cried Oyuki, sniffling. "What good does it do to read a book when you're half asleep! Stop it and go to bed."

In the next room, partitioned off by paper doors, Sankichi was

* A loose-fitting trouserlike garment worn over a kimono.

reading under a feeble lamp light. The snow on the north side of the house never thawed during the winter, and each new fall accumulated on top. The garden trees and grasses were buried deep. Trickling water from the thatched roof froze into brown icicles, some already two feet long. At night the chill of the frozen snow seeped through the house, and sometimes the wooden posts creaked loudly and split from the cold.

"If you'll excuse me, sir, I'll say goodnight," said the maid, opening the sliding door a little and bowing low. Soon Sankichi heard her sobbing as she prepared for bed by the fireplace. Poverty on one hand, and a ruthless climate on the other. The almost constant sobbing of the women and child only increased his helplessness. He pulled a quilted blanket around his knees and sat at his desk until late into the night.

When Sankichi was finally ready for bed, Ofusa began to cry again, and she was still not asleep when the clock struck twelve.

Oyuki was exasperated. "Who's crying so much? Get off of me. You've a tummyache because you want to eat everything."

Ofusa cried even more. Her screaming voice reverberated off the cold walls. The mother's angry scolding made her shriek only louder.

"Sleep, baby, sleep. Rock-a-bye, baby," Oyuki softened her voice, coaxing the child. Ofusa grew calmer but continued whimpering as she sucked at her mother's breast.

"Don't you know mommy's sleepy too!" Ofusa burst into tears again at Oyuki's harsh voice. Finally the mother and child began to cry together.

In the adjoining house, the preparation of rice cakes began and the pounding noise sounded loudly through the thin walls. Sankichi's household was also busy with New Year decorations. The traditional pine-bamboo-plum ornaments were hung at the gate. Sankichi selected a sunny spot in the south room to make simple decorations for each room. Customary New Year's garland materials such as ferns, *daphniphyllum,* and bitter oranges lay scattered all about.

Sankichi pondered over New Year, that came even to the house of a poor school teacher. He hung a round decoration with long ferns on the pillar of each room.

"Why do you let the child cry so much? Surely you can manage to keep her more quiet, can't you?" said Oyuki, standing before the maid. Sankichi heard her voice and made a grimace, thinking she was again having trouble with the child. It was his nature to blame his wife rather than the useless maid. Whether or not she had reason to scold the maid, he invariably regarded the employer responsible.

"That's why she gets spoiled," Oyuki had muttered about Sankichi's attitude many times.

"You're asking too much of her," Sankichi said. "She's still only fifteen. She's a child. You mustn't blame her so."

"I'm not blaming her," Oyuki replied resentfully, thinking that her husband knew very little about the maid and cared less how disobedient she was and how harshly she treated Ofusa.

"You say you don't blame her, but I can hear you," repeated Sankichi.

"When did I blame her?" Oyuki was offended.

"Your tone is accusing."

"My tone is my natural way of speaking."

"The tone you use to your father and the one I just heard sound very different to me."

"Whoever heard of anyone speaking to her father and to a servant in the same tone? You don't have to drag my father into this in front of the servant."

"You don't make any sense. I didn't disgrace your father by mentioning him. How can you manage your servants unless you are as grateful to them as you are to your parents?"

They argued, oblivious of the maid. Ofusa was puzzled and looked from one parent to the other, while the trembling maid retreated into a corner.

"It's silly to quarrel about a servant," thought Sankichi. He was irritated when he realized that their marriage had now reached the stage of quarreling over trifling matters.

A local rice merchant came in from the front gate and shouted in his peasant voice, "Good morning! Your rice cakes are here. Sorry to be so late."

"Rice cakes, it's rice cakes!" the maid explained to the child. Ofusa raised her hands in delight. All she could do was coo.

The peasant led a horse loaded with rice cakes right to the entrance of the house. "Whoa! Whoa there!" he cried and tied it to the larch-tree hedge.

Chapter 8

Two summers later, Tatsuo and Otane passed through the small town where Sankichi lived.

Otane was on her way to the Itō Spa on the Izu Peninsula for her health, and Tatsuo, in order to accompany her, had combined a business trip to Tokyo. This time, Otane left her daughter, Osen, and her daughter-in-law, Toyose, at home. She chose a route that would enable her to see Sankichi and his wife at the railroad station. The brother and sister had not seen each other since he visited Kiso some summers before, and she had never met his wife. Much as Otane would have liked to stay overnight and see Sankichi's children, Tatsuo's busy schedule would not permit it.

Sankichi and Oyuki dressed up the children and hurried to the station. They were now the parents of Ofusa, who was three, and another daughter, Okiku, one. Ofusa walked from the house to the station hand in hand with her mother. A young neighborhood girl carried Okiku on her back.

"It would be better if you held Okiku," Sankichi suggested when they arrived at the station. Oyuki took the child into her arms. They waited on the platform for the Tokyo train with Otane and her husband on board. Soon a puff of white smoke rose beyond the castle ruins, and porters in large leather shoes scurried about the platform.

The train pulled in, carrying its assortment of travelers. Leaning from the window of a second-class car, Tatsuo and Otane called to the couple and their children. They gathered by the window and Oyuki exchanged warm greetings with the in-laws she was meeting for the first time.

Sankichi held a child up to the open window. "Ofusa, this is your Aunt Otane."

"Is this Ofusa?" Otane put her head out the window and said, "Dear, I have a present for you."

108

"Oh, she looks like a very healthy child, all suntanned." Tatsuo laughed cheerfully.

Otane wanted to hold Ofusa for a brief minute, but there was no time. She hastily took out the presents she brought for the children and gave them to the parents.

"Are you planning to stay in Tokyo for any length of time?" asked Sankichi.

"No, Tokyo comes later," replied Tatsuo, leaning out. "First I'll get my wife settled. Then I go back to Tokyo to take care of business. If we weren't in such a hurry, I'm sure Otane would like to talk to you about a lot of things."

"Oyuki, forgive us. We can't even have a decent conversation today. But we'll see you again soon," added Otane.

Oyuki bowed, still holding Okiku, and Otane touched the baby from the window. Before they had exchanged more than a few words, the train began to pull out.

By the time Otane leaned out to look at her brother's family again, the train had left the station. Ofusa's country-red cheeks, Oyuki, smiling with Okiku in her arms, and the hat Sankichi was waving—all disappeared quickly from the sight.

"My prayers have been answered at last," Otane said to herself as she leaned back in her seat.

For a while, Tatsuo and Otane talked only about Sankichi's family. She was more nervous than usual with the strain of traveling, but she tried her best not to show her worries to her husband. Tatsuo was in low spirits, which he also was trying to conceal.

When the train descended the mountain, a woman in the next car squeezed the surplus milk from her breast through the window; watching her, Otane thought of her own childless daughter-in-law. She felt very far away from her family.

The trip caused Otane much anguish. For some reason, she felt defenseless and forlorn. Her failing health began to force her to stay in bed about the time of Sankichi's wedding; wracked with headaches or pain in her limbs, she spent a great deal of time in bed. She already once followed Morihiko's advice and made the trip to the Izu spa for rest. This was her second journey to Itō. Somehow she had no desire to leave home, and had obstinately protested, but her husband finally persuaded her.

It was close to evening when they got off at Akabane Station in Tokyo and changed to a train on the Eastern Seaboard Line. After settling in another car, Tatsuo lay down for a while, and Otane, covering him with a woolen comforter, sat at his side and listened to the rumbling of the train. He soon sat up again, unable to sleep, and his fine, dignified face seemed to show a hint of trouble. His eyes had the look of a man pursued by an invisible enemy.

"Is anything wrong?" asked Otane, concerned. "It would be nice if you could arrange to rest awhile in Itō too."

"Oh, no, I can't waste time like that. I've got to see to the business in Tokyo, and I may have to go home right away. Right now, one day counts very much."

Tatsuo was not the man to be satisfied with merely inheriting the family business. At present he held an important position in the bank in his hometown. The time for the annual report at the close of the fiscal year was drawing near.

To help pass the time Otane bought some apples from a platform vendor who came to the train window; she offered one to her husband. Tatsuo took out a knife and began to pare away the skin. His hands shook strangely, and he nicked his finger slightly.

"Something is really wrong with me," he said, trying to laugh it off. Otane looked at him, very much puzzled; it was so unlike her usually well-poised husband. Cutting himself? She had never seen him do such a thing.

Late that night, Tatsuo and Otane arrived at the inn in Kōzu quite exhausted by the trip.

The sound of the waves through the night prevented the two mountain travelers from sleeping. They took breakfast in the room overlooking the sea.

Otane was concerned for her husband's busy schedule and made a suggestion: "If you are so pressed for time, why don't you go on and attend to your business? From here it's only a boat trip, and if the sea is calm, there's nothing to the trip to Itō. I'll go by myself."

"Would you? I'd appreciate it. But are you sure you will be all right alone?"

"Of course. Since you've brought me this far, I'm quite all right. Besides, this isn't my first trip. And when I get to Itō, the whole Hayashi family will probably be there. There's nothing to worry about."

"Well then, I suppose I can say goodbye here. Let me see, I'll go to Tokyo right away for the bank business. . . . I'm going to be pretty busy."

While they were talking, a maid brought them the boat schedule. A train was evidently about to leave for Tokyo, and some travelers were setting out from the inn.

"There's a train going out," said Otane, listening to the noise outside. "That's perfect. Why don't you take it?"

"Think how much time it would take if I go all the way to Itō," answered Tatsuo. "If I don't go with you, I don't have to rush so much. There're plenty of trains to Tokyo."

"But you said you couldn't waste any time. I should think you'd want to take the earliest one possible."

"Well, anyway, I'll see you off to the boat."

For a man who had so little time to spare, Tatsuo now showed no sign of moving and sat passively. He began to smoke again. Somehow he had lost his usual composure.

A train whistle sounded at the station. He paid no attention to it but continued to gaze pensively at the sea.

Soon the time for the ferry arrived. They left the inn and walked down to the beach along a promenade lined with ancient pines. They crossed the fine sand beach down to the water's edge where the waves washed pebbles and rocks. Travelers were gathering. All the passengers had to be carried to the launch on boatmen's backs through the foaming, breaking surf. Otane said goodbye to her husband as she clung to the back of a strong, muscular man. The man waded through the white foam, splashing the water as he strode out to the launch.

As the launch approached the ship, pitching and tossing as it moved, Tatsuo's figure standing alone on the beach grew smaller and fainter. Otane had no qualms about the crossing, for she had already made one trip, and now the weather was beautiful. But the thought of her husband weighed heavily on her mind. Once aboard the steamer, she became more troubled, for he was no longer at her side.

The steamer crossed Sagami Bay and reached a sunny beach, and the passengers rushed to get on the launch. It took them to the spa town, where the sulfur odor of the hot springs filled the air.

At the inn, Otane found the Hayashis, old Mrs. Hayashi, and their student houseboy, all of whom she had met before. They vacationed almost every summer at the same place. The Hayashis occupied a second-floor suite along a long corridor facing the garden. Otane was led to the room next to them. She wrote to her daughter-in-law, Toyose, as soon as she settled down.

From then on, she thought of her home day and night. Strangely, there was no word from Tatsuo. One week, two weeks passed, but not a single letter came from him.

She waited a whole month, and still nothing. Letters from Shota and Toyose made no mention of him, but repeated assurances about home, recommendations to take care of her health and to rest well, all were phrased in a tone obviously meant to minimize her worries. She sensed that something extraordinary was happening. She could readily conjecture the real reason she was sent away alone, so far from home that she could see Ōshima Island from the beach: Tatsuo did not want her to see the trouble at home. She thought constantly about the grim trip she made to Itō at her husband's insistence and about his hands shaking so much that he cut his finger. Every time she thought about it, she felt a chill run through her veins.

Two months passed. The Hayashis returned to Tokyo leaving the mother and houseboy. As she saw them off, Otane felt their departure was more than she could bear.

Finally, a letter from Morihiko in Tokyo told her something of the situation at home. For the first time, she realized that her husband had absconded with money. Morihiko advised her to follow the wishes of the family and stay in Itō a while longer: nothing could be done at home even if she returned now. She was finally able to understand some of what had been puzzling her. Obviously no one had told her the entire situation at home, knowing how excitable she was.

There was no news from Tatsuo. If he was troubled and suffering, all the more reason to write from his hideout, at least to his wife, she thought. Otane still relied on his confidence in her. She waited another month.

The young Hashimoto couple, Shota and Toyose, arrived in the morning boat one day. They were concerned about Otane.

As she received them in her room, Otane felt as though the children were a boat coming to save a shipwrecked woman, and she did not know where to start or what to ask about first.

Her spirits rose as she looked at her son and daughter-in-law, and she tried not to show her dejection to them.

"Did you come to the spa to make babies, since you haven't succeeded at home?"

Shota and Toyose looked at each other. "Mother, this is no time for joking," replied Toyose sadly.

Shota interrupted them and sent his wife to take her bath, shortly he followed her to recover from the journey.

The bath was at the end of a maze of staircases, and the young couple stopped briefly in the hallway where they could see the blue Izu sky.

"If we came to make babies! I wonder if she's serious," remarked Toyose. "When can we tell her?"

"You know what she's like. We can't tell her all the bad news at once. It would be best if you stay with her for a while and break it to her gradually."

Shota went to the men's area and immersed himself in the bath with several other guests. He would have to go home immediately, leaving Toyose in Itō. The prospects were bleak. He had to straighten out the affairs of the apothecary which his father left in shambles, and pay off all the debts that had accumulated. In his youth he often thought he cared little what happened to his family. But once he saw signs of collapse, he willingly threw himself into the breach.

After the bath, he joined his wife and mother. "Old Mrs. Hayashi is in the next room," Otane said in a low voice. "I was joking before; I know what's happening at home."

"It might not have happened if we hadn't helped Uncle Minoru," said Shota. "But it's like crying over spilled milk. Father helped Minoru because he was in financial trouble. After all, it was Father's fault."

"Why did Uncle do such a thing? He must have been taken in by someone," Toyose said.

"Remember," Otane rejoined, "just before I came to Itō, an investigator from the district court came to ask about Minoru. It has bothered me ever since. In a small town everybody talks a lot."

"After that, we couldn't get credit at any bank," said Shota.

"I thought it was probably something like that. I don't know how many times your father went to Tokyo with bank business. Obviously he couldn't get enough help in Tokyo to cover the deficit. And what did you do after that?"

"Things will take their own course," Shota said pointedly. "I'm going to ask Uncle Morihiko to come."

"And what happened to Kasuke?"

"Old people are no help at a time like this. He hardly knows what to think."

Otane plied them with questions, but Shota avoided answering. Then Otane asked the whereabouts of Tatsuo.

"He sent his registered seal from somewhere. That was the last we heard from him. He probably intends to go to China," mumbled Shota, not wanting to say more.

"Is he going to try his luck so far away?" Otane sighed disheartenedly. Toyose was suddenly choked with tears, and the two women wept together.

Shota could not stay long. On the day he was to leave Itō, he was alone with Otane and told her what had happened to Toyose. As Shota went on with the story, Otane opened her eyes in amazement. Not only was her husband no longer hers, but her daughter-in-law too was about to be taken away from the family.

As soon as Tatsuo's flight was reported, Toyose's family wired her. The telegram said that her grandmother was ill, but Toyose easily read between the lines. She suspected that she might not be able to return to her husband. And sure enough, when she arrived home, she was forbidden to go back to the Hashimoto house. The separation made her realize that she was Shota's wife, and she fled her own family. Now that it was difficult for her to stay in her home province, she intended to live in Tokyo a while and work out some way of earning a living. Having told his mother this much, Shota took his leave.

What an outrageous thing to do—reclaim a married daughter! It humiliated Otane, and her anger led her naturally to thoughts of the inherited weakness for women of Hashimoto men. It was her first thought every time something happened. She was convinced that their inherited philandering led people like Toyose's family to point a finger at Tatsuo and Shota. They must think: like father, like son; there's no hope for them.

"I warned him," she sighed to herself. She felt like putting her arm around Toyose and crying. The entire family seemed to be going insane.

Her next-door neighbor walked by, down the long corridor. "No wonder your husband deserted you, Mrs. Hashimoto," he teased, "just look at your hair!" Otane was leaning against the balustrade, looking at the sky over the spa. Now almost at the end of the year, the Hayashis had returned to the hot spring.

Since Toyose joined her, Otane lost all interest in her hairdo and put it up in a perfunctory knot every day. But such criticism from a man rankled her very much.

"He's very wrong to think that. I've not been deserted by my husband!" she said to herself. But whatever she thought, it probably amounted to the same thing as desertion in other people's eyes. She could not believe that Hayashi had said it jokingly.

As soon as she returned to her room, Toyose left. When the two women began to talk about home, they invariably ended up crying. It was painful for them to sit together, and so they took turns going to town, the fishing villages, the nearby historical sites, or the rooms of the neighbors or other spa guests who had become their friends. Each avoided as much as possible being with the other.

Otane lay down alone, thinking of home. The desk, the lamp,

her husband earnestly writing a letter. It was one night last winter. Puzzled by Tatsuo's behavior, she pretended to be asleep until about one o'clock. When he finished writing, she suddenly confronted him and demanded he let her read the letter. How could he still be writing such things? she said, and threatened to call Toyose if he did not let her read it. Tatsuo begged her to let it pass just that once. If she would, he swore, he would give up the woman. Subsequently Otane heard that the woman left town to go to Tokyo. Occasionally a parcel arrived from her with a letter, and Tatsuo still continued to send her money.

Her thoughts dwelled on the young geisha, young enough to be his daughter, who had seduced Tatsuo. She also remembered that he had not written her since they parted on the shore of Kōzu, even at the year's end.

Otane and Toyose had to see the New Year come in at Itō without their family. On the second floor of the inn, they feasted with the Hayashi family on the customary dishes: small dried sardines, herring roe, chestnuts, spiced sweet wine, and other New Year dishes. Near the end of the eve, a hairdresser came to their room. After Toyose's hair was set, Otane had hers done for a change, adopting an unusually prominent chignon that struck Toyose as curious.

Otane did not sleep well that night. She rose before dawn and dressed neatly.

"Good heavens, mother, are you using powder?" asked Toyose, getting up.

"Certainly. Why not?" she laughed, a little excited. "When I was young, I used plenty of powder."

"That's expected when you're young. But I haven't seen you make up since I first came to the Hashimotos'."

"Come on, Toyose, fix yourself up. Let's go see the Hayashis and wish them a happy New Year."

Someone had suggested a New Year's party to break the monotony of spa life. Each guest thought up something different to do for entertainment. When Toyose returned from the bath, her mother-in-law had borrowed a man's *hakama* and was tying up the hem with a cord.

"Toyose, old Mrs. Hayashi and I are putting on a funny skit. I've already talked with her."

"What on earth are you going to do, mother?"

"Don't worry. Let me have your coat."

Toyose's kimono coat was lined with a colorful silk print of a crane against the sunrise. Otane borrowed it and put it on wrong side out.

"What are you doing? Mother, don't do anything you'll be sorry for afterward." Toyose was perturbed.

"You mustn't say such things in the green room. Look, the sunrise and a crane. It's made to order. If I wear this with the *hakama,* I'll make a fine *manzai** dancer."

Toyose didn't know whether to laugh or cry.

"The proverb says, 'No shame away from home,' doesn't it? I'm going back to my childhood and have fun. Now, will you go to Mrs. Hayashi and ask her if she's ready?"

Toyose left the room, uneasy and wondering whether a woman like her mother-in-law, usually serious and stern, could go through with such a ridiculous plan.

The spa guests gathered in the large hall on the second floor. Not only were the regular guests there, but also bored visitors from other hotels. They were all to dispense with ceremony and have a good time. Even cooks and maids were invited to join.

There were bursts of laughter as the guests' talent show began.

Young girls and maids in the audience whispered to each other. One after another, talented guests and trick performers presented themselves; they seemed to feel that there was no better chance to exhibit their talents and eagerly volunteered. Affected by the applause, some became unnerved in the midst of their performances.

After observing the scene, Toyose returned to her room. On the way, she saw Mrs. Hayashi in the corridor. "Mrs. Hayashi," she said nervously, "do you think our mothers will be all right? I'm so worried."

---

*Professional well-wishers who customarily visited homes on New Year Day to present dances and music and wish good fortune to families in return for food and money.

"I hear our grandmother is the main dancer," Mrs. Hayashi laughed, her ample body shaking.

"I think mother's worried too much about home. She's too keyed up. I've never seen her like this."

"But Mrs. Hashimoto's a sociable, entertaining person. Think about *my* mother."

They could see at the end of the curving corridor the two rooms the Hayashis were using. From a gap between the sliding doors, they could glimpse a ceremonial hat and a cap moving.

The masquerading female *manzai* were ready to make their appearance. Otane took old Mrs. Hayashi's hand and passed by her daughter-in-law.

Otane was trying to convince herself that surely husbands don't like wives who can't entertain them; if she tried, she could of course make people laugh. She was confident she had made herself look sufficiently comical. It never occurred to her that her daughter-in-law might be worried to death.

A round of applause sounded in the hall. All the guests enthusiastically welcomed the old folk's skit, ideal for the New Year's celebration. Toyose was distressed, wondering what her mother-in-law was about to do. Mrs. Hayashi watched, laughing.

Old Mrs. Hayashi was a quiet woman who had never done anything like this in public, and as soon as she appeared in front of the large audience, she hung her head in fright. Beside her, Otane was eager to keep the guests amused and shouted random words of congratulation, improvising the patter of *manzai* entertainers. She mimicked the sounds and gestures of a drummer and strutted around the main dancer, who stood fidgeting and shaking.

"Where in the world did mother learn such things! When did she ever pick that up?" marveled Toyose.

"Grandmother!" Mrs. Hayashi cheered her mother-in-law.

"She's just chattering and chattering away." In her consternation, Toyose spoke in her dialect. "Mrs. Hayashi, do you think we should let her go on? I'm terribly embarrassed."

"She does seem a little carried away, doesn't she?" As the two women talked, Otane finished her lines successfully and stood giggling with the old Mrs. Hayashi. The poor old woman took off her ceremonial hat and ran to her room with Otane close behind.

Even in her room, Otane was uncontrollably excited. Toyose came in behind her and helped her take off her coat and the *hakama*.

"Calm yourself a little, mother."

"What are you worried about?" laughed Otane. "I'm going to have a good time with the guests. Why don't you compliment me instead of complaining?"

Toyose did not know what to say. Otane's mind must have been overwrought by her concern, she thought sadly.

Otane remained in the garden until evening, chatting with the spa guests. That night neither she nor Toyose could sleep. Toyose found no peace until the next day, when her mother-in-law fell into despondency as if in reaction to the strain of the previous day.

Toyose could not stay with her mother-in-law indefinitely. She had to go to Tokyo as soon as possible and find a way of earning a living. For Otane, who was used to living in a large, old home, this separation from a family member was unbearable, and she was unwilling to let go of her daughter-in-law.

"Toyose, you talk as if you were worried only about me. But you are acting all upset. There's no need to get worked up about leaving."

There was something ambiguous in what Shota and Toyose had said about Tatsuo's whereabouts, thought Otane. They must be hiding something. If Toyose knew where Tatsuo was, Otane wanted to cajole her into revealing it. Otane postponed Toyose's departure from day to day.

"Mother, here's what we'll do. Since I don't know what to do myself, why not ask Uncle Morihiko for advice? If he says I should stay here, then I'll stay."

Morihiko's reply came, saying exactly what Toyose wished to hear. He told her to come to Tokyo as soon as possible and start planning for her future. He wanted Otane to rest in Itō a little longer; he would come and visit her soon. At the end of February, Toyose finally decided to leave her mother-in-law.

"I wish you'd stay a little longer. You have no idea how lonely I'll feel staying here alone," said Otane disconsolately.

"I would stay longer if I could, but. . . ." Unhesitatingly Toyose began to change her clothes, and rapidly packed for the trip. Both old and young Mrs. Hayashi offered to see her off to the boat, and encouraged by them, Otane left the inn with Toyose. It was still morning as they walked along the steaming river and passed the old-fashioned streets, and soon they came to the shore where they could see the boat to Kōzu. The boatman was getting the launch ready.

It was already the season when boats from the Shimoda area came to sell wreath shells for the spring festivals. The climate was completely different from that of the distant mountain country. Otane realized she would see spring come to Izu. As she thought of the time that had gone since she parted from her husband, she felt a sudden dizziness and almost collapsed on the sand.

"Mother, please get well. I'll be waiting for you in Tokyo. I really wish I could stay with you," Toyose said, and hurried off to the launch.

Otane stood with her neighbors and gazed at the steamer. The boat whistle reverberated in the sky above the harbor as though in farewell. Only the bright blue ocean remained before her eyes.

Returning to the inn, Otane found herself all alone again. Everything that happened to her during these months was completely beyond her comprehension: the old Hashimoto family, which had continued since the days of Chikuo, collapsed almost overnight; the father, not the son, had destroyed it; and she herself was about to be cast away in the group of the most helpless women in the world. Toyose was gone.

In the afternoon Otane descended the meandering staircases and let her weary body sink into the bath—the flowing hot water, the misty vapor, the opaque light filtering through the glass window—all was completely still around her, with no other bather about. She pressed the nape of her neck against the edge of the tub as she lay immersed in the water. She stayed immobile for some time, as though she were dead.

Outside the window a warm rain had begun to fall. The sound took her back to a distant past when she was young and living at her parents' home, just about the time her marriage was being arranged. Her father was alive in those days, and her mother and grandmother were well. Someone from her grandmother's family asked for her in marriage, and the arrangement with the Hashimotos, which she preferred, was almost broken off. It was her grandmother who tried to break it, and her mother was about to reject the Hashimoto proposal out of a sense of duty to her mother-in-law. Had Otane not been resolute enough to attempt suicide, most likely she would not have become Tatsuo's wife.

That episode and subsequent scenes came back to her: the youthful determination with which she tried to kill herself, and the discovery and rescue by her mother.

She married Tatsuo after all those complications. Her devotion to him never diminished, even after she had Shota and then Osen. Her long illness, whose nature she could not disclose to others, was in fact the result of her husband's dissipation. She endured the pain of her slowly corroding body, for she adored him.

Recollecting her past, she became terribly confused and could no longer think coherently.

"I'm still not good enough, to hold these things against him," she checked herself. "Without me taking care of him, how he must be suffering," she thought as she dried herself.

She was about to put on her clothes when she found herself in front of a large mirror. As she wiped off the clouded surface, she saw in it the very image of her father, who had died insane.

Some of the female guests staying at the inn came to know Otane. "Mrs. Hashimoto, you are a really lucky person, having money sent to you from home and enjoying yourself here as long as you wish," one of them commented. She was hard put to answer.

"That's right, there's no one as carefree as I am," she replied, but she swallowed her sobs in her room.

The Hayashi family soon returned to Tokyo. Otane lost the old woman who had kept her company, consoling and encouraging her. Every departure she saw off at the beach made her wish she could leave and at least go to Tokyo to join her daughter-in-law. But she was not permitted to do so even in March. She received letters from everyone telling her to keep calm.

Money from home now came only intermittently. Instead, Morihiko sent funds from Tokyo. Otane could do nothing but stay in

Itō until she had the family's consent to leave. In spring when the fern shoots appeared in the hills, she often took long walks with other guests to gather them. Looking over the sunny hills of Izu Peninsula, she brooded over her husband. She carefully dried and stored the fern shoots, with hopes she might possibly find some way to send them to her husband, who reportedly had gone to China.

June came, and early in the month the day arrived for which she had been eagerly waiting. She packed quickly for the trip to Tokyo.

Even then, she had received no word from Tatsuo, but she could not give up hope for him.

She said goodbye to the friends she had made at the inn. She felt like a completely different person from the woman who arrived almost a year before. But when she retraced the long shoreline and the same ports of calls for cargoes, she recalled the earlier boat trip and her sorrowful parting from Tatsuo.

The steamer arrived at Kōzu, and all the passengers hurried off for landing. High waves soon lifted the launch and carried them to the shore. Shortly she was standing on the spot where Tatsuo had so forlornly seen her off.

A bright June sun lit Sagami Bay and she found it difficult to leave the beach. She felt the hot sand she had once walked on with her husband; she saw the same pine trees lining the promenade and the inn where they spent the night perched on the top of the cliff.

When she stopped for lunch and asked various questions at the inn, the proprietor recognized Otane and greeted her. "Oh, you're going home now. It was a very long stay for you, wasn't it?" Quite unaware of her situation, he flattered her, rubbing his hands together in his eagerness to please.

She arrived in Tokyo while it was still light, looking forward to seeing Toyose, Morihiko, and Minoru's family in his absence.

Chapter 9

Toyose's apartment was in the heart of a congested district. It was one of many barren, boxlike rooming houses built on both sides of a narrow, dusty street. Soon after reaching Tokyo, Toyose enrolled in a bookkeeping course, and she chose the location because it was close to school.

Otane came to see her there. The two met in a small upstairs room. The friendly couple who owned the house ran a retail shop in front and lived in the rear of the first floor. They barely scratched out a living, though both worked very hard.

"This is an awful hole," said Otane after she settled in. "But Toyose, I would much rather nibble on a bread crust here than have a banquet alone in Itō."

To Toyose, Otane appeared less fretful than when she saw her in Izu. She mentioned that her own mother—she was a Terashima— was visiting in Tokyo. She came to be hospitalized for treatment but expected to be released shortly.

"Oh no!" Otane was flustered. "I couldn't possibly face Mrs. Terashima."

"You shouldn't feel like that. It doesn't really matter," Toyose said.

"It doesn't matter to you, but it does to me. In the first place, how can I face her letting you live in a dump like this?"

Otane thought of the people who sent false telegrams to Toyose after the Hashimoto bankruptcy. It was not only a sense of shame that Otane felt.

"I have an idea. I'm going to ask Morihiko to let me stay with him. Then I'll come back again. Yes, that's what I'll do. Don't think badly of me but I really can't see your mother this time," said Otane. Toyose felt sorry for her rather than offended. She decided to speak frankly.

"I was in such a bad way. When mother came, I had absolutely nothing. I couldn't even buy a post card. When she asked me to write home about her arriving safely, she had no change and told me to get some cards for her. I couldn't even do that and I was wondering what I should do. Mother realized it and said 'You don't even have money for a post card!' She began to cry. Then she gave me a hundred yen so I could breathe a little."

"It must have been terrible. Money stopped coming to me too. If that's any sign, they must be having serious trouble at home. But as soon as things are worked out, Shota will never let you get into such straits again." Otane had only a hazy notion of financial matters. Until recently the head clerks managed the accounting of the Hashimoto household. Her only responsibility was to be wife and mother.

Otane decided to move to Morihiko's inn the following day. After hearing Toyose's story, she realized that her apartment was not her home either.

So Otane moved to Morihiko's for a fortnight, and when Mrs. Terashima left for home, she moved back with Toyose. It was the first sunny day after weeks of rain, and as Otane returned slushing through the mud, the road was beginning to dry in spots outside the rooming house. The glass door of the store glinted in the sun. She climbed the dark staircase to Toyose's room, feeling as if she had entered a stiflingly hot cave. Toyose was still at the school. In the room with makeshift kitchen utensils, only Toyose's splendid kimonos, stretched on hangers, were incongruous in the squalor around. Otane now could find no place to rest her back comfortably, nor a pillow on which to sleep peacefully. But from then on, she lived with Toyose in the second-floor room, and the two developed an intimacy that had not existed before. Otane discovered Shota had deeply hurt Toyose in the same way Tatsuo had hurt her. Toyose learned about a woman with whom Shota was having an affair and was wracked by a grief she could not reveal to others. Otane felt as though she was seeing a portrait of her own youth.

Otane was brought up by her father to believe that fidelity was woman's primary virtue. As far as she was concerned, Tatsuo's infidelity was by far the most serious shortcoming in their marriage.

From her own experience she had formulated ideas on how to keep a husband happy. She wanted to impart this knowledge to Toyose in minute detail, explaining how a woman could charm a man, how she could protect him from other women, and all the schemes she could possibly devise. Before they fell asleep those summer nights, Otane spoke of things one does not ordinarily tell to a daughter-in-law. The reserve between the two women was broken, and they began to feel they were really mother and daughter.

One day Toyose said to Otane, "Mother, I've been hiding something. . . . Shall I tell you what happened to father?"

Otane stared at her daughter-in-law. "Are you trying to tease me again?"

"No, I'm not."

"Toyose, are you really going to tell me something? Wait a minute. I get the chills just hearing you talk that way."

For the first time Otane learned of Tatsuo's whereabouts. She believed he had gone to China, but he was not very far away. The young geisha with whom he had had an affair at home had come to Tokyo. Her release was purchased from a Shimbashi geisha house, and now she was living with him.

"I thought it was probably something like that." Otane hid behind a grim smile, but a thousand suspicions crowded her mind.

In August, Otane expected Sankichi in Tokyo. She was excited also at the happy prospect of getting together with other members of the family. Toyose too talked about the uncle-in-law she had never met.

Sankichi came searching for Otane early one evening, just as the lamplight began to glow inside the glass door of the store. "Is this Mrs. Hashimoto's lodging?" The proprietress of the house came out to greet him and told him that Otane and Toyose had gone out for a stroll and some shopping.

Sankichi, deciding to see his sister at his inn, left a message for her to visit him the next evening.

He returned to the inn. Sankichi was on a brief stopover on his way to the north to see Oyuki's parents and relatives.

The visit to Tokyo was his first in a long while, so he waited at the inn all the next day to receive his relatives. Morihiko arrived at the appointed time. Sankichi led him upstairs and introduced him to one of Oyuki's younger sisters, Oai, who was just visiting.

"Is she a daughter of the Nakuras?" said Morihiko, looking at Sankichi. "What happened to the young lady who was studying in Tokyo before?"

"You mean Ofuku? She's graduated and gone home. She already has a husband."

"Time goes so fast. I'm amazed how fast young people grow up. Minoru's daughters are quite big too. Speaking of daughters, I guess I'll have to send mine to some Tokyo school next year."

As he looked at the young girl with a blue ribbon in her hair, Morihiko thought of his own daughters at home.

"Oai, why don't you go back to school now? You'd best stop at your guardian's and have his seal put on your visiting permit." She blushed and gathered her things to leave.

Sankichi was now alone with his brother. Morihiko took off his summer coat and seated himself by the window, crossing his legs. They began to talk about Tatsuo and Minoru.

"Well, it's causing serious consequences," Morihiko said. "The fire is spreading all over the place."

Sankichi moved closer. "But I'm sure this didn't happen overnight at the Hashimotos'. When I visited them in Kiso, Tatsuo was doing very well, working very hard. Those were probably his best days."

"Anyway, they say he spent fifteen hundred yen for Shota's wedding. He had a lavish way of doing things and everything was overdone."

"I wonder why Otane didn't suspect."

"I'm sure she was worried. But whenever she wanted an *obi*, her husband bought one for her; if she wanted a kimono, he got it for her. He was generous because he had a guilty conscience. But she didn't think so. She was probably worried, but she didn't realize how bad things were."

Sankichi tried to go on to things involving Morihiko more directly. There was much he wanted to know about Tatsuo too. But first he asked that dinner be sent up.

From the window of the midcity inn, Sankichi could see only

the walls of storage buildings, roofs of houses, and branches of tall trees. But it was relatively quiet, good for conversation.

"I wonder how a quiet man like Tatsuo could do such things," said Morihiko. "M and I went all the way to Nagoya to urge him to reconsider."

"How did you ever find out he was in Nagoya?" Sankichi poured fresh tea into Morihiko's cup.

"Tatsuo withdrew money from the bank when he left home; after quite a lot of investigation, we found that he paid for the geisha and took her with him. She was working someplace in Shimbashi. M guessed that he must be in Nagoya and asked me to go with him to look for Tatsuo. We went down to Nagoya and put up at an inn, but we didn't know where to start. The owner of the inn was a former geisha, so we explained the situation, promising her a reward if she could locate the couple. After all, she is a professional about this sort of thing. She said the way of the geisha world is to get men to spend money as fast as possible. Give me ten yen, she said. My health is not too good, I'll go to a hot spring where they might be. She went to the spa, and in about a week sent a telegram to come right away. I hurried there. When I went into Tatsuo's room, the mosquito net was still hanging. The mistress of the inn was sitting on one side of Tatsuo and on the other, M. They spent all night watching him. And the look Tatsuo had when he saw me!" Morihiko made a gesture as if something had struck him in the eyes. "M and I tried to reason with him. Tatsuo said things he ordinarily would never had. He'd given up everything. He no longer considered himself husband or father. He didn't give a damn what happened to everything. After that, there was nothing we could say. So we left."

"What a way to leave home! Others think of going to a monastery—but he takes a mistress," commented Sankichi. But he had read Tatsuo's diary that day long ago in the Hashimoto godown and he felt in a way he understood the contrived grand climax to Tatsuo's dissipation.

"I made a report of the meeting and sent a copy to Shota for the records. I kept a copy myself," said Morihiko as if to bring the discussion to a close.

"Does Otane know about this?"

"That's another problem. It would have been disastrous if she had gone mad or something. We decided to let her in on it little by little. That's why we made her stay in Itō as long as possible and kept the news from her."

A maid came up with the dinner, and Sankichi dismissed her so the two could talk as they ate.

"Well, shall we eat?" Morihiko said as he quickly picked up the chopsticks. "Minoru's family's such a headache. His wife came to see me some time ago and explained why you couldn't send any money for a while. I had to do something. But I appreciate what you've done for them for a long time. We've both worked hard. It hasn't been easy since we all have our own families."

"I had several reasons actually. My school is a poor one to begin with. Then the number of teachers had to be increased in spite of a reduction in the township and county subsidies. I couldn't just ignore the school's predicament so I decided to take a cut in my salary. I'm afraid I won't be able to help them for a while. But I'll take Otane home with me. We decided to do it before I came."

"Fine! It'll be wonderful for Otane if you can."

After talking a while longer, Morihiko put on his kimono coat as if to signify he had exhausted both food and conversation.

"Otane should be here soon," said Sankichi. "I guess she decided to wait until after dinner."

"A man is coming to see me on business," said Morihiko, tying the cords of his coat. "I'll have to be excused. Thanks for dinner."

"You don't have to go yet, do you? Stay and talk a little longer."

"Not tonight. If I can manage, I'll see you again. Give my regards to the Nakuras and the others."

Morihiko left, carrying a stylish summer hat. Sankichi saw him to the door. His sister arrived shortly afterward.

Otane brought Toyose along to see Sankichi. It was the first reunion for brother and sister since Kiso, except for the brief meeting at the train window when Otane was on her way to Itō. He had been worried about her in his own way, and he felt relieved to see her looking so well.

Sankichi and Toyose were introduced to each other and exchanged greetings.

"If you had come a little earlier, you could have seen Morihiko," he told Otane.

"I know, but I didn't want to bother you with too many visitors."

"Uncle, I'm sorry we weren't home last night." The word "uncle" seemed a little new and strange to Toyose.

"We are staying in a ghastly room," said Otane, taking out her tobacco case. "You'd be shocked to see it. Our bedroom is kitchen, parlor, and study. We've so many mosquitoes that we borrowed a net from Minoru's house, and it's too big for the room. Even when we hang it as high as possible, it's still too long. We laughed ourselves to death."

"Sometimes it's good to experience hard times," Sankichi remarked.

Otane and Toyose glanced at each other. After a few puffs on her pipe, Otane said, "I stayed in Itō for quite a while. Thanks to Morihiko, I got my health back. If you could let me stay with you as Oyuki suggested in her letter, I'd come and take care of your children or do anything you want."

"Certainly, come for a while. The quiet country will be good for you. But we won't be able to treat you to fine food."

"Who needs it? These days I go to Morihiko's inn once a week to read the newspapers, take a bath, and get treated to dinner. That's how I spend my time and I have no other pleasures."

Toyose listened in her slightly hunched position, smoking the slim silver pipe she borrowed from her mother-in-law.

"When I was in Itō, a woman said, 'Mrs. Hashimoto is a lucky person. Here she is, enjoying herself at a spa, while the money comes from the country.' People don't know anything, you see."

Otane's unexpectedly placid tone came as a great relief to Sankichi. He was anxious to talk about Tatsuo, but first he had to tell her his summer plan of going to visit his father-in-law.

"When Oyuki was in Tokyo some time ago, I saw her at Minoru's."

"I met her in this same inn," Toyose said, "when Uncle Morihiko and I came to visit."

"She met your wife before she met you," added Otane.

Toyose sat as unobtrusively as possible beside her mother-in-law, sensing that her newfound uncle was examining her in minute detail.

The summer evening fell, and the lamp lit up the three faces. Sankichi stated what was on his mind, watching his sister's face.

"I understand Tatsuo's in Nagoya."

"So I hear," Otane answered, managing a wry smile to mask her depression.

"Widows all around."

"Sankichi, I don't consider myself a widow, yet!"

"You may not think so, but the fact is you are," he chided.

"Don't talk nonsense!" Otane pulled herself up and glared at her brother as she placed her hands squarely in her lap.

He sighed. "Otane, you'd better give up on your husband. His style of doing things is just too fancy. I heard all about it from Morihiko. What's the use in devoting yourself to a man like him? It's better to think of yourself as a widow. Believe me, it is!"

"Stop calling me a widow! I won't have it!"

"Nonsense! If I can find some good man I'll arrange a marriage for you." Sankichi pitied his sister and tried to make it as light as possible in an offhand way. But by now Otane was trembling.

"Sankichi, look how you've shocked Toyose. It's because you say such mean things. When we were at home, Osen and the boys were always talking about 'Uncle Sankichi,' and Toyose was looking forward to meeting you." She looked at her daughter-in-law. "Isn't it true, Toyose? Who needs such a dreadful uncle?"

Toyose could not help laughing.

"All joking aside," said Sankichi, looking at Otane, "do you think it's so bad to be a widow?"

"What's so wonderful about being a widow?" she snapped.

"Probably there's nothing worse than being a young widow. But what about an older woman like you? Being a widow gives you a chance to be free and spend the rest of your life peacefully, doesn't it? It may depend on the person, but to me becoming a widow at your age and thinking about the children seems rather nice."

"Speak for yourself," Otane retorted, and said nothing more.

She intended to stay at Sankichi's inn that night and have a long talk with him. When the streets quieted down, she turned to her daughter-in-law.

"Toyose, you'd better be going now."

"I'd like to stay too, if you don't mind. It sounds like it's going to be an interesting talk tonight."

Otane agreed, and Toyose returned to her rooming house to inform the landlady and then came back to the inn. The three lay down under one mosquito net, and the brother and sister continued their talk. Otane pulled her tobacco set toward her and smoked, but her agitation was now visible. Often in Itō a dot appeared behind her tightly closed eyelids, whirling faster and faster as it grew in size. She described it to Sankichi with her hands, and told him in a quaking, troubled voice how she felt she was eventually sucked into a whirlpool.

Sankichi realized that she was not completely well yet, and Toyose too could not fall asleep after she heard this.

The next morning, the two women left, promising to visit again. They talked as they made their way back to the lodgings.

"If I wait at Sankichi's home, it would be easier for Shota to send for me."

"Yes, if you went there you'd practically be home."

The last days of August came quickly. Otane started her preparations for traveling again. She had to visit Morihiko at his inn, Naoki's family, and all the other relatives to say goodbye.

One hot, humid afternoon Otane visited Minoru's family for this purpose. She had postponed this call until the last. Since her marriage into the Hashimoto family, she had only few opportunities to call on the main branch of the Koizumi family. She remembered one time in particular when she saw her mother there shortly after the family moved to Tokyo. Tatsuo was having an illicit affair, and one of the head clerks who had managed the pharmacy for many years quit the shop in anger. Unable to cope with the grief, she herself seriously thought of leaving her husband. She remembered also that it was the last time she saw her mother.

The Koizumi family took a smaller house every time they moved. Otane turned into a narrow alley and walked on the gutter coverings. The people who scratched out an existence by odd jobs formed a dismal world in this alley. Otane came to a latticed door at a dimly lit entrance.

"Who is it?" a young voice called, and Oshun's face appeared. "Mother, Aunt Otane's here," she said.

Okura came out from behind an old bamboo screen. She suffered from beriberi almost every year, and she was in and out of bed while she waited with her two daughters for her husband.

Otane and Okura talked together in front of an oblong charcoal brazier that was incongruously large, a remnant of past affluence.

"Sankichi was very sweet to invite me, so I'm going to be living with him for a while," said Otane.

"That's wonderful. He stopped in to see us." Okura smiled dolefully. "I looked like a ghost with such messy hair, and I think I frightened him away."

"I'm at the end too," said Otane in dialect. Oshun, who had just brought in tea, heard the provincial speech and giggled.

"Oshun," her mother glanced at her. "We still have the good tea someone gave us, don't we?"

"It's too old now, Mother." She blushed slightly.

"Ordinary tea is fine, Okura. Please, if you stand on ceremony, you'll make me feel like a stranger," said Otane, laughing understandingly. "Sankichi said something odd when I went to see him at his inn. 'Widows all around.' Can you imagine? I lost my temper."

"But it's true. We're all as good as widows, though you're better off than I am. Look at me, there's no one as unlucky as I am. Since I married Minoru I've lived with him hardly one-third of the time you spent with your husband. One absence after another. I've spent my whole life waiting for him."

Without dye, Okura's hair was like an old woman's. Yet for all her complaining about her misfortunes, she was relaxed and easygoing. This irritated Otane all the more.

Otane looked around. Could this be the main house of Koizumi? Minoru in prison, Osugi dead, and Sozo living with strangers. The Inagakis, once such frequent callers, stayed away these days, and Okura managed somehow to live, but completely depending on the meager assistance of her two brothers-in-law. The two rooms she rented rarely saw a ray of sunshine. After so many relocations scarcely any furniture was left from the opulent past. Otane found some calligraphy of her father's mounted as a scroll on the wall of the back room. Tadahiro's spirit seemed to live only in it, watching the declining fortunes of the family.

Even in this squalid atmosphere Oshun grew rapidly, and now she was about to graduate from high school.

"Oshun's grades are always outstanding, and the school principal is very much interested in her future." Okura turned to her daughter. "Bring your paintings to show to Aunt Otane."

Oshun brought some drawings and spread them on the floor. She was wearing an *obi* she painted herself.

"Finally she's permitted to use colors," said Okura, pointing at the sketches. "Sankichi suggested that she should stop the painting and poetry lessons and concentrate on school. But we've managed this far, and she likes painting so much, I want to let her continue at least the art lessons."

"It would be such a shame to make her stop now," Otane agreed.

"I don't care what else I have to do without. I want to give her everything I can. But do you think she listens to me at all? These days she talks back to me and every time she wins."

"Naturally. She's getting a better education."

"Yes, that's true. When I was young, there was no such thing as a girls' high school."

"Where is Otsuru?" Otane inquired about the younger daughter.

"I think she went to see her friend," Oshun replied.

"Oshun, where's her certificate of merit? Why don't you show it to Aunt Otane. She does very well at school too. She gets the honors at every examination."

As she talked, Okura cleaned the mouthpiece of a long pipe that she lit and hospitably offered to Otane. Sunbeams leaking through narrow gaps in the eaves brightened the window. Through the bamboo curtain they could see the next-door neighbor making clogs. A putrid smell drifted into the room from the gutter.

Prompted by her mother, Oshun went to Minoru's paulownia desk in the next room and brought a recent letter from her father.

Okura showed Otane the letter in a gray prison envelope. "He says here he wants to be remembered to Mr. Hashimoto," she said, lowering her voice.

"Minoru probably knows nothing about what happened in the outside world," sighed Otane.

The two women fell silent.

"I must admit," Okura began in a pleading tone, "since he has been gone so long, I've had very difficult times. Sankichi tells me to move out of the city, to someplace where the rent is lower. But every piece of furniture here is attached by creditors. And then we couldn't move any place that would be inconvenient for the girls to go to school. And our debts. . . ."

Okura's voice grew more and more supplicating. Digression was habitual for her, and she struck off on so many tangents that her conversation usually grew unintelligible.

"Morihiko is not a man to talk about his work," Otane interrupted. "Supporting you and his own family, and paying his bills at the inn . . . it's not easy for him. When you think about it, he's really doing a lot."

"Yes, and I'm very grateful."

"His room at the inn is always immaculate. He doesn't drink or smoke. I'll never know how he can be so stoic. I'd really like to see him succeed in what he's doing."

The conversation then shifted to another member of the family.

"Now, about Sozo. . . ." Okura did not hide her aversion for him. "The people taking care of him often tell us he is absolutely in-destructible. Even in my condition, I've got to send him a fixed sum every month. So, Morihiko's burdens are enormous."

"Sozo is the black sheep of the family. I don't know how such a man was born among us."

"If only he would act a little more like an invalid, but he's terribly spoiled. You know how blunt Morihiko is. He says if Sozo were an insect, he would squash him under his heel."

All three laughed. No one but Morihiko could make such a state-ment.

It was soon time for Otane to leave.

"When you get to Sankichi's, please ask him to remember the care of Oshun and Otsuru," said Okura earnestly. Otane left the Koizumi house.

She took a morning train, and Toyose, Oshun, and Otsuru came to see her off. Toyose stayed by the train window, looking up at her mother-in-law with tears in her eyes.

Chapter 10

Since leaving her own home, Otane had drifted from one place to another for more than a year, and she finally settled down at Sankichi's house. Sankichi had made the long trip back from the Nakura house and was waiting for her with Oyuki.

Once Otane was escorted by the couple to the back room, the children gathered around her full of curiosity. She was delighted to be away from the crowded city and come to live with her brother's family in the country, where the sound of a water mill echoed in the air peacefully. She had been able to make the trip without her usual travel sickness, she said.

"Ofusa, do you remember your Aunt Otane?" Sankichi asked his daughter.

"She couldn't possibly remember me from saying hello at the train window." And turning to the child Otane asked, "Do I look like your aunt?"

"Don't you think they've grown?"

"I'm amazed that Okiku's so big. She's almost as tall as Ofusa," said Otane, comparing the two girls before her.

Oyuki brought the infant who had been asleep in the next room. "This is our addition this year. See."

The third child was also a girl. Her name was Oshige. She was frightened by the stranger and began to sob, hiding her face in her mother's bosom. Oyuki smiled and offered her breast to pacify her. Otane laughed and said she would keep her distance until Oshige got used to her.

"How old are you, Ofusa?" asked Otane, taking out the gifts she brought.

"Your aunt is asking how old you are."

The little girl first held up four fingers, then folded back two of them. "I'm this old, and Okiku's this old."

"Hm . . . you're four and Okiku's two. My, you're smart. I'll have to give you a prize, and a present for Okiku too."

"Presents! Presents!" screamed the two girls, dancing around gleefully.

"Auntie will laugh at you if you don't behave. They're so full of mischief." Oyuki apologized.

Ofusa stayed by her parents in the beginning, but now she came to her aunt and, urged by her mother, sang "Turtle and Hare."

Her young voice reminded Otane of her own childhood long ago. "My, how well she sings!" Otane kept time by nodding her head. "Will you sing me another? I don't remember the last time I heard a children's song."

The thatched roof was a novelty for Otane, who was paying her first visit to her brother's house. Oyuki took her around to show her the vegetable garden in the rear. Then they returned to Sankichi's room.

"I see there's a persimmon tree." Otane stooped to examine the hanging branch in a corner of the garden. "Kasuke told us how much he appreciated your hospitality on his yearly business trips here. He said you have persimmons, plums, and nice azaleas."

There were also cherry trees and rhododendrons; an apple tree stood near the eaves, and the shade of its boughs added to the serenity of the surroundings.

Oyuki brought the infant to Otane. "She cried a minute ago, but now she's all smiles."

"Yes, I see she's in good humor again." Otane took the baby. "What a nice baby!"

"Having children as we do is a lot of work, but your family might have at least one. . . ."

"Seems like Toyose can't."

"I wish I could give you one of ours," Sankichi laughed.

"And I'd accept it," replied Otane as though joking. "If you're meant to have children, you will. The human body's like that. You can't do anything about childlessness."

"We started our life like a couple of students, you know," said Sankichi. "When Okiku was born, I had to let Ofusa sleep in my bed, and that was the worst period. She wouldn't fall asleep unless she was with Oyuki. On cold nights, she cried all night. I never realized bringing up children was such an ordeal. Sometimes I felt like crying myself."

"We all go through this as we mature."

"When I was a student, I used to think it's cowardly to give up your dreams just because you have a family. But as I think about it now, I can understand why many men get so discouraged."

"Oyuki, don't you have a maid now?"

"No, we don't. We thought we found a good girl, but her parents wanted her back during the silkworm season."

"Then I know how difficult it is," Otane said as she looked around the house. "But, Oyuki, I'm going to help you. Just think of me as a family member."

Otane was still high-strung, and her efforts to control herself occasionally showed through her pallid face. Sankichi wanted her to rest.

"Come on, Okiku!" Calling out in her provincial accent, Ofusa came in with her younger sister through the back door.

"Mommy, look!" Ofusa called from beyond the hedge; and Okiku gave a cry riding piggyback on her aunt.

In the evening after Otane's arrival, they had just returned from a walk to town.

"Oh! How nice of auntie to buy you lanterns," said Oyuki, standing on the veranda of the south room.

"We just took a trip to see the town," said Otane over the hedge. The older child came in first, holding a red lantern. Otane followed and put Okiku down.

Oyuki took the lanterns from the excited children, lit the candles, and gave one to each.

"Okiku, you mustn't wave it around so much. The candle's a little too long," warned Otane.

"See how red and pretty they are," said Oyuki, holding Oshige to show her the glowing lights.

"Let's go show daddy." Otane led the children to his study.

"Daddy, a lantern!" cried Ofusa, stretching out her arm. Sankichi was resting at the moment, smoking a cigarette.

"What pretty lanterns your aunt bought for you!" he responded as the children walked around holding the red lights high overhead.

"May I have a puff too?" said Otane as she sat down beside her brother. "How can you do any work with all the noise? Having children certainly makes a great difference."

At every opportunity, she changed the topic to her husband. The question why he deserted her and the children was always on her mind.

"It's a curious business," she reminisced. "Once when Tatsuo was still at home, he suddenly said, 'Otane, don't worry, I'll never leave you.' And that was before I ever suspected him of anything, and naturally I was startled."

"You might have guessed something about the finances then."

"How could I? We had one visitor after another from morning till night. He insisted that I wine and dine them, and if I didn't, he became angry. There was always such confusion that I never had time to ask him anything."

"When I visited you, he was working very hard."

"It would have been wonderful if he had only continued. But he gets tired of things so quickly. And when he's bored, his sickness takes over. That's his pattern."

"I wonder what he's doing now."

"I wonder."

"Do you think he's still with that woman?"

"If he is, it certainly can't last very much longer. Once he runs out of money, that kind won't cater to him. It'll be his turn to be thrown out. That much is sure."

"I suppose you're right."

"That's exactly what I'm worried about. My husband was born into the Hashimoto family. I'd like to see him die in his own house."

A quarrel broke out, and one of the children began to cry. Otane left to tend to them.

Her young nieces soon grew indispensable to her. Letting them cling to her shoulders and chest and trail after her everywhere brought great satisfaction to her mothering instinct. In some measure it brought her consolation for the loss of her husband.

Ofusa and Okiku were sitting at the dining table near the hearth. Otane had prepared some parched-barley cereal. Ofusa savored the sweet powdered cereal as she ladled it into her mouth with a wooden spoon; the younger girl was always spilling hers.

"Give the bowl to me, Okiku," said Otane and stirred some hot water into the meal. "Come, I'll feed you so that your clothes won't get soiled." Trying to make the child open her mouth, Otane involuntarily opened her own.

Having finished her portion, Ofusa licked her lips. "That was gooood!"

"Children, when you are finished, run out to the back and play awhile. Go see what your mother's doing. Is she washing?"

"Aunt Otane, come play with us," cried Ofusa.

"Later. Auntie wants to talk to your daddy now."

The children ran out.

Sankichi had launched on a long, demanding project that spring. The hours not taken up with schoolwork were invariably spent at his desk, and he didn't so much as go out to the vegetable garden any more. Despite the enjoyment he received from it, he turned over the gardening to the school janitor, who came periodically carrying his hoe on his shoulder.

Otane went to the back room, tobacco pouch in hand. For a moment she hesitated. "Sankichi, are you working?"

"Come in if you want to talk," he responded, turning around. Otane was going through her menopause. The periodic tide that had started when she was a bashful child was at last receding. She no longer had the patience of a younger woman, and her feeling of helplessness only increased.

"It's a curious business," she said. This opening always made Sankichi laugh. Whenever she prefaced her remarks in this manner, she was about to bring up her husband.

"Tatsuo will be fifty next year. Imagine a man his age still acting the way he does. What a disgrace! But a man's a sinful creature, and if only I could have kept him company when he drank, and sung a song or two. . . . Sometimes I feel it might have worked out, Sankichi."

Tears began to stream down her cheeks, which were twisted in an unhappy smile. She talked about the Tatsuo who was once hailed as a bright young man, and about his study in Tokyo while she kept the house in the country. It was during that period that he first began to show signs of sickness.

"Once after he came back from Tokyo, I suspected his 'sickness' was starting up again. I asked him a few probing questions. He said, 'Oh, that woman? She has no redeeming feature,' and went on to tear her apart. Imagine, Sankichi, he was already having an affair with her! Then she got pregnant. I thought of adopting the baby and bringing it up as my own. But then I thought about the people who would point at me and say I couldn't keep my husband. It was an embarrassing business however you look at it. She had the baby soon enough, but prematurely, I was told, and since she had no milk, it didn't live two months. . . . But he's really an honest man. And he's gentle. When he felt he was in the wrong, he always bowed all the way down to the floor and apologized to me. Then I would feel more sorry than angry. Even now, if he would think it over and come back. . . . Yes, yes, I still trust him completely. I told Toyose, if only our love could reach him, he would be sure to come back."

After returning from the town bathhouse with Oyuki and the children, Otane went to the room with her belongings and opened her vanity kit. "Auntie, are you putting on makeup?" Ofusa asked, looking up at Otane. "Certainly, even auntie does. Every woman tries to look nice." It was the most secluded room in the house, previously occupied by the houseboy, and Sankichi occasionally brought his work there. The mirror she brought with her was large and thick. Facing it now, about to apply bath powder, she suddenly remembered that paragon of old-fashioned womanhood, Grandmother Koizumi, who, even when she was over sixty, daily put on her light makeup. The realization that her husband had been stolen by a young upstart of a geisha also came to her and overwhelmed her. The mirror, cruelly honest, spared nothing. It returned the image of a dried-up old woman, as if to say talking about fidelity was pointless when one no longer possessed an attractive body.

Ofusa's smiling red cheeks appeared at her back in the mirror.

"Ofusa, I'll put some powder on you. Oh, you have such a lovely color after the bath." Ofusa held up a suntanned face to her aunt.

Otane then took her to Oyuki, who was putting up her hair.

"Mommy!" Ofusa showed her white cheeks.

"Look at her, mommy. She's so pretty," chuckled Otane.

Oyuki could not contain her laughter. "She's so brown that the powder makes her look like a monkey."

Otane stood for a while, gazing at Oyuki's hairdo. She finally cried out as though she could no longer stand it, "Come, let me do it. Your hair looks so countrified. I saw what Toyose used to do with hers. I'll set it in the latest Tokyo style."

And while the women worked, Ofusa strutted through the house, singing loudly.

Oyuki chose her usual place near the south sliding doors to spread out her sewing things. Otane sat opposite her, engrossed in helping prepare her autumn clothes. It was a warm, bright spot, comfortable for sewing or taking clothes apart for cleaning.*

"Okiku, show me those photographs. I haven't seen some of them."

Otane took the pictures given to her by the little girl. Oyuki's whole family was there. "Oyuki, is this your sister's husband?" she asked, holding a picture of Tsutomu.

"Yes, it is."

"Sankichi told me he's met him. He's an adopted son-in-law of Mr. Nakura too, isn't he? Tradespeople somehow always look like tradespeople, even in photographs," she said, examining the picture.

"Okiku, you mustn't play with the pictures like that." But the mother's words made no impression on the child. Otane finished her work and stood up, brushing off her apron. "Come with me, children. Let's go see the castle site."

She tightened her *obi* and left with the two girls. Only Oshige in her bed remained with Oyuki. Through the opening of the sliding doors Oyuki could glimpse an autumnal tint in the sky. White, cotton clouds drifted past, driven by the wind.

"Where's my sister?" Sankichi asked when he came back from school.

"She took the children out for a stroll to pick some plantain fruit."

"What's she going to do with it?"

---

*Kimonos are traditionally made in such a way that they can be readily taken apart for cleaning.

"She said it's for her hair. You boil it and put the juice on your hair and it improves the texture. She probably heard about it in Itō."

Sankichi took off his cotton *hakama* and stretched his legs on the veranda.

"By the way, Otane wants to take one of the children home with her. What do you think of giving her Oshige?" Oyuki did not answer.

"We can't make ends meet with so many children," he continued, looking at the sleeping baby. "If Otane takes one, it will help a lot. She keeps talking about it."

"How could I do such a thing?" Oyuki replied firmly.

He sighed. "Otane must be lonely, you know. Of course she may want to keep her for a long time, and she may ask to adopt her, since Shota and Toyose are childless. We'll discuss it again if she wants adoption. Anyway, she is bent on taking care of Oshige for a while. What do you think? I don't mind letting her."

"You may not, but I do. Do you think I'd ever give up a child of mine?"

"There's no reason to worry about the baby. You know Otane; she'll take good care of her."

"I don't care what your sister says. Oshige is mine!"

Otane had spoken only to Sankichi and Oyuki would not hear of it.

One day in midautumn, Shota paid one of his rare visits to Sankichi's house. He had gone on a brief trip to Tokyo, and on his way home he took the mountain route to spend a night at his uncle's house.

Voices and laughter mingled in the back room. Otane was beside herself with excitement, tripping lightly between the kitchen and her son's side.

"Shota, are you ready to take me home?" she asked as they sat together.

"No. I still have some business to take care of on the way back. I'll send Kasuke to bring you home very soon."

"Well, that's all right then. I just wanted to know your plans. It doesn't have to be this time, of course." Otane realized that her return home was approaching at long last. With this happy news, she went back to help Oyuki.

It was a long time since Sankichi and Shota had the opportunity of talking together. Since the summer Sankichi spent in Kiso they had met only once, immediately after Tatsuo's departure. The reunion filled the two men with mixed emotions. Shota was well and showed his high spirits and determination to assume the responsibilities brought on by his father's failure.

"Shota, don't you think your mother has calmed down quite a bit? When she came to our house, she really wasn't herself. I've been teasing her that when she gets home, she should put on a pair of straw shoes and go out peddling medicine."

"It would be fine if she felt lighthearted enough for that. But I think she's well enough to come home at least. Of course she'll be shocked. Things were so bad I didn't know where to begin. I finally put everything right on the table and told the creditors to take anything they wanted."

"It wasn't an easy decision, I know."

"As a result—and only because I did what I did—all the debts have been paid. They took everything! Even the calligraphy on the sliding door was torn off. But I didn't let them touch a single thing that belonged to Toyose. I'm glad Mother wasn't there. If she'd been, I couldn't have made such a drastic decision. There's one good thing about country people. We didn't have to give up the house, and we keep on living pretty much as we did. Our medicine still sells as well as ever. Kasuke's way of running things was out of date, so we've put the shop into the hands of younger men. And I'm thinking of going to Tokyo. Everything depends on my hard work from now on."

"So you're going too. I've been planning to return to Tokyo with my new novel."

"I'll probably be there before you are."

"Yes. . . . I've lived here too long."

Otane wanted to know the last detail of everything, including about Osen, but Shota took leave of her and his uncle the next day.

Otane began preparing to return to a husbandless home. She imagined all the painful yet precious things Tatsuo left behind: his room, his clothes, his bed.

"Sankichi, I'm planning to stop at Toyose's parents' home on the way back. If I talk to Mrs. Terashima frankly, I'm sure she'll understand how I feel." While talking to her brother in the next room, she took out her wicker trunk and exchanged some summer kimonos with Oyuki.

Soon Kasuke came to meet her. He seemed to have aged suddenly. As she was fond of plants, Otane took with her some lilies of the valley that Sankichi had brought from a nearby farm, and yellow wild mums that she dug up at the castle site. At last she said goodbye to Sankichi and his family. When she left with Kasuke for the trip home, her eyes showed fear and emotion at the thought that she was soon to see her changed house.

The following March, Sankichi finally decided to give up the country living he had become accustomed to and move back to Tokyo. But many difficulties lay before him. His job did not allow him to make much progress with his writing, and even if he gave up teaching entirely to concentrate on his novel, it would still take at least a year to finish it. Now the father of three daughters, he had to set aside sufficient funds before making the move to provide for the entire family. Nevertheless, he determined to leave this mountainous region to write the novel. As the first step before the move, he decided to visit his friend Makino and seek help.

"Put out my suit, will you," he said to his wife.

The chilly, piercing sound of a horse-drawn carriage horn sounded near the station. A friend had promised to go with Sankichi, but the temperature dropped so sharply that she gave up the idea. Sankichi turned up his coat collar over his ears and left the house with a worried look on his face. The horse struggled up the slope, pulling the bus and exhaling white vapor from its nostrils. He waited at the street corner and boarded the carriage.

Snow still lay deep on the ground. As the carriage circled the foot of Mount Asama, the passengers clamped their knees together, trembling in the cold. After traveling about five miles on the carriage Sankichi got off; before walking deeper into the mountains, he felt he had to thaw his frozen body by the fireside of a teahouse. The next four miles were traveled by few pedestrians. The once flooded valley lay blanketed under pure white snow.

Makino lived in a remote mountain village. Sankichi had met the wealthy young landlord by chance and friendship developed between them. Whenever Sankichi called on him, he looked forward to seeing the quiet study, the garden with its many trees, and the well-cultivated fields of the Makino family. But today he had too much on his mind to enjoy the visit. Makino, his wife, and children received Sankichi in the spacious, old-fashioned drawing room. Yet in this warm family atmosphere the future weighed heavily on Sankichi's mind. He wanted to tell his friend his desperate need and appeal for help. But he could not bring himself to broach the subject even the next day.

Sankichi left the Makino house without saying one word about the purpose of his visit. He retraced his steps over the snowy road, trying to overcome his feeling of despair. He waited at the coach terminal for more than an hour. A group of carriage drivers had congregated, and there was a good deal of chatter and laughter. Sankichi himself, as if mesmerized, was drawn into a mirthless laughter. After a long wait the cold coach left. Trembling, he watched the setting sun filtering through the trees and the color of the golden sky fade.

When he reached home, Sankichi did not tell Oyuki the details of his visit. The youngest child had been put to bed beside the foot warmer, and Ofusa and Okiku were playing noisily with their beanbags by the scratched wall on which a calendar and some woodblock prints were pasted. Headless dolls lay strewn about. He looked at them broodingly as he warmed his body at the foot warmer. How could he support these children and also finish his novel? Oyuki took out the grape jam the Makinos had sent to the children, and looking like a mother hen feeding her chicks, she sat the two girls before her, gave them bread with jam, and let them lick the spoons.

Ofusa, who resembled Sankichi's mother very much, was a cheerful girl with red cheeks. Oblivious of his mood, she came to her father and sang gaily:

Rabbit, rabbit, why are your ears so long?
When my mother was young, she swallowed a bamboo leaf,
well-known in the province.

That's why my ears are so long.

Oyuki had taught her the song; it was Ofusa's favorite. It was a song Oyuki learned as a little girl from a maid from the Aomori area.

Sankichi suddenly felt encouraged, and that night he wrote a long letter to Makino.

Fortunately Makino understood his dire straits and his need for assistance. The answer came, and Makino became Sankichi's patron. Makino promised to keep his help a secret. Sankichi was deeply touched by such thoughtfulness and generosity and was determined to do his best to complete his writing and repay this kindness.

Sankichi made a brief business trip to Tokyo in April and looked for a house. The children missed him and made daily trips to the station. On the northern side of the thatched roof the remaining snow began to thaw, and water trickled like raindrops from the eaves.

Sankichi returned and told Oyuki about a new house he found in a Tokyo suburb on the grounds of a nursery. It was a one-story structure facing the street, and the walls had not been plastered yet; the carpenters were still busy on the interior. It seemed too small for the family, with three children, and for him to work. But the quiet, treed surroundings appealed to him. He made two more trips, and then, pledging he would await the completion of the house, he signed a lease. He told this to Oyuki as if the very thought of house-hunting made him perspire.

"There's nothing worse than looking for a house. To top things off, I got caught in the rain."

But his wife and children were ecstatic over the idea of moving to Tokyo.

That night before bedtime Ofusa and Okiku played around Sankichi.

"Were you both good little girls while I was away?" he asked. "Now stand there together."

They stood noisily before him.

"Now then, Ofusa, you're number one, Okiku is number two, and Oshige is number three. All right?"

"Daddy, am I number one?" asked the oldest.

"Yes, you're number one and Okiku's number two. When I call your number, answer me. Ready?"

The little girls looked at each other, delighted with the new game.

"Number one!"

"Here!" the younger promptly shouted.

"Okiku, you're not number one! I am," her sister protested, grabbing hold of her.

Bedlam broke loose as the two girls pranced about the room. The maid, who was recently hired from a nearby village, brought the baby to Sankichi.

"Oshige's vaccination took. Please look at it." The baby was still so bundled up she could not crawl, but she could clap her hands and do a few other things. Her head no longer wobbled on her neck, and she had become the charmer of the family.

"All right, all right. That's enough. Now all of you, off to bed," Sankichi ordered. Ofusa and Okiku ran to their mother, who changed them into nightclothes. The maid pressed her red cheek against Oshige's tender skin as though caressing a doll. In no time the three were sound asleep all in a row.

Number one, number two, number three. Sankichi's improvisation turned against him. His mother had borne eight children, including some who died in infancy. Oyuki herself was one of eleven. Her eldest sister had five, and the second sister was already the mother of six. He was surrounded by fecundity.

The next day he sent his school a brief letter of resignation, and the family started packing. They often talked about the new house and what it might hold for them. When it rained, they worried about how well the walls would dry, and on sunny days they wondered how far the work had progressed. The house gradually took definite shape in their minds and grew more habitable every day.

The couple was busy with preparations. Oyuki worried about what to wear and what to put on the children on moving day.

"Come here, Ofusa," she called to her eldest, taking out the child's best kimono. "Let's try this on. We won't take you to Tokyo unless you behave yourself." The kimono sleeves were decorated with Ofusa's favorite ribbons. Oyuki decided to dress Okiku in a checkered, yellow silk kimono.

Everyone commented that Okiku's fair complexion made her look lovely in anything. The neighbors who had become the couple's friends over the years came one after another to say goodbye.

"Well, I guess this is the last time . . . ," said the school janitor at the entrance garden.

"I have nothing adequate to give you as a farewell present, but I thought you might like the hoe and I put it aside for you," said Sankichi, pointing to the instrument, which stood in a corner of the entrance enclosure.

"Thank you very much. I'll be very happy to have it. You'd be surprised; things like hoes last to your grandchildren's generation."

The janitor rubbed his large peasant hands together and took the hoe.

On moving day a warm shower passed early in the morning. The pressure of the longstanding snow and the weight of the icicles had partially broken the eaves on the north side. Smoke from next door filtered through the gap and curled along the wall. The flowers in the garden were in full bloom.

The woman next door brought some steaming hot rice with pickled vegetables to the back door, and Sankichi and his wife sat on the soiled mats with their children and ate their final breakfast in the house where they had lived for seven years. For a short time the sun broke through. Ofusa and Okiku, escorted by girls from the neighborhood, were the first to leave for the station.

In front of the station, where dirt was piled for road repair, Sankichi's colleagues and students and the many townspeople he had befriended all gathered to express their regrets on seeing the family move away. The confectioner and the wife of the bean-curd merchant brought their modest gifts for the couple. One of Sankichi's colleagues, an old science teacher, presented a bouquet of flowers to the couple through the train window. Makino was there too, wearing a Western-style suit, but he saw Sankichi off silently from a distance.

"Make it stop! Make it stop!" Okiku was panic stricken. Having never been on a train, she clung to her father when the scenery on either side began to slide back.

Undulating thatched roofs, earthen walls, branches of persimmon trees, mulberry patches with their stone walls—all slipped by each window.

When the train reached the Jōshū plain, Sankichi put his head out and tried to catch a last glimpse of the mountains, but the smoke of Mount Asama was hidden behind the clouds.

After they changed trains, the cars became crowded and Sankichi had to stand. There was space for only one child in addition to Oyuki holding the baby, so Ofusa and Okiku took turns sitting. Oshige began to cry as she lay in her mother's arms; neither her mother's milk nor gentle rocking could soothe her. Not knowing what to do, Oyuki alternated carrying the baby on her back and sitting and standing by the window.

About four o'clock in the afternoon, the family of five arrived at Shinjuku Station. They had not brought a maid because they had to economize, at least until Sankichi's work was completed. Ofusa and Okiku were in good spirits as their parents led them along the unfamiliar road, but Oshige was exhausted by the journey. Her head drooped on Oyuki's back, and her eyes remained in a vacant stare. Sometimes Oyuki stopped to admire the scenery.

"Look, Oshige, look!" she spoke to the child on her back, but Oshige did not stir.

The suburb was developing rapidly. They saw their new home, its roof gleaming through the fresh green leaves.

Chapter 11

Making his way toward Sankichi's house, Hashimoto Shota reached the suburban street bursting with green. Sankichi's home was on the spacious grounds of a nursery, cut off from the road by a hedge of Chinese hawthorn and a narrow dry gutter. It was past noon, and all was hushed; not even the noise of a cart disturbed the early summer air. Oyuki stood at the window, leaning against the lattice as she watched the road. Shota stopped in front of the window where a little girl about four was engrossed in play.

"Aunt Oyuki, is she a friend of Okiku's?" Shota called in a friendly tone. The child seemed shy of the stranger, but did not run away. In her short kimono and narrow *obi*, she reminded Oyuki of Okiku, who was just about the same age.

When Oyuki moved from the remote mountains to the city with her husband and three children, she anticipated a happy life in the new house. But soon after the confusion of moving was settled down, Oshige, just past her first birthday, died. And one year later, the second child, Okiku, also passed away. The little girl who was so fond of wearing her wooden clogs and singing her favorite songs around the house, was gone forever. Unlike her sister Ofusa, Okiku had few playmates. The little girl outside was one of the few who used to come calling Okiku to play with her.

The road was bathed in sunlight. The brightness of the fresh green seemed to pierce the brain. Oyuki's eyes were red from the brilliant light and grief.

"Oh, Shota, come in."

Shota looked into the house and asked where Sankichi was.

"He said he wanted to take a walk . . . over there behind the owner's house."

"Then, I'll go round back too," he said, deciding to look for Sankichi in the nursery garden.

Two low houses similar to Sankichi's stood on the grounds. Their shingled roofs were opposite the high thatched roof on the main house, separated by groves. It was the season for the nurseryman's family to make new tea, and at the end of the garden for flowers for sale on holidays stood a wicket leading to the tea patch and vegetable garden. Shota caught up with his uncle in the narrow lane that ran between the patches.

The vista stretching before them was very much that of a developing suburb. Here and there among the trees, new house tops glinted in the sun, and blue smoke curled from their chimneys.

Sankichi gazed into the distance. "How do you like it, Shota? Don't you think the area changed quite a bit in one year?" He spoke in a friendly tone about new buildings and about the chicken coop that had just been put up near the tea garden.

Shota seemed depressed. He had come to Tokyo before Sankichi and rented a small house in Honjo to live with Toyose, but they soon moved out. He sent his wife home and tried to make business contacts on his own. His temperament did not let him take an easy walk. With minimal resources, he traveled as far as Hokkaidō and Sakhalin, only to return empty-handed. Coming home from Kolsakov, he was stricken by a serious illness and had to stay at an Aomori inn until he recovered. All his schemes were attempted without much capital. Once he planned a sale of Iwaki coal; another time he started lessons in conversational Chinese, intending to go to South China. He still had not found any promising work and was at the end of his patience.

His eagerness for business success was spurred by the fact that all his uncles were now gathered in Tokyo: Minoru, in prison for so long, had come back in good health; Morihiko, having settled the Forestry Incident, was about to move in another direction; and Sankichi had just published a long novel, the draft of which he had brought with him from the mountains. Showa was impatient to establish a house in Tokyo too, and this desire was uppermost in his mind.

Sankichi and Shota talked for some time under the shimmering young leaves before returning to the garden. They skirted the greenhouse for hanging ferns, turned in by the shrubbery nursery, and came upon shelves of dwarf trees. Flowers bloomed in profusion with scentless yet seductively beautiful petals. The daughters of the gardener, all barefooted, with their skirts tucked up, were busy helping their father. While one of them drew water from the well, another sprinkled the flowers with a watering can. Sankichi spotted his child. Shota saw her too and called out her name. She languidly shook the thick hair hanging around her ears and looked at the two men with her dreamy eyes. Her weak condition made her childish features even more feminine.

They talked as they made their way toward the well, leading Ofusa by the hand.

"Isn't Ofusa completely well yet?"

"Her fever comes and goes for some reason. I've had a couple of doctors examine her. She's not really sick, but she's not well either. They talk about some intestinal fever."

"But she's grown quite a bit," Shota said as he passed a fragrant olive tree.

The flowering tree had a very old trunk, and its long, thin branches stretched in all directions. It made part of one border, and the rest of Sankichi's garden was partitioned off by a simple bamboo fence.

"Oyuki, did you give Ofusa her medicine?" Sankichi called from the yard. Shota sat down on the veranda.

"We don't know why, but Ofusa's been like this for some time," Oyuki said as she joined them, looking at her daughter. "She goes off for a minute, then comes right back and lolls about. I had to force her to go out and look for her daddy just now."

After an arduous struggle to finish his novel, Sankichi was exhausted too; yet he was unable to rest. He went into the room off the garden with Shota, fighting his fatigue.

Oyuki brought tea. "Shota, our landlord gave us some new tea leaves. I'd like you to try some."

Sankichi offered him a cup, which gave off the fragrance of budding leaves, and sipped some himself. While talking about his work during the past year, he mentioned a famous Russian writer in whose biography he read how his wife prepared *prostokvasha*, or sour milk, for her husband when he was exhausted by his writing. "I was amazed," he said, "to learn that even Europeans with such great stamina get tired. I did some senseless things to finish my novel, and I can't describe how I felt when I finally finished and threw my pen down on the desk. I wanted to roll all around the room!"

Shota laughed.

"I thought I'd push through as far as possible," said Sankichi. "Nothing else was on my mind. But I had to worry about living with so many children, you know. I had a tea crate when Oshige died—remember, the one I brought my books in from the mountain. I had it planed down and made into a coffin. My landlord and I took it over to the temple. That was the best I could do. I said half seriously to Oyuki I was rather grateful that she'd died. Soon after that Oyuki developed night blindness from malnutrition."

"Oh yes," Shota recalled. "It was terrible then. Once I went all the way to Shinjuku to buy her some chicken."

"I went through hell to complete that novel, and then just when I managed to finish it, Okiku died. I was stupefied . . . beyond grieving. It was like she was blown away by a tornado."

After they moved into the house in the suburbs, the first baby boy, Taneo, was born. Leaving the infant in the care of a young maid, Oyuki now came to listen to the two men.

"How terrible it must have been for you." Shota turned to Oyuki. "Mother wrote me about it."

"We really miss Okiku," she replied.

"The other day, a fanatic landed on us," Sankichi said. "She had bobbed hair and wore a black *hakama*. She stormed in and began to rant at us, berating Oyuki outrageously."

"She's a relative of our landlord," Oyuki explained. "According to her, I'm too much of an atheist. She claims that's why we had so many misfortunes. You know the people in this area are very religious."

Sankichi glanced around restlessly. Near the pillar in the middle room, Ofusa was playing with a box of ribbons. He rose, went over to her, and checked her temperature by putting his hand on her forehead, then he returned to his seat.

Someone rattled the lattice door at the entrance.

"Okiku's friend is here," said Oyuki as she went to see the little girl. She stayed some time at the entrance.

"Dear, why don't you give her something to eat?" Sankichi suggested and Oyuki opened the Buddhist altar doors in the middle room and took out the cake that had been offered before the new name tablet.* Long after the child had thanked her and run away, she remained, listening to the clatter of the little wooden clogs.

Onobu, the oldest daughter of Morihiko, now lived at Sankichi's house and commuted to school by streetcar. She returned home dressed in a high school *hakama*.

"Hello, Cousin Shota," she greeted.

Oyuki visited the graves of her two children almost every day at the nearby temple where they were buried. She decided to take Onobu along that day. Sankichi and Shota stayed behind and continued to talk, one stretching his legs on the floor, the other lying down.

Shota had not mentioned his father until then, but now he suddenly sat up.

"We've finally located my father."

Sankichi rose at the mention of the long-lost Tatsuo.

"The other day, Mr. U came from Kobe to see me." Shota lowered his voice. "According to him, father's teaching school there. He's earning enough to live on. But he might have done something better than teaching. After all, he left us in total ruin to be free."

"I wonder what happened to the young geisha. I heard that Tatsuo paid for her release and took her along."

"You know what they're like! I'm sure she left him long ago."

"Do you think so?"

"Well, Mr. U says that all things considered, he can sympathize with Father too. It's not good to leave him alone, and he wants us to get in touch with him, at least by writing."

"Well, do you want to send a letter?"

"No." Shota's eyes grew bright. "Of course I couldn't write, and father couldn't either. He treated the employees so miserably that he couldn't possibly face them. But I feel sorry for mother. I want to let her write him privately. Mr. U says he's willing to be the intermediary."

His story took Sankichi back to the house by the murmuring Kiso

* A wooden memorial tablet bearing the new name given to a dead person.

River. He could visualize the Hashimoto house, just as it was the summer he stayed there.

"It's beyond me, everything has changed so much. Your mother, Toyose, you . . . Tatsuo doesn't know anything about all that. Remember, when I was there, he was working very hard, and he worried so much about you. You and I often talked in the big guest room. I remember very well what you said to me then."

"I had no idea what I was doing." Shota laughed as if to silence Sankichi. "But just look at my family. Grandfather and then Father both ran away from home when they were young."

"Oh? Did your father leave home to study without permission too?"

"Yes, and so did I. We must have gypsy blood running through us," Shota said. He could not laugh when he thought of his assassinated grandfather and his unfortunate father.

Soon, the new leaves of the fragrant olive tree in the garden began to shine. Oyuki and Onobu returned, Oyuki carrying a small present for her daughter in her sleeve. She gave her some wool yarn she purchased at a notions store on her way back from shopping.

"We're late because we stayed at Okiku's grave until just a while ago. We cried our hearts out," she reported to her husband. Then she hurried to the kitchen to work.

Usually when Shota visited them, Sankichi was always busy and rarely kept him company in the relaxed manner he did this day. The two men talked in the small front room until dinner was ready. Farmers were returning from the fields, hoes on their shoulders, and the nursery workers hurried back from job assignments in town and passed under the window.

Sankichi looked out sadly and said, "Sometimes I feel so lonely on evenings like this, it becomes unbearable. It wells up inside with no reason at all."

"I know exactly what you mean. It's even more true with me in my circumstances. But at times like this I feel terribly sensitive to things."

The darkness gradually enveloped them. Another, smaller window, cut through the dim wall for ventilation, gathered a pale blue light on its small screen. Shota watched it, lost in reverie.

They finished the dinner Oyuki had prepared before the rest of the family sat down. Shota seemed to have something on his mind that he was unable to bring up, and after much hesitation he asked for a small amount of money. He had asked for five or ten yen at a time on many occasions, and even his travel expense to Sakhalin was paid by Sankichi.

"Are you that hard up?" Sankichi looked at his nephew. "Why don't you write home for money?"

"That's just it," said Shota, disconcerted. "I don't want to ask for money if I can help it . . . because the shop is really run by our young employees."

Seeing Shota in such low spirits, Sankichi placed some money in front of Shota and asked no more questions.

When Shota returned to his rooming house, Oyuki, her work in the kitchen finished, joined her husband under the lamp.

"Isn't Shota working at all yet?"

"He doesn't seem to be able to find a decent job," Sankichi murmured as he walked over to see Ofusa. "He always comes up with a different story. First he wants to sell coal, then something else. I hope he finds himself soon. It'd be fine if all he had to do was be the family figurehead."

The little girl had been running a high temperature for some days. Her bed was in the room facing the garden, and medicine bottles on a tray were placed beside her pillow. A ball, some shells, a woolen coin purse, and her favorite dolls were there too. Ofusa could not keep still and alternated between sitting up and lying down.

One day when Sankichi returned from shopping in town, Ofusa sat up in bed, listening enviously to the healthy voices of the neighborhood children playing outside. She looked at him with large innocent eyes.

"Ofusa, I brought something for you," he said, taking out some brightly colored ribbons. He had also bought a milk drink for this child with no appetite.

"Oh, what pretty ribbons daddy brought," Oyuki said, tying one in Ofusa's hair.

"Did she eat anything at all?"

"She had just a spoonful of porridge for lunch. She wouldn't drink milk because she doesn't like it. I'm worried most when she won't eat."

"Ofusa, listen to what the doctor says, and you'll get well soon. Then daddy'll get you a nice *hakama* that will look very pretty on you."

The little girl only nodded in response and lay down.

"Daddy's tired too," Sankichi said as he stretched out at her side. "The house is suddenly very lonely with Okiku gone, isn't it? Remember, when daddy was working, I made both of you sit in front of my desk and asked whom you liked best, daddy or mommy. You said 'daddy' right away, but Okiku thought for a minute and then said 'daddy and mommy.' She was quite a diplomat, wasn't she?"

"I don't know who was more diplomatic." Oyuki laughed lightly.

To amuse the sick child, Sankichi improvised stories. He talked about the rabbit song Ofusa used to sing when they lived in the country and reminded her of the frog story, the one told by the maid who was always falling asleep. Almost every summer for seven years the croaking of the frogs on the stony slope provoked a feeling of nostalgia in Sankichi. It still sounded in his ears, and he imitated the croaking for the child.

"Hyoi, hyoi, hyoi, hyoi . . . gu, gu, gu, gu."

"Silly daddy . . . ," said Ofusa, looking at her father as she lay there. Her lips showed a weak but irrepressible smile.

Oyuki brought in a spoon and a cup of the milk drink Sankichi had brought home. "Ofusa, mommy's made you something delicious. Will you drink a little for me?" she coaxed. The child tasted one spoonful but made no attempt to swallow the delicious-smelling liquid.

That night her temperature climbed higher. Something very strange was happening. Sankichi's eyes were fixed as though he were possessed.

"This is getting really serious!" He said to his wife they must do everything to save Ofusa. A terrible fear took possession of him, and Oyuki could not sleep either.

Two days later they decided to move the child to a hospital. Oyuki, supporting Ofusa's emaciated body, changed her soiled night-dress and put her arms through the sleeves of her best kimono, the one she wore when she came to Tokyo.

"Dear, she's burning!" Oyuki cried, and Sankichi touched the child fearfully. Her body was on fire.

"The doctor will make you well at the hospital. Don't worry, darling," Sankichi encouraged the child.

"Mommy, will you tie my hair?" Even in a raging fever, the little girl wished to look nice. Oyuki tied her hair with a ribbon.

Oyuki got in the ricksha that had been waiting. Sankichi carried Ofusa out and placed her gently in her mother's arms. The maid, holding Taneo, followed in a second ricksha.

Sankichi called to his niece: "Onobu, I'm going to the hospital too. I want you to stay and look after the house." Deciding to go by streetcar, he left in a hurry.

During the family's absence, relatives and friends living nearby called constantly to inquire about Ofusa's condition. The woman schoolteacher next door often came through the garden and comforted Onobu. When they learned that Ofusa's illness was very serious, both Oyuki and Sankichi kept vigil at the hospital. Onobu's father, Morihiko, arranged to stay with his daughter every night and returned to his inn in the morning.

As usual, the house was quiet. A rooster's crowing sounded from the farmhouse across the road. A solid, heavyset man in formal kimono, bowler in hand, passed through the gate. It was Morihiko. It had been a week since Ofusa was admitted to the hospital. Today Morihiko first stopped to see the sick child and then came a little earlier than usual.

Onobu met him at the door. It was rare for him to spend so much time with his daughter, for he had lived at inns ever since he left his hometown years ago. He noticed her provincial speech as she discussed Ofusa's illness and realized that, coming only recently from the country, she would never talk like one born and bred in Tokyo.

"How's your headache? The other day Sankichi told me you didn't look too well. He was considering taking you out of school for a while. You mustn't be such a weakling!"

Morihiko slipped into his native dialect without realizing it. Then in a tone typical of the head of an old family, he expounded upon such human virtues as universal love, perseverance, and frugality. Not knowing her father too well, Onobu listened in awed silence.

"Oh, I forgot to give you this candy," he chuckled, taking a package out of his sleeve. He then looked around the room and commented, "This house has very poor ventilation. I've known that for some time. If you smoke all the time the way Uncle Sankichi does . . . I make sure all the windows are open and the bad air is out before I go to bed. Even a whiff of cigarette smoke's enough to keep me awake." And asking for a knife, he slit the top part of the paper in the sliding doors in every room.

"Well, Onobu, I'm going now."

"Oh, must you . . . so soon, father?"

"Sankichi told me he was coming back today, so it's not necessary for me to stay. That suits me fine because I've got another stop to make. I'll be back again."

Sankichi hurried back from the hospital that evening and listened to Onobu's reports on all the visitors who came during his absence.

As Sankichi called across the garden from the veranda to his neighbor, the teacher answered from her house, "Oh, Mr. Koizumi, are you home?" She noisily opened the lattice door, stepped outside, and circled around the well and the bamboo fence to come to Sankichi's house. She was the mother of a teen-aged boy, and she spoke politely and distinctly, with a hint of the province in her speech. "How is little Ofusa?" she asked from the garden. "When I went to see her at the hospital the other day, she was very ill and I felt terrible for her. I couldn't bear to see her suffering so much."

Sankichi briefly described Ofusa's condition, and with a sigh said there seemed to be no hope. Onobu listened to the conversation at his side.

"If there is any change, the doctor will send a telegram, so I came home on some errands."

"I wonder why all your children. . . The landlord's grandmother says you chose the wrong direction when you moved.* I

* A belief involving omens and consulting fortunetellers before making a trip, moving, or doing routine chores, especially in connection with direction in any movement. It is based on a blend of ancient Chinese geomancy, the Yin-Yang philosophy, and Shintoism.

doubt if there's any truth in what she says, but to see all of them go in one year . . . ," said the teacher. Then she added sympathetically. "Ofusa was calling for her mother at the top of her voice, loud enough to be heard all over the hospital. How terrible it must be for her mother. We all feel deeply for her."

"She's been calling for a solid week, but now her voice is getting weaker."

By the time the teacher went home, a yellow glow appeared in the sky between the gardener's thatched roof and the dark mass of pine branches. Sankichi paced up and down in the garden, lost in thoughts of his child.

"Onobu," he said after dinner, "I haven't slept for at least a week. Do you mind if I go to bed early tonight? If you have a headache, you should go to bed early too."

Thoughts of the impending telegram interrupted his sleep. The distinctive hospital odor had saturated his entire body and the smell now returned to him and took him back to the child's bedside. There were the lamp and the bed. Above Ofusa's head, a black cloth shielded the light. Oyuki was sitting by the bed with the attendant, while the maid held Taneo at their side. Nurses in white uniforms moved in and out of the sickroom. Ofusa was screaming with all the strength of a little girl, as though refusing to give up until her brain was completely destroyed. Finally exhausted by the thought, Sankichi fell into a deep slumber.

He spent the following morning at home, and Onobu straightened the house in the afternoon.

"I wish I could stay with Ofusa all the time with Aunt Oyuki, but I've got to worry about money too, you know," Sankichi said to his niece as he went out on an errand. When he returned, he stretched out and immediately fell asleep.

After dinner he talked for a while with Onobu about the hospital. And once more he went to bed early.

"Mommy!" Sankichi awoke with the cry ringing in his ears. It was already late but he had no idea how long he had slept. His niece slept soundly in the adjacent room. As he sat still, he could hear his child frantically calling her mother. Her cruel cries pierced his ears and drummed in his brain no matter where he went or what he did.

Suddenly, as in a nightmare, he heard the dreaded rapping on the gate. "Telegram! Mr. Koizumi, telegram!"

Sankichi bolted from his bed. Dashing to the door, he snatched up the piece of paper. *"Pulse fast, come immediately,"* it said. He went to awaken Onobu. "Coming!" she replied but sank back into deep sleep.

"Look! The telegram!"

"Oh! Oh dear!" Onobu, still sleepy, lapsed into provincial dialect. "I thought I was dreaming," she said, sitting up in bed.

"I'm getting ready and going right away. I'm sorry, but will you call a ricksha?"

Onobu went off rubbing her eyes.

Sankichi went outside to wait. He heard streetcars still running. It was the night of the harvest god festival, and the sky shone brightly above Shinjuku. A dog barked in the distance. The ricksha arrived shortly, and he decided to ride to Shinjuku to catch a train.

"Will you be all right, Onobu?" he asked his niece as he left. She went back into the house, locked the front door, and crept back into her cold bed, where she imagined all kinds of things as she lay trembling. Her uncle should have reached Shinjuku just as raindrops began to drum on the shingled roof.

Once again, it was still inside the house.

The ricksha drew up in front of the house, and Shota jumped out and pushed through the closed gate. "Onobu, we're home" he cried, opening the lattice door. Onobu ran out and Morihiko appeared in the doorway too.

"So she didn't make it after all?" Morihiko asked.

"I hear she passed away this morning . . . early. Everyone will be back any minute now," Shota replied, and they looked at each other.

After a while three more rickshas arrived. With the baby in her arms, Oyuki entered her home for the first time in two weeks. The maid, followed by Oshun, carried the luggage.

Sankichi's carriage was the last to arrive. The ricksha draped in black slowly drew up and came to a stop in front of Ofusa's playmates, who were gathered in the sunny road, watching and whispering to each other.

"May I help you, Uncle Sankichi?" Shota approached.

Wrapped in a brown shawl, Ofusa lay in her father's arms. Sankichi carried the inert body from the ricksha into the house.

In a corner of the middle room with the Buddhist altar, the family prepared a bed for Ofusa. They laid the cold body on it and covered the face with a white cloth.

"When you see her like this, she's much taller than you remember her. What do you think, should we bend her knees now?" said Morihiko.

"She's only a child. I'm sure she'll fit into the coffin just as she is," said Shota, measuring with his eyes.

"Still, it may be better to bend them a little," said Sankichi, lifting Ofusa's knees slightly. The cold legs were no longer pliable, and he had to put on some pressure. Oshun and Onobu brought a pitcher of water and some flowers and placed them beside the pillow. Oyuki's second younger sister, Oai, arrived from her school dormitory. She sat down at her sister's side, and they wept together.

In the afternoon the teacher next door came in through the kitchen to have a last look at the dead child's face.

"I honestly don't know how to express my sympathy. Mr. Koizumi must be very sad, but he's a man and it's easier for him. But I'm truly sorry for Mrs. Koizumi," said the woman.

Oyuki told her that Ofusa's fever was not from intestinal infection but from a virulent meningitis. Everyone agreed that death was preferable to surviving as a mental defective.

Sankichi leaned against the wall near the window, absently watching the yellow of the candle burning in the daylight.

"Uncle Sankichi, you must be exhausted," Shota said as he came over.

"I was so involved in trying to save her during the first week that I don't think I slept at all. And the second week I was up thinking it might be my last chance to be with her. Toward the end I practically slept on my feet taking care of her. If my head so much as touched the pillow, I was fast asleep."

"I sometimes wish we had a child. But when I see you and Aunt Oyuki suffering so much, I'm thankful we don't."

"Do you have any cigarettes? Let me have one."

Shota fumbled in his sleeves and handed him one. Sankichi lit it and took a deep puff. The house was in chaos with funeral preparations and the mourners' visits. Sankichi sat and rose as if he were a robot.

On the day of the funeral, all the relatives gathered around the small coffin. Naoki came, representing his family. He had graduated from high school some time before and had already started a career of young businessman.

Oshun arrived and said, inferring that Minoru was still doing his penance, "Uncle Sankichi, father would be here if he could. I came in his place."

Oai arrived in a long purple *hakama*. In Minoru's absence, Morihiko was the oldest of all the relatives in Tokyo to attend the funeral. He was amazed by the rapid growth of the younger members and looked at Oshun, now in junior college, and the elegantly dressed Oai. He could not help comparing them to his own daughter.

Shota went out and bought several bouquets of flowers, and he arranged them around Ofusa, who appeared to be sleeping. "O-yuki, let's put these toys in with her," said Sankichi.

"Yes, you should," agreed Shota. "They will only stir up sad memories."

He placed a ball, a pocketbook, and other toys in the corners of the coffin.

"She liked the wool yarn so much. Even when she couldn't see any more, she was still talking about it," Oyuki said as she took out the toys she purchased while the little girl was in the hospital.

"Put them all in."

Ofusa was soon carried away to rest beside the graves of her two younger sisters. Oyuki stood by the gate and watched the tiny coffin fade in the distance. Standing close to the hedge of budding Chinese hawthorn, she realized Ofusa was no longer with her. Tears welled in the mother's eyes, and she returned to the house weeping.

The novel Sankichi had finished in the mountains was received with considerable acclaim. Rapidly the number of callers increased, and hosts of friends came to visit him. Sankichi did not stir outside the privacy of his house, and the front gate was not even unlatched on most mornings.

Sankichi had said that he did not care what happened to his children, but now remorseful, he could no longer be so callous. He wondered why his struggles to reach his goal, surmounting many difficulties, should give him so much grief in the end. He turned repeatedly in the direction of the little graves, drawn by the thought of three children who lay there. The flat road from his house to the cemetery was bordered on either side by bright green foliage. Yet in every sunny spot in the grove he saw a gloominess that matched his own heart. His wanderings were confined mostly to the perimeter of the temple, for he could not bear to look at the three little graves. If he forced himself to approach, the blood rushed to his head, and he felt a blinding dizziness that put him close to collapse. Whenever he set out for the graves, he invariably turned back on his way.

"Daddy's heartless," Oyuki complained frequently. "He never visits the children's graves."

At the slightest pretext, the family talked about the children, and Sankichi was drawn into the conversation in spite of himself.

Oyuki often chatted with Onobu while nursing Taneo. "When Oshige passed away, Ofusa was still too young to understand. But when Okiku died, she knew very well what was happening, and she cried with the rest of us."

"Yes." Onobu nodded. "When I think about those days, I can just see Ofusa right here."

"They were both so excited when Oshige died. I told them Oshige was dead, but it didn't upset them at all. They sang and danced around the coffin, 'She's dead! She's dead!' And they would peek at the baby and start giggling."

"Oh, dear!"

"I used to take them to Oshige's grave and pick mulberries behind the grave. I told them the mulberries belonged to Oshige, and they always asked, 'Oshige, may we have some mulberries?' The tree is tall, so they used to ask me to do the picking."

"Let's talk about something else," Sankichi interrupted. Whenever the children came up in the conversation, he would sooner or later suggest changing the subject.

"Taneo," Onobu called to the baby.

"I wonder why the baby's so weak." Oyuki watched his face.

Sankichi looked at him with guilt-ridden eyes, and the couple glanced at each other. Will this child . . . too? Fear gripped their hearts, but they said nothing. Having watched the development of three daughters, they were afraid that the frail baby might not even grow normally.

Sunlight burst through the clouds, the damp ground in the garden turned a warm tawny color, and the leaves of the fragrant olive tree cast deep shadows on the ground. Sankichi picked up his hat and said he was going for a little walk.

"I suppose there's nothing left of Oshige by now," Oyuki said to her niece with a sigh. She went to the veranda, holding the baby, and looked across the garden.

It was the kind of day when the sun moved in and out behind the clouds. Onobu stepped into the garden and began to sing "Violets," a song Ofusa and Okiku often sang around the house when they were well. Oyuki joined her softly as though looking for her daughters. Another voice in the kitchen joined in the chorus.

Sankichi returned toward evening looking disheartened.

"I feel as if I'm going mad." He said he decided to take a trip to the Isobe hot springs, and began to pack. His friend in the mountains, Makino, had repeatedly invited him to visit. But he wanted to go someplace where he could be alone, where he could forget everything. He set out early in the morning.

"Oh, look! Uncle Sankichi's back already!" Onobu cried, standing in the garden at the entrance.

Sankichi had been at the hot springs for only a few days when the news of Oyuki's grandmother's death reached him. He returned as soon as he received the telegram.

"Taneo, daddy's home!" Oyuki came out with the infant in her arms to meet her husband. "How did you manage to come back so soon? We were all worried about your health."

"Oh, that's why Morihiko sent a telegram asking after me! I thought it was odd. But I was worried about you." Sankichi heaved a sigh and began to talk about Oyuki's grandmother.

The death of the matriarch reminded him of the immensity of the Nakura family. Two granddaughters had established branches with the name Nakura. The grandchildren who were still in school and the great-grandchildren taken together amounted to a very large number. Oyuki was the only grandchild who lived far away from home. She wanted to attend the funeral at all costs, and Sankichi had cut his trip short, deciding to send her with Taneo and the maid.

"Now it's your turn to go away," he said. "I'm glad this happened after I finished my work. Why don't you go buy whatever you need. You'll have to take some gifts too."

"They don't need gifts. If I buy a gift for everyone in my family, we'll never have enough money."

Oyuki enumerated the sisters, the nephews and nieces, and the distant relatives.

But Sankichi insisted on buying gifts for her to take to the Nakura girls; it had been such a long time since she was home. When he returned from town with the traveling money and the purchases, Oyuki was already packing.

While she prepared for the trip, a thousand thoughts raced through her mind. She was going to see her family after all the difficult years she went through; she was going away from the house she had seldom left in the past, to rejoin her parents, sisters, and friends. Dazzling sails, billowing waves, the cries of seagulls . . . . Nostalgic scenes from her childhood at the seashore were not all that she looked forward to. She was also going to see Tsutomu, to whom she had once given her heart; he was now the husband of her younger sister.

Shota came in the next morning. "Aunt Oyuki, are you going home?" he asked and looked at the luggage, the baby's clothes, and her things scattered about the room. "I see you're really busy."

"Excuse me, Shota," she apologized, tying her *obi*.

"Bring the baby here for a minute," said Sankichi, and the maid came over holding the sleeping infant. "You must take very good care of him on the way."

"He sleeps very quietly," commented Shota.

"You know, he still needs an enema every day," Sankichi said. "He won't move his bowels otherwise. But give him a toy or something, he'll lie there all day without complaining. Compared to the girls, he's much weaker."

"But at Aunt Oyuki's home in the country, he may get stronger."

"Yes, he'll stay there for the summer."

"It's a lot of work for Aunt Oyuki. It's not easy for a woman to travel."

Oyuki pulled on her white *tabi* as she listened to the conversation. "Sankichi won't be able to eat while I'm gone, so I'm going to ask Oshun to come to stay," she said. The packing done, she drank tea with her husband and Shota, praying for a safe journey. "I'll give Taneo something to drink too." Oyuki opened her kimono and guided her dark nipple into the baby's mouth. Onobu ran out to the ricksha station.

Sankichi asked Shota to look after the house and set out for Shinjuku Station to see his family off. When he returned, Shota was waiting with a troubled look on his face.

"Shota, have you had breakfast? I forgot to ask."

"Yes, I ate early, before I left home."

"That's not like you."

"Yes, I usually sleep late, but this morning I got up very early. I thought about a lot of things at the breakfast table. It's been more than a year since I left home, and I'm still not doing anything." He snorted as though he were indignant. He went on to say he saw a gleam of light in the future, but he hesitated for a moment to go into detail, uncertain of his uncle's reaction. Then he said that he had no choice but to have a go at Kabuto-chō, that he had made up his mind to start life afresh as a stockbroker.

Sankichi, gazing at his nephew, listened as though to an adventure story.

"But you know, Minoru, Morihiko, and all the rest have been trying so hard to make money. Lots of experienced people do their best and still don't make any. That's the truth of it. You can't make money just by joining Kabuto-chō."

"I belong to a different generation from Uncle Minoru," he said earnestly.

"Well, to a layman like me, the safest thing would be to master a trade or some profession first and then to start thinking about making money. Look at my father-in-law. He first developed his business, then he made money. For some reason you seem to put the cart before the horse. That's why you think about the stock market. Isn't that so?"

"That's just the point. I'll make the stock market my business. If it was a matter of trying for awhile and giving up right away, I wouldn't even get involved. First of all, I'm going to start out as a clerk. I'm determined to stick with it."

"If you're that determined, I guess you could give it a try. My philosophy is to let anyone do anything he wants to."

"I'm glad to hear you say that. I don't know what Uncle Morihiko will say, but . . . ."

Shota invariably would think like Morihiko when talking to him, and like Sankichi when talking to *him*. The husband of the schoolteacher next door was familiar with the stock business, and Shota asked Sankichi to speak to him about some introductions.

Shota went home leaving a vague impression of insecurity. "I wonder if he's really serious," Sankichi muttered to himself, but he decided to do what he could for his nephew. In the afternoon, he went over to the shelves where the dwarf plants were kept. This section of the nursery formed a part of the teacher's garden; her son, a high school boy, was there seated on a tripod stool, absorbed in sketching.

The teacher's husband was a retired government official who now had a secure job at a brokerage firm in Kabuto-chō. Sankichi approached the cluttered veranda and spoke to the older man standing there.

The husband's answer was friendly after Sankichi explained the situation. "If that's what you want, I'll be happy to see what I can do. I know Mr. Hashimoto by sight. How old is he?"

"He's three years younger than I."

"That's quite young. The best years are ahead of him. What sort of person would you say he is? I'd like to know more about him."

"Well, let's see. Right now he's not working, but in general I'd say he's rather flamboyant."

"That's just right. A person thinking about becoming a stockbroker should be showy. Would you send me a brief resumé? I'll ask around some of the firms I know."

Sankichi returned home where Onobu was waiting alone and immediately wrote a letter to Shota.

"I guess Aunt Oyuki is well on her way by now," said Onobu.

"She would never have gotten away if her grandmother hadn't died. It was a good opportunity for her."

He himself was trying everything to forget the grief of losing the children.

Chapter 12

W hen the schools closed for summer vacation, Oshun came to her uncle's home with her younger sister, Otsuru. A tall Indian lilac tree stretched its branches over the hedge of the farmer's house across from Sankichi's. Forlorn vermilion blossoms hung over the road.

Oshun opened the lattice door and came in, her sister a step behind.

"Oh, it's Cousin Oshun!" Jumping joyfully Onobu welcomed them. Sankichi appeared from the rear of the house.

"Uncle Sankichi, I should have come much sooner, but school kept me busy. It must have been hard with only Onobu helping you."

"I'm so glad you came too, Otsuru," Onobu said happily.

"I brought her along because her school is closed today."

"Isn't her school out for the summer yet?" Sankichi asked.

"Their vacation is shorter. Father told me to give you his best, Uncle."

"I'm so happy Cousin Oshun's here," Onobu repeated.

Oshun and Otsuru finally had their father living at home after years of his absence. They had just managed to survive with their uncle's support and their mother's careful husbanding of the frugal resources. At the times of Sankichi's marriage, Oshun was just finishing elementary school, but now she was old enough to run the household. It was the first time in years for her to spend a summer with Sankichi.

"Otsuru, why don't you go look at the back garden," Oshun suggested.

"How she's grown!"

"Yes, her kimono's too short now. She outgrows everything so quickly."

Embarrassed, Otsuru smiled and went to the garden.

"Oshun, what is your father doing?" Sankichi asked.

"He hasn't started anything yet . . . but he gets up very early. He says he made us suffer long enough and he'll make it up to us. He gets out of bed while it's still dark and lights the fire. He says he just can't sleep late anymore. By the time mother's up, breakfast is all ready."

"I feel kind of sorry for him."

"While father was away, we didn't bother too much about the house. But since he came back, everything is clean and orderly. It's strange, isn't it?"

Laughter came from the garden. Otsuru had slipped and fallen, and Onobu rushed to her aid. Oshun, laughing, went to brush the mud from her sister's clothes.

That night Sankichi's house was unusually gay. The girls enjoyed the cool summer night with Sankichi, who stretched out on the veranda to catch the night breeze. In the room facing the dark garden, the only bright area was where the three nieces sat; he said he had no desire for light. A lamp stood in the corner and cast its glow on Otsuru's white summer kimono and Oshun's pink *obi*.

"Otsuru, why don't you dance for uncle," Oshun suggested.

"Which one shall I do?" Otsuru thought a minute. "How about 'Turtle and Hare'?"

" 'Urashima' would be better."

The girls began signing to entertain their uncle. The Koizumi daughters grew like young grass in the midst of the degeneration and decline that had overtaken the house. Otsuru retied the ribbon on her braided hair and stood up, smoothing the wrinkles from her short kimono. Accompanied by her sister and cousin, she danced around the room.

Sankichi watched her from the veranda. "Very good! Very good! Now I'll have to treat you to something special."

"That's enough, Otsuru," said her sister, but she was too caught up by the mood. She was not satisfied by one or two dances.

Otsuru went home the next morning. The sound of youthful laughter continued in the kitchen from that day on.

After several days of intermittent rain the bright sun came out, and Oshun carried a washtub out to the well to finish the laundry before the day grew too warm. Onobu came around the bamboo

fence, holding a wooden bucket. She drew water and passed it to
Oshun, who tucked up her sleeves and began washing.

Onobu kept her older cousin laughing. "Oh, ah. My body feels
like a jellyfish this morning. I can't walk like a celery stalk." Oshun
called for fresh water and kept scrubbing. The garden was large
enough to hang out the wash. She arranged the laundered clothes
on a long bamboo pole and raised it in the air.

"Oh, I'm so happy!" she suddenly shouted. Onobu stood and
looked at her.

"I just thought of the problem my teacher told us to solve during
the vacation," Oshun exclaimed as she came in with Onobu. They
looked at each other, breaking into smiles for no particular reason,
and dried their wet bare arms in the kitchen.

The sky was a marine blue. Sunlight filled the house, reflecting the
dazzling white of the laundry. In the afternoon the girls leaned
against pillars, lounging. Sankichi strung a hammock near the
south window and sank his steaming body into it. Heat waves
rose from the earth and combined in a curious way with the cool
breeze passing through the window. Lulled by the monotonous
chirping of the locusts, he quickly fell asleep.

The sting of a horsefly bite wakened him bleary-eyed from his
nap. Oshun ran to fetch her hair oil and offered it to him.

"Onobu, come and look," Oshun cried, tittering. "Uncle Sankichi has so many white hairs! "

Onobu hurried from the kitchen.

"Hey! Hey!" Sankichi said in a bantering tone. "Don't insult me
that way. I consider them my medals of honor!"

"If that isn't sour grapes!" giggled Onobu.

"Well, Onobu, he can't help it if his hair's getting white," said
Oshun, coming closer to Sankichi. "Uncle, hold still and I'll pull
them out for you. The front isn't so bad, but your temples. . . .
Good heavens! There are too many. I'll never be able to get them
all!" She isolated one white strand after another to pull it out. Sometimes she caught black hair with shiny white ones.

On another occasion Oshun came from the kitchen and stood
beside Sankichi. "Uncle Sankichi, I wonder why my hair doesn't

stay in shape," she said in a familiar tone. She had grown quite dependent on Sankichi and confided in him things that girls usually reveal only to parents.

She turned her back partially to him so that he could see the nape of her neck. "Why does it look like this in summer?" She grasped the roots of her dissheveled hair and shook it to emphasize the difficulty.

The laundry dried in the garden, and the girls, singing together, took down the clothes. Sankichi found their lively, light-hearted voices charming. He stood on the veranda and watched their carefree movements as they folded the dry clothes. A generation younger than Oyuki and Shota's wife was now budding all around him.

Cool, refreshing air wafted in under the eaves. In the evening Sankichi and his nieces talked about Oyuki. The farmer's family had dragged a bench out to the road and was enjoying the cool summer night. The three tossed to see who should go out to buy ice, and Onobu lost. She soon returned, and Oshun brought glasses and the sugar bowl.

"Let's see. Let me concoct something special," Sankichi said, getting a bottle half filled with red wine; he poured it over the crushed ice.

The girls' conversation turned to the topic of letter writing. Oshun explained that a stamp pasted on upside down indicated enmity, and one tipped slightly to the side meant love.

"Isn't it strange that enemies would write to each other?" Sankichi heckled, but undaunted, Oshun argued. "You should know all about such things, Uncle Sankichi."

She then began to talk about her life at school. Sankichi listened to her, bemused, and occasionally held his glass up to the lamp to see the color of the wine.

"I love the word nirvana," said Oshun, carefully munching a piece of ice.

"How weird!" exclaimed Onobu, clinking the contents in her glass. "Well, in that case you shall be called Miss Nirvana from now on."

"The very sound of the word is lovely." Oshun continued, saying that she often walked in the cemetery behind the school. Her idea of pleasure was to sit there on an old stone and read, surrounded by the aroma of burning leaves.

She went on, "My teacher told me that I'm the type of person no one will dislike, but being loved by too many people can mean harm. He said I must be firm, otherwise a great deal of misery could come to me." As she spoke, she pulled her kimono collar together in a typical gesture. "I don't mean you, Uncle Sankichi, because you're too close to me, but among all my acquaintances there's no one I can really respect. I can see right through the people who have great reputation and fame. I know it's peculiar, but I begin to see through them after a while."

Onobu glanced at Sankichi and then at Oshun.

"When I'm twenty-five, I'll tell you all about my past, Uncle Sankichi," said Oshun. "You read all sorts of things in novels, but that's nothing compared to my own experiences. I've had the strangest things happen to me."

"Well then, let's have the true confession right here," Sankichi said in jest.

"No."

"What's the difference whether you tell me now or when you're twenty-five?"

"When I am more calm, I'll tell you. Right now I'm easily upset."

For a while Oshun was silent. In the quiet dusk one could hear the farmer's family across the road busily fanning themselves.

"But when you listen to me, Uncle Sankichi, you must think I'm talking nonsense."

"Not at all."

"I'm sure you do."

"No," Sankichi said, looking at his niece. "But I never knew you could talk so much. I've discovered something new tonight."

"I'm a chatterbox all right. Aren't I, Onobu?" said Oshun as she shyly hid her face behind her sleeve.

A post card had come from Morihiko the day before, inviting the girls to the "opening of the Sumida River" at Ryōgoku. Oshun and Onobu looked forward with excitement to the fireworks.

The next day the newspapers announced the postponement of

the event due to high tides. News that the water level rose to a dangerous point came as a great disappointment to the girls. But even if there had been no fear of flood, the cool summer rain that started early in the morning would have caused a cancellation.

Sankichi asked Oshun where Onobu was, and she answered she was probably visiting the next-door neighbor. Onobu called on the schoolteacher almost every day.

The rain revived the trees and grasses in the garden. The continuous heat had withered the fragile garden balsams by the foot of the fence, and the leaves and red flowers had drooped. They were now coming to life again. Sankichi looked wistfully from the veranda.

"Shall I tell you why I like cemeteries?" Oshun said. Sankichi came back into the room and listened to her as he gazed at the pleasant rain.

Oshun told him haltingly the story of her young, unhappy life. She grew fond of wandering in the cemetery when she was sixteen and lost a close friend. She was so deeply hurt that she even contemplated suicide. The thought of her mother and sister barely dissuaded her, but she was convinced she was born to endure such trouble and suffering.

"But I certainly don't want to develop a warped mind, no matter what. I constantly worry I may be growing cynical." After a few moments of deep thought, she said, "Shall I tell you one of the things that happened to me?" She added no one but her mother knew about the incident. From her tone, Sankichi surmised that it involved some man among their relatives, but he had no idea who had tried to make love to her.

"You've probably guessed by now, haven't you?"

"No," Sankichi shook his head. "Perhaps you misunderstood his intentions. You may be making more out of it than it really is."

Tears began to roll down Oshun's cheeks, and she covered her face with her hands. Remembering it all seemed to make her cry. She walked out to the veranda and immediately came back.

"What sort of man do you think Shota is? I wonder if he's the kind of person you think he is."

Sankichi stared at her. "You were talking about Shota?"

"I said I would tell you when I reached twenty-five. This is only one of the things. I wonder how Toyose would feel if she ever heard about this. It's disgusting! Hideous! I won't be able to hate him enough even if I hate him for the rest of my life."

"The whole thing is unpleasant. Why are you telling me this?"

"You kept asking me."

Puzzled, Sankichi looked at her in silence.

"Let's talk about something more pleasant." She smiled. Then she went to her room and returned with a letter in her hand. "You probably know who wrote this, Uncle Sankichi."

What she showed him could scarcely be called a letter. Rather it was a few elegantly worded phrases delicately written with a nibbed pen on a piece of pure white paper.

"I have never met anyone with such a fragrant personality as yours. I shall call you my White Lily."

It was simple and there was no signature, but Sankichi immediately recognized Naoki's hand.

"He's always been like a brother to me. So I've asked him to become a real one. That's all for today," added Oshun. Her closing line made Sankichi smile.

The girls called both Shota and Naoki "brother." The first was their cousin, while the second was the son of Sankichi's benefactor. But Naoki was as close as any relative. In order to distinguish between them, the girls called them "Cousin Shota" and "Cousin Naoki."

From Oshun's stories, Sankichi learned many things—things he had been completely unaware of.

Chapter 13

Minoru paid his first visit to Sankichi's house since his marriage to Oyuki. This man who was the principal heir to the old Koizumi line spent years in misery and despair, but serveral of his boyhood friends among the gentry in his native province had also experienced the dwindling away of their fortunes. Naoki's father, a partner in many of his schemes, passed away during Minoru's imprisonment, and Tatsuo, who had shared the same hopes and dreams with him, was now destitute in self-imposed exile.

Minoru was not as weak as his family feared he might be after such a long confinement. He was the tallest of the brothers and had inherited his father's strong constitution. He had the famous Koizumi nose, a mark of ambition that had come down to him from remote ancestors, and his complexion was still surprisingly fresh.

And now he came to see Sankichi. The girls were out when he arrived, and Sankichi brewed tea to offer his brother at the oblong brazier.

Very much aware of the errors that had marred his life, Minoru avoided his brothers as much as he could. He had still not called on Morihiko since his release, and this was only his second meeting with Sankichi.

"Where's Oshun?" Minoru asked.

"She went to Shinjuku . . . shopping with Onobu."

"Is she managing things all right?"

"Yes, she's doing very well. Today I told them to buy summer kimonos."

"That must have made them happy. I was sorry to hear about your children passing away one right after the other. Bad luck never stops, it seems. But don't be too upset. Don't get involved. That's my answer. With anything—wife, children. . . ."

Minoru avoided involvement with his brothers as much as possible. He was like someone maneuvering skillfully through a crowded street. He made no attempt to confide in Sankichi, to tell him anything of his past difficulties; nor did he offer a single word of gratitude or apology for all the trouble he had caused him. He sat there, imperious before the youngest, therefore least significant, of his brothers, and his manner was that of a family head to a subordinate.

Minoru was proud, and discussions about financial matters were difficult for him. The invalid Sozo belonged to the family and was his responsibility; but with Sozo now being cared for by outsiders, Sankichi was obliged to pay the expenses. All financial burdens had been transferred to Sankichi, and yet Minoru had come once again to demand more money.

"I borrowed forty yen from Mr. N," he stated. "I assured him you would pay him back in due time. You've got to raise the money . . . any way you can."

Perplexed, Sankichi tried to speak, but Minoru promptly cut him off by taking out a minutely itemized list. He told him that with the forty yen Sankichi was purchasing the pieces of furniture listed there—a chest of drawers, a set of serving tables, a rug, a cigar case, a set of sake bottles, a basin for wine cups, and other items.

"You'll take care of this, won't you," he said and hurried from the house.

"Couldn't he at least say thanks for taking care of the family while he was away?" Sankichi sighed to himself. But he knew very well that Minoru was inherently incapable of it.

Oshun and Onobu came back, each carrying a package of kimono material.

"Let's show Uncle Sankichi what he bought us." They unwrapped the summer fabrics and the latest bright patterns appeared. The drygoods store had many, and only with the greatest difficulty were they able to select two medium-sized print fabrics. They fully expected their uncle's approval.

"Why in the world did you choose such gaudy patterns?" Sankichi said disapprovingly.

"But even Cousin Toyose wears ones as colorful as these. Doesn't she, Onobu?" Oshun glanced at the younger girl. But Sankichi embarked on a lecture expounding the cause for the present low state of the Koizumi fortune, how the girls never thought of it and followed flighty fashions while wearing worn-out socks.

"But, Uncle Sankichi, all the others looked awful on me," said Oshun, crestfallen.

But after a while Sankichi recovered his good humor and told them about Minoru's visit and why he had come. Oshun then talked about what had happened at home. The day she returned from school, a public auction was being held at home. Those items of furniture necessary for everyday living were bought by an acquaintance, who arranged to return them to the family. Bailiff, pawnbroker, secondhand shop—words connoting the miseries of life—fell from Oshun's lips.

Sankichi paced the floor. He could see the last of the catastrophic waves now sweeping the family away. Bankruptcy followed bankruptcy, Minoru always repeating the same mistake, losing more and more each time. He was forced to relinquish the last of the valuable art objects he had collected over the years, and even the homespun clothing woven by his mother with such care and patience at his old homestead was taken away. Everything was seized by the creditors, and after the auction, the family was moving into an even cheaper house.

Whenever the conversation turned to her parents, Oshun could not hold her tears.

She spoke about personal matters, about the time she closed her ears to her mother's pleas for help because she was studying for examinations. She talked, sobbing more and more, and she looked up at Sankichi through her tears as though appealing to him for understanding.

"I can't apologize to mother. Even when the words are on the tip of my tongue, I still can't say I'm sorry. I can bow to her, but I can't put it into words."

Late that night Oshun walked out alone.

Onobu asked after Oshun and Sankichi replied, "She probably went out to mail a post card or something." Oshun came in and locked the front door after her.

"Oh, you were crying outside!" said Onobu.

"No, I was not!"

The next evening the girls spread out the sewing things under the lamp, while Sankichi sat on the veranda. Oshun was working on Onobu's kimono. The younger girl glanced at her cousin from time to time, pleased to see the garment gradually take shape. They planned to wear the new kimonos on the night of the river festival. On the way to see the fireworks at the cool river bank, they would stop at Morihiko's inn, then visit Naoki's house. Excitedly, they chattered on and on.

Though there were clouds in the sky, the earth was bathed in moonlight. Sankichi strolled past the chicken coop, through the woods, and as far as the foot of the hill. The luminous yet dusky shadows of trees fell across the road, the nursery gardens, and the veranda of Sankichi's house. After returning home he still looked outside. His nieces prepared themselves for bed, said good night to him, and retired under their mosquito net.

The pleasant night air enveloped the house. All was hushed. Even the trees seemed to be asleep, their leaves limp, but Sankichi could not sleep. He lay down under the net, but crawled out again and sat leaning against the open door until the small hours of the morning.

Dawn brought an end to the short summer night. Already it was the first day of autumn by the calendar. Oyuki had written him asking how he was in the summer heat. She had written the girls separately and thanked them for their work in her absence.

In the afternoon Oshun said she did not feel well, and found a cool spot and lay down with ice on her chest. Onobu, complaining of a headache, wrapped a towel about her head.

"I worry a lot when someone's sick in the house," said Sankichi, as if speaking to his own children.

"I'm sorry," Oshun replied, half rising.

Sankichi was still unable to visit the graves of his children. But he sometimes stretched his empty arms in a futile hope to enfold his dead daughters. If only the girls who spent these days with him were his own. . . . The idea astounded him. Oshun was too close to being grown-up for him to embrace as he would Ofusa.

The neighbors were sprinkling the gardens. By the time Sankichi stepped out barefooted, Oshun said she was already feeling better and began to work in the kitchen. She seemed better than he expected, and he was anxious to show his appreciation for his nieces. After dinner he made a trip to town to purchase a large watermelon. The girls brought fans and cooled themselves on the veranda as they ate the watermelon, away from the lamplight.

Onobu took a slice of watermelon to the schoolteacher but returned soon through the garden.

"Her husband's so funny. He said, 'Oh, oh, how Mine's grown up! Now he can climb Mount Fuji all by himself; no wonder I've gotten so old!' I couldn't help laughing."

Oshun smiled at Onobu's childish story.

Moonlight had stolen into the garden, and Onobu lay down under her net earlier than usual. Caught up in enjoyment of the night scene, Sankichi took a walk as he had done the night before, and this time Oshun came along.

Breakfast was ready. Onobu brought a large bowl of steaming rice from the kitchen. Oshun sliced the pickled eggplant she had prepared and served the slices in small dishes.

Sankichi did not begin to eat at once, but embarked on a sort of self-criticism.

"I'm such an idiot. From now on, I'm going to be a different man. I'll be a better person!" he said, bowing to his two nieces in a ceremonial way.

The girls giggled and, without understanding his meaning, returned the bow. At length he took up his chopsticks and inhaled the delicious aroma of the *miso* soup.

That morning he was not at all himself, not at all the uncle who made funny faces that sent his nieces into stitches. He spoke seriously, and long after breakfast was over, he lectured his nieces on one and a hundred subjects, explaining how grateful he was to be alive and reasonably healthy, unlike his dead children, how Minoru's family owed its very existence largely to Morihiko—Oshun was never to forget that—and on and on.

Despite his moralizing, he was unable to conceal his inner turmoil. Sauntering to the window, he watched his children's playmates in the street and the chickens pecking at the ground around the farmhouse. All the while he vividly remembered the events of the previous evening. It was a night when trees and grass smouldered in the bluish light. He followed the familiar path past the chicken coup to the woods, Oshun behind him. As they strolled in the moonlight, he could hear the faint chirping of crickets. This was the area where Ofusa and Okiku had so often played. He used to lead them by the hand, stopping now and again to pick flowers. And now, on some strange impulse, he suddenly took his niece's hand. He could not help himself. "Would it be peculiar if we held hands like this?" he asked half jokingly. Oshun seemed to trust him completely. "Why should it? You're my uncle," she answered with her usual candor. The question he had put to his niece now returned to plague him.

Idiot! he thought as he stood by the window.

Oshun and Onobu carried a table to the center room and opened up writing paper on it, saying they were going to write to Oyuki. Oshun also intended to write to friends, both boys and girls. She laid out several postal cards she had illustrated herself and showed them to Onobu.

"Cousin Oshun, paint one for me too, please." The younger girl begged, admiring her cousin's talent.

It was Sankichi who had initially recommended that Oshun take art lessons. Her mother expected a promising future and was determined to let nothing interrupt the course, even in the most desperate financial straits. Oshun studied, imitating classical models of flowers and birds for several years. And during her stay at Sankichi's he gave her many lectures on various aspects of painting, trying to teach her to work directly from nature. But he began to speak less and less on aesthetic subjects.

The garden balsam by the hedge had been blooming for some time. Oshun picked a flower and drew a beautiful picture of it on a post card. The colors delighted Onobu.

"You mustn't look!" Oshun cried, covering her painting with her hands as Sankichi drew near to see.

Oshun started to gossip about her friends, then shifted to an appraisal of her teacher, whom she respected. According to him, she said, there were ten ideals in the world. Combined, they made one great ideal. . . . She could list only seven and could not think of the rest, though she tried throughout the summer to think of the answers. She added that the teacher was just like Grandfather, and argued heatedly when Sankichi commented that her teacher sounded quite different from Koizumi Tadahiro.

He started to say, "So that's how you idealize your grandfather?" and stopped himself. He shrugged his shoulders and retired to his room.

Evening came, but it was still as bright as day outside. Drawn by the fluorescent light, Sankichi again felt the urge to stroll out to the woods. Once more Oshun accompanied him.

It was quite late when they returned, and the farmhouse doors were closed. Several large dogs lay in the road; some raised their heads, others perked their ears. One started off in the moonlight as Sankichi walked apprehensively by them, shielding Oshun. They reached the gate and went down the narrow path between the hedge and the window. The teacher's family had already gone to bed, and the darkened windows facing Sankichi's house were like slumbering eyes.

It was a deep, hushed night, and moonlight bathed Sankichi's lap as he sat on the veranda. Oshun had gone to sleep at her cousin's side but soon returned wearing a white nightdress. She was too wide awake.

Suddenly the entire pack of dogs crawled through the bamboo fence and dashed into the garden. They romped around snapping at each other, wagging their tails all the while, and darting around the trees. Suddenly one of them barked from across the road. First, one dog ran off, and then the others dashed after him in hot pursuit, their barks echoing in the night sky.

"It's really too beautiful to go to sleep, isn't it?" Oshun said and then fell silent. As Sankichi sat by her side, listening to the barking, he found himself quivering like a dog.

"Are you going to stay up for a while?" she asked.

"I think so. Don't bother about me, just go to sleep."

Oshun lay down once again. Sankichi sat alone, gazing into the tremor he felt.

The next morning he repeated the performance of the previous day before his two nieces. Again he berated himself. He was going to reform, he didn't think he was such a bad sort, and so forth.

What's happening to me? What on earth's the mater? he thought. He regreted the walks he had taken with Oshun on the two nights.

The turmoil in his mind was not easily stilled. He went to the well, soaked his hands and feet in the cold water, and doused his dry hair.

"Strike my back for me," Sankichi requested, and the girls walked around behind him, giggling.

"Don't you mind how hard we hit?" Oshun asked.

"Go ahead. You two are not strong enough to hurt me. But I don't care if you break my back."

"I don't want you to scold me later," Onobu laughed.

Sankichi directed them, "A little higher, down a little," letting them strike him until the pain penetrated to the deepest part of his body.

The day arrived when the postponed river opening was to be celebrated at Ryōgoku. Oshun and Onobu still planned to visit Morihiko on their way, and they began to get ready in midafternoon. Oshun's mother, Okura, came to pick up the money her husband had requested from Sankichi.

"Mother, excuse me while I change," Oshun said. She and Onobu began to put on their new summer kimonos.

Sitting with Sankichi, Okura looked at her daughter. "Uncle Sankichi was very kind to buy you such a pretty kimono. We're wondering at home how you're managing Aunt Oyuki's house. While you're on vacation you can learn a lot from your uncle."

Sankichi looked at mother and daughter.

"She's not much help, I'm sure. Don't overlook her faults please, and don't hesitate to scold her."

"Mother, how's Otsuru?" Oshun asked as she dressed.

"She studies hard every day," Okura answered, helping her daughter with her *obi*. Then she went to inspect the kitchen.

Onobu came up to Sankichi. "Uncle Sankichi, will you please see if my ribbon's straight?"

"Mine too, does it look all right on me?" said Oshun, half turning her back.

Sankichi placed the money in front of his sister-in-law. She

thanked him and tucked it safely under her *obi*. She then asked him
to continue to pay Sozo's expenses, gossiped about Shota's intermittent dallyings, and expressed hope that Minoru would do well this
time.

The girls were impatient, fearing that the fireworks might start
at any moment. They were going to accompany Okura halfway
home.

"I forgot to bring my tobacco. Could I borrow a cigarette, Sankichi?" Okura lit the cigarette he gave her and chatted on and on: how
was Otane, she heard head clerk Kasuke passed away, and Toyose
should be sent for as soon as possible for the good of Shota.

"Mother, let's go!" Oshun said fretfully.

"I'm coming," Okura replied, turning back to her brother-in-
law. "This time I think my husband finally learned his lesson. I
scold him these days quite openly and he laughs at me. He says I
have turned into a terrible nag, that I used to be sweeter. But you
know very well if he doesn't give up his big ideas, he's bound to fail
again. He doesn't know what we went through. It's wonderful that
you've always had your two feet on the ground."

Sankichi put his hand to his forehead in embarrassment.

Okura left shortly with the girls, while fussing over Oshun.

It was a beautiful evening, and no doubt the crowd was gay at
Ryōgoku Bridge. Sankichi sat trembling in the unlit, dusky room.
He felt temptation slowly leading him into destruction. He had
to stop it now. He thought of his wife, whom he had put out of his
mind for some time. Darkness gradually enveloped the room. Fireworks flashed in the distance.

Sankichi received a letter from his mother-in-law.

Dear Sankichi,

In this persistent heat at the end of summer, the news that you
are well was indeed welcome. When grandmother passed away,
you were very kind to let Oyuki come so promptly, and we are
truly grateful. Thanks to everyone's help the memorial service
went smoothly. We have our late mother to thank for the impressive attendance. Many guests stayed on with us. We have
kept Oyuki with us far too long, and I am sure you have been

inconvenienced. We have also inflicted Oshun and Onobu with too much work, and we are greatly indebted to both of them. Nevertheless, what with this heat and with Taneo to bring along on the return trip, Oyuki will surely have a difficult time on her way home. Therefore we would like to keep her here just a little longer, until the worst of the heat is over. I beg you to grant this favor. Please do not think ill of me for this additional imposition.

When the letter arrived, the damp air already carried a hint of autumn. Oshun came to Sankichi and spoke more frankly than ever.

"Uncle Sankichi, I have nothing else to do. Would you like me to massage your shoulders?"

"No, thank you."

"You want me to pull your white hair, don't you?"

"No. Thanks."

"Is something wrong today?"

"Nothing's wrong. Leave me alone . . . do whatever you want," he answered in an unusually curt tone, sitting upright at his desk. Oshun feared she must have done something to displease him. For lack of anything better, she returned to the kitchen.

"Oshun, Naoki's here," Onobu called.

The young businessman was as gentle and diligent as ever. Having been reared by an able grandmother, Naoki was invariably well dressed. Even for an informal visit such as this, he looked neat in the summer coat that had belonged to his late father. He was liked by old and young.

Sankichi tried to make the girls and Naoki good friends. Living as he did in the suburbs, he was anxious to hear news of the midcity business district. But he wanted more than that. He called in his nieces so that they might hear the tales of vicissitude and learn how the character of Tokyo was changing; how ancient Edo with its shadowy storage buildings and its indigo curtains typical of Edo stores was disappearing; how the prosperity of the merchants, in their rows of tall buildings, was rapidly becoming a thing of the past; how the mother of a famous large store owner who had lived in such unprecedented splendor when Sankichi was a houseboy in Naoki's house, was now destitute, adding to the sorrow of her old age.

"Oshun, why don't you take Naoki to see the nursery gardens?" Sankichi said. Naoki, fond of plants, accompanied her to the shelves of dwarf trees where the flowers were in constant bloom. Onobu went with them.

Sankichi remained on the veranda and heard peals of young laughter coming from the garden. He looked in the direction of Naoki and his nieces, who were having innocent fun, and tried to overcome his shame and sadness.

In a little while the young people returned and picked some garden balsam. They spread a white handkerchief on the veranda and stained it with juice squeezed from the flowers. The balsam contained too much liquid to get the desired result. Naoki picked a leaf from a hanging fern under the eaves, and Oshun pounded it with the blunt end of a pair of scissors. The shape of the leaf was beautifully transferred to Onobu's new handkerchief.

It was dark when Naoki left, and Sankichi told his nieces to accompany their guest to Shinjuku Station.

One evening Sankichi came to the kitchen, where Onobu was peeling an eggplant, and asked where Oshun was.

Oshun had left for a brief visit to her home. "She isn't back yet," Onobu replied from her seat at the sink.

"Did she say anything to you?" Sankichi asked worriedly.

Onobu shook her head and picked up the knife again. Peelings of eggplant fell on the cutting board.

Sankichi anxiously waited, but Oshun did not return, not even after dinner when the lamp was lit. Eight, nine o'clock came and went.

"She must be spending the night at home," he convinced himself and went out to close the gate, but he left the latch off. He waited until after ten, but still she did not return.

Fear was gradually taking possession of him. He went to Oshun's room to check if her clothes and books were still there. Relieved to see them there, he returned to his room. Is she planning not to come back? He began to wonder as the night wore on.

A framed enlargement of Ofusa hung on the wall, and the glass glinted in the lamplight. Sankichi watched the reflections and tried to imagine a conversation between Oshun and her mother. Perhaps she was telling in her low, sharp voice that there was no difference after all between Uncle Sankichi and Shota. The very thought sent a pain stabbing through his heart.

Why did she misunderstand? He did not mean it that way. His guilty conscience made him try, like some coward, to make a joke of the entire episode. She trusted her uncle completely, and her manner was entirely innocent as she massaged the soles of his feet and cleaned his ears. But he could not be blamed if he found temptation in the physical closeness. He said to himself he was never like this before he was married, and sighing, he went to bed.

The next morning Oshun came back. There was nothing unusual in her attitude.

"What happened?" Sankichi asked her in Onobu's presence. He was secretly grateful for her return.

"I had a sudden urge to see my parents. So I surprised them at home." Onobu was holding her cousin's hand sweetly while she talked. Oshun was sorry she had been the cause of such concern to them.

At last Sankichi felt relieved. He thought of Oshun affectionately, realizing that she worked for him devotedly, trusting her father's brother.

From that moment on, he avoided his niece as much as possible. But the more he withdrew, the more he felt involved and degraded. He could no longer look directly into her eyes without feeling a stab of pain. Sometimes he detected a delicate hint of feminine fragrance from her body when she was overheated or from her hair, or some other stimulating odor he had never caught before. At such moments he was irresistibly drawn to the innocent girl in spite of himself. If he went on like this, what would finally happen, he wondered. There's nothing left for me but to run! He shouted silently at himself like a lunatic.

Two men, apparently merchants, roughly pushed the lattice door open and strode into the house, each holding an apron in his hand. One was Shota, the other Sakaki, whom Shota had brought along.

"Hello!" Shota greeted as he walked into his uncle's room with his friend.

Oshun prepared tea and called Onobu, who had just fetched the tobacco set. "Serve this to the guests, will you?" she said, filling the cups.

The young man, Sakaki, was the owner of a large soy-sauce manufacturing plant in Mishima; Sankichi knew him and had spent a night at his house some ten years earlier, and he had not forgotten this old acquaintance. But Sakaki's sudden appearance with Shota took him by surprise. He was further astounded to learn that this owner of the huge establishment with numerous white storage buildings was now in Tokyo, running a fruit shop. But when he was told that Sakaki's young wife was selling fruit in the shop, he was convinced his guest was joking.

"As a matter of fact, it all started when I went to buy some fruit," said Shota. "I hadn't been feeling well and spent some time in bed. I sent out for fruit several times. From the description, the lady in the shop didn't sound like an ordinary merchant's wife. I asked the owner's name and learned it was Sakaki. I remembered hearing about him from you. I thought it might be a coincidence, and I went to the shop to see for myself, and my hunch was right. It turned out to be the same Sakaki. Since then we've become good friends."

"We talk the same language," Sakaki explained, his eyes sparkling. "Sir, you never know where you will run into an acquaintance. It's a small world." Out of habit, Sakaki called Sankichi "sir."

Shota spoke, glancing at Oshun. "Thank you for your help, Uncle Sankichi. The position your neighbor inquired about for me fell through, but there is a possibility of an opening with another firm. Sakaki's applying at the Kabuto-chō for a position himself."

Shota was in good spirits, dapper in his new summer coat. His virile eyes glowed with determination, and he seemed unable to suppress his swelling ambition.

While he talked, Sankichi had his eyes fixed on Shota; he could hear Oshun crying, "Oh, help me! Cousin Shota's naughty!"

Sakaki looked at the two men and said, "Here we are, the two of us exactly alike. Forgive me for mentioning it, Hashimoto, but you also had a large business in the country, didn't you? We've followed the same road to disaster, in a manner of speaking."

Shota adjusted the apron in his lap with his delicate hands.

"Don't you agree, Hashimoto," continued Sakaki, "that we both should work for success? The fruit shop's only a steppingstone. I'll close it shortly and send my wife home."

"Sakaki will probably get a job before I do," said Shota.

Sankichi thought back and wondered what happened to the castle-like Sakaki house in Mishima, to the guest room on the second floor where he slept, to the bath, and to the spacious godowns and storage buildings, where the giant tanks of soy sauce stood in rows. Sakaki would not talk about them; he spoke only of the future. After a while he rose to leave with Shota, his youthful laughter still ringing behind him as he left the room.

At the entrance while taking the hat handed to him by Oshun, he asked Onobu. "How's your headache?"

"It's all right now," she answered, smiling simply.

"The doctor said there was nothing wrong," Oshun explained, keeping her eyes on Onobu. "Now she's too embarrassed to take her medicine."

"It's only natural when you move from the quiet country to a noisy city like this," he remarked, crossing over to the door.

Onobu covered her face with the sleeve of her kimono, thinking they were making fun of her, and Oshun chastely pulled her collar together.

From the laughter of the cousins and their uncle, Sakaki sensed the closeness of the family.

Indian lilac flowers dropped and lay strewn along the road. The blossoms that had made Sankichi both hot and melancholy all summer were fading, but some still clung to the branches in front of the farmhouse. There was a festival in the district and the girls were getting ready to go. They planned to spend the night at Oshun's.

"Your dinner's all fixed," said Oshun.

"All right," Sankichi answered. "You'd better be leaving pretty soon. I'll look after the house and enjoy being here by myself." He gave each girl some pocket money, and they left chattering about the fun of the following day, which was also the day of the star festival. Once they were gone, Sankichi shut the entrance gate and locked up.

From the window he could see the Indian lilac withering in the sun. He closed that window too. The house was now as hushed as the innermost recess of a temple.

"At last I feel better," he mumbled to himself, rubbing his hands together. He went to the room that opened onto the garden.

The soft afternoon light seemed to hint the approach of September as it fell on Ofusa's photograph. She was still there, on the wall. Lying under the white coverlet of the hospital bed, she still looked up at him with her large eyes. As Sankichi stood before the framed portrait, the play of light superimposed his own reflection on the child beneath the glass, and he saw his own dejected face staring back at him.

As he paced the lonely room, past events flashed through his mind. Oyuki's absence for the entire summer made him examine in greater depth the significance of the bond that united them. He was amazed how much he had changed since he married. The sexual abstinence the summer had imposed brought back memories from the past. It was as if he were on a guided tour of some famous old temple where young acolytes take the visitors through, pointing out a treasured painting on an old wall, relating the important episodes of the life of some celebrated priest. *His* guide whispered of an incident that took place the year he was married, then of something else two years later. Long-forgotten episodes paraded through his memory. It was not that his life compared in any way with the wondrous stories of noble priests. Each picture he recalled contained the image of some woman or other. They were all memories he wanted to keep hidden. He was appalled by his vileness and hypocrisy.

Thunder rumbled in the distance, signaling the approach of a late summer storm.

"I'm home," Oyuki cried as she stepped off the ricksha with Taneo in her arms. The maid got down from the one behind.

"Aunt Oyuki is home!" his nieces shouted to Sankichi as they ran to greet her. They carried the luggage from the two carriages into the house.

"Thank you both very much for being such a big help for the whole summer," said Oyuki as she paid the ricksha men. She looked at the faces of her husband and nieces that she had not seen for so long.

"Taneo, I'm sure you're hungry too. I'll have to feed you first," she said, opening her collar. Listening to the baby's hungry suckling noise, Sankichi could think only, "Thank God she's back in time."

The girls prepared tea, and after quenching her thirst, Oyuki began an account of her journey. Soon the luggage with the boat stickers was brought out.

"Will you please open this one, dear? Father tied it up so tightly," Oyuki said. "You'll find presents for Oshun and Onobu in it."

The visit home after many years meant numerous presents from various relatives. Oyuki took them out one at a time, identifying each as a present from her oldest sister, or as one from the second oldest, the mistress of Maruna, and one from the sister who was the mistress of Yamana. Yamana was the trademark of Ofuku's store. Gifts marked "From Oyuki's mother" were placed before Oshun and Onobu.

Surrounded by the clutter, Oyuki prattled on, mixing the stories of the trip going and the one coming back. "When I first got home, Father didn't come down from his room. And when he finally did, he went to the sink and washed his face before he said hello. He could hardly speak when he saw me."

"He must've been overwhelmed with happiness."

"Later he said he was glad I could get there so quickly. Grandmother's funeral was postponed until I arrived, you know."

Then she shifted to her return trip. On the day of her departure, all the sisters and children gathered at the harbor to see her off. Ofuku came on board the steamer and then waved her handkerchief on the launch as she returned to the pier. After a moment of hesitation, she told Sankichi that Ofuku's husband came with her on the return voyage.

"Oh, Tsutomu. . . ?" said Sankichi.

"Yamana came along part of the way on business."

When Oyuki referred to Tsutomu, she called him either "Ofuku's husband" or "Yamana." She was trying to bury the past as best as she could. She wanted to think of Tsutomu simply as a "member of the family." Sankichi appreciated this, and he referred to Tsutomu in the same casual way.

Oyuki unpacked new summer clothes, a present from her mother. Next came a round package, a going-away gift from an acquaintance. All this time the maid had sat stolidly, very much as though she herself were a guest, but catching sight of the package, she exclaimed, "On the boat the master of Yamana asked what this was. 'If it's a watermelon,' he said, 'let's eat it right away'."

"It is only a blue vase," giggled Oyuki.

When Sankichi visited the Nakura house the previous summer, he and Tsutomu introduced themselves to each other. He had been favorably impressed by the youthful, intelligent, good-natured merchant.

"Well now, let me offer some incense," said Oyuki, going to the Buddhist altar, before the small tablets she had not seen all summer. She made an offering of incense and some sweets and fruit that she brought back with her. Then she joined her nieces again.

"I'm sorry I had to impose on you girls so much. I gather Tokyo's been very hot."

"Oh, the heat this summer was terrible."

"It was very hot in the north too." As they talked, Oyuki looked around the familiar interior of her house. She wore a delicate new ring on the fourth finger of her left hand. After a while she took off her white, travel-soiled *tabi* and went to work in the kitchen, resuming her position in the house.

Two or three days later, Oshun thanked her uncle and aunt and returned home. Did her eyes say she had seen through Sankichi? Now she knows what sort of man he is. Every time he remembered how piercingly she had looked at him, he broke into a cold sweat. He could no longer look upon himself without pain, nor could he regard others as before. The intricate, nebulous, and unfathomable interrelations of people bound together in the same family began to weigh heavily on his mind: uncles and nieces, cousins, sisters and younger brothers-in-law, brothers and younger sisters-in-law. . . .

Chapter 14

Beyond the chicken coop near Sankichi's house and past a copse lay a meadow. The ground sloped gently toward a shallow basin and gave one standing in the meadow the illusion of being on a hill. The path from the woods led to a leafy cryptomeria grove where it divided to become two hilly, back-country roads, one stretching to the left and the other to the right. Occasionally a man on a horse came trotting along it.

Even in this quiet pastoral scene with its typical Musashino features, one could discern astonishing changes. The nurseries and vegetable fields were being ruthlessly dug up and one after the other new houses were springing up.

Sankichi looked across the meadow. Crickets were singing in the sunny grass. When the family first moved to the area, Okiku thought she was still in the country and she used to say, "Ofusa, let's go to the castle site and pick flowers." They followed Sankichi to the meadow, holding each other by the hand. Oshige died, Okiku died, and Ofusa too. He could not help wondering why he moved to this area with his family.

Cotton clouds floated across the distant sky. Sankichi imagined the mountain, where his friend Makino lived, ablaze with autumn foliage. He stood motionless for a long time. He had decided to begin an even longer novel than the one he finished in the spring.

The low rumbling of a streetcar reached the house from the direction of Shinjuku. He listened to the noise, just as he once did to the train wending its way over the mountains in the lonely province. From the mountain to the suburb, from the suburb to the city, he was somehow drawn toward ever greater noise. And his children's playmates only served to sharpen his painful memories. He needed a less quiet place now. He thought of moving to the center of the

194

city; perhaps the chaotic noise would help him overcome his grief and start on his new work.

As he turned back through the woods toward home, he saw a man just inside the gate drawing a map of his house. It was the landscape painter who lived nearby. Oyuki was standing at the entrance telling him the location of each window and the direction it faced.

The artist took a compass out of his coat pocket and marked the precise orientation on the map he made. He told Sankichi about a friend who knew all about geomancy. In a kindly tone he remarked about the death of three children in this house. It might be well-advised to look into the lucky directions of the house. If Sankichi by any chance were thinking about moving, he would do well to investigate the directions. The painter said he would send the map to his friend for his advice, then left the house.

"I didn't know that artists bothered with geomancy," said Sankichi, but he appreciated that the man had taken the trouble of drawing the map.

Oyuki looked at him. "When a man pays no attention whatsoever to such things, like you, it's not so good either," she said. "Sometimes you should listen to what people have to say. When we left the mountains, we were told it was an unlucky day and we should postpone the moving. But you ignored the advice and went right ahead. That's why people now talk about us. Anyway I'm beginning to dislike the place."

So as much for his wife's sake as for his own, Sankichi decided to move. The superstitious gardener's family wanted them to leave as soon as possible. They felt that Sankichi had brought bad luck with him and polluted the newly built house. When such accusations reached his ears, Sankichi wanted to leave all the more.

The September sun poured in brilliantly on one side of the Outer-Moat Line trolley. Sankichi selected a seat on the shady side. He was on his way home from house hunting, and he had taken this route because it passed by Morihiko's inn.

The car stopped at a station, and two impressive-looking men boarded with the other passengers.

"Mr. Koizumi!" one of them exclaimed. Sankichi looked up. It was Professor Oshima, whom he had not seen for many years.

The car was crowded, but Professor Oshima found an empty seat opposite Sankichi. Conversation was impossible in the crowd and they remained silent.

Sankichi's erstwhile teacher had known the same hellish torment that plagued Sankichi throughout the summer. Following the death of his wife, Oshima was reputed to have fallen into a dissipated life and become the talk of the town. Once he had been a fanatical reformer, lashing out with self-righteous indignation against any evil. Now all voices of condemnation came back to him. Justice, love, high ideals—all the principles he had advocated were buried and vanished as if in a dream. Now he was known as a defector. He had often extended a helping hand to his younger disciples, but now he hung his head before them expecting their condemnation. Most of his friends abandoned him, and in turn, he isolated himself from everyone.

He had put on a good deal of weight since the former days, and he was dressed more impressively. But his rueful expression revealed he was no happier than when he was poor.

Sitting across from him, Sankichi mused while listening to the deafening clatter of the trolley. Certain passages in Oshima's writing reminded him of a dog howling in the night. Such sudden and un-related flashes of memory mingled with a feeling of nostalgia, and blurred his ability to discern his own past from the professor's. They passed through his mind like the houses and willow branches out-side the trolley window.

After a while Sankichi was able to move to the opposite side. Oshima turned his heavy body toward him as if to grasp his hand, but they were unable to talk as they used to.

"Oh, this is Kajibashi." Oshima rose quickly to look out the win-dow.

"Are you getting off already?" Sankichi asked, standing up.

"Mr. Koizumi, forgive me. . . ," he muttered as he got off the trolley.

Sankichi turned for a last look. "He arranged our marriage," he thought, watching the lonely man. He was walking with his com-panion by the bridge where some old willow trees stood.

The trolley moved on.

"Is Mr. Koizumi in?" Sankichi inquired at Morihiko's inn. The old proprietress had been replaced by a woman who used to be a maid. The new owner, with a stylish coiffure piled up, greeted him at the entrance.

Morihiko was on the phone downstairs and told Sankichi to go up to his room. Oshun was waiting in his room too. Morihiko finished his conversation and came up.

Sankichi and Oshun looked at each other with some discomfort. He was nonplussed by his niece's silent feminine stare in the presence of the puritanical Morihiko. He could not face her with the carefree, affectionate feeling he had when she first came to look after his house that summer. He sat stiffly, ill at ease.

"Uncle Morihiko, I'm on my way home from school," she said, obviously anxious to leave.

"Of course. Well then, will you take care of my kimono? Ask your mother to do it any way she thinks best."

Living in an inn, Morihiko left the laundering and sewing of his clothes to Okura's care. Oshun adjusted the belt of her long *hakama* and said goodbye.

Sankichi regained his usual self and told his brother about the daylong hunt for a house. Naoki's neighborhood was rife with memories of Sankichi's childhood and adolescence. Given a choice, he preferred to live near his relatives and acquaintances. With this in mind, he found a two-story house with the help of a woman who once worked for Naoki's family.

"By the way, I've decided to send Onobu to the same school as Oai," Sankichi reported. "It will be better for her."

Morihiko seemed to resent having his daughter transferred to a school inferior to the one Oshun went to, but he consented. "Well, I leave the matter of her schooling in your hands. I wanted Onobu to concentrate on foreign languages to prepare her to become a diplomat's wife. I was eventually going to send her abroad to study."

"But it depends on her personality too."

"You'd think she would have a lot more spunk, being my daughter. But things don't always turn out as you expect," he sighed, lamenting his inability to control his daughter's future.

"I hear Minoru's family is also moving."

"So I understand. He's really a troublemaker. If only he'd consult with me before starting business, I would not have let him make such mistakes. I can't tell you just how much damage he's brought on my work. People always say 'he's a brother of a man with a prison record' whenever I do anything. You can't be too careful about him. So, let's get together at Minoru's house to talk to him, shall we? We mustn't let him stay in Tokyo. We've got to send him to Manchuria or somewhere. You'll see, I'll really put it to him straight when I see him."

Morihiko's voice grew louder; he was concerned for the name of the Koizumi family and for Minoru's future. He seemed unable to find a comfortable position for his solidly built, heavy body; his energy overflowed into his voice. His diatribe included Shota and his presumptuousness in planning a quick killing in Kabuto-chō. In his childhood Shota lived in Morihiko's household, and the uncle still regarded the nephew a stripling.

They could see the green paulownia leaves through a slit in the sliding doors. Sankichi stood in the corridor and looked across the roofs of the town.

"You say your new house is going to have two floors?" asked Morihiko. "That has its merits, but it's not safe for children. I heard Osen fell down the stairs when she was a baby; she's been retarded ever since. Tatsuo and Otane were asleep upstairs and didn't know a thing about it."

"I thought Osen had the same sickness Ofusa had."

"Well, I heard different."

Sankichi looked directly into Morihiko's face, wondering just what the stairs had to do with it.

He left Morihiko's room thinking to himself how could his brother tolerate living alone for so long. He boarded a trolley and got off at Shinjuku. He walked along the tree-lined streets, watching the dinner-time smoke rising from the roofs. He hastened home to tell his family about the new house.

They started to move the furniture: bedding, dinnerware, and other things were all piled high in the moving van that stood at the gate.

"Taneo, we're going to our new house," Oyuki said, pulling a hood over the child's head as he hung on to the maid's back. She then went to say goodbye to the families of the schoolteacher and the landlord. Oyuki departed before her husband, leaving behind her memories and the graves of her daughters.

Onobu was already waiting when Oyuki arrived with the baby and the maid. The new house was found by a hairdresser Naoki's mother used to patronize. Her daughter also worked for Naoki's father as a maid and was already the mother of an adolescent girl. They lived in the immediate vicinity and came to help, bringing a teapot and a kettle to make tea. In the midst of cleaning, Oyuki had to snatch the towel covering her hair off every time a visitor came to call.

She had grown accustomed to the quiet of suburban life and the loud cries of venders amused her. The sardine men's voices, the bean-curd vender's horn, the clog repairman's drum—sounds unfamiliar in the suburbs now noisily passed by the house. Almost none of the other housewives on the street wore their hair like Oyuki's; she was astonished by the modish coiffures of city women who tried to keep up with the latest fashion.

A chest of drawers, a set of serving tables, and other pieces of furniture were delivered from Minoru's house in place of the money he had borrowed. All were relics of Minoru's earlier days in Tokyo, each a genuine antique and carefully preserved. Oyuki felt sorry for him and slightly guilty for decorating her own house with them.

Sankichi arrived with a van of furniture. "Won't it be interesting to live like country folk in the middle of a city?" he said.

Oyuki worked without pause, and by evening the house was for the most part habitable. Miscellaneous possessions brought by the van somehow found their appropriate places and Oyuki joined the others at the dinner table, enjoying sitting on the new *tatami* floor.

The women of the family took turns going to the public bath after it grew dark, and on returning, they all remarked how embarrassed they were by the brightness of the bathhouse. The maid rushed back, her eyes wide with amazement. "Around here, even the woman at the general store plays the samisen," she told Oyuki. The fact that traditional Japanese music pervaded not only the gay quarters but also ordinary homelife astonished the country girl.

"Onobu, let's take a walk and have a look," Oyuki invited her niece.

The thousands of brilliant lights, unknown to rural nights, reflected in Oyuki's eyes. Illuminated signs of all shades of red, blue, and yellow set the city night glowing all around them. They looked at each other's brightly lit faces and linked hands as they walked homeward, passing by the dark, quiet river that flowed through the city. She was again reminded of the fact that they moved into Naoki's neighborhood.

Sankichi was already immersed in the noise. When the clamor of the morning traffic subsided, the screeching and groans of the trolley and the throaty whistle of the riverboat reached him in his room.

"Are you patching up the sliding doors?" Shota called as he came up the stairs. He recently found employment in Kabuto-chō, almost at the same time Sakaki did.

Sankichi leaned the completed sliding door against the wall. "Can a stockbroker go around visiting people at this hour of the day?" he said laughingly.

"No, but I'm still new and more like a customer. I just took a look at the exchange and then came here." Shota stood at his uncle's side smoking. He took out the cord he had bought on the way, to hang some framed pictures for his uncle. In matters like this he was very thoughtful.

On the wall hung a painting of the garden of a country house. Shota changed the cord on the frame and tied it more attractively. The picture by the landscape artist who lived in the suburbs was an unforgettable memento of life in the mountains for Sankichi.

Sankichi stared at the painting, and said as though recalling a bit of ancient history, "I wonder what Mr. S is doing." A long time before, Shota was interested in dyes and weaving, had taken up the study of painting, and since then had kept track of the landscape painter.

Sankichi sighed. "I rarely see Mr. S. It's always sad to lose friends."

"Didn't you both live in the same town?"

"That's just it. . . . When he painted this for me in the mountains, we were very close. We had almost no one to talk to, and saw each other nearly every day. I would stretch out in the grass by the rice field, and he would come back from the valley smiling and carrying his easel. We talked about painting on the way home, and I would stop at his house to look at his sketches. Sometimes we talked late into the night. This was his garden. It was so enjoyable then. We'll never be able to have those talks again."

"So many friendships seem to fall by the wayside."

"I could never understand why ours did. Neither of us did anything to hurt the other's feelings. But when I stopped to see a friend the other day, he said, 'Koizumi, S said you use guinea pigs.' I asked what he meant by that, and he explained that in the research labs of universities, doctors inject all sorts of chemicals into guinea pigs for experiments. He said that my friends were the guinea pigs and that I was like a doctor."

Shota burst out laughing.

"Just a minute. When I thought about it, I found it quite true! Unconsciously I've become the doctor. Suppose someone stood by you and watched your every move—you wouldn't feel very comfortable. So I realized for the first time just why S drifted away."

Shota chuckled.

"But Shota, I didn't become a scientific naturalist by accident. I really wanted to see things, to reexamine the world. This is at the bottom of my torturing others—and myself. But you know, when one goes through a terrible experience, one starts rethinking things. Since I lost my children, I stopped thinking that research is all that important."

The sunlight fell on the framed watercolor of a sunny garden. The scene showed the peaceful days that followed the busy silkworm season. The mulberry trees were now budding again after leaves had been picked, and the apple tree flung its shadow across the garden. Oyuki came up the stairs.

"You've finished the sliding doors!"

"Look at the picture. Shota hung it beautifully."

"He's good at such things, isn't he?" Oyuki looked at the watercolor and then stepped out to the veranda.

"Look, Aunt Oyuki," exclaimed Shota, pointing to the rows of roofs and the clothes of the pedestrians in the narrow streets that retained the atmosphere of old Edo.

Shiose was the name of the brokerage house where Shota was employed. He was hired as a trainee with an introduction from an acquaintance with Sankichi's guarantee for him. Sakaki's office was larger, his sponsor better, and he was treated more like a client than an employee. Shota and Sankichi still knew very few people. Even Shota's employer did not know him.

Autumn dragonflies flitted across the city sky. The books of the Shiose firm had been examined for the day, and as the afternoon session was over, the officers and employees were anxious to go home. One rushed to the phone, another tried to persuade his friends to join him for a drink. Shota passed through the curtain hanging at the front entrance and walked to the office where Sakaki was waiting, and the two set out toward Sankichi's house. They followed the narrow, zigzag streets lined with tall buildings as far as a streetcar stop. Pedestrians bustled about, exhausted by the strain of following the rise and fall on the stock board all day. The two young men took the streetcar as far as the Sumida River embankment, where they resumed their stroll.

Sakaki stopped in the middle of the street. "Look at that fellow in the ricksha . . . nouveau riche," he said, looking back at the haughty man in the carriage, who might well be rushing off to see his mistress. Both men felt an unvoiced humiliation. Then and there Sakaki decided to squander his hard-earned wages on one evening's pleasure.

At the end of a bridge, withered willow leaves drooped over a stone wall by the river. Through the long, slender branches, they could see the tide surging up from Tokyo Bay. Sankichi's house was quite close now.

"Sakaki, there's the first Western-style restaurant in the country near uncle's. It's a tiny old building, but the interesting thing is that the house was there way back when my father used to go out drinking, in his otter-fur hat that was all the rage then. Let's go over with my uncle and talk about the old days."

"Come on, don't be a cheapskate," said Sakaki. "We earn so much that we'll blow a whole month's salary on just one night on the town. So what? We're stockbrokers, and we're going to hit the jackpot, aren't we? Don't worry, tonight's on me."

They laughed as they walked on.

Shota recalled his father's ambitions. Enchanting phrases in classical Chinese poems such as "golden bodkins" and "fragrant shadows," with their descriptions of gay quarters, kept returning to his mind. He recalled wistfully the episode he once read in his father's diary, how a famous geisha, dressed in a kimono with a black satin collar and barefoot, entertained him. Shota forgot momentarily the hard times in Sakhalin and his sickness at the Aomori inn. As he walked, he tried to picture the ways of the sophisticated world symbolized by the elegant pleasure boats along the river.

"Oh, you've both come." Sankichi welcomed them, leaving his desk and leading them to the room upstairs.

Sankichi had not seen Sakaki since he went to work in Kabuto-chō. Both Sakaki and Shota retained the elegant air of scions of old families. Their speech alternated between extreme politeness and oafish adolescence.

"Aunt Oyuki, you look so different," Shota remarked about her Japanese-style coiffure when she brought tea to them. She had changed her Western-style hairdo for the large topknot popular in the commercial section of Tokyo.

After she went downstairs, Sakaki looked at Sankichi and Shota.

"Hashimoto, don't you think our career is really like a geisha's? We cater and kowtow to customers to curry their favor as if they were gods or something. Compared to us, your uncle is what's known as an 'artist,' and what a difference it makes!"

Sankichi grimaced in annoyance at this familiar remark.

"I'll dispense with 'sir' today," Sakaki continued. "Mr. Koizumi, what is your opinion of me for getting into this business?"

"He has no thoughts about that," interrupted Shota.

"Don't think that I'm sitting here, but a professional clown is," Sakaki said and turned to Shota. "Hashimoto, you agree we're buffoons, don't you? By the way, how did you like the market today? I just can't sit back any longer watching others rake in all those millions."

"You're talking pretty big," scoffed Shota.

"Come on, let's work together and see how much we can make."

Flutes and drums sounded, and a procession of tall banners advertising some theatrical production passed beneath the veranda. The din that followed was enough to drown out the conversation. The barker's voice echoed down the narrow street. Someone opened a downstairs door and carried Taneo out to watch the parade. Sankichi heard the laughter of his nieces with the rest of the hubbub.

Sakaki turned to Sankichi. "I don't like to get personal,"he said, "but you remember my wife, don't you? She's back in the country now. Sometimes she writes me long letters that make me cry. I often can't fall asleep after reading a letter. I lie wide awake, thinking. But then in three or four days I forget it completely. It's the truth. You know the story: I inherited a debt of thirty million yen from my father and doubled it in my time."

Shota was stirred and nodded, profoundly sympathetic. He then took out his watch. "Sakaki's going to treat us to dinner tonight," he said. "Uncle Sankichi, will you give us the pleasure of your company?" He bowed slightly and Sakaki followed suit.

The girls trooped noisily up the stairs.

"I'm going now," said Oai as she came in to take her leave.

"What have you done about the note for school?" asked Sankichi.

"Oyuki wrote it for me."

"Uncle Sankichi, I'm going home too," Oshun said rather formally, bowing to him and the other men. "Goodbye," her younger sister, Otsuru, whispered behind her.

Sankichi, followed by his guests, went downstairs to see them off. He explained to Shota that Minoru's family moved again and that Onobu was going to live with them.

The rooms downstairs temporarily grew crowded. Oai's elegant outfit was conspicuous among the girls. Oshun wore an *obi* on which she had painted autumn flowers. She seemed saddened when she noticed the dresser that had until recently belonged to her family. They took turns bidding farewell to Oyuki and left. Sankichi joined the two men waiting outside the gate. It was still twilight, but a lamplighter was already making his rounds, and the city began to twinkle in the gathering dusk.

The river flowed slowly outside the sliding doors. Sakaki and Shota led Sankichi to a room with electric light. The bluish water of the river, which Shota saw from the end of the bridge earlier in the afternoon, now murmured nearby.

Sakaki spoke as he opened all the sliding doors, "Hashimoto, one can really enjoy this sort of place only if one has—"

"Money, money, money!" shouted Shota.

Sakaki gripped him by the shoulder and shook him hard two or three times in complete agreement.

Sankichi stood looking at the water as the maid brought in several trays. The heaviest drinker of the three, Sakaki began toasting a hundred different causes.

"Here's a drink for you too," he said, handing a cup to the maid. "What do you think we do for a living?"

She put down the cup and looked at Sakaki and Shota.

"What would you say I do?" Shota asked, impatient for an answer.

"Well . . . you might be. . . . Could you be salesmen . . . in lady's bags?"

"Good god! Do we still look like amateurs?" Shota scratched his head pretending embarrassment.

Sakaki burst out laughing. "The two of us are beginning stockbrokers. We're still wet behind the ears."

"Oh dear! So you're from Kabuto-chō? The geishas go wild over stockbrokers," she said flatteringly but apparently still believing this was the customers' usual practical joke. She smiled meaninglessly.

Since they were not habitués of the place, a middle-aged geisha, the sort willing to serve anyone, arrived to entertain the undistinguished party. A burst of laughter resounded from a bright room across the garden. Festive samisen music reverberated joyously over the water. Apparently someone who could afford a lavish drinking party was in the suite. Sakaki and Shota soon abandoned their role of humble "clowns" and changed into dauntless customers.

"The guests over there are getting very good service," Sakaki said. The two younger men felt resentment. Their pride was further damaged because the maid was hardly capable of dealing with them, and the geisha, not knowing them, remained distant. Sakaki was particularly displeased and drank incessantly.

"Won't you offer me a drink?" the geisha asked as though not quite sure of herself. She was the type who was unaware of her unpopularity, a wet blanket for any party.

Shortly a younger girl came to help, and the singing started.

"What about a popular song," said Shota, who began to sing in a clear baritone much like his father's.

"What a wonderful voice! I've never heard Hashimoto sing," exclaimed Sakaki in admiration.

"And this is the first time I ever sang in your company, isn't it?" He smiled at Sankichi.

"I've never seen Koizumi tipsy. We've got to get him drunk tonight," Sakaki said, offering a cup.

The geisha held out the bottle to Sankichi. "Come on. Down it goes!" she urged.

The wine had its effect, and Sankichi grew red yet felt strangely clearheaded. He downed drink after drink in an effort to get drunk, but he could not.

He merely bantered easily, as though he were having dinner with close friends.

"This gentleman's not doing much drinking," the young girl remarked to the older one.

As the evening progressed, the party cooled.

"Tell me something. Sing me a song of your heart," the older geisha repeated mechanically. The younger one rudely took out a small mirror and made up her face in front of her guests.

Sakaki was not drunk. When the younger girl made her bow to leave, he seemed to resent the very sight of her and swore to her face. After she left, he called her a parasite and laughed at her. The older woman sat bewildered before these customers who had come to amuse themselves and could not. She idly shook the sake bottle to see if it was empty and trembled with fear of her angry guests.

The sake had grown cold.

A temple gong boomed across the dark water, and the entertainers' boat offering impersonations of kabuki actors drifted by. Sakaki lay with his head resting on Shota's lap, and they listened to the plaintive dialogue between a man and a woman. Sankichi stretched out on the floor.

It was late when the three left the room. Once outside, Shota declared as though persuading himself not to feel disappointed, "One of these days I'm going to have a big time here, you'll see!"

Sakaki, tugging at Shota's hand, tottered away.

"Koizumi, are you going home? What a bore you are!"

Sankichi received a letter from Morihiko. The note suggested tersely as usual that they meet at Minoru's house to help him come to a decision about his future, that he would not be at peace until such an understanding was reached.

But the younger brothers were thinking not only of Minoru's future. After the havoc caused by his repeated failures, they were forced to think of themselves. And so, on the first sunny day following the rains, Sankichi set out. The streets were awash, and life was at a standstill in Minoru's neighborhood. Gutters ran deep, roads were all but impassable, and pedestrians sloshed through the mud. Beyond all this was a quieter residential area, and there Minoru's family lived in one of the modest houses.

Oshun was waiting for Sankichi. "He's here!" she called to her parents, and Onobu peered over her shoulder.

"Has Morihiko come yet?"

"He's been waiting for you," Oshun answered. She seemed to be uneasy, disturbed by thoughts of the coming discussion.

"Otsuru, go play with your friend," she suggested to her sister.

"Yes, that's a good idea, Otsuru," Okura agreed. Oshun hoped that Onobu would be considerate enough to slip away too, and she tried to signal her cousin with her eyes. But having moved into the house only recently, Onobu was still very confused.

Minoru was waiting for Sankichi, straightening the room and preparing tea. Now the three brothers sat down to drink it before they started the discussion. Minoru walked over to a cupboard and took down an old box, dusted it off, and placed it before Sankichi.

"I'm going to leave this with you," he said. It contained their father's last calligraphy. Tadahiro's numerous literary manuscripts were now scattered among various hands. This box was all that remained.

"Well, let's get down to business," said Morihiko.

Oshun anxiously glanced at them all. Her mother was listening intently by the sliding door, and Onobu sat by the brazier with her head bent forward. At her seat by the desk in a corner, Oshun decided to listen carefully to remember the talk for a long time.

"Such shilly-shallying will never do!" Morihiko was shouting. "If you decide to go to Manchuria, you've got to have the guts to leave right away."

"You're right. And my health is good," Minoru answered. "As long as family matters are clear, I can leave even tomorrow."

"Your family will be taken care of. I'm here, and so is Sankichi."

"You will look after them? I appreciate that. If you two would agree to that, it would be a big load off my mind."

Oshun stared at her father, shocked by the casual manner in which adults made such important decisions. He brought out a detailed list of all his debts. Suddenly Morihiko burst into a torrent of accusations that had accumulated over the years. Discarding the protocol he usually observed, he spoke as though to an inferior. Without raising his voice, he accused Minoru in such severe tones that Minoru's face turned white.

Oshun wondered what was going to happen. Her father listened patiently in utter silence to the tongue-lashing. As always, Morihiko tended to exaggerate, and her heart went out to her unfortunate father.

"Oshun," he finally called, "bring the lunch you've prepared." When she heard him speak, she sighed in relief and helped her mother set out the food.

Minoru resumed his head-of-the-family tone. "Now then, help yourselves. There's plenty." The brothers sat at the table. Although no one mentioned it, this was going to be the last meal they would share. Morihiko's anger evaporated when he began to eat. "Hm, this is delicious," he said, complimenting Okura on her soup.

"Do have some more," she urged with Koizumi hospitality.

They ate in high spirits.

In a short time, Morihiko and Sankichi took their leave. After trudging through half a block of mud, Morihiko turned to his brother.

"I really told him off today. I dare say he must have felt it quite a bit," he said jokingly, but neither of them could laugh. The burden of supporting Minoru's family and Sozo still weighed heavily on them.

Once her uncles were gone, Oshun went looking for her sister. "Father's leaving tomorrow. Where is she playing?" she said to herself nervously. She was told at one of the houses that Otsuru just left and she hurried home again.

Oshun never dreamed that her father's departure would come so abruptly. Looking around her, she could not hold back her tears— her father laughing as he packed, her mother completely bewildered, her sister so innocent and unaware.

It seemed just yesterday that he came home to his family after so many miserable years. And now he was about to leave again; those who drove him away were none other than her uncles. They were going to deprive the family of its head. Oshun's heart was filled with resentment toward them. The pain of being forced to bend to them so that they would continue their help was intensified by the misery of being reduced to such poverty. She dissolved into tears.

Yet at the same time, hostility strengthened her resolve to be independent. She realized that this was not the time for tears as she thought of her fragile, aging mother. That night she stayed up late helping her mother get the traveling clothes ready.

"Mother, let's try to get some sleep—though I don't think I can," she said as she stretched out near her father.

She could still clearly see the red, lonely blossoms of Indian lilac near her uncle's home. In the dark room she thought of the suburban home where she spent the summer with Sankichi. If the separation was to come so soon, why didn't she spend the summer at home with her father? Why did she grow so close to Uncle Sankichi instead of keeping him at a distance? "How terrible! How hateful!" she kept saying as she lay in bed. All thoughts raced through her mind. Her father also seemed unable to sleep, and she could hear him tossing and turning.

Minoru left his bed before dawn, and Okura and Oshun got up immediately after him.

"Mother, listen to the rooster crowing," Oshun said as she dressed.

The hanging lamp cast a feeble red glow in the house. A fire was burning in the kitchen. Okura carried a few embers in a small shovel and put them in the oblong brazier. Onobu and Otsuru were up by now.

The Koizumi family had not observed Buddhist rites since Tadahiro's time, and the house contained only a Shinto shelf for the "August Spirit" of god. Minoru now went there to pray. His father still seemed to be present behind the sacred branch in the altar and to bless his son before the long journey. Minoru clapped his hands in farewell to his ancestors.

Okura and Oshun served breakfast at the table they had placed by the brazier. Mother and daughter wept as the family gathered to drink one last cup of tea.

Again the rooster crowed as the sky whitened, marking the end of night.

"You mustn't see me off," Minoru said to his family as he left alone. "You must stay in the house, everyone." Although already fifty, he was strong and courageous. In his pocket was only enough money to last until he reached Tatsuo's lodgings in Kobe. The plains of Manchuria were far away. It was probable he would never return; but Minoru left the city and his family with a resolute heart.

Chapter 15

Oyuki stepped out, her sleeves tied back with cords, carrying the fulling board. She propped it against the fence. Sankichi was away. In the late October sun the cloth dried quickly, and just as she was about to take in a dried board, an unexpected guest appeared.

"Oh, it's you, Toyose!" she cried, quickly untying the cords around her sleeves and leaving her work.

"It's been such a long time," Toyose called from the garden entrance. Her silk kimono rustled as she stepped up into the house.

It had been many years since she was in Tokyo, and she did not know where to start with the news. Before settling down on the cushion, she offered her condolences for the deaths of the children. She relayed messages from her mother-in-law in the country, and then expressed gratitude for the care they had taken of Shota.

"Imagine," she laughed. "I'm a stockbroker's wife now!" She seemed amazed at the sudden turn of events in her life.

"Taneo, say hello," Oyuki told her son, who approached with big round eyes.

"How he's grown!"

"Taneo, this is your Cousin Toyose."

"Come here a minute, Taneo. Do you remember me?" Toyose called to the boy, "I brought something for you." But the bashful child hid behind his mother.

"How old are you, Taneo?"

"He's already two."

"How time flies. We're hardly aware of getting older, but the children certainly make us realize it."

The baby, who was sleeping by the wall, suddenly began to cry. Oyuki took him in her arms and showed him to Toyose.

"So he's the new one," Toyose said. "You had only girls before,

211

and now you have only boys. But you're lucky to have more children."

Oyuki called to the inner room. Oiku, her youngest sister, was going to the same school as Onobu and had come for a visit. She prepared some tea for the guest.

"What happened to the young lady I used to see?"

"Do you mean Oai? She's graduated and gone home. She is getting married soon."

"Is she really! But of course Oshun will also. It's only natural."

Life was monotonous in the mountains where Toyose lived for the last several years. She took in everything she saw and heard with fresh amazement. Shota had rented a house across the river not far from Sankichi's, and leaving her mother-in-law behind, Toyose came to Tokyo with great expectations. She did not stay long, but reported that she went to see the wife of Mr. Shiose, Shota's employer, and also stopped to see Morihiko. Now she wanted to go shopping so that she could decorate the new house exactly to her taste.

"Aunt Oyuki, you have no idea how much I've been looking forward to coming to Tokyo. I'd like to see a lot of you if I may, since we live so close," she said sweetly. She soon left, and Oyuki went back to the fulling boards.

It was dark when Sankichi returned. He had begun to work on a new novel. He went to look at his child who went to bed early, exhausted from playing all day, before changing into his everyday clothes.

"Toyose was here today," Oyuki said, taking his jacket. "She brought some wild game your sister sent us."

"Oh, that was nice. You used to talk so much about Toyose. How do you like her now?"

"I can't even approach her. She's too smart for me."

"You really won't know until you come to know her. Anyway, it's good to have all our relatives living around the river."

As Sankichi was taking off his shirt, Shota dropped in. He chatted about the theater and the concert of Japanese music he had attended. He then said he had not yet had dinner and wanted Sankichi to come with him to spend the early winter evening at a nearby restaurant.

"Oyuki, give me my suit again. He says he's inviting me out. I'll go with him so we can talk."

"Men have such freedom," Oyuki laughed. He put on the shirt and suit he had just removed and left the house with Shota.

"You've become quite the Kabuto-chō dandy," Sankichi remarked, looking at Shota's get-up. He was wearing a long blue silk scarf around his neck and noisy leather sandals. "By the way, where are you taking me?"

"My surprise, Uncle Sankichi. You've done a lot for me, and it's my turn to treat you," he said as they walked along.

The city lights seemed to draw him inevitably to the pleasure quarters. His restlessness was stimulated every day by the deafening noise of the stock exchange with people madly buying and selling at each rise and fall of the index, by the swift reversals in fortunes, and the insane gleam in people's eyes. He could not stay at home, and like a moth drawn irresistibly to a flame, his steps automatically led him in the direction of the gay quarters. They took a streetcar to the station, where Shota ordered two rickshas. They crossed over a large bridge and then a shorter one.

The night was still but chilly. At the restaurant they were shown into a quiet, spacious room. Through the glass pane in the sliding door, they could see that both the storm shutters and the glass doors facing the river were tightly shut against the night.

The maid brought in a charcoal fire and put it in a brazier by the dining table. Sankichi, who had been shivering, gladly drew close to it.

"Call Kokin for me," Shota said after he ordered food.

"She's at another party now."

"Tell her 'excuse me for telephoning a while ago.' She'll understand."

The maid nodded and left the room.

Shota took a calling card from his wallet and placed it on the table.

"I can go anywhere with one of these. Shiose's a top company in Kabuto-chō."

He began to talk about his life in the brokerage house. Finally he came to be recognized by his chief and was made one of the senior employees. In order to win confidence, he worked very hard and even volunteered to balance the books, something the others hated to do. He lost two nights' sleep doing it. He described the showy but insecure life of a stockbroker, illustrating it by how clothes prepared for New Year invariably went straight to the pawnshop without ever being worn, basting stitches all intact.

"It's a frightening time all right," he continued. "The other day I stopped at Oshun's house and asked her younger sister what sort of man she is going to marry. What do you think the child said? Military men have no money, doctors have money but are too busy, so she wants to marry the owner of a large clothing store who has beautiful clothes and plenty of money. When I heard that, chills ran down my spine."

During their conversation, food was brought to the table. Then Kokin arrived, greeted Sankichi, and sat down intimately beside Shota. Young and gentle, she would have made a dutiful daughter in any home.

"Shota, let's invite Oimatsu too. She's at a party here tonight." Kokin went out rustling her sumptuous kimono.

The girls born and raised in this district preserved the aura of the old Edo geisha, and Shota wanted his uncle to see them. Like a sophisticated connoisseur, he longed to enjoy the fragrance of the old city and to hear the sound of the music that survived.

Kokin, Oimatsu, and a middle-aged geisha joined the men to enliven the party. Oimatsu was no longer young, but she retained some of what must have been ravishing beauty. She poured sake with thin, white, heavily ringed hands.

"Oimatsu, I've brought this gentleman along," said Shota, "so that he could hear your singing."

She glanced at Sankichi with nervous eyes.

"Look at us," he continued. "Who do you think is older?"

"I think this gentleman's the younger," answered Kokin, pointing to Sankichi.

"I think so too," Oimatsu agreed, examining the two men.

"See, everyone says so." Shota chuckled. "This is my uncle."

Oimatsu clapped her hands in amazement. "Your uncle!" She began to laugh.

"You must be joking!" cried the middle-aged geisha, who sat between the two women. She too broke into laughter.

"But he really is."

"Uncle, uncle," Oimatsu and Kokin chanted playfully. Each turned to Sankichi and bowed, giggling, and he joined in their laughter.

"I guess I do look older," Shota admitted.

Kokin waved her plump hand back and forth in denial. "You don't have to lie to us, Shota. You're always teasing."

"Here, uncle, have something to drink." Oimatsu offered the sake bottle.

"May I have a drink too, please?" asked the middle-aged woman, shivering with cold.

The electric light illuminated their faces. Outside, the night was quiet, and beyond the glass doors and beneath the stone wall the river flowed silently by. Oimatsu sang a cheerful song in a pleasing voice. At Shota's request, the three women tuned their samisen and played a subtle old kabuki number. Shota did not hold his liquor well, and he soon passed into a state of subdued euphoria, his long, handsome face slightly flushed.

"Won't you sing something?" said Oimatsu, sitting down at Sankichi's side.

Sankichi laughed. "I'm enjoying just looking at you."

She smiled back disdainfully.

"Uncle Sankichi, to tell you the truth," Shota said, "a friend of mine introduced me to Kokin a long time ago when I was still jobless. But every time I went up the river by steamboat, I'd stare over here and wish I had a job in Kabuto-chō."

"Hear, hear!" cried the tipsy women.

"Shota." Oimatsu rubbed her hands, warmed through by the wine. "I hope you'll be rich soon."

Gradually it became quiet. Shota seemed to have forgotten about going home. He whispered into Kokin's ear for a long time right in front of Sankichi, who sat smoking in silence.

"But I can't dance," she finally protested loud enough for everyone to hear.

Oimatsu sang snatches of popular songs. She was intoxicated enough to be in a singing mood.

"Youth has gone," she sighed softly, as though lamenting how quickly women of the frivolous world aged. Several dishes of food ordered for the women were on the table. The middle-aged one pulled the leftover fish paste and the mashed sweet potatoes nearer and silently gorged herself.

It was close to midnight when at last Sankichi asked the maid to look after his drunk nephew and ordered a ricksha so he could start for home. She and the three geishas went to the entrance to see him off and were still giggling when he entered the carriage.

"Uncle! Uncle!" they cried, waving goodbye.

Receiving a post card from Morihiko, Sankichi went to his brother's inn. The paulownia leaves he noticed outside the upstairs window on his previous visit were gone now.

"Ah, there you are." Morihiko's greeting was brief as always. A guest with close-cropped white hair and pipe in his mouth sat across from Morihiko; a go board was between them. The man was a close friend who participated in some of the ventures Minoru and Naoki's father had planned.

"Sankichi, wait till I finish this game. We're at a crucial point. Either I lose some black stones or capture some white ones."

The guest greeted Sankichi too, and the two men resumed their concentration on the board. The slow, intermittent clicking of stones suggested their long friendship and approaching old age.

When the game was over and the guest had taken his leave, Morihiko turned his sturdy body toward Sankichi and plunged into the matter at hand, "I sent you a post card because I just heard that Shota's been sowing some wild oats. Before he's made any money to speak of, the rascal's already spending heavily."

Sankichi had to smile.

"In fact, Toyose came to complain a couple of days ago," he continued. "I questioned her in detail, and she has good reason to. It seems he's lost his head over a geisha by the name of Kokin. Toyose saw the president of Shiose, and he was concerned about Shota too. He warned her that Shota had better watch his step. He worked hard to get where he is now, and it would be a shame to lose the confidence of his boss. She wanted me to talk to him."

"I met Kokin lately when I went out with Shota," Sankichi said. "Is she worried about *her*? She didn't seem to be a dangerous type. She seemed rather good-natured, in fact."

"Toyose is worried he might follow in Tatsuo's footsteps."

"But they say men in Kabuto-chō do their business at drinking parties. Besides, I heard that the head of the Shiose Company has several mistresses. I'm sure he thinks nothing of his employees' visits to places like that, and he's not likely to give such a lecture. Isn't she making a lot out of nothing?"

"Well, I don't really know."

"Better not pick on him about it for a while. It would be better for him if we took him to task for not making money than for spending it."

Morihiko rubbed his hands over the brazier. "Anyway, there's something wrong with him. All he'll ever make will be some paltry sum, and then he'll just spend it on women. Sometimes he laughs in a very cheap, common way, and he gapes like an idiot. You can see right through a man who laughs like that. Both his mother and his wife are worth a lot more than he is. Of all our relatives, I think Toyose's the most remarkable. A man who lets his wife worry will never amount to anything."

"But I don't underestimate Shota or overestimate Otane and Toyose the way you do. Maybe Otane and Toyose are what you say they are, but don't they think an awful lot of themselves?"

Morihiko gazed at his brother. "I don't know. You may be right. They do seem to have a pretty high opinion of themselves."

"They are obsessed with *the other woman*," Sankichi continued. "They think Tatsuo and Shota would be just perfect if only they didn't have that failing for women. It's their basic thinking. Isn't there anything else they should be worried about? The trouble is that they're convinced that Tatsuo deserted his home because he had a weakness for women."

Morihiko seemed amazed that his younger brother spoke so reprovingly.

"But," continued Sankichi, somewhat disheartened, "it may well be true that Shota is a second-rate broker."

"He'll probably never make any money in the stock market. I'll believe it when I see it."

"Last summer some special productions of Chikamatsu plays were put on, remember, for the kabuki's summer season. Shota, Oshun, and Onobu all went. I saw 'The Girl from Hakata, or Love at Sea,' and when I got home, I looked up the text of the play. There's a man called Soshichi in it, a young merchant who appreciated the elegance and gentility of Osaka life in the early eighteenth century. Yet he's an extremely emotional, adventurous, and reckless sort of man who goes to Nagasaki and starts foreign trade. When he likes something, he goes all out. He somehow reminded me of Shota. I keep remembering Soshichi whenever I see him."

"Tatsuo is Soshichi, and Shota is Soshichi Junior," said Morihiko, and the brothers broke into laughter. "Anyway, I'll talk to him. He shouldn't worry Toyose the way he does. I want you to say something to him too."

"Last summer, I realized I have no right to preach to anyone," Sankichi said enigmatically and smiled. "But, I'll tell him to be more careful."

After talking about Minoru in Manchuria and Oshun's forthcoming marriage, Sankichi left.

Shota was in his office at Kabuto-chō. It was the hour when everyone at Shiose was exhausted from the day's work. They sat around the desks or gathered in front of the safe talking about the theater. Cigarette smoke rose in white swirls and floated toward the back of the office.

In a sunny room toward the front of the company's storage building, Shota was at his desk, drinking tea with other employees, when an office boy brought a letter for him. It was from Sankichi. Puzzled that it had been sent to his office rather than his home, he opened it and found a single piece of paper, a talisman from the shrine of the marine protector.

In a flash he understood its meaning, and banged the desk with his fist hard enough to make the pen jump.

"What's wrong, Hashimoto?"

Shota laughed and bit his lower lip. "Well, yesterday one of my uncles phoned me, and I stopped in to see him on the way home. He really gave me hell about my love life. I've been expecting a lecture from my other uncle too, and sure enough, he sent me this."

"What's the big joke?"

"He's saying 'don't get drowned.' "

"That's one way of getting the idea across, I suppose," said one colleague, and they all laughed.

Sankichi's advice made Shota ponder. For the time being, he sent Sankichi a post card saying that he had a sense of honor and that he would never abandon his goal in business. He hurriedly closed the book and slipped out through a side entrance. A vender was selling warm milk at the corner of a narrow alley. He drank a bottle and then caught a streetcar to Sankichi's house, where he found the family and Toyose sitting around a brazier.

Toyose offered her husband her own seat opposite Sankichi.

"Shota, didn't you receive something strange?" Sankichi asked casually with a smile on his face, and started to change the subject.

"I certainly did," replied Shota. "I wrote an answer, but I suppose it hasn't arrived yet."

"I've been visiting for some time," Toyose said to her husband and then looked at her in-laws. "Do you know, whenever I say something, Shota always tells me to go to Uncle Sankichi and ask."

She wanted a cigarette and Shota and Toyose shared one, passing it back and forth.

Taneo came up to Sankichi. "Peek-a-boo!" Sankichi made a funny face at the child.

"Aunt Oyuki, I often wish I had a child," said Toyose.

"Yes, I think you would enjoy it if you had at least one," agreed Oyuki as she poured tea.

"I don't think we'll ever have a baby," Toyose said resignedly.

"What about seeing a doctor?" Sankichi suggested, holding Taneo on his lap.

"Shota says it's my fault, but I wonder whose fault it is."

"I prefer not to have children," Shota said suddenly.

"Sour grapes!" snapped Toyose, and the two women laughed.

After his wife went home alone, Shota followed Sankichi up the staircase, thanking him again for the letter. "A girl like Toyose doesn't understand," he said. "Of course there are all sorts of geishas, and some have no scruples. But you know those at the top are not at all what people think. They have their own spirit. If they didn't, who'd ever prefer them to a wife with education and class."

Sankichi interrupted his nephew. "As long as you don't forget the days you were stuck in a rooming house, out of a job."

"Thanks for your advice. I'll keep the talisman in my wallet. I did a lot of soul-searching today," Shota said, his eyes excited and emotional. He seemed unsure of himself, whether he was serious or not.

They talked further, and at one point Shota said, smiling, "When it comes to sexuality, I think amateur women are much more sex-conscious than the geishas."

"Shota, I wonder why everyone worries about you so much."

"I don't know, Uncle Sankichi."

"Plenty of people act exactly as they please, and no one objects. You shouldn't have to have so much advice from everyone. Somehow you give them a feeling of insecurity."

"That's it. My colleagues tell me the same thing. Something must be wrong with me. Well, I'll have to give that a lot more thought."

"Papa, Yamana's here," Oyuki came up the steps and said.

Realizing there was another visitor, Shota followed his uncle downstairs to leave, and Sankichi introduced him to Ofuku's husband, who was in Tokyo on a quick business trip. He presented Oyuki with a package from her mother containing dried squid, bonito, and herring roe.

On the day for the semiannual housecleaning, carts full of trash passed Sankichi's house, and dull thuds sounded in every street as mats were beaten. Even the women in the pleasure quarters, who normally walked in long-sleeved silk kimonos, spent the day amid soot and dust, their hair wrapped in towels. The policeman made his rounds, and pasted an inspection tag at the entrance of each house.

Evening came early. Oyuki took off her soiled duster, and accompanied by her children and the maid, she set out for the public bath. In her absence, Sankichi received Kosaku from the Hashimoto

apothecary, on the freshly cleaned *tatami* flooring. The young head
clerk came to see him on one of his rare visits to Tokyo.

"Master Shota's wife brought me here on her way shopping.
It's been so long since I was in Tokyo that I can't get around at all,"
he said. He displayed the typical good manners of the Hashimotos.
With a tradesman's apron on, he carefully moved closer to the
brazier.

Kosaku used to be an apprentice to the former head, Kasuke. He
was younger than Shota, but his managing ability and devotion had
saved the Hashimoto business to this day.

He looked with curiosity at the cramped city home, for he was
used to the shiny black pillars of the spacious old house. They talked
about Tatsuo and naturally of Otane, who was still in the country.

"Mrs. Hashimoto seems to think that everything would work out
fine if the master would come back. I wonder if something can't be
done to calm her down."

In his honest, straightforward way, Kosaku showed genuine concern for Otane; Sankichi was anxious to find out more about her.

"Is she still sickly?"

"Lately she's been in and out of bed again."

"That's too bad."

"I'm at a loss. We can't possibly invite the master back at this
time."

"Right. Even if Tatsuo himself wanted to come back no one would
accept him, I'm sure. I feel sorry for him, really. But it's not good
for him either if we break down now."

"I rather think so, too."

"It would be different if he were really destitute or sick. But think
twice before you do anything for him."

"But Mrs. Hashimoto has a one-track mind as you know, and I'm
caught in the middle. I really don't know what to do."

"I wonder why she can't calm down and help you in the store
or just think about her children. That would be so much better for
her."

"I would be grateful if she could."

"Tell my sister, 'if Tatsuo is suffering, he's getting what he deserves.

Tell him to think over what a terrible thing he did and that the house isn't his anymore.' Tell her that if he really repents someday and apologizes, then everyone may make a place for him and let him come back."

Kosaku heaved a sigh. "I feel strange. I can be adamant to her because I realize I've got to be firm. But I dream about the master at night . . . after all the misery he brought us! I dream he's still sitting in front of the big pillar, calling me. Then when I wake up, I feel I've got to do whatever he tells me to."

They were still talking when Oyuki returned from the bathhouse. "Kosaku brought us some Hashimoto medicine," Sankichi said to her.

She thanked Kosaku. "We use it for the children all the time," she said. She was flushed from the hot bath.

The young man turned to discussing Shota and Kokin, worried about Shota's future. "In fact I received a letter from young Mrs. Hashimoto. She said she wanted to talk to me. That's why I came up when I finished the business in Nagoya."

"Oh, you didn't have to go to so much trouble. Toyose worries too much."

"But she seemed very upset. I came without telling old Mrs. Hashimoto."

"It's better not to make too much fuss," Sankichi said.

Kosaku left for Shota's house, where he was spending the night.

Balmy weather returned. Two blocks from Sankichi's house, the familiar yellow-green willow hung over the riverbank. At the foot of the stone wall was an inlet where freight barges were moored. Streetcars crossed over the bridge under which, in spring, the muddy blackwaters sent up a ferment of bubbles.

From this season until early summer Sankichi habitually suffered from his migraine headaches. The pains had come every year since Okiku and Ofusa died. He had never been subjected to such suffering before the loss of the children. With invalid's eyes, he paced up and down beneath the willow trees. White walls reflected the warm rays of the sun. The diaphanous light increased his annoyance at the slowness with which his book was progressing and at the pressure he constantly felt as family provider. He felt as unstable as the boat now floating past the stone wall. He retraced his steps through a narrow alley that ran between warehouses, avoiding busy main streets.

Oshun's mother was waiting when he walked in.

"Okura's been here for quite some time," Oyuki said sitting by the charcoal brazier. She was offering a lit cigarette to her sister-in-law.

Money often exposed the ragged edges of family relationships. When Okura saw him looking gloomy as though he had just come out of bed, hair unkempt, and beard unshaven, she was all the more discouraged to bring up the reason for her call. Even under normal circumstances she had difficulty making a point.

"In other words," Sankichi interrupted, "the people say they can't take care of Sozo any longer, is that it?"

"No, it's not that," she said, smiling sadly. "They're out of work and they do want to take care of him, but he's such a difficult patient, and besides, the cost of living keeps climbing."

As always, she began to go off on a tangent, and Sankichi pushed for some conclusion.

"I should think the present amount would be plenty."

"That's my point. They say they simply can't manage unless you increase the monthly payment by about two yen."

"I've got an idea," Sankichi said half jokingly. "Wouldn't you like to take care of Sozo? Suppose I give you the same amount I give them every month. I'm sure we'll both save money."

"No thank you!" Okura shuddered. "Over my dead body! I'll never have him under the same roof again!"

Beside her husband, Oyuki smiled as she listened.

Sozo spitefully persisted in living, while despised by Minoru's family and while everyone said he could not last much longer. Since Minoru's departure, Sankichi had assumed responsibility for his expenses and punctually made the payments to Okura every month. No matter how great Sankichi's headache was, the expenses had to be met. Poverty forced Minoru's family to come often to Sankichi for help.

"You've come all the way over here, but I'm afraid I just don't have the money today," he said, pressing his hand against his forehead. Nevertheless, he agreed to the monthly increase and told Okura to send Oshun the next day.

They talked about Oshun's approaching marriage.

"Thank you for everything," Okura said, looking at Oyuki. "We've exchanged betrothal gifts. I feel much better about it now."

Morihiko and Sankichi had to share the role of Oshun's father in her forthcoming marriage. Morihiko had suggested that he and Sankichi jointly provide her with an adequate trousseau.

"Why don't you stay and talk for a while? I must be excused. I have a lot to do," said Sankichi as he went upstairs.

Yet he could hardly work. The sun from the direction of the river reflected on the sliding doors. The same light that struck the white walls along the riverbank also illuminated the yellowed walls of his room. As he watched the play of the light he began to think that all his hard work over the years served no other purpose than to support his relatives.

"I'm going on an errand. Will you get my kimono out," he said to Oyuki as he began to change clothes. Okura was still talking there. Oyuki took out several pairs of laundered white *tabi*. "He wears these once or twice and throws them away. No wonder we run so short," she laughed as she picked out the best pair. He quickly broke the thread tying them together and forced his feet into the tight-fitting cotton socks.

"Have you heard from Manchuria?" he asked his sister-in-law as he fastened the clasps.

"Yes, he's well and working hard. He sends you his regards . . . a letter came just a few days ago."

"I hope he'll make a go of it this time."

"I hope so too."

"Can't he send home any money yet?"

"Not at all. But the people there are very kind and they are taking good care of him." Okura emphasized the words "very kind." Sankichi walked out, leaving her behind.

Morihiko was at his inn; he had just returned to his room from the telephone downstairs and he told Sankichi to wait for a few minutes while he wrote a brief letter at his desk. He quickly read it over, sealed the envelope, and clapped his hands for a maid.

"This letter is urgent. Be sure to mail it immediately," he said to the girl, and then turned to look at his brother.

"I have a request to make today," Sankichi began. Morihiko was always intuitive, and immediately knew what to expect. He asked Sankichi to wait and took an unopened can of cookies out of the cupboard.

"I wish you'd take over payment of Sozo's expenses for a while," said Sankichi.

"Ah, you too?" Morihiko smiled wryly. "And I was hoping you'd be able to help Oshun's family. So far, I haven't sent anything this month. It seems we've all been hit at the same time."

Their conversation centered on Sozo and Minoru's family.

"Sozo's really hopeless. He's lived this long only because he's a human being. If he were an animal, he'd have been eaten a long time ago."

"But even if he doesn't want to, he's got to live as long as there's life in him. It's hard for him too, you know."

"His attitude is all wrong. An invalid should act like one. He should respect other people's wishes. But not Sozo—he bites the hand that feeds him. No wonder nobody wants to take care of him anymore."

"You know, I'm beginning to wonder whether it's really a good thing for us to spend our lives helping relatives. I'm not sure anymore. What do you think?"

Morihiko remained silent.

Sankichi continued, "All our help for our family has turned into something completely different from what we originally intended. We saw Oshun through school so that she could earn a living for her mother. But she's grown into a young lady unsuited for teaching. We've pampered Otane and treated her like an invalid, and she's really become one. We've worked long and hard, and what we've done is teach our brothers to depend on us. According to my father-in-law, we are wrong to help them when we have to borrow money to help."

"He's right about that," said Morihiko, laughing cheerfully. "Your father-in-law speaks out of conviction. I admit it's one way of looking at life, and that's how he built the Nakura family. But I have my own philosophy. Others probably wonder what I've been doing for the last ten years, living at inns, pottering about. But I've never given anyone any trouble, and I didn't ask for so much as a sen from my brother when I left home. Now I'm supporting *his* family and I don't complain. I'm doing what I think is right."

"It's all right for a month or two, but after all, it's been years. Sometimes I feel I can't carry the load anymore."

"Oh, I know it's hard going," Morihiko laughed.

Encouraged by his brother's cheerful voice, Sankichi decided to borrow money elsewhere. In spite of his complaints, he still could not cut off his support for the helpless ones, even Sozo, who generated fatalistic strength in his prone body taking the attitude of "I'll eat if you feed me. If not, that's all right too."

"Are you going already?" Morihiko said as he saw Sankichi off. "Sorry you had to make the special trip for nothing."

Oshun hurried to Sankichi's home. She had chosen to marry a young man from an old family, a refreshingly placid youth she had met by chance, and she had made strenuous efforts to bring their engagement to the final stage. It took a long time, and the negotiations broke off completely at one point before they were resumed. All along, her uncles urged her to reach some kind of agreement, often oblivious to her feelings. She was even forced to say that they should do whatever they thought best, while silently yearning for the marriage to take place.

She was occasionally amazed at Sankichi's contradictory behavior. Once he was asked to lecture to a gathering, and Oshun and Onobu sat in the ladies' section in the audience. She would never forget what he said: "Women must open their eyes when they look at men." But when it came to his own niece opening her eyes, he seemed interested only slightly. He frequently made self-centered, unreasonable demands. At the base of all this was the downfall of the Koizumi family, and every time she thought about it, Oshun could not hold back her tears.

As she approached the house, she saw Oyuki at the gate pointing out to Taneo, on her back, a band marching down the street.

"Taneo, did you have a good time on Mommy's back?" Oshun said as she followed Oyuki into the house.

Sankichi was upstairs putting the finishing touches on his novel. As Oshun came up the steps to see him, he suddenly put on a stern face.

"Uncle Sankichi, thank you for listening to Mother yesterday," she said, bowing formally to him.

"Oh yes, I've been waiting for you. Come in." He was a completely stiff, different person from the man with whom she had spent an enjoyable summer. He used to make funny faces, wrinkling his nose or twisting his mouth—droll expressions often seen on old noh masks—sending Oshun and Onobu into gales of laughter. Such feeling of camaraderie and warmth was no longer there.

He himself was fully aware of the transformation, and was deeply ashamed of his involuntary reaction and hypocritical moralizing before Oshun. He sounded false even to himself. Yet he was incapable of acting differently. In his own way, he was concerned about Oshun's marriage and very much wanted to give her friendly and helpful advice. But he lived in fear that she might tell someone how he had held her hand while Oyuki was away, and he found himself tongue-tied when he saw her. He felt that whatever worthwhile things he might say or do would be negated by that single fact. He took out the money he had promised and handed it to his niece. His eyes showed how painful it all was for him.

Oshun wondered to herself why he had been acting so unnatural lately. She took the money for Sozo's care, and feeling too uncomfortable to stay, quickly thanked him and went downstairs.

Oyuki had spread her sewing out on the floor. She poured tea for Oshun by the brazier and brought steamed taro roots. They talked about the cherry blossoms in the parks at Ueno and Mukō-jima.

"Tea is ready!" Oyuki called from the foot of the stairs, and Sankichi joined them. With the three of them there, he talked in his usual good humor, making the two women laugh. Determined to speak what was on her mind before she left, Oshun said, "I understand you spoke to mother yesterday about Uncle Sozo coming back to live with us. I want to make it clear that we'll never agree to that." She sounded almost angry.

Sankichi smiled stiffly. He protested to himself that he had no intention of forcing them to live together. He was merely joking;

Oshun shouldn't take everything so seriously. But her resoluteness discouraged him from speaking out.

After she left, Sankichi sighed deeply. "I wonder what makes her act like that," he said to Oyuki. His niece did not understand him, nor did he understand her.

Another misfortune struck Minoru's family. Oshun's younger sister was rushed to the hospital, and Onobu hurried to Sankichi with the news. The little girl ran a high fever, and after a week in the hospital, she died of meningitis.

It was the season when the willow fluff was falling along the riverbank, and Sankichi went to attend the wake for the unlucky child at Oshun's house. Oyuki was already there, having left the children in the care of the maid.

The family without its head had gathered; Morihiko, Shota, Toyose, relatives both close and distant on Minoru's and Okura's sides, came to offer their condolences. Sankichi slushed through the early spring mud and arrived at the height of the confusion. The women were working in the kitchen. "Poor dear. Poor Otsuru," everyone was saying.

"Your family follows Shinto rites, doesn't it?" Morihiko looked at Okura. "I suppose we'll have to call in a Shinto priest."

"One of Sozo's poetry friends is a priest," she answered. "We often asked him to perform rites while Mother was alive."

"Good. Shota, I'll have to ask you to go get him."

"I'll come with you," Sankichi offered, joining his nephew.

When they returned from the long trip to the priest's house, all but the closest relatives had left. Okura was still in a complete daze and did not know what was to be done. Oshun had to take charge of the funeral arrangements including the accounting.

Sankichi called to Oyuki, "You'd better excuse yourself now."

"Yes, please go home, Aunt Oyuki," said Oshun.

Morihiko looked up from the desk in the inner room where he was writing announcements. "That's right, those with children should go home. I'm leaving too after I finish addressing these post cards. We've got to send as many notices as possible. Oshun, can't you think of anyone else? We'd better collect a lot of sympathy gifts from home." Everyone laughed despite the presence of the coffin.

When evening fell, those remaining for the wake gathered in one room. Toyose sat close at Shota's side.

"I hear I'm known as a henpecked husband," he said sarcastically, looking at Sankichi and Okura and chuckling. Toyose lowered her eyes, perceptively hurt.

Okura approached her daughter's coffin to check the oil in the altar light. "I understand you have moved, Shota," she said, returning to her seat.

"Yes. Now that you're alone, come and visit us. We're on the same side of the river as Uncle Sankichi."

"Uncle already came over once," Toyose added.

"Your new house is very nice," said Sankichi, turning to Shota. "You have a wonderful view of the river."

"Onobu, come see us with Oshun," Shota said to the girls.

The oil in the earthenware dish was burning low, as if it were the last flicker of a life. Otsuru had been destined to carry on the Koizumi name, but now she was gone. Okura began to reminisce about the house in the country. All eyes focused on the unfortunate woman who dwelt in memories of the past, clinging to them as if they were the very source of life.

And she remembered a great deal. When Minoru's grandfather, known as the restorer of the family, inherited the house from his father, he found only one hundred *mon** in the cashbox and two sackfuls of rice in the storage. The storebin for beanpaste was empty too. The grandfather and grandmother were looking at each other in despair, wondering how they would ever survive, when a daimyo procession arrived at their gate and requested lodgings. The house was a traditional stopping place for traveling dignitaries, so that night the Koizumis put up a large crowd of guests. Starting with this windfall, they managed to revive the business. Okura moved on from this episode to one about a Koizumi girl who was a celebrated beauty of the Kiso Road. Okura vaguely remembered what she looked like.

* The smallest unit of currency in the Edo period, worth one-thousandth of a yen.

"You really have a wonderful memory, Aunt Okura." Shota complimented her, longing after bygone days.

Okura reminisced about the last years of Koizumi Tadahiro, her father-in-law. For some time before his death, he was tortured by invisible enemies and constantly referred to some adversary who was coming to attack him. One day he set fire to a paper screen in the family temple in an attempt to drive his enemies away. The incident forced Minoru's hand, known as a model filial son. After consulting with the village elders, Minoru sat before his father and deeply bowed. "I go against the code of filial piety in committing you," he said. "Forgive me, father, I do this only because you are ill." Then he tied his father's hands behind his back, and Tadahiro was carried into a locked room that had been prepared in a wood-shed. The building, flanked by a storage bin for rice, had a large bamboo grove to its rear and a pond to the front. As befitted a man considered the father of the entire village, he was attended by every-one in the community, who took turns keeping watch, which they called "nursing the master." A separate matted room was provided next to the prison for Minoru's mother for preparing food for him. Sometimes Tadahiro would call to his wife from behind the bars, "Come here a minute!" He would catch her off guard and suddenly grasp her hand so hard that she felt it must be torn off. In the dark-ness of the makeshift prison, he would scribble anything that came to mind. To the very last he was fond of patriotic poems. He also drew up strategies for his imaginary battles. He once planned a battle in which he used his own excrement, following the historical precedent set by Kusunoki Masashige. He threw it out from between the bars. All his relatives, including his wife, and even the villagers were Ashikaga forces defeated by him.

Everyone laughed.

"I didn't know very much about father's last years," said Sankichi to his sister-in-law. "But thanks to you, I've learned a lot tonight. And what sort of man was he when he was normal?"

"When he was calm, there couldn't be a gentler person. You know how bad Sozo was as a child. He had to be punished over and over with burning moxa. Father used to get so upset and shaken up. 'Come quickly, someone. Stop me!' he begged of us, trembling. He was so gentle and sweet . . . and considerate of the servants too."

"I want to know more about father," Sankichi said eagerly. "He was pretty strait-laced. I suppose he didn't bother much about women."

"Not much, but sometimes he made advances to Osue, and she would come running to mother or us for help. Remember Osue, the maid?"

"Even a man like father!" said Sankichi, glancing at Shota. Someone chuckled.

Sankichi, Shota, and Toyose stayed that night after they sent the immediate family to bed. Okura was unable to sleep, thinking of her husband, of her daughter who was to marry, of a hundred different things. She leaned helplessly over to Oshun. "I have no one to depend on now that Otsuru's gone. I'm completely alone."

"Mother, don't talk like that," Oshun said.

After Otsuru's funeral, Sankichi brought Shota to his house. "Thank you for helping us," he said as they went upstairs together.

Opening the sliding doors, Oyuki brought her husband's favorite tea. The two men sat facing each other.

"Aunt Oyuki, my house looks a little better now. Won't you come and see us? We had a paper hanger redo all the screens, upstairs and down."

"I understand it has a wonderful view."

"Yes, you can see the river quite well. But we have an awful lot of slugs . . . shiny silver trails all over the place. I hear the neighborhood's teeming with them all along the river." He looked at Sankichi. "You must come soon too. It's only seven or eight hundred yards from here—just enough for a good stroll."

The setting sun reached into the room. The rays, coming from the direction of the river, falling on the streets, slipped between the roofs and set the highest windows in a nearby factory aglow. Oyuki stood on the veranda scanning the city sky. The child began to cry so she went downstairs.

"Shota, the women have been mulling over a problem," said

Sankichi. "Minoru's family is faced with a dilemma. They have a daughter but no one to carry on the family line. When Oshun marries into her fiancé's family, it'll be the end. When Minoru left for Manchuria, he was counting on taking a husband into the family for Otsuru. But now that she's dead, what's Oshun to do? The women are of two minds. One says she should stay with the parents, and the other thinks it's perfectly all right for her to marry into another family."

"I'm opposed to the idea of breaking the engagement. Things would be different if they hadn't exchanged betrothal gifts, but now that they have, I think they should be married."

"I suppose so."

"What if Oshun had been married well before Otsuru died? What could they have done then?"

"I guess we should respect the wishes of the young couple too. I hope Oshun will handle the whole thing in a sensible way. Otsuru's dead, and Oshun will soon be gone. I don't know how Minoru will manage in the future. To put it bluntly, the main branch of the Koizumi family seems to have come to an end."

The two men sat silently awhile watching the setting sun.

"Shota, it's as if you, I, and Oshun are new buds on the old tree. We're all young shoots. We've got to start new families."

"But there's a good chance I'll be the last of the Hashimotos," Shota said pensively.

"We criticize the old people, but our generation's not exactly dependable either," Sankichi said.

"Very true."

Just then Taneo crawled up the steps, and when Sankichi saw his head suddenly bob up, he hurried over to the child.

"Oyuki! Why aren't you watching Taneo? He could fall and hurt himself."

"But he climbs all over the place these days," Oyuki replied from below.

"It's dangerous just the same. Come and get him"

"Come here! Come on, Taneo!" she called.

"Oh, he's up here already!" Shota laughed as he looked at the child.

In the gathering evening, the roofs of the houses gradually faded into the twilight, but a gleam of color still lingered in the factory windows. The maid brought a lamp from downstairs, and when Sankichi lit it, light filled the room. Staring at its brightness, Shota's thoughts went out to his own home, where the lamps were probably burning too.

Chapter 16

N ews reached Shota that his mother was preparing to come
to Tokyo with his sister. Otane sometimes deliberated on
her trips for as long as six months, but at last she wrote she
was coming late in July. The long letter confirming the departure
said, "The day I have awaited so long has finally arrived. Kosaku has
been legally adopted and is now a member of the family. We chose
a bride for him, and they have already been married. Now I can
leave the house in their care and come to Tokyo. How have you
and Toyose been? Not a day goes by that Osen and I don't talk about
you. I want to show her the city where you live, and I want her to
get to know her uncles and aunts."

Shota wanted to tell the news to his uncles after stopping in his
office. His new house faced the Sumida River, as did Sankichi's and
Naoki's, although much closer to the Umaya Bridge. It stood just
above a high stone wall that demarked the Komagata district, above
a street built on what was apparently reclaimed land. Shota set out
down the stone steps. The morning sun bathed the wall above the
river. He imagined his mother and sister in their traveling clothes
and was pleased that Otane had made the decision on her own to
come to Tokyo, even though she firmly believed women should stay
home at all times. He could but think of the deep pain and sorrow
she had known under the heavy roof of the mountain house.

He hurriedly finished his work, and using the company ricksha,
he stopped at Morihiko's inn and then headed for the river to call on
Sankichi. In the second-floor living room, he confessed to Sankichi
that he had made a number of unsuccessful speculations on the
market, that the losses would now oblige him to cut corners, especially with his mother's visit.

"So she's coming up with Osen?" Sankichi said in surprise, cocking
his head skeptically. "It's a little too soon to live with her, isn't it?"

"You think so too, don't you?" said Shota worriedly. "I suspect mother's really coming up to see father. She probably has hopes of inviting him to meet her at some spa. It's only a hunch, but I can't see her making the trip just to be here."

He quoted Kosaku's latest letter in support of this hypothesis, and added that his parents had been secretly corresponding.

"I don't know what sort of letters she writes," Shota continued. "Father's are addressed to Toyose, and she relays them to mother under her name. I get to read them sometimes."

"What sort of things does he have to say?"

"I'm shocked to see what he puts down, at his age," sighed Shota. "We'd never write anything like that."

"What would happen if Tatsuo came home?"

"If he does, he'll be offered a decent position by the township. They have very few capable men. And that's the point. If he's given a job, he'll just do the same thing all over again. That's as sure as the day."

As he talked with Sankichi, things became more clear to Shota. His father's flight, the subsequent bankruptcy—all sorts of memories came to him.

Looking into his nephew's face, Sankichi was somehow frightened. "If that's the case, Otane should think twice."

"That's why I'm planning to stop her," Shota said emphatically.

"I really think you should. We'd be foolish to permit a reunion now."

"If mother comes to see you, please explain it to her carefully."

Sankichi counted back how long Otane had been waiting for her errant husband. He could understand how she had been driven to Tokyo by the desperate hope of seeing him again. She was counting on rekindling his love for his daughter. Her only dream was to live again as one family, parents and children, husbands and wives, all together under one roof.

Shota's carriage was still in front. He called to the ricksha man and hastily left for home.

Two days after Otane and Osen reached Tokyo, Shota visited San-kichi briefly to deliver the latest news.

"She arrived safely the day before yesterday," he reported, standing somewhat formally in the vestibule.

"He says they're here," Sankichi said to Oyuki, who came smiling to the entrance, holding her youngest son in her arms.

"Please come for dinner, both of you, at the beginning of next month," Shota said. "Mother was overworked the day she arrived. Toyose and I thought it was a bad sign, but yesterday she began to calm down a bit."

Shota suggested they wait until early the next month, but Sankichi was anxious to see his sister after the long separation and decided to visit her that evening. He had Oyuki change Taneo's kimono and took him along. When the streetcar brought them to Komagata, the lamp above the stone wall with the Hashimoto name was already lit. Sankichi held the child closely as he climbed the steep steps.

"You're with your daddy, Taneo! How nice you could come," Toyose cried.

"Here, come right in," the old maid called to Taneo.

Toyose, childless herself, was delighted with the boy. "Such darling little wooden clogs!" she exclaimed.

While Sankichi talked with his sister and niece, Taneo walked freely about the neat rooms. Otane held him tightly in her arms. "Taneo, I'm your aunt from Kiso. I used to hold your sisters and carry them on my back." She turned to Osen and said, "Dear, give me the little dog."

Osen took a toy animal down from the dresser top and gave it to Taneo.

"Come upstairs, Uncle Sankichi," Shota said, showing the way.

"Yes, let's all go up. We can talk upstairs," Otane added, letting the boy hold onto her back. "Come along, Osen."

"Be careful, mother," cautioned Toyose, who brought up the rear holding a lamp.

On each visit Sankichi remarked that the upstairs room had the atmosphere of a waterfront pavilion, with their fine view of the river. Lights on the opposite bank sparkled gaily in the rippling water. Osen sat near the balustrade listening to her mother and uncle. Occasionally she edged her youthful cheeks close to Sankichi's face to express her pleasure in being with her family. It was difficult to believe she was now twenty-five or so; she appeared much younger.

"How do you feel, Osen, about seeing Uncle Sankichi?" At her mother's gentle question, she placed a delicate, white hand over her mouth in embarrassment.

"You've no idea how happy she is," Otane explained. "She's been talking about you day and night. When she was taken back to Kiso, she was only six. Of course she couldn't remember anything about Tokyo. This is really her first trip here."

Taneo did not stay still for a moment. The room was decorated artistically and reflected Shota's taste, but the boy paid no attention to the care that had been taken with the decor. Any object became his private toy.

Toyose called to him, "Come here, Taneo, I'll give you a piggyback ride. Let's go see what's outside." She took him downstairs and soon called up from the street, "Osen, would you like to take a walk with us?" Osen left with them to see the night sights of the town.

Shota repeatedly climbed the stairs trying to make the guests feel at home. Sankichi and Otane sat near the veranda, a tobacco set placed between them. Melancholy crossed Otane's broad forehead. But she was much calmer than he had anticipated, and he felt no constraint in talking of his dead daughters. Otane had so much to tell that she seemed not to know where to begin. Much had happend since she left Sankichi's mountain home.

"Considering how healthy the three girls were, I was surprised that Taneo was so fragile; but he's growing nicely now. He was just a bundle of troubles."

"He does seem very frail."

They had not been talking long when Shota came dashing up the stairs.

"Mother, Toyose says Osen's lost!" he announced breathlessly. The three looked at one another.

When Sankichi returned from an initial search through the streets, he learned that the others had gone out looking too. Only the old maid was waiting at home.

"She's still not back?" he asked from the garden and walked into the living room. Taneo, who had been sleeping on a cushion next to the wall, was also gone.

" Where's the boy?"

"He woke up, so the older Mrs. Hashimoto put him on her back and went out to look."

It was a lovely summer evening, and cool breezes from the river wafted into the room. Sankichi stood at the glass door with its light blue curtains, watching the pedestrians walking along the stone steps, the lights twinkling in the houses, and the night sky over the water. Almost an hour had passed since Osen wandered off.

He turned to the maid. "I'm going out to have one more look."

"It's really high time she was back, isn't it?" she mused.

"Where was she last seen?"

"I understand that young Mrs. Hashimoto took her shopping at the little notions store on the boulevard where the streetcars run. She thought she was beside her as she was showing something to your son, but when she turned around to look, Osen had already disappeared. It was a matter of minutes. . . ."

After hearing her story, Sankichi left the house.

The second time he came back to the dark stone wall, he saw Otane standing behind the glass door, looking distraught.

"Is she back yet?" he called up from the street.

"No, not yet."

He grew more alarmed. Otane waited until he came in and then asked, "You'll stay here tonight, won't you?"

"Yes. I'll just take the child home and come right back."

"Yes, of course. He's so delicate—Oyuki will worry. I want him to have the doggie, but maybe I'll bring it with me when I come to visit you."

Sankichi took the sleepy child from her arms.

"What shall I do about his clogs?" the maid asked.

"Just wrap them in a newspaper and tuck them in my sleeve," replied Sankichi. "Taneo, we're going home." He coaxed the child onto his shoulders. The boy sleepily nestled his head against Sankichi's neck, letting his arms hang limp.

"Oh, poor thing, he's so sleepy," the maid said.

At home Sankichi deposited his son in bed and returned by streetcar. As he approached Shota's house, nearby fire bells were ringing loudly, and the narrow alleys and streets were churning with people.

He was stunned. It was bad enough that Osen was missing, and now a fire! It was raging just half a block away.

"What a thing to happen now!" Otane exclaimed, following Sankichi upstairs.

When they opened the storm doors, they immediately saw the fierce flames shooting up from a warehouse on the waterfront. It was somehow contained to one building, and as they watched, it soon began to die down.

"It's under control now," Shota said, coming upstairs. No words were spoken as the three watched. At last they closed the doors and made their way to the first floor. The street was still crowded, and some spectators even came up the stone steps to inquire about Shota's family, since they were so near the fire. Shota seemed unable to control his agitation. "Uncle Sankichi, I hate to ask, but will you go to the Shitaya police? I've already reported to the Asakusa precinct."

"She's like an innocent baby," Otane said. "She may well come back completely unharmed."

"She won't remember the address, will she?" Sankichi questioned.

"I'm afraid not," Otane sighed.

"She doesn't have sense enough to catch a ricksha," added Shota. "Besides, she doesn't have a sen."

Sankichi turned to the maid. "Will you go to the alley and watch the crossroad? I'm going to the Shitaya police."

It was growing late. Everything was now very quiet after the clamor of the fire. Now and then a pedestrian passed under the pale streetlights along the boulevard where the willows cast long shadows. After a while, Sankichi came back to the corner where Toyose and the maid kept their watch.

"Did she come back?" he called to them as he approached.

"No. What shall we do?" Toyose asked remorsefully.

"Well, let's go home and talk things over." Toyose walked slowly behind Sankichi, and the maid followed in silence.

The family gathered once more.

"What time is it?" Sankichi asked.

Shota took out his pocket watch. "It's past eleven." He paced the room for a while, lost in thought. He walked over to the glass door and peered up into the black sky. Rejoining the group now and again he cast baleful glances at his wife. "I've always been concerned about her," he mused, "but I never dreamed she would be so vulnerable."

"It was all my fault for bringing the boy," Sankichi said.

Otane interrupted. "If anyone is to blame, I am . . . for bringing Osen. It's no one's fault. It's her fate. I just have to accept whatever happens to her. We'd better work hard from now on, together for the good of the family. That's all we can do."

"When it comes to work," Shota said to Sankichi, "I can do anything. The more I work, the sharper my mind gets. But I just can't cope with emotional problems like this."

"You mustn't let things get you down," said Otane bravely, trying to cheer him up.

"Oh no, I'm not discouraged. Not at all. The future of the Shiose company is the only thing on my mind. Besides, tomorrow is the last day of the month." His eyes glinted with determination.

"Come." Otane adjusted the collar of her kimono and looked at her family. "You can do nothing about what's happened. Why don't you rest until about one. Then, I think Sankichi and Shota should go look for her again. Get a little sleep, Sankichi." She turned to the maid. "You too, why don't you lie down over there. We can't do any more for now."

No one could really sleep, least of all Otane herself. Even those who tried hard soon got up again and rejoined the discussion. About midnight some snacks were served.

When the clock was almost one, Sankichi and Shota prepared to leave once more.

"Uncle Sankichi, let me give you an extra undershirt; you may catch cold," Shota said. Turning to Toyose he told her to give him some long underwear too.

Well then, I'll borrow one of yours." Sankichi slipped into the underwear and tucked up the hem of his kimono. Shota put on his summer hat, and they left the house.

Sankichi dashed into the house shouting, "I hear Osen's back. Great! I heard the news at the corner police box."

"Osen, say thank you to your uncle." Urged by her mother, the girl blushed a little and bowed formally. The poor girl was completely bewildered.

"Uncle Sankichi, she had such a narrow escape," Toyose explained standing behind Osen. "A stranger was following her, but fortunately a policeman saw him, and they kept her at the station until a few minutes ago."

Shota arrived shortly and was delighted to hear about Osen's safety. "I was worried to death. We'll never, never let her out of sight," he sighed. "If she were lost for good, I was ready to beat the daylights out of Toyose."

Toyose turned her back and wiped her tears. "Of course. If Osen hadn't come home, I was going to kill myself."

The family surrounded the girl and plied her with questions. She wracked her weak brain for the answers, waving her hands and swaying her body. "Anyway, this man wanted my address. I ignored him, but he kept asking, so I told him it was Kiso."

"That was good," Sankichi laughed.

"He must have thought it strange." Toyose looked at Osen. "She doesn't seem to have been frightened at all."

Sporadically Osen was able to remember little bits of incidents. "I didn't want him to steal this package in my handkerchief. It's some powder Toyose bought me. I was holding it tight like this. He kept telling me to put it in my sleeve. So I did. Then, wouldn't you know, he grabbed my sleeve and wouldn't let go."

"Oh, she thought he was only interested in the powder," mumbled Shota.

"Yes," smiled Osen. "Then we went from one dark place to another until we came out to a bright place with lots of trees. He said I must be tired and told me to rest. So I sat on the bench and rested."

"They were in the park after all," cried Sankichi. "We covered every inch of it!"

"He asked if I smoked," she continued, "and he gave me a cigarette. I took only one puff. Then he asked me to become his wife. Such nonsense!"

"Oh good! You were smart not to become his wife!" Otane exclaimed, and everyone laughed. Osen joined in, rocking with merriment.

"Let's all go upstairs and rest. Shota, you have to work tomorrow, so you'd better get some sleep. Come along." Otane led the way. "The beds are all ready," the maid told them.

The family went upstairs, put on their nightclothes, and tried to get some sleep. Unable to doze off, Sankichi finally crawled out of the mosquito net and lit a cigarette. Osen got up too. Toyose was next to join them, and finally Otane could no longer stay in bed and crept out from under the net in her white nightdress.

Sankichi looked under the net. "Shota's sound asleep."

"Let him be. He has a hard day ahead," Otane whispered.

Toyose rose and went to the storm door facing the river. "Uncle Sankichi, let's open the door. It must be nearly dawn."

The night's events were indelibly marked in everyone's memory. Otane became fearful of having Osen go into town, even though she brought her daughter all the way to Tokyo. She preferred just staying with her children in the house by the river.

In August, Shota was able to spend some days at home. When the laughter of the young people sounded in the house, Otane was carried back to happier times. One could see little patches of green plants growing beside the stone wall just outside the living room. She loved the green and flowers as she did in her own garden; she cleaned the area and tended them daily.

Otane walked down the steps carrying a grass broom in her hand. She was busy weeding beside the wall when Sankichi appeared on the narrow path. Unaware of his approach, she stretched back and looked at the results with satisfaction, when, standing behind her, he suddenly covered her eyes with his hands.

Startled, she let out a shriek. The broom flew from her hand. Shota and Toyose opened the window and looked out. They saw Sankichi laughing heartily in front of Otane.

"Oh, it's you. I was really . . . I didn't know who it was." Otane smiled and urged him to come into the house. They climbed the steps together.

"I came to tell you we are expecting you tomorrow," Sankichi said as he entered the house. "We want you to come and talk to us."

"Thank you very much. I've been anxious to see the children, and Oyuki too, after all this time." She seemed much more composed than the night Osen was lost, and her quiet tone was reassuring to Sankichi.

Once alone with Shota, he asked about Otane's condition.

"It looks as if mother's finally begun to think," Shota said, referring to the incident of that other night.

"Well, after all, she'd just arrived in Tokyo when it happened. That was a horrible experience," said Sankichi.

"It took at least ten years out of me."

"Remember when we came out of the park on the boulevard? There wasn't a single person in sight, and it's usually a busy place. We said good-bye to each other there. I told you to look around Shitaya, and I went back to the Asakusa Bridge street. I had this horrible sense of impending disaster at that moment."

"That's right. I felt we'd all be doomed if I took one wrong step. As I walked alone to Ueno, I really had to pull myself together."

The midnight streets had been hushed, as if a water sprinkler had just passed. The only sound had been their own footsteps receding as they went their separate ways.

The women joined them, and talk shifted to relatives. When Minoru in Manchuria came up, Otane seemed to miss her own husband all the more. Oshun's approaching marriage and a suitable date for the event came next, after which Sankichi went home.

Otane went to visit Sankichi without Osen.

Oyuki dressed the children up and brewed fresh tea while waiting for Otane. She received her with some formality, for Otane was not just a casual visitor. She was the oldest of the relatives, and that put Oyuki even more on her guard. Otane began to talk about the deceased children.

"All the girls you knew are gone now," Sankichi said, sitting down beside her.

Otane nodded pensively.

"Taneo, come say hello to Aunt Otane," Oyuki called.

"We already know each other, don't we? I brought the doggie I kept for you the other night."

Sankichi scooped the second boy, Shinkichi, up in his arms and showed him to her. The child had just reached the crawling stage.

"Oh, Shinkichi!" Otane laid her cheek against the baby's face.

"What a healthy child! He has the same round eyes Sankichi had at his age. Let's see, I must give him a present too. Such good boys."

Taneo proudly showed the stuffed dog to everyone.

"Oyuki, bring Ginzo over here," said Sankichi.

"But don't disturb him. He's sound asleep," Otane stopped him. She walked over to look at the sleeping infant.

"He's our sixth child, Otane. Don't you think we've had quite a few?"

"You can still have many more. Oyuki's healthy too."

Embarrassed, Oyuki escaped to the tea shelves.

"Children make such a big difference in a family," said Otane, who seemed to be comparing this household to Shota's. She tried valiantly to appear cheerful, but every now and then tension was apparent in her voice. Oyuki was concerned about Otane's inability to sit still even for a moment. Otane was curious about life in the crowded city and wanted to see even the untidy kitchen, adding to Oyuki's discomfort.

Sankichi invited his sister upstairs. The sound of a samisen carried through the dry city air.

"Don't you think Tokyo has changed a lot?" he asked. She quickly shifted the subject to her son. "On this trip I found a peculiar thing in Shota's house . . . a talisman of some sort, he says. He's become terribly superstitious, even about the slightest things. He says all stockbrokers are, but he wasn't at all like that when he was younger."

"But he has many good qualities. We all hope he'll do well."

"Well, he has more determination than his father."

Hesitantly, she asked about Shota's affair she had heard about from Toyose.

"You mean the geisha from Mukōjima?"

"Yes."

"Is she still worried about it? I thought that was all finished."

"Quite the contrary. That's why we're concerned. Toyose says she can talk to Morihiko about anything, but it's hard to talk to you." Otane smiled, and he laughed uncomfortably.

Oyuki brought up the sushi that had been ordered from a nearby restaurant. To keep her children from disturbing the guest, she did not come to join the conversation.

"Oyuki's afraid of you," Sankichi teased.

"She couldn't be," Otane glanced at her sister-in-law as she started to go downstairs. "We've been friends ever since we lived together in Komoro, haven't we, Oyuki?"

Hearing Otane's nervous laughter, Oyuki hurried down to the screaming children.

Sankichi went to the cupboard and took out the calligraphy their father had done. It had been entrusted to him before Minoru left for Manchuria. He dusted the box and put it in front of his sister. It contained a collection of Tadahiro's poems artistically written in *Man'yōgana.** The last sample in particular, written in classical Chinese, caught Otane's eyes.

> How lamentable it is!
> The righteously indignant and patriotic man
> Is treated like a madman.

The writing in black ink was bold and strong, not at all the shaky hand of a man near death.

Sankichi had always wanted to ask about the last days of Tadahiro's life, but Otane did not remember them as well as Okura, who told stories to the family at Otsuru's wake. But she did recall something that had escaped Okura.

She smiled. "He once wrote a big character for 'bear' and showed it to me through the bars of his prison. He said everyone was conspiring to turn him into a bear."

"That's good," said Sankichi.

"His mood changed so often. When something struck him as funny, he laughed as though his sides would split. Then the next minute he would turn melancholy. I can still hear his voice. He used to recite this poem:

> In the frosty night when crickets chirp,
> I lie on my mat, alone, but for my garment.

He would scream it out and then burst into tears."

Otane shuddered. The old poem seemed to express precisely her

---

* Chinese ideographs used phonetically to represent Japanese sounds.

own unhappiness, and she recited it with much feeling. Sankichi imagined he could hear his insane father talking through Otane and stared at her face silently.

Sankichi expected that at any moment Otane would propose meeting with Tatsuo. Shota had claimed that it was her primary reason for coming to Tokyo. But she said not a word, and when she finished telling of all the changes that had taken place at home, they went downstairs.

Oyuki was holding Ginzo, who was now awake. "Aunt Otane, look at the baby."

"What a good baby, nice, quiet baby. And what a pretty white apron," she cooed, as if playing with her own grandson.

"I have my hands full with these children, as you can see, but I'd like to visit with you some evening," Oyuki said.

"Please come, Oyuki, and meet Osen too. I'll be waiting."

Otane stayed in Tokyo one more week. Learning she was already preparing to go home, her relatives came to see her one after another. When Sankichi arrived to say goodbye, Oshun and Onobu were also visiting, and so was Morihiko's second daughter, Okinu, who was studying in Tokyo.

Otane was seated in front of a mirror near the staircase. "Excuse me, Sankichi," she said. "I'll be through very soon." A hairdresser in a white apron behind her was arranging her hair.

Shota seemed pleased by Sankichi's timely visit. "I'm going to go home with Mother for a short visit," he said. "I was just about to come to see you because there's something I wanted to talk to you about."

The two men went to the upstairs room with the river view. A steamboat with red windows heaved into sight, chugging rhythmically. It passed by and was quickly lost to view.

Sankichi gazed at the muddy wake. "I guess she plans to leave without saying anything to me. By the way, what did you want to see me about?"

Shota groped for a way to begin. It was about money. He wanted to borrow two thousand yen, and apparently some acquaintance in his hometown would advance a loan if Sankichi were cosigner. He would not let any trouble come to Sankichi if he endorsed the loan.

"Mother told me about this man," he explained earnestly.

Otane, having finished with her hair, came upstairs. "Sankichi, I've visited all the relatives, and I don't want another experience like the other night. We're quite ready for home."

Osen joined them and looked at her uncle as if to say how much she hated to leave. Every now and then she glanced out at the street.

"Well, Osen," Otane said, "you saw Uncle Sankichi, and I'm sure you're happy. Let's pack up and go home."

Looking at the faces around her, the girl answered, "Yes. I feel more comfortable in the country. It's nice to be with my brother and sister in Tokyo, but . . ."

The street lights had begun to glow when Sankichi took his leave. He returned in a short while, however, bringing Morihiko with him.

"Oh, Uncle Sankichi . . . and Uncle Morihiko too!" Toyose greeted them at the entrance. The two men went into the first-floor living room with a businesslike air.

"Would you like to take a bath?" Toyose offered hospitably. "I prepared bath water specially for mother and Osen before they go back to the province."

"I think I will," said Morihiko.

On this last night before the guests' departure, the house was buzzing with activity.

After dinner the men sat down near the veranda on the second floor and waited for Shota to finish his bath. It was now completely dark outside. Osen came to check the coals in the tobacco set.

Morihiko crossed his legs and relaxed. "Osen, is your brother still in the bath?" he asked.

"No, I think he's out. We're about to take one," Osen replied, walking out on the veranda. The heavy air made the scene across the river seem far away. The water was as calm as a lake. Before going downstairs Osen leaned against the balustrade and looked up at the night sky for a while.

Shortly after, Shota came up, tobacco pouch in hand. His eyes glinted momentarily, seeing his two uncles.

Morihiko turned his solid body toward him, but his eyes stayed on Sankichi. "I bumped into Sankichi on my way here and heard that you came to him about a loan. I wanted him to reconsider, so we came together to talk to you."

"Oh, that business." Shota forced a smile.

Sankichi was staring at the river. Morihiko began to say eloquently that he could not stand by and watch Sankichi being swindled. Both Minoru and Tatsuo had brought ruin to their families by having a relative endorse a loan.

"In that case, let's just forget the whole thing," Shota said firmly.

By the time Otane joined the group, Morihiko's voice had risen. Once he got started, he always went overboard. He vehemently attacked the Hashimoto father and son in front of Otane and Shota, firing his verbal broadsides without mercy: Shota's experience in the brokerage house was, in his judgment, close to nothing; he was not yet qualified even as a freshman broker.

Toyose and Osen came up dressed in summer kimonos. Morihiko's voice grew so loud that it not only reached the old maid downstairs but carried outside the house as well. Osen nervously fidgeted beside her mother, glancing back and forth from Shota to her uncle.

"We understand very well what you're saying," said Otane. "We do indeed. Shota, you've got to pay strict attention to what your uncle says. You've got to rebuild the family fortunes. It's your responsibility. Don't ever forget that." She was so upset that her voice rasped.

Toyose, at her mother-in-law's side, puffed thoughtfully on her delicate pipe. She raised her head and said, "Family tradition has kept us too silent. Mother, we should speak out what's on our minds from now on."

Osen laughed merrily. At last the family returned to a more cheerful mood, and Morihiko flashed his charming smile. "A man must earn the confidence of others in everything he does," he said. "Take me, for instance. I've been working on the same project for the last ten years, on something that may well be more than I can handle, but I can continue with my work because I've been able to keep the trust of others."

"That's right. You don't drink, you don't smoke. It's very difficult to be like you." Otane nodded.

"You know, since I began to live at inns, I've visited the gay quarters only twice. Both times I couldn't avoid it for business reasons. Once was when Mr. M came to Tokyo, and the other time—"

"At least you admit it was twice." Sankichi laughed.

"But it's true," Morihiko answered seriously, staring at him. Then, throwing his head back, he burst out laughing.

"Otane," He turned to his sister. "There's something I've always wanted to ask you. I heard that when you were still living in Tokyo, Osen fell down the staircase and struck her head . . . hard. You and your husband were asleep and didn't know anything about it."

"That's not true," Otane said heatedly.

"One way or the other, it's better to bring things out in the open the way we did tonight," Sankichi said to Shota.

"Yes, it's good . . . once in a while," Shota agreed, regaining his spirits.

"Sankichi," Otane said, "I understand you've been saying that I came to Tokyo with the intention of getting together with Tatsuo." She spoke as though she were talking about some third person.

"Yes, the subject did come up," Sankichi smiled. "You've got to think about your children too, you know."

"Yes, yes, of course!" she said emphatically.

Morihiko had been looking at Otane's profile for some time. "How about that!" he exclaimed. "She's still thinking about sex, at her age!" he said bluntly, cutting to the truth of the matter. They all burst out laughing and looked at Otane.

"Yes, I am. Of course I am!" she retorted sulkily in an angry tone. She was visibly trembling.

"Ah, the target's shifting now," Sankichi remarked playfully.

"It looks like it's my turn to be picked on," Otane laughed. Osen giggled too, flapping her hands like a child.

"All joking aside," continued Otane, gathering the collar of her kimono, "this is an occasion, having everyone here. Toyose, if you have something to say, say it now in front of your uncles."

"I . . . no, I have nothing in particular." She bent her head and pressed one hand to her breast.

By the time the men put on their summer *haori* and at last rose to go, most of the lights on the opposite shore had gone out. The family said goodnight with mixed emotions.

"Well, that was a close call," Morihiko remarked to Sankichi after they left the house.

Chapter 17

Fireworks rose in the daytime sky.
It had become an annual custom for Sankichi and Oyuki to
invite the young girls in the family to see the opening of the
river at Ryōgoku. Toyose arrived before the rest as she had said.

"Aunt Oyuki, I don't know how you manage to take care of the
children so well."

"I don't know if I do, Toyose. I don't like children that much,
you know."

Toyose looked surprised to hear this answer. She peered at the
child sleeping peacefully under the netting around the crib. The maid
came in from the street leading Taneo and carrying Shinkichi on her
back.

"Let's change your clothes, children. Your cousins will be here
anytime now," Oyuki said.

"Come to your auntie, Taneo," called Toyose, beckoning to the
boy. "I'll dress you nicely."

The two brothers were outfitted in matching new cotton kimonos by the time Sankichi returned from an errand, holding a fish-
bowl with some goldfish he bought for the boys.

"Is Shota coming?" he asked Toyose. Shota had already returned
from taking his mother back to the country.

"He said he'd come later. You know he isn't going to stay put on
a day like this." She smiled.

"I just heard from Toyose that the Shiose Company's gone bank-
rupt," Oyuki said.

"Haven't you heard about it, Uncle Sankichi?"

"No, I didn't know anything about it. It looked like such a solid
firm. That's a bad break for Shota."

"One thing about being a stockbroker: you never know what's
going to happen next," Toyose said gloomily. "I remember, when

we were living on the other side of the river, he never carried less than a hundred yen in his wallet. . . . Speaking of money, I'm glad Uncle Morihiko said what he did the other day. If Shota had borrowed it, can you imagine what would have happened to him?"

Sankichi and Oyuki exchanged glances.

"I'm so depressed," she sighed. "I've decided to watch the fireworks and try to enjoy myself."

Oyuki changed into a better kimono. Toyose asked Sankichi for a cigarette, narrowing her eyes as she smoked it. Sankichi smoked awhile too, then went back upstairs.

A yellow pall from the fireworks floated across the city sky. Sankichi stepped out to the veranda and watched the display from behind the bamboo screen that hung on the street side.

He was going over in his mind a passage from a letter a former boyfriend had sent Oyuki: "Since you have often written me that you should never have married, there is a chance that you have already returned to the Nakura family. I am writing to your present address hoping that somehow you will receive my letter."

He was overcome by an indescribable disillusionment and the feeling had persisted ever since. He was hurt that the wife who had shared so many difficult years with him never really understood him. And he did not know how to interpret her feelings, exposed as they were in this letter from a stranger. The young man was obviously of a different philosophy, personality, and background from himself.

Noise exploded along the river, and smoke wafted by the wind trailed in the air like willow branches. Sankichi watched, feeling dejected.

Shota came up the steps calling his name. Sankichi smiled as though he had been rescued from the depths of a pit, and they began to talk about Kabuto-chō.

"I heard that the Shiose Company is finished," Sankichi said.

Shota looked at him sharply. "Did Toyose tell you that? Actually, Shiose started to go under before I ever went to work there. They put up such a good front that even their own employees didn't know. I found out when I got to be one of the consultants. This time they've really had it. There was a run on the bank, and the customers began to accuse us. Once a firm starts going down, it's hopeless.

They'll probably close and then open again on a smaller scale under the name of Hirota. I'm still advising them because of my past association, but I'm as good as out. All my efforts have gone up in smoke," he sighed. He would have to join some other company if he wanted to earn his living.

"I wonder what happened to Sakaki," Sankichi said suddenly.

"He failed and went home. He seems to have lost any desire for another trial."

As they talked, they could hear girls' laughter downstairs, so they decided to go down. Oshun, Onobu, and her sister Okinu, and Oyuki's youngest sister, Oiku, had all arrived. One of them was showing the goldfish on the veranda to the two boys, neatly dressed in their cool kimonos printed with blue wave-patterns.

"Oyuki," Sankichi called to his wife, "let's have our pictures taken. You and the girls go to the photographer's with the children. I'll take one with Shota later." Oyuki smiled, delighted with this idea. The stream of pedestrians never stopped in the streets.

In the evening they had a supper of cold noodles behind the airy bamboo screens, and the entrance gate was left open to let the fresh breeze in.

"If things were different," Shota said, "we could rent a whole boat and have a wonderful time on the river." He snapped his white fan moodily as he walked out the gate with Sankichi.

"Oshun, girls, come along!" Oyuki called as she stepped out to the garden with Toyose. Inhabitants of the midtown district often carried benches out to the street corners where they could cool off. While cooling they could watch the smartly dressed strolling crowds.

"Why didn't you put up your hair in Shimada style?" Toyose asked Oshun. "Shimada is so becoming on you."

Okinu answered for her. "The other day we teased her about rushing the wedding by wearing her hair in Shimada. That's why she won't wear it like that." All the girls laughed.

"Okinu doesn't have any trace of country accent," Toyose commented with admiration.

"I practiced at home before I came to Tokyo," Okinu confessed, modestly lowering her eyes.

"Onobu speaks like a native Tokyoite already," said Oyuki, amazed by how rapidly young girls learned.

The crowd had been drawn like a tide to the river area beyond the streets. Frenzied shouts greeted every burst of fireworks. When Shota and Sankichi made a circular tour of the embankment and returned, the girls just stood up to go for a walk.

"How stylish she is!" Onobu cried, calling Sankichi's attention to a young girl walking along the street, and she then followed the others.

Oyuki went inside to check on the children and brought out a tea tray for the men, who were cooling themselves on the bench. Toyose followed with a tobacco set.

"Oshun told me today that she would like to borrow my *obi* for her wedding," Oyuki whispered to her husband.

"Doesn't she have one of her own?"

"It doesn't go with her wedding kimono, she says."

"Well then, let her use yours."

As she was speaking with her husband, Toyose invited her to take a walk to the river bank. Their husbands remained on the bench.

"How's the Mukōjima girl?" Sankichi asked with a grin, refering to Kokin.

"Toyose worries herself sick. She gives me a pain," Shota sighed.

"How about introducing her to Mukōjima?" Sankichi suggested playfully.

"I've already done that, but it didn't work. Toyose's not broad-minded enough. I took her to a teahouse by the bank and Mukōjima came. But she must have thought it strange, because she didn't show up right away in our room. If only Toyose would laugh it off. . . . "

"But she couldn't, of course. They're both women."

"Mukōjima is a professional, after all. She knew how to handle the situation. She ordered two carriages when we were ready to leave. She put Toyose and me in the love-seat ricksha and followed in a single-seated one to escort us home. What do you think Toyose said afterward? 'You mean you like that sort? I expected to see someone much more glamorous.' You know, for a mistress I prefer the quiet type, but I want all the glamour in the world in the entourage. . . . "

Red, lavender, all colors of fireworks exploded in the night sky and then faded away. They had an excellent view from their bench. Sankichi, ever concerned about his children since he lost three, went periodically into the house to check on the sleeping boys. Each time he rejoined Shota to continue their talk.

Sometimes he looked up at the sky. "I wonder why families are always loaded with problems," he said to his nephew as though thinking aloud. "Mine, for instance—you'd think we'd get along better."

Soon Toyose and Oyuki returned hand in hand under the bright gaslight. They were about the same height, and both wore their hair in the Japanese style popular in downtown Tokyo. Oyuki was thirty-one, and Toyose almost thirty. Compared to Oyuki, who had rounded shoulders and a well-molded bosom, Toyose was slender. But they were both mature and well-developed women. They were engrossed in conversation as they approached the bench.

The girls also came back holding hands, whispering and giggling. Young couples strolled past the family.

After the last of the spectacular fireworks had been set off, Sankichi and Shota wandered back to the bridge.

Lanterns on the departing boats glowed in the night. Several of them bore the trademark of one or another of the Kabuto-chō brokerages. Shota was depressed as he slowly walked homeward with his uncle.

It was late, and the girls divided into two groups to stay overnight. Oshun and Okinu went home with Shota and Toyose, while Onobu and Oiku remained at Sankichi's house.

It was a typical summer night in the center of the city. The mosquito net was used for only twenty or thirty days during the season, unlike in the suburbs, where it was a necessity four or five months out of the year. But that night they all slept under netting.

Sankichi suddenly awoke. His family was sound asleep, but he was bothered by the buzzing of mosquitoes and could not go back to sleep even after some time. He could see several of them gathered around the pillow, drawn by the odor of milk that lingered on the baby, and some of them had made their way inside the net. He crept out of bed, fumbled for matches, and lit the candle. No one stirred, even when the linen net glowed green by the candlelight.

"Taneo's rolled himself way over there. What a sight! You're all restless when you're sleeping," he whispered reprovingly. He quietly stepped over his sleeping children.

He came closer to Oyuki as he searched for mosquitoes inside the netting. She was quietly asleep, completely free of any trace of guilt, one mothering arm outstretched to the infant. He held the candle close to her face as if to read her thoughts but nothing was out of the ordinary under the flickering light. She was deep in untroubled sleep and not a muscle moved in her face. Even her white arms seemed to be sleeping.

After exploring the room outside the netting, Sankichi snuffed out the candle and crawled back into bed. This time he fell asleep at once.

The next morning the two girls ate breakfast with Taneo sitting between them, while the maid fed Shinkichi at one end of the table.

"What is it, Sankichi?" Oyuki asked as she ate. "Why are you looking at me like that?"

"I have the right to look, don't I?" he teased.

"You don't have to stare that much."

The girls giggled.

"Do you know something? I awoke in the middle of the night and went burning mosquitoes, and you never opened your eyes." He added in a playful tone, "I even heard Onobu talking in her sleep."

"Oh, Uncle Sankichi! I never talk in my sleep!" she protested.

Oiku grinned. "I heard you moving around, but I pretended I was sleeping."

Sankichi went up to his room by himself. He kept the desk he had brought back from the mountains on the second floor. Sitting and working at it, he viewed the rooftops of the city and the sky above the river. Often the light burned late into the night while he continued to work long after all the neighbors had retired.

The voices rising from the first floor interfered with his concentration. He berated himself, realizing how foolish it was to be angry with his wife. It was distasteful even to think about it. But he always became involved in quarrels against his better judgment. In despair, he wondered when their two minds would understand each other.

He was a faithful protector in his role as husband, but he did not make a good companion. He was unable to remain in her company for any length of time, and was quickly bored by any conversation with her. Compared to moody Sankichi, many men were far more companionable. Some of them sometimes visited the Koizumi household and made everyone laugh. Hearing the merriment downstairs, Sankichi felt lonely. Occasionally he would dash down the steps and snatch his child from the visitor's arms.

He thought of the man who had the audacity to send letters to his wife, addressing her: "Oyuki dear." Yet, when she said innocently that he was a kind, entertaining sort of person, Sankichi was powerless to do anything to castigate her.

Even a slight disagreement would crush her, and Sankichi would come down from the second floor to bow deeply before her, clownishly apologizing. "I hope I'm forgiven this time."

About the time of Oshun's wedding, Oyuki's mother came to Tokyo on a visit. She served as an indispensable mediator in the large Nakura family, and Sankichi often told Oyuki that Otane and her mother were the two opposite poles. She was good not only to the various adopted sons-in-law but even to Sankichi, who did not belong to her family, showing him the most delicate considerations. On this visit to her daughter too, she immediately put on her eyeglasses and began mending her grandsons' clothes. Tirelessly, she helped Oyuki with the house chores.

Tsutomu came to Tokyo on business at the same time and lodged at his usual place not far away. With his mother-in-law staying at Sankichi's, he dropped in frequently on errands, and she was always surrounded by cheerful voices.

Sankichi felt melancholic in such an atmosphere. He often went for walks around sunset to hide this from his mother-in-law's perceptive eyes. He had no destination in mind; he simply fled the house to mingle with the crowds in the streets. His feet often took him to the bridge. As evening fell and the city lights began to twinkle, he looked at the tree-lined promenades and the crowded buildings from the bridge. He also got into the habit of visiting a popular vaudeville house in the neighborhood. The professional raconteur's trite love stories and cheap impersonations on the stage did not particularly appeal to him. He only tried to forget his vague depression in the crowd of strangers, placing his cushion in a secluded spot in the rear and sitting by himself as he silently smoked his favorite cigarette.

Mrs. Nakura stayed for some time, and Oyuki often asked her to look after the house when she went out to see Toyose or her old schoolmates. As the mother of three boys with no dependable help, she had had far too few such opportunities. Now Sankichi began to feel uneasy about her going out.

One evening she left home to visit Naoki's family, and when by ten she still had not returned, Sankichi began to worry.

"Mother, I wonder what's happened to Oyuki. She's so late. I'm going to take a look," he said and set out toward Naoki's house to meet her.

He saw her coming back at the foot of the bridge near home. "Sankichi!" she called brightly.

"You worried me quite a bit. Why did you stay out so late? I was about to go all the way to Naoki's."

Oyuki drew close to her husband. It was so rare for them to be out together alone. Deep in thought, Sankichi retraced his steps along the dark road with his wife.

"Sankichi often asks me what made me decide to marry him," Oyuki said to her mother.

"What does he mean by that?"

Tsutomu was visiting dressed in his tradesman's attire. He sat by the brazier and told the two women about his business trip to Osaka, about his errands in Tokyo, and about the merchandise shipment to the north. He said he would be leaving for home the next day.

Mrs. Nakura called from the foot of the staircase, "Sankichi, Tsutomu's here to say good-bye. Will you come down for a minute?"

Sankichi joined them. He enjoyed listening to this cheerful and sociable brother-in-law describe a merchant's life.

It was many years ago that Sankichi discovered and absolved the secret love between him and Oyuki. Tsutomu and Oyuki's sister were now parents of a child Taneo's age. Sankichi and Tsutomu had maintained friendly relations and come to know each other well. Oyuki's romance was treated as something long forgotten, yet the anxiety that plagued Sankichi recently brought back the nagging pain. He felt himself freeze stiff when Oyuki joined Tsutomu and him for a chat.

"You must be working very hard," Tsutomu said, looking at Sankichi's pale face.

"Yes, he's very busy," Mrs. Nakura said, glancing at him. "Sankichi, why don't you go back to your work. Don't feel you are obliged to keep us company."

She made fresh tea and offered a cup to her son-in-law.

When Tsutomu returned to his inn, Sankichi went out to buy a gift for Tsutomu's child and handed it to his wife. Taneo spied the package and clung to him. "Daddy, may I have something?" he whimpered.

"This is not for you. It's for your uncle," he answered and said to Oyuki, "will you take it over to Tsutomu for me?"

"Oh, that wasn't necessary!" Mrs. Nakura said.

After dinner Sankichi returned to his work. "Idiot!" he muttered. He tried to convince himself that he was content to remain outside Tsutomu's and Oyuki's relationship, and that it should not matter to him. But he could not be a mere observer. In spite of himself, he began to visualize her visit to the inn. He even imagined the words they would exchange.

He looked desperately around the room. What's the matter with me? he wondered. He sadly remembered a passage he once read in a French novel: "Have you ever been jealous?" A jealous man—when he realized that it was his own story, he felt deeply ashamed. He repeatedly assured Oyuki and himself that he had forgiven them completely, but had he really?

The children were put to bed. Oyuki, ready to leave, called from the foot of the steps, "Sankichi, I'll be back soon." He could sense her happiness as she opened the wicket to leave the house, as he listened to the diminishing sound of her wooden clogs.

He awaited her return trembling in body and soul. He ruefully realized that such were the times that made a man think of divorce. After vacillating for some time, he finally arrived at a solution that had never occurred to him before: he would lead the celibate life of a monk. As desolate as such an existence might be, he could think of no other way to support his family and still ease the pain. He would regard the house as temple and cloister.

Oyuki returned from Tsutomu's inn and said that he had gone out.

The next day a post card came from Tsutomu thanking them for their gift and apologizing for his absence when his "sister" took the trouble of bringing it to him; he added that he was about to leave for the north and asked to be remembered to his mother-in-law.

At the end of October, Sankichi went to bed with a persistent cold. His mother-in-law was still there. Oyuki carried medicine and food up to her husband daily. Sometimes the children followed her and held on to her shoulders or playfully pulled her hand.

And Shota came to see how he was. Sankichi was feeling better and sat up in bed wrapped in a heavy gown.

"I'm sorry for not getting in touch with you for so long." Oyuki apologized to Shota and asked him how Toyose was. As she left the room, she heard her husband's laughter, which she had not heard for some time.

"How's Kabuto-chō?" Sankichi asked. "How's the new firm doing? What was the name . . . Hirota?"

Shota managed a wry smile. "Well, all you can say is that it's there. Most of the staff have moved into smaller offices. None of the old Shiose image survived."

"But you go to the office, don't you?"

"Yes, but it's like a game these days. In fact, just recently I drew up a plan for saving the Hirota company. I took a chance and stormed into the office of another firm and threatened the staff to either kill or save the Hirota company. It was practically extortion. I did it nine times in a single day, each time rushing over by ricksha in a downpour, but the head of the firm refused to see me, so it didn't work out. Then some people at Hirota began to criticize me, traitors that they are. They said my way of doing things was too reckless. They're such cowards. How can they do anything when they're all so chicken-hearted? That made me realize I must start all over and make new connections."

Shota's eyes glistened, yet he was obviously discouraged. Fumbling in his sleeve, he took out a silkworm cocoon that contained a lead weight. He explained that he was devising children's toys, since he had so much time on his hands. He talked about a plaything invented by Kibun, the cultured millionaire merchant of the Edo period who was interested in many projects. As sunlight fell on the roofs of the houses and splashed into the room, Shota demonstrated how to roll the cocoon, while Sankichi sat pensively in bed.

The husband might regard his house as a monastery, but the wife was by no means a nun. And having gone through hard times since his childhood, he was particularly sensitive to the feminine tenderness with which he was cared for in his sickness. When he recovered completely, he was voluntarily "defrocked." He was perturbed, even humiliated. He decided that his relationship with Oyuki should be like that of a brother and a sister.

It was a November day, and the sky was leaden. In a rare good mood, Sankichi accompanied Oyuki to go shopping. She was wearing a blue coat over an attractive holiday kimono. As she followed her husband, pulling on her gloves, she was still full of amazement. "I wonder what's gotten into him—this might bring a change in the weather," she thought.

When they reached the busy street, Sankichi stopped and said, "Don't be so timid. Hold yourself straight when you walk. You embarrass me."

"But I can't help it." Oyuki blushed.

After they finished shopping, Sankichi took her to the second floor of a Western-style restaurant. No other customer was in the dining room. He selected a table near the window and sat down, while Oyuki removed her gloves and placed her hard-working housewife's hands on the white tablecloth.

"So this is the restaurant you patronize," she said, as she looked curiously around the dining room. It was decorated with flowers, mirrors, and some old-fashioned oil paintings. She walked to the window and looked out over the roofs of the city.

A waiter in a white jacket brought several dishes. Sankichi raised a spoon and looked at his wife.

"Do you still envy your old friends? Remember the girl who came to see you in the heavy black silk *haori*? When I saw her the other day, she had aged so much I didn't recognize her."

"She's had so many children. . . ." There was a faraway look in Oyuki's eyes. They sipped the soup as they talked.

"What happened to your friend who went to America, the one who said she was going to work and support her husband? Come to think of it, there was another one who left her husband and child and went off somewhere. Some sad stories are circulating about her. When you think about yourself, do you really envy her?"

"Actually, I admire her a lot."

"I don't."

The waiter came with the next course, and for a while the couple ate in silence.

"How about the woman in Shiba?" Sankichi asked again. "The one you always go to see."

"Her husband's not well. She complains all the time."

"Whatever else you say about women, they certainly live longer. Look at Naoki's family. Grandmother's the only survivor. That shows you. I have to laugh when big fat wives call themselves frail creatures."

"Yes . . . but I do envy men. I hope I'll never be born a woman again."

The setting sun turned a brilliant red. Each window in the dining room became a distant picture, as the city beyond sank gradually into the gathering dusk. Shortly the couple went out to the street. Sankichi escorted his satisfied "sister" home, trying to hold out against his weariness of life.

Chapter 18

Slowly Shota walked from his house in Komagata toward Sankichi's, passing along the river to the Umaya Bridge and zigzagging through the narrow back streets. At length he came out on Kuramae Boulevard, a long, tree-lined thoroughfare.

Sankichi had just returned from a trip. Shota called from the garden entrance, "Uncle Sankichi, come take a walk with me, if you have the time."

"All right. But first come in for a few minutes," Sankichi replied and ushered his nephew into the living room.

Oyuki's father had traveled the long way from his home to join his wife, who had extended her visit and spent the New Year with their daughter.

The old man greeted Shota. The vigorous man was finally showing the signs of his advancing years, his beard now quite white.

After he finished his cup of tea in Sankichi's room, Shota relaxed, seating himself more informally. He looked at Sankichi's suntanned face and said, "We heard that Father's finally gone to Manchuria." Sankichi interrupted the account of his trip.

"He was in Kobe for a long time. Apparently he did something underhanded and had to leave. I guess Uncle Minoru helped him. I didn't know anything about it, but Aunt Okura got a letter from Uncle Minoru and came to visit last night—she's lonely now that Oshun's gone—and stayed over and told us everything."

The news that Tatsuo and Minoru were together in Manchuria moved Shota and Sankichi, and they speculated about what lay in store for the heads of the two families.

Sankichi resumed the story of his week-long travels. He and his companions, who had left the noisy city for the sound of a mountain stream, began to miss their homes well before the end of the week. They talked constantly about their families at the hot springs and on the trip back, and once in Tokyo, they all hurried home to their wives.

He brought out picture post cards of old harbor towns, seascapes with lighthouses, and women in curious costumes of the region. Breaking into a mischievous smile, he said, "How would you like to send a card to Mukōjima?"

Shota was amused by the idea. He addressed one with a white lighthouse to Kokin and on the back he wrote, "From you know who." This made Sankichi chuckle, and he added a few words of his own.

"Toyose will make a face if she hears about this," Sankichi said, laughing as he stood up.

But soon Shota was dispirited and ready to leave. He tucked the picture post card in his pocket and went downstairs, passed by Mr. Nakura, and walked out. Sankichi said a word to Oyuki in the kitchen and followed after him.

They walked through narrow alleys between rows of warehouses and came out at the white-walled waterfront. The embankment was Sankichi's favorite spot for strolling. The Kanda River lay just beyond. It was so quiet that it was difficult to believe they were in the heart of a busy district. The late February sun reflected dimly in the black water.

Above the steps of the pier, square stone blocks were piled up into a low wall, and an iron chain hung at one end. The two men leaned against the wall and talked about their two relatives in Manchuria.

"When the two get together and drink, they'll probably get all choked up," Sankichi said sympathetically.

Shota pensively watched the chickens playing at their feet.

The stark willow branches along the waterfront added to the wintry desolateness.

"How's your work coming, Shota? Are you still unemployed?" said Sankichi as they walked beneath the drooping branches. Taking out cigarettes, he offered one to his nephew.

Shota smiled sadly. "There was a good position, and I was supposed to get it. But Hirota went to the firm and told stories behind my back, so I lost it."

"Did he really? But he was your colleague."

"Stockbrokers' ethics are another story. They think nothing of double-crossing their colleagues. They will sell you at the drop of a hat and go to any length for a profit. They specialize in bragging about their own success, in being jealous of others' success, and in laughing at their mistakes. . . . They're merciless even between father and son. Stockbrokers' jealousy is probably even more fierce than artists'."

He asked Sankichi if he knew anyone who had connections in Kabuto-chō, and if so, to keep him in mind.

They left the stone wall together and slowly walked downstream. At the end of the bridge where the water of the Kanda River met the Sumida, the entertainment district extended along the water. The area had been Shota's territory when he used to entertain his customers. In those days the Hashimoto name had been well known. "I haven't been here for some time," he mumbled as he walked down the gentle slope toward the estuary.

They could see the Sumida River from that point. Graceful white seagulls hovered above, and on the opposite shore a cluster of houses with smoke rising from the chimneys was visible through the veil of polluted air.

"Even the smell of the river is different now. It's not like the old days," Sankichi mused, looking at the water. They strolled along the bank toward Ryōgoku. Pedestrians hurried by the little park, and many strolling couples passed Sankichi and Shota.

"Shota, what do you feel these days when you look at a woman?"

"Well . . . . I don't know."

"I feel all tense when I see one," said Sankichi.

They passed the vegetable market and walked toward the Hama-chō waterfront, where a large smokestack stood on the opposite bank. The Fukagawa district was now limited to the section beyond the reclaimed land. Shota recalled the days when he lived there and how Sakaki used to visit and rant on and on with his tall stories.

"Speaking of Sakaki," Shota said, walking to the river's edge. "His idea of pleasure and mine are entirely different. He's indiscriminate in his choice of women, and he has an insatiable desire for material possessions."

An electric train thundered by from the direction of Ryōgoku, and its roar silenced Shota for a time. Then he smiled and added, "But I'm particular. If it's not first-class, woman or anything else, it's not for me. I have no desire to take second-rate women when I go to the teahouses on business. I used to fill the customers with wine and then lie down alone in the next room and read a book. The maids used to talk about how strange I was."

The two men came to an area where the sound of the train no longer reached them. Naoki's house was nearby; in former times, Naoki's father, fishpole in hand, would walk the six blocks from his home to spend his limited leisure time under the willow trees. The rocks on which he used to sit and the trees along the bank had for the most part disappeared. Only two or three willows remained. The two stopped and looked about. The tide was coming in, and most of the boats were sailing up river.

"The fire tower of Ohashi still looks the same," observed Shota.

The light reflecting on the blue water soon tired their eyes. Sankichi could not stand it much longer and urged Shota to walk on.

After they reached Ohashi and turned back again, Sankichi noticed Shota was particularly depressed. "Do you see Mukōjima often?" he asked.

"Not at all."

"Oh?"

"She told me to come to her lodgings because it's too expensive to meet at teahouses all the time. Her employer wasn't pleased about that. Besides, visiting a geisha at her private quarters isn't very elegant. . . . The president of that company," he said, pointing to a factory building on the opposite bank, "has taken a liking to her and took her to the Hakone springs. He's even talking about buying her out of the profession. She asked me what to do. I told her not to ask me, to do whatever she wanted. But the poor girl's even gone into debt for me. She often complains, but of course we can't get married." Shota fell silent. Sankichi lowered his eyes and walked along in silence.

"Oh yes." Shota began to smile as he remembered. "Do you remember the snowy day a few days ago? The next day, I took the steamboat up to Azuma Bridge and I ran into Mukōjima with a couple of apprentice geishas. She asked what had happened to me, why I never came to see her. She said she thought I would surely come in the snow and waited all day. She held on to me and would not let go. I said I couldn't stay that day, I didn't have a sen in my wallet. She said that money wasn't the object. She called to the girls at the foot of the bridge for help. They joined forces and held me captive the whole day."

Sankichi suddenly realized that his nephew was exhausted by his worries over love. The two men walked on to the landing at Ryō-goku, where Shota boarded the boat for Umaya Bridge. Sankichi stood at the foot of the iron trestle as the white boat was drawn away from the pier by a coal-burning steamer.

He had been talking cheerfully, but after his nephew left, he suddenly felt dizzy, and a persistent oppressive pain attacked the back of his head. Fighting his fatigue, he retraced his steps to the Kanda estuary.

Boats were sailing on the flowing tide under the bridge. Others were moored near the bank. Trying to organize his thoughts, Sankichi stared for a while into the water as it moved back upstream.

"It's a lifetime no matter how I struggle," he mused. Husband was husband, wife was wife. They held no power over one another. The conclusion sent him close to despair. He heaved a long sigh and started to walk home rapidly.

His father-in-law had just begun a before-dinner cup of sake, which he savored in little sips as he sat by himself.

"Please don't bother about me," he said to Sankichi as he poured more sake for himself. "I'll feel more at home if you don't fuss."

Oyuki came in from the kitchen holding a plateful of food she had prepared. Whenever he became tipsy, Nakura habitually launched on his life history for the edification of anyone who happened to be around. He enjoyed talking with gestures about the hardships, his success in amassing wealth, the prosperity of the clan, and the long trips he had taken after his retirement. He was never concerned about his appearance and wore the simplest of clothes, but his inner dignity showed through. He was unmistakably an extraordinary man.

"Father's at it again," Mrs. Nakura said, sitting down at his side.

Sankichi asked, "How did you feel when you saw your house burn to the ground right in front of your eyes?"

"I didn't feel a thing," the old man replied, as if not to give in. "It was destined to burn down. Everything has a fate of its own from the moment it's created."

Nakura was a man who built up a large fishing concern, often sleeping on the ice. He had lost none of his former spirit in his old age, and none of his adaptability to the vicissitudes of life. The two women smiled at him affectionately. Taneo and Shinkichi sneaked up with hungry glances at the food.

"Mind your manners," Oyuki warned.

"They are both growing fast. They're both good boys," Nakura said, looking at his grandsons with eyes that began to redden from the alcohol. He quickly popped an appetizer into each child's mouth.

"Stop it!" Oyuki exclaimed, striking the floor.

The children ran away chewing on the tidbits. The maid brought in a lamp, and Nakura said he had enough to drink. At the end of each meal he habitually offered a prayer of grace.

After dinner, as Sankichi went upstairs to his work, the rain began to patter outside. He told the maid to bring up a half-full bottle of wine. It would help him forget his fatigue.

Oyuki joined him, holding Ginzō.

"This wine comes from southern Europe," Sankichi explained. "It has a nice bouquet and even women can drink it. Would you like a little?"

"Are you sure it's not strong?" said Oyuki, shifting the baby to her lap.

Beyond the shutters, the soft rain had apparently changed into sleet. Oyuki, shivering with cold, held the little glass in her right hand and the baby in the other arm. The light glowed in the wine, showing a color more beautiful than ripe grapes.

"Oh, it's so strong!" she exclaimed innocently, savoring the slightly bitter taste.

"I'm already all red on just that little bit," she exclaimed, covering her burning cheeks with her hands. Sankichi looked at her silently.

A post card from Morihiko requested that Sankichi join him at his inn to discuss something. Nakura, who had just returned from a sightseeing tour of Yokohama with his wife and Oiku—she had come from her school dormitory—was sitting by the charcoal brazier smoking a pipe. He examined the post card closely.

About three o'clock in the afternoon, Sankichi left the house. "I'm going to find out what he wants," he said to his wife.

Morihiko was waiting for him at the inn. As usual the room was orderly; a bear skin lay on the floor. The central area with its brazier served as a living room, and the area by the window as a study. Tea was ready when Sankichi entered.

Morihiko's greeting was laconic.

No matter how old they grew, they always treated each other with brotherly protocol. The older brother had become quite bald, and the younger's temples were flecked with gray, but Morihiko still looked on him as a child. He offered some cakes and said, "I asked you to come today . . . as a matter of fact about money."

His funds had been temporarily cut off. The colleague on whom he normally depended was now sick, and there was no way of raising money. Unless a solution was found, his struggle for many years would come to naught. Everyone was in difficulty at one time or another, and he needed a helping hand now. He had no intention or desire to cause any trouble to his relatives, but he absolutely had to have two hundred yen.

Sankichi was speechless.

"I know you don't have a regular income," Morihiko continued. "But can't you help me out somehow? It's only temporary. A man can accomplish so much yet be blocked by so little."

Sankichi pondered as he drank his tea. "You got into trouble by helping others," he began, "so naturally you're in trouble yourself. I've thought about us many times. Our lives have been full of troubles that no one else knows about. And what do we have to show for our efforts? The gains from our work have been swallowed up by relatives, for most part."

"There's no use talking about that now."

"Yes there is. It's good to look at the way we think and maybe change our attitudes."

"But I'm still in a bind."

"I don't mean temporary things. It's the basic philosophy I'm talking about."

Puzzled, Morihiko looked around the room. "I help my family. That's why I'm helped by others. In the game of go it's called sacrificing a stone to benefit the next move. I help my relations for the next move."

"How about changing your tactics?"

"What do you mean?"

"You might make a completely new start. How about going home? That seems a sensible move to me. What's wrong with being simple Koizumi Morihiko in the country? I think it would be fine if you retired, cultivated land in your spare time, planted fruit trees and other things, and came to Tokyo only when you had business."

Morihiko's eyes bored into Sankichi's. "So you're saying I should leave here and go home? How can I ever do that? If I gave up now. . . ."

"It would be interesting to find out."

"Don't be ridiculous. The people who have helped me until now would drop dead from the shock."

Sankichi offered to treat Morihiko to an eel dinner, and he asked his brother to order it.

"We've got to talk over this sort of business once in a while. Let's eat first and then talk some more," Sankichi suggested, relaxing on the floor. Morihiko clapped his hands for the maid.

After dinner Sankichi tried to get Morihiko to talk about his life from the beginning. Morihiko had devoted eight years to the forests of his home province. Sankichi knew something of the difference between Suyama and Akiyama,* and about the poor peasants who illegally took trees from government property. Morihiko, talkative as usual, spoke about his initial visit to Tokyo as provincial representative, about paying his expenses out of his own pocket and not receiving a sen, about negotiating with the government over the long, troublesome dispute. And the government finally decided to award an annual subsidy of ten thousand yen for the towns and villages of Kiso. He also spoke about the five formerly proscribed trees that were now being planted in many mountainous regions.

"At the time," said Morihiko, rubbing his hands over the hibachi,

* Suyama was an area for raising and training falcons for the shōgun. Akiyama was the area in which the people of Kiso were legally permitted to cut trees, except for five proscribed species.

"Mr. M was the delegate from the province. He asked me how much I had spent and told me to submit an itemized claim for reimbursement. I sent him a statement that came to thirty-three thousand yen. They never offered to pay any of it, and I didn't ask about it. The governor felt sorry for me and tried to get the government to pay, so finally they deposited six thousand yen to my bank account at home. As you know, Shota's father left my affidavit with the bank as collateral. So the bank took action and immediately seized the money. I got part of it back in the end, but I lost about fifteen hundred yen because of the Hashimoto family. The people at home are such ingrates. What did they think the money was for? Who do they think I worked for so hard and so long?" Morihiko became too emotional to continue.

"Why didn't you quit then? If you had said at the time that you had done all you could and that they should do the rest and gone home, the people at home would never have let you starve. You needed money badly because you had to see the negotiations through. You had to scheme a way of making money."

"That's pretty much the case, but I didn't do all that work for profit. How could anyone sacrifice eight years for such business if he wanted to make money? I still remember passing the entrance of the Imperial Palace late one night and making up a poem on the spot to express my feelings. I actually wept as I recited it there out loud." Tears of self-pity rolled down Morihiko's cheeks.

"I guess it's my nature," he continued, looking at his brother. "Once I start something, I've got to see it through. I don't give a damn if the people at home don't appreciate me. I think I'm beyond worrying over that. I don't expect them to understand. Maybe a hundred years from now somebody will be grateful."

"Well then, keep faith with yourself. Don't lose sight of your past. But what happens now? I'm worried for you."

"I'll make money this time. I'll go to work."

"But I think it will be difficult for you. You're not the kind of man who can work just for money."

"Yes, I can. So far, I haven't made any because I didn't try. From now on I'll make a lot. I can do it."

"I'm worried that you'll fall into the usual pattern. Somehow I feel Father is haunting us. Wherever we go, whatever we do, he's always there. Do you ever feel that?"

Morihiko stared at Sankichi in silence.

"I often wonder," Sankichi continued pensively, "if there is any difference between Tadahiro, who went through agony in prison, and us children. Otane is neurotic, you stay on and on in this inn, and I brood in my room. Wherever we go, we carry our family on our backs."

"I suppose so. . . ."

"I want to destroy that. For a long time I've been looking for a chance to talk to you about it."

"Wait a minute. I'll be fifty soon. When I'm fifty and still haven't finished what I've set out to do, I'll take your advice and retire in the country. But wait until then."

"I'm not talking about that."

"But what about the money I mentioned?"

"I'll see what I can do. I'll let you know."

"Don't be so vague. Give me your word now." Then Morihiko changed his tone. "You came here today determined to put me down, didn't you? But it was fun." He laughed loudly.

Sankichi left the inn about eight o'clock in the evening. He was immersed in thoughts about Morihiko's life as he took a streetcar home. When he entered the house, Oyuki came and took his hat and coat. "What did he want?" she asked.

"Money," he answered casually.

"Father was saying it would probably be that. He thinks you are too good to your brothers."

The warm rain, which had started about midnight, let up briefly in the morning and then turned into light snow.

In the afternoon the maid took Taneo, Shinkichi, and Ginzo to the public bath. Oyuki was the last to return, splashing through the mud under an umbrella.

Gossamer snow drifted steadily down from the luminous sky. Oyuki was not even wearing her *tabi*, and she was dressed in thin clothing. But she inhaled the crisp air with pleasure, warmed by the bath and her good circulation. The wet roofs along the street were barely white. The snow melted under her feet, and the pleasant coolness not only cleared her steam-clouded eyes but also refreshed her heated skin.

"What a long bath!" her mother scolded when she saw her.

"But I was with the children," she said as she walked to the kitchen.

Cold water from the faucet refreshed her, and she wiped the beads of perspiration from her brow. She stood before the mirror on top of the chest of drawers and inserted thin boxwood combs into her wet and disheveled hair.

Shota came in unannounced. "Aunt Oyuki, are you just back from the bath?" He passed behind her and climbed the stairs.

Sankichi welcomed him. "How did you manage to come out in this nasty weather?"

Shota, wearing a long, navy blue silk scarf around his neck, sat down before his uncle. "I have no place to go but here to forget my troubles." He looked at the snow through the glass in the sliding door. He seemed to be thinking of Kokin. "It feels like a spring snow, doesn't it?" he said.

"Shota, I went to see Morihiko, and we talked about all kinds of things from three in the afternoon until eight at night. The matter of money came up and I even said he should go back to the country."

"That was a lot of talk. I can just see the two of you."

"But we seldom understand each other. I have the feeling I didn't get through to him. I probably didn't express myself too well, so he took my advice as a suggestion for retirement in the country."

"Uncle Morihiko couldn't possibly retire. He's the kind of man who always stays at first-class inns and pays the highest prices. Even with his money troubles he still has to do that. He could never wear straw shoes and plough through the land; he can't attend to business in his leisure time."

"He looks like a simple person," Sankichi said, "but underneath he's quite an aristocrat. After all, he was born into an old family. If he sees anyone in difficulty, he can't help saying, 'Just leave it to me. I'll take care of you.' That's our ancestor in him talking."

As they talked about Morihiko, they gradually realized they were unwittingly discussing themselves. They detected in each other the typical decaying impracticality of an old family member.

"He asked me to raise two hundred yen," said Sankichi, coming back to the original subject. "If it's really going to help, I'll do anything to get it. I'll write something expressly for it, but if I'm any judge, it's not going to do much good. None of my efforts has, and I can't keep it up."

He cocked an ear as he detected Nakura coughing downstairs. "Take my father-in-law. He's a strong man and he's just watching me, thinking I'll go down any minute along with the others. He never tries to help. Well, I do whatever I can to help and just tolerate it. I've asked him to help me out with my publications, but I've never asked him for any living expenses. He doesn't offer it either and just stands by and looks on, as you can see. That's the interesting thing about him."

They heard the entrance door open and a man come in. The family downstairs began to talk.

"Oh, it's Tsutomu," said Sankichi, looking at Shota as Oyuki came up to announce her brother-in-law's visit. Sankichi nodded to Shota and went downstairs alone.

The Nakuras and Tsutomu were sitting around the charcoal brazier. Sankichi asked in a friendly tone, "Is this one of your business trips?"

"Yes, I have to come up once or twice every year," Tsutomu answered amicably. "By the way, Sankichi, I received a message from Maruna. You told him you would be needing another maid, and he's going to bring a girl along very soon now."

"Oh, thanks very much. How is Maruna? Is he looking after the store as usual?"

"He says he's very busy."

After chatting for a while, Sankichi told Oyuki to serve refreshments and went back to Shota. "It's Ofuku's husband," he said. "Merchants from the north are just like the ones from Osaka. They're all aggressive and hard working."

Shota had not yet found a job, but he was evidently not trying hard to find one. He seemed to have lost weight. They spent the snowy afternoon talking about the *yōkyoku** recital, culinary arts, and the

* Texts of Noh plays, often sung to the accompaniment of a flute and drums.

exhibition by a painter who had recently returned from Europe. Shota went home after a while.

Sankichi's thoughts returned again and again to Morihiko's difficulties; to compound the expenses, he had two daughters in school. Sankichi felt he must help and decided to raise the money without letting his in-laws know.

By the time Mrs. Nakura ended her prolonged visit and left Tokyo with Tsutomu, Sankichi had come out of his brooding. He no longer went directly to his room after each meal. He used to sit at the table with his eyes fixed and staring, and Mrs. Nakura commented on how frightening they were.

These days he sometimes came down the squeaky staircase for no special reason and sat leaning against the pillar in the living room. "Oyuki, who do you think will die first? You or me?"

"I'll live longer, I'm sure," she replied. "But then what shall I do? We haven't provided for the children yet. Even with your royalties, I don't know if I can send them all through school. I know I can't depend on it. . . . Widows have such hard times. I don't think I'd make a good teacher. I'll probably have no choice but to become a hairdresser or something like that."

Nakura let his wife precede him home while he stayed on with his daughter. His legs, in excellent condition since his youth, easily managed the walk from Sankichi's house to the Shinagawa area. He was inexhaustible. He would rise early and walk to the remotest corners of the city to see the roads under development, the new bridges, houses, water system, and other construction sites. He claimed he covered every inch of Tokyo.

"But father doesn't walk as much as he used to. I guess he is getting old," Oyuki remarked.

Finally the day came for the old man to say goodbye to his daughter and grandchildren. Sankichi and Oyuki saw him off at the station. The baby remained with the maid who had been brought to Tokyo by Maruna, but Taneo and Shinkichi went along.

"Grandpa is going home. Let's walk fast," Oyuki coaxed, but after about two blocks she had to carry Shinkichi on her back.

From time to time Nakura and Sankichi stopped in the street and waited for Taneo to catch up. A flock of birds suddenly appeared and dived almost to the ground, only to soar up again, warbling as they climbed. Then they scattered, darting to the eaves of various houses.

Sankichi stopped to watch. "It's already the season for swallows."

The family took a streetcar to Ueno Station, where they waited for the northbound train. The old man did not stand still for a minute, laughing occasionally as he talked with Sankichi.

The two boys watched the gathering travelers at Oyuki's side with great curiosity. Nakura called to them, "Be good boys now. Grandpa will come back again with presents."

Oyuki repeated his words to the children.

Nakura turned his eyes to Oyuki and muttered, "Grandpa can still make another trip," and he assumed the heavy silence of an old man.

The train time arrived, and the group hurried to the platform. Sankichi took the children close to the second-class car. "Taneo and Shinkichi, say goodbye to your grandpa," he said. Oyuki held Shinkichi up high for one last look.

Nakura's white-bearded, smiling face was framed in the window. He held on to the windowsill and looked at his daughter and grandchildren, but soon sat back in his seat and sadly hung his head. Porters scurried between the train and the people as the heavy wheels slowly began to turn.

"This just might be his last visit to Tokyo," Sankichi said to his wife after the train departed.

In May, Shota was still not working. Morihiko left for Nagoya in high spirits, with a plan for a new enterprise.

"I wonder if there's nothing Shota can do," Sankichi said to Oyuki. "It's a shame to waste time like that." To check on his nephew, he decided to visit the house in Komagata.

He walked all the way to the familiar stone wall. On Shota's house he noticed a prominent sign reading Second Floor for Rent, visible from the road. Somehow the house had a lonely air about it. Sankichi climbed the stone steps and found the old maid alone and dejected, when she answered the door.

The young couple had gone shopping, but they should be back

soon, the maid said. Sankichi chatted with her as he waited. The furniture had all been moved downstairs to make the second floor available for renting. Shota's desk was now by the window, a pot of sweet flags placed upon it. The faded blue curtains were still hanging.

The old woman offered him a cup of tea. "When I came to work for them," she told Sankichi, "I had never seen such a close and affectionate couple. But I came to know them better . . . well, I have to take Mrs. Hashimoto's side. After all, we women must stick together." She spoke quietly. She had been torn between the two. She herself had apparently suffered much in her life but was sincere in her concern about her employers, unlike ordinary servants.

"But Mr. Hashimoto is nice too," she added.

Sankichi looked outside through the glass door. A ball of peat moss wrapped in silk floss hung from the eaves—it might be Toyose's invention—and green millet shoots were growing through the floss. Sumida River was visible, and the early summer water flowed by a pier of Izu rocks.

"Uncle Sankichi's here!" Toyose exclaimed as she entered after her husband.

"Mrs. Hashimoto, someone came to look at the room," the maid reported. The couple smiled at Sankichi.

The two men sat down facing each other with the river in view. Shota explained, averting his eyes, that he thought of moving to reduce his expenses, but he had spent so much money on the house— even built a bath—that he hated to give it up. So he decided to rent the second floor.

"I walked over to see how you are," said Sankichi. "I saw a store on the way selling potted poppies. I was surprised to see them in the middle of the city. It took me back to the mountains I had forgotten all about. Remember the poppy field near the house in the country?"

"Uncle Sankichi, do you see what we've started?" Toyose said, pointing to the silk floss ball. "They're millet shoots. People stare at it from the street wondering what it is."

Shota seemed restless. He signaled to his wife to leave him alone with Sankichi. "As a matter of fact, Uncle Sankichi, I was coming to visit you. I haven't had the chance, but I've decided to go to Nagoya in a few days. Someone's invited me. I'll try my luck for a couple of years with the stockbrokers there. I'll start as a sort of apprentice."

"That's a fine idea," Sankichi said enthusiastically.

Shota hoped for success this time. He showed Sankichi the charts of market prices of the years before and after the Russo-Japanese War and the Nagoya newspapers he had sent for. "As you've advised me time and again to study the market, I'm paying a lot of attention to the daily fluctuation of Nagoya stocks. I'm not going to rush in headlong this time. My colleagues here are all watching me; they are impressed with my preparations."

"Luckily, Morihiko's there. You can consult with him."

"You're right. He is not in my field, but I can still talk to him. I think this is probably going to be Uncle Morihiko's last try. I'll see the fruit of his work there."

"He's picked a strange road for himself. Even his family doesn't know what he's up to, but he doesn't care. He's an interesting person."

"Toyose always says he'll do something big."

"He'll never give up his dreams as long as he lives, and he has many admirable qualities. For instance, he supported Oshun's family all the way. Most anyone would have given up a long time ago."

When Toyose brought in a sweet cake, a gift from an acquaintance, the two men changed the subject.

"It would be a shame not to see the view from upstairs as long as I'm here," Sankichi said, and Toyose led him. The second floor was empty; only the pictures remained on the walls. Sankichi walked out to the veranda and stood beside the railing.

"You don't look well, Toyose. Is something wrong?"

"It's nothing serious. . . . But Shota stays home most of the time, and even if he doesn't have a job, I'm thankful he eats at home these days."

They talked as they watched the pale green water of the river. "Sometimes I have such sharp pains in my chest," she said plaintively. Sankichi looked at her for a moment and then went downstairs.

Empty boxes for the toys Shota had designed were piled high in a corner of the vestibule, and a large signboard of the Hashimoto pharmacy especially ordered from home was leaning against the wall. Sankichi took leave of his nephew, assuring him he would call again soon.

"You're the only one who has anything nice to say about Shota," Oyuki had just remarked to Sankichi when Toyose's voice was heard from downstairs.

"Please excuse me, Aunt Oyuki, for coming over without being invited," she said warmly.

With Shota in Nagoya, Toyose had taken to visiting them frequently. For a long time Oyuki had remained reserved and critical with her, for she went to extremes in liking or disliking people, and she had never accepted Toyose. But after she found out about Shota's affair with Kokin, she abruptly took Toyose's side, and they had grown much closer. Toyose often came to talk about her husband, to complain of her loneliness, or to gossip about the singing instructor who had rented the rooms upstairs. Less than two months after Shota's departure, the voices of green plum venders were heard in the streets, and the humid weather added to her restlessness.

She had borrowed some novels from Oyuki and came to return them.

"Toyose, we received a letter from Shota," Sankichi said, smiling. "You wrote something disturbing to him, didn't you?"

"Did he say anything?"

"He said that he regarded himself a young man with much future, but his wife already feels like an old woman."

The two women looked at each other and smiled uneasily. Toyose explained that Shota had not sent her any money as he had promised.

Nothing in sight was dry. The roofs and houses seen from the window were wet with the imperceptible drizzle in the air. They fell silent and irritably looked up at the sky from time to time as if from under the water. Sodden birds were seen flying in the distance like the shadows of swimming fish.

"Toyose, what do you think of the woman from Mukōjima?" Sankichi asked.

She looked back at him painfully. "I have a premonition that Shota's going to desert me."

"Nonsense!"

"You don't know him, Uncle Sankichi. When we were still on the other side of the river, I made a trip home. Late one night she came and asked him to let her stay. The maid told me later—she had the audacity to sleep in my bed. And then . . . Shota promised to take her and her mother to the theater and told me to get money for it. He said he absolutely had to have it. I told him I didn't want to raise money for something like that. Then he got angry, and suddenly . . . Uncle Sankichi, he struck me and I had to pawn my clothes." Unable to continue, she wiped her tears with the sleeve of her elegant underkimono. "Tell me what a woman has to do to please a man," she said after a while, looking at Sankichi sharply, as though bent on learning what men really desired.

"I don't know the answer to a question like that," he said lamely, hanging his head.

"Don't you wonder too, Aunt Oyuki?" Toyose asked.

Sankichi replied passively, "I guess there's nothing you can do but leave him alone for a while."

"What sort of woman do you like, personally?"

"Well, let me see," Sankichi smiled. "To be honest with you, no woman is that special. I've found some interesting people in classical literature—a woman who lies alone, clad in a crisp kimono, lightly made up in mid-August, on a colorful mat spread in a cool, breezy shade. . . . Someone like that sounds interesting to me."

Toyose and Oyuki looked at each other, completely baffled.

The quarreling voices of children rose, and the two women hurried downstairs. After a while they called out that tea was ready, and Sankichi went down to the living room.

"Idiot!" Taneo suddenly shouted at his father.

Sankichi laughed. "You say that to everybody. But your kind of name-calling is harmless, I guess."

"It's become his favorite word," Oyuki said apologetically to Toyose. "It's embarrassing when we have company."

"How about a cigarette, Toyose?" Sankichi said, lighting one himself. He inhaled contentedly.

"Thank you, I will." Toyose held out her hand. "I don't particularly want it when I'm alone, but when I see someone smoking, I feel tempted."

Oyuki asked for a cigarette too and held it between the index and middle fingers of her left hand.

"I don't understand my husband," Toyose said to Sankichi. "Just before he left for Nagoya, he slept through every day. He said you told him not to worry and sleep, and that's just what he was going to do."

"He was really down for a while," Sankichi answered sympathetically. "Sometimes he was terribly depressed when he came to see me."

"He always said he could start breathing when he talked with you. Sometimes he used to say, 'Uncle Sankichi is my true love.'"

Sankichi burst out laughing. Oyuki listened, knocking the ashes from her cigarette.

"You would think he'd be more successful," Toyose said pensively.

"In a way, he's a born hedonist. You find men like him in old families. Among our relatives, no one is his equal for appreciation of painting, music, theater, and cultural things in general. But when it comes to work, his kind is often a talented amateur. He can't become a professional, not even a mediocre one."

"Do you think so?"

"First of all, he has a lot of charm. That's why women make such a fuss over him."

Toyose smiled in a bittersweet way.

A few shrubs grew in one corner of the front garden; among them only fatsia seemed to thrive. The bright green leaves sparkled gemlike in the rain and, through the pane of the sliding door, lent an aura of quiet to the room. It was the quiet of a snakepit.

Oyuki rose and took out Oshun's wedding picture. The bridegroom was clad in a formal kimono and she in one with a long train.

"I hear Oshun's husband is a very nice person," Oyuki said, looking at the picture. "I envy her very much."

"I do too." Toyose nodded.

"Why are you so envious?" Sankichi asked, looking at them.

"I like a close relationship in marriage. It's wonderful to live with a lot of laughter," Oyuki answered, her eyes on Toyose.

"Pretty soon Oshun won't be laughing all the time," Sankichi snorted, and the women giggled.

Sankichi looked around the house. The passions and furies that had stirred him and his wife had long since passed. Love and desire no longer preoccupied him. He was able to regard both himself and Oyuki with the objectivity of a connoisseur enjoying sculpture or the taste of a good wine. They had come to be quite inseparable—bound to each other.

Chapter 19

Late in August, Toyose came to see Oyuki. "Aunt Oyuki, I'm going home," she said. "Shota told me to in his letter. He says they don't seem to be getting along at home. I wonder what's happened. Before Kosaku married, he was the apple of Mother's eye. I'm so discouraged because I just keep moving from place to place and never can settle down. Uncle Sankichi, could you come and talk to my mother-in-law? It would be so helpful."

Then she talked about her husband. "I wrote to him about the beautiful moon over the river and asked him how he was enjoying the moon there. He answered that he was looking at it over the clotheslines on the roof top. Nagoya must be hot too."

She said that the house was left in the maid's care and that she planned to stop in Nagoya on her way to the country; she left Sankichi's house in a hurry.

Sankichi decided to order a gravestone for his parents, who had been laid to rest in the mountain village. He wrote to Kosaku asking him to inquire about a tombstone. The reply included figures for the sizes and costs of several choices. In late September a post card came from Toyose, written with her thin-pointed brush.

> Dear Uncle and Aunt,
> Hope you have been well. I've been home a month now. The Situation here is not good and I worry about our house in Tokyo. I'm very anxious to return to Tokyo as soon as possible.

At the end of autumn, Kosaku sent word that the stonemason finished the carving, and Sankichi prepared at once for the trip. Concerned about his sister, he made arrangements to travel by way of the north so that he could visit the Hashimotos en route. Then he could stop in Nagoya on the return trip and surprise Morihiko and

Shota. Oyuki busied herself with helping her husband pack. They talked about Otane, Kosaku and his bride, and Toyose as they worked in the cluttered room.

"Otane worried about her husband and her son, and now about her adopted son. You would think she's had enough," Sankichi sighed and Oyuki thought of all the trouble in her sister-in-law's life.

Sankichi went to Iidamachi Station because the Chūō Line was under repair. To reach Otane's home, he had to stay overnight en route, then go by foot over a mountain pass, and on the far side of the mountain catch a horse-drawn carriage.

This was his first visit to the Hashimotos in twelve years, and in to his home village in fourteen years.

It was near evening when the carriage approached Otane's town. Electric lights twinkled through the deep foliage, and Sankichi counted them as the carriage rolled on.

They came to a stop at the town limits and the horn sounded by the coachman echoed through the mountain air. Some Hashimoto servants hurried down the entrance steps. Kosaku came out too. Accompanied by them, Sankichi climbed the familiar stone steps that zigzagged as they approached the top. The old gate with the pharmacy signboard was exactly as he remembered it. As he entered the house, the hearth fire under the high ceiling caught his eyes first. There he was introduced to Kosaku's bride, Oshima, and the maid. Osen came from the rear apartment to greet him.

"Where is my sister?" he asked.

Kosaku answered with his characteristic directness, "She went to town on an errand. Toyose went with her. I have sent an office boy to get them. They'll be back soon," He no longer called Toyose "Mrs. Hashimoto."

"You have no idea how eagerly Mother's been waiting for you." Oshima said hospitably. She had married into the family on Morihiko's recommendation; she spoke the standard language of city women.

"They'll be here any minute," Osen looked at her uncle.

Dinner was served to the guest who arrived at such a late hour, and he talked about his trip while eating. Otane and Toyose returned before he finished his dinner. Otane blew out the candle of her lantern and sat down heavily, facing Sankichi. She could not speak.

"It was so good of you to come," Toyose said in greeting to Sankichi, then turned to Osen. "Why don't you get some hot water for mother. She didn't expect Uncle Sankichi tonight, and she's too happy to speak."

Otane was pale, and after drinking a mouthful of hot water offered by Osen, she put her hands in her lap and lowered her head. After a few minutes she barely managed to speak. "Sankichi, I can't say anything. This is my greeting." Once again she was the mistress of the Hashimoto home, sitting in front of the central pillar.

When Sankichi woke up, he saw the white-shaded electric light recently installed in the back parlor. This had been Tatsuo's room, and the large alcove with the shiny black pillar had not changed. His desk still stood in front of the bright paper sliding door opening onto the garden, and the same yellow-patterned woolen tablecloth, though now quite faded, still covered it.

The aging Otane got up before her brother, who had trouble sleeping during the trip, and by the time he came out to the garden, she was diligently sweeping among the moss-covered rocks.

"So now you have electric lights here," Sankichi remarked.

"That's the least of the changes. Just come and see." She smiled sadly as she led him through the garden toward the kitchen entrance. At the top of the stone steps that once led to the storage buildings, Sankichi stood looking into a quarry below.

The sharply excavated fresh red clay slope and the half-finished railroad crossing the center of the garden lay before his eyes. The *miso* storage and the white-walled godowns with their loft windows, under which he read Tatsuo's diary, had vanished. The pear garden, the grape arbor, the large stone well where the maid Oharu had so often come to draw water—everything had been swept away. Otane pointed with a broom at the devastated ruins of the garden. Only a small log house still stood at the top of the opposite slope. A crew of workers arrived for work under the cliff, carrying rail tongs on their shoulders.

Otane was bewildered as she walked back to her room. She looked as if she had seen some dreadful scene. Kosaku came from the front to tell Sankichi that the gravestone he ordered was quite impressive and that it had already been sent to Sankichi's home village. While he talked, Otane maintained a strange reserve.

As usual, the entire family gathered around the hearth for breakfast. Everything was the same as when Tatsuo was the head: the master to the youngest servant all sat in front of the shiny cupboard in the room with the high ceiling. The maid served soup by the hearth, and everyone followed the ritual of cleaning his own bowl and chopsticks with his napkin at the end of the meal. But the relationship of the family and clerks was no longer one of master to servants. Each now worked for a salary.

"Thank you for the breakfast," Ichitaro, the son of the former manager, Kasuke, said mechanically as he left the table. He had worked there as long as Kosaku and was now head clerk. Kosaku glanced at the gruff man as though to say, "Do whatever you're supposed to do and be happy about it."

There was no laughter, and Otane sighed, displeased with everything she saw or heard. She did not take up her chopsticks but stayed at the table to keep Sankichi company. Toyose and Osen ate quietly, looking from face to face as they drank their tea.

"Mother, won't you please eat a little?" Oshima asked timidly.

"I just had some milk. I'll eat later," she replied abruptly and disappeared into the back parlor.

Sankichi remained by the fireside, questioning Kosaku about the fastidious old Sawada. He learned that this friend of Tadahiro died some time earlier.

Suddenly Sankichi's ear caught the faint sobbing of Oshima behind the medicine signboard. He rose and walked from the hearth through the small room, where Osen was standing absent-mindedly, to Otane's room.

In the center of the room was a large lacquer table Shota had made when he was young. Otane sat in Tatsuo's seat in front of it, behind her the old picture scroll that had been handed down for generations. She looked very much the mistress of the house in Tatsuo's absence. Toyose took out a tea set and brought it to the table.

Sankichi looked around the room, the adjacent one, and the storage chamber. Much of the furniture had disappeared since the bankruptcy, and the spacious house appeared even more roomy.

"But you have more furniture left than I expected," he said.

"Thanks to everyone's help, yes," Otane answered. "When I came back from your house, it was like after a typhoon." She shuddered.

"I hear Tatsuo went to Manchuria."

"So they say."

"Do you now feel you've been deserted?"

"I didn't think so while he was in Kobe. I felt he just might come back. But when I heard he finally went to Manchuria, I thought it was the end."

"You can do nothing about it. You'd better give him up."

"It's easy for you to say, but I'll never be able to." She smiled helplessly.

A thunderous roar rose from beneath the garden at the foot of the cliff. It was the railed truck transporting gigantic boulders. Otane listened until the noise faded; it seemed to sink into her brain. She then began to talk about Shota in Nagoya, shaking her head again and again and repeating how she hoped he would do well this time.

Tea was ready, and Osen, who had been folding medicine envelopes in the next room, joined her mother, while Toyose went off to fetch Kosaku and Oshima. When the couple came in, Otane suddenly became rigid. Kosaku related the story of a man who had been discovered copying one of the Hashimotos' patent medicines and had come to apologize. He brought out a box of cakes the man had presented.

"Let's all have the forger's cakes," Kosaku chuckled as he offered them around and helped himself.

Otane looked sharply at her younger daughter-in-law. "You have a sweet tooth, Oshima. You'd better eat a lot."

"Thank you, I have enough," she said amiably, sitting down next to Kosaku.

"Look at her gobbling them up happily!" snapped Otane with a forced smile.

The young couple did not stay long, and when they left, Sankichi said to his sister: "I wonder why your face has grown so scary."

"What do you mean? Do I really look so terrible?" Otane stroked her forehead as if to soften the lines by smoothing the deep furrows. "Even a woman's face stiffens when she gets old. I'm trying to keep my mind at peace, and I stroke my forehead every day."

"But your tone's so sarcastic. You've turned bitter because you've suffered, but you shouldn't pick on young people. They can't take it."

"Do I sound all that sarcastic?"

"You're asking me? 'Look at her gobbling them up happily!' What sort of bride can go on eating after hearing a remark like that?"

Toyose and Osen giggled while Otane smiled mirthlessly.

"Sankichi, don't be so hard on me. Just look at me, at what I'm like these days," said Otane, opening the front of her kimono. She was nothing but skin and bones, and her withered breasts hung lifelessly. Sankichi saw there the sum total of Otane's past.

"Isn't this something!" she cried, looking down at herself, and then hurriedly covered her chest.

She rose to fetch a letter from Minoru on the writing desk to show it to Sankichi. She yawned rudely, so loudly that the sound probably carried throughout the house.

Kosaku, the young, progressive-minded businessman now managed the store and worked on the ledger in place of the elegant, generous, aristocratic old master. He learned a hard lesson from Tatsuo's failures and was trying to improve all procedures. Living expenses were cut; so was the working staff. Quite indifferent to whether or not there was merriment in the workshop or around the hearth, he was preoccupied only with the volume of medicine sales. When the old master had the store, he had many more workers and did not sell half as much as they now did. What were they doing then? All the women, from mother on down, were kept busy just preparing food. The many rooms with their remembrances dear to Otane were white elephants to him.

Kosaku had a practical mind, and Oshima had not been exposed to the atmosphere of an old family before her marriage. The young couple came from an environment entirely different from that of Otane and Tatsuo, and they did not know how to console her.

Sankichi went to the front, where the young coupld lived. In that very room he had spent a summer with Naoki. The garden had not changed, and from here he could hear clearly the sound of the Kiso River in the valley below. A framed watercolor sent by Shota hung on the wall. Even Kosaku had an appreciation of art.

Kosaku sent for Toyose, and she came out of the dark parlor looking somewhat bewildered. He prefaced his statement by saying that he would have no other chance if he did not speak now. He told how he prayed for Shota's success, and how he had been sending whatever he could to help Shota in his new work. He described the depth of Otane's disappointment since her return from Tokyo.

"If my brother succeeds, I'll have nothing to say. I'm doing everything I can to help him. It'll solve many problems if he's successful," he said emphatically.

Now that the situation was made clear by the old woman and the young couple, Sankichi found it impossible to rest. And that night once again, he was forced to listen to Otane's grievances. She did not let him go to sleep, and the later the hour, the sharper her awareness became.

"Otane, why don't you leave everything to the young people?" Sankichi said.

"Of course. I don't intend to criticize. I'm leaving everything to them." Sometimes her tone revealed her distress. The new life Kosaku and his wife were building, and the ruthlessly encroaching railroad served to irritate her raw nerves all the more. She was unable to sit and observe the destruction. Bracing her shoulders as if preparing to meet an enemy, she stared in the direction of the front rooms.

"They act as though our way of doing things was all wrong. They say we squandered so much money. . . . They only blame me. You think I'll give in to those youngsters? Just let them try!"

A brisk fire was burning in the hearth. It was the third day of Sankichi's visit, and he was to leave on the next. Toyose, Oshima, and Osen were by the hearth, roasting a Kiso specialty, rice cakes made with walnuts and soy sauce. Otane came to join her brother, leaving the kitchen to the young people.

Sankichi was pacing the back parlor garden, the same place where the family photograph was taken twelve years before. He walked to where Tatsuo had stood in front of the azalea, spotting where Shota had sat and where Kasuke had worried about his bald pate. He stood between the same two boulders against which he had then leaned. He proceeded to climb on top of one.

At times, Otane thought Sankichi a child. "Sankichi, you are acting just like Shota," she said as she made her way down to the garden from the back parlor. She showed Sankichi the various plants and flowers she was growing. The lilies she had brought from Sankichi's mountain home now bore coral-like red berries. Caring for her flowers, dreaming of former days, she was still waiting for her husband.

Osen stood on the veranda of the room next to the back parlor. Her oval face with its broad forehead and prominent eyebrows looked like her father's. She glanced vaguely at the garden and walked away toward the kitchen.

The red sun, reminiscent of autumn leaves along the Kiso pike, shone on the wooden roofs weighted down by large stones. Otane seemed to be dreaming of her home village.

"If you're going to visit the cemetery, I'd very much like to go with you, but I guess I'd better stay home this time," she said half to herself, then she invited her brother to the fireside.

In the afternoon, Oyuki's letter arrived. Sankichi read it with Otane as they stood near the veranda. Otane asked Kosaku to bring out the old ceramics for Sankichi. The ancient teacups, which had been made specially for customers of the apothecary, and Tatsuo's old rice bowl with an elegant classic pattern had all been carefully stored away.

"Would you like to see something we found?" Toyose asked, bringing out a dusy paulownia box. In it were letters written by an ancestor to his children on his deathbed, some sketches of armor and harness apparently done by Tatsuo's father, documents of mobilization plans, and other old papers.

Sankichi found a "Black ship" picture, which he examined with keen interest. The woodblock print the size of copy paper featured the vessel that frightened people in the midnineteenth century.

"It looks just like a ghost!" Sankichi said looking at the "Dutch Ship." "This is what drove Father insane," he said to his sister. Otane glanced at him with a strange glare in her eyes.

"I'd like to have this. May I?" He slipped the picture into his bag along with Oyuki's letter.

Her uncle's departure provided Toyose with an otherwise impossible pretext to leave her mother-in-law.

"Please, Uncle Sankichi, please take me with you. I'll start packing right away." She entreated him and began to gather her things.

Sankichi was a little annoyed. "To be honest, I want to travel alone. Besides. I don't want to be responsible for somebody else's wife."

"You'd better not if you have any doubts," Otane said.

"But I am going," Toyose insisted from the adjacent room.

"Then I'll take you to the train," agreed Sankichi.

Otane seemed not able to sleep now that their departure was imminent. She retired to the back parlor with Sankichi, and the two sat up talking until late. Worried about Otane, Sankichi got up again after lying down once and took out cigarettes to keep her company. They talked about Osen. Sankichi commended Otane for having accomplished the difficult task of bringing her up. It was a good idea, he said, to teach her how to fold medicine envelopes; that obviously developed her natural aptitude for quiet handiwork.

"I've survived mainly for her," Otane said, pulling the tobacco set over beside her.

Toyose and Osen were sleeping quietly in the next room. To calm her, Sankichi changed the subject to the Hashimoto family and remarked how hard Kosaku was working. Shota was her own flesh and blood, but Kosaku was not. She must not try to find fault with her adopted son and his wife, and as far as faults were concerned, Shota had many. Did she ever think of the true cause of Tatsuo's running away?

"Sankichi, do you think . . . I did something wrong? Do you mean that's why the family's gone down? What . . ." Suddenly she sat erect, as though Sankichi had touched her raw nerves. She was visibly trembling and her reproachful eyes tried to say that she was blameless, that she had been faithful, the most important of feminine virtues. She looked at him as if saying that even her own brother had turned into an enemy.

"Stop it! You mustn't get upset like that before you've heard what

I have to say. Why do you get so worked up? Look at things more calmly," he cajoled, half rising. Otane, so agitated that she was incapable of talking coherently, immediately changed the subject.

"But isn't it true that Tatsuo was on the verge of going to prison?" Sankichi insisted.

"Yes, that's true. And because we didn't want him to go . . ."

"Everyone worked so hard to pull the Hashimotos through. Just think how hard Shota's working. This is no time for you to be complaining."

"I understand. I was petty about the young couple."

"It's not a matter of being petty."

"I understand. I understand!"

She grew more confused, and finally neither knew what it was all about.

"What do you really want, Otane?"

"I want to go to Shota. I don't care how difficult it is; I want to live with my children."

The conversation ended with neither one satisfied. And Otane did not fall asleep until dawn.

When the sky started to lighten, Toyose left her bed and began gathering her baggage. Otane lit a candle and went to Toyose's room. Osen was still asleep.

"Toyose, are you really leaving?"

"Yes. You two were talking until late last night."

"I hardly slept at all."

"I heard your voices, but fell asleep soon."

"I'm so unhappy." Otane sobbed, sitting by her daughter's pillow.

When Otane sat down to have morning tea with Sankichi, however, she was a different person from the night before.

"You took the trouble of coming all the way from Tokyo," she said cheerfully. "I'm sorry I exposed to you such unpleasant business."

"We talked for three whole nights, didn't we?"

"It certainly was a lot of jabber, jabber, jabber!" They laughed together.

Toyose was ready, and it was soon time for their departure. Otane, Osen, Kosaku, his wife, and the clerks gathered around the hearth to drink a parting cup of tea.

Oshima and Osen went as far as the edge of town to see the travelers off.

Toyose was not used to traveling on foot, but they were obliged to walk because the old Kiso Road was torn up. Sometimes the noise of rocks being dynamited could be heard, and huge boulders rolled crashing down the high cliff into the valley colored by autumn.

"This is hardly the road for a woman alone, is it?" Toyose said as she followed along.

Occasionally a group of ten or twenty workers blocked the road, leaning on their picks as they rested from carrying rocks and earth; Toyose's elegant clothes drew their attention. A large forest stretched before them, the Kiso River was visible through the trees, and inviting teahouses stood along the way. Sankichi stopped at one to give Toyose a rest. A middle-aged woman brought out tea.

"Where are you from, madam?" she asked. Toyose was not shy, but she did not answer the question; instead she pointed to Sankichi and said, "This is my uncle." Her smile made the woman think that she was only joking. The two left the teahouse laughing.

They arrived at a recently opened station toward evening. Checking the train schedule, Toyose said she wanted to stay for the night and then take the first train to Nagoya in the morning. Sankichi felt relieved when he saw her off the next morning.

By the time he reached Morihiko's home village, he was thoroughly soaked by the autumn rain. There, he had to veer away from the Kiso River and climb a wooded slope. The hamlet, situated next to Sankichi's home village, was the seat of Morihiko's foster parent's home. The family name was also Koizumi. The foster father was long since dead; but Morihiko's foster mother and his wife and children all sat around Sankichi and chatted about Morihiko in Nagoya and about Onobu and Okinu, his daughters at school in Tokyo. The old turnpike ran right in front of their typically Kiso-style house. Morihiko's wife was devoted to him and seemed to miss her husband very much.

Sankichi left his brother's village and climbed the hilly road in the mountain near the end of the Kiso Valley. He trudged on for some five miles, and at the top of the mountain pass he came on a man from his village dressed in peasant clothes. As they walked on, Sankichi saw once again the rolling mountains he had known as a child.

"Master Sankichi, let me carry your coat," his companion said with the same deference he used in their childhood; though he was already carrying Sankichi's luggage on his shoulder, he took the coat, ignoring Sankichi's decline.

"I would feel better if you didn't bother about me. I've just come to visit the family graves," he said as they continued along the sunny mountain road. He wanted to revisit the scenes of his childhood before his old friends found out about his arrival. After a while his companion said goodbye and went off toward a temple.

Sankichi, a lonely traveler dressed in Western clothes and straw shoes, entered the village. There was a terrible fire some years back and very little remained of the old post station. He stood on top of the mountain on whose other flank ran the Mino Road. On either side of the sloping road among the trees next to surviving houses stood several new houses. Some sites were made into vegetable fields.

A girl of eleven or twelve was playing on a stone hedge. She wore a little sleeveless "monkey *haori*" coat, and she looked inquisitively at Sankichi, who was searching about, trying to find a familiar place.

"Family by the name of Koizumi used to live around here," he said to her. "Do you know where they lived?" The little girl made a strange face, then pointed to a mulberry field directly before him.

His companion reappeared, and the two crossed the village and continued along a narrow path between fields and then up a low hill. At the top was the old temple built by Sankichi's ancestor. He entered alone the cemetery situated midway up the slope. Passing a tombstone engraved with his forebear's posthumous name, the same as that of the temple, he walked to the far end of the cemetery. In this quiet, scenic spot, his parents had been laid to rest. The new tombstone stood in front of a mound.

He was filled with memories of his childhood as he looked out over the village houses, now more visible since the trees had been thinned out. Most of the houses that had belonged to the gentry were destroyed by the fire. Many new ones had been built, but they were all in that part of the village where the poorer inhabitants used to live.

Sankichi was soon surrounded by old family friends and acquaintances. The following day, in the large hall of the temple, he found himself the center of a considerable crowd. Distant relatives who came to visit the grave, peasants who had worked for the family, and others who had not forgotten the glories of the Koizumis assembled to see him.

On the third day Sankichi moved to the house of a former neighbor, a family of important vintners; the original site of the Koizumi house had become part of their holdings. The second-floor guest room was located on the same side as the Koizumi guest room, and its window overlooked the extensive Mino Plain. The present head of the family showed Sankichi to his room. The mulberry field lay beyond the stone wall surrounding the house, and Sankichi could make out some traces of his old home: his father's study, the center room in which his mother and Okura frequently did their sewing, Minoru's den, the elevated room reserved for nobility, the meeting room, and the quarters separate from the main building.

The host was gentle and had the looks of a man of means. He also seemed to be reminiscing; he stood with Sankichi on the veranda, pointing out the location of the well, the storage buildings, and other sites. The area around the log cabin that had served as Tadahiro's quarters was just as Sankichi remembered it. And his host told him that the two-story building where Sankichi's grandmother lived after her retirement now housed his own mother.

"I have something for you," said the man. He clapped his hands to summon wine and then brought out three stone seals that once belonged to Sankichi's father. They had been unearthed while the mulberry fields were being tilled.

He remarked that an old mirror had also been found, and that the peonies in front of Tadahiro's study survived the fire and to this day large white flowers bloomed.

Old school friends and other villagers came to the sunny second-floor room, to pay their respects. The landed gentry of the area, who once called him by his nickname, now addressed him formally. Most of the visitors had been Tadahiro's pupils at one time or another. Some of them spoke of the old days in high-pitched, tipsy voices. "When the master was alive, they said the family fortune was pretty much gone, but even then there were sixty or seventy bags of rice in storage. Your oldest brother squandered them all."

Sankichi slipped out to the veranda. Though the house had long since been destroyed, the panorama of the mountains remained unchanged. Below the rise he could see the wooden roofs weighted down with rocks. It was now late autumn; a few colorful persimmon leaves still clung to the boughs, and the mulberry field had already been blighted by frost.

A fall shower was quietly gathering in the sky.

Sankichi took the sorely neglected turnpike from his native village toward the Mino Plain. Several villagers saw him off, a few walking the entire five miles to the small town where he boarded the train for Nagoya.

There, Shota was staying at a young stockbroker's house. Sankichi walked along the streets lined with quiet, clean, lattice-windowed houses until he reached Shota's address.

"Who is it?" said a voice, and the brown curtains at the entrance were drawn back, and a woman's face appeared. She was about fifty.

"I am Koizumi, Mr. Hashimoto's uncle."

He was ushered to a quiet room at the rear of the house. Shota and Toyose were out, and Sankichi learned from the woman that Shota had already lost money in the stock market. Her young adopted son speculating with Shota also lost a large sum.

Shota and Toyose returned about four o'clock. The room he rented was at the second floor front.

"Toyose, why don't you get Uncle Sankichi something to eat." Shota sent her out and led Sankichi to his room through the corridor. They passed by a room where the elderly mother of the landlady was sitting and came to a staircase adjacent to a high wall.

The second floor was dark. Sankichi and Shota sat down at the window and looked at each other. Sankichi sensed his depression; before Shota opened his mouth, he began to talk about his trip. "I have a lot to tell you."

Toyose came into the room. "Uncle Sankichi, thank you very much for everything," she said. "I feel that I've acquired another mother since I came here." She told Sankichi that the landlady was very capable and knew a great deal about stocks, and she was concerned about her adopted son's fiasco. After a while Shota signaled with his eyes that Toyose was to leave them.

"Uncle Sankichi, at last I've been baptized," he said, hanging his head. Sankichi was mystified.

Shota continued gravely, "We took a trip to Atsuta, and on the way back I got the signal. I coughed up blood twice."

Then his voice resumed its usual tone. "I'm going to work hard from now on. The doctor told me that I brought on my sickness myself, from mental fatigue, and that I had nothing to worry about right now. It isn't fatal for the next three or four years, and he assured me I could live for ten years under his care. I asked him if I could work, and he said yes. So, I've made up my mind. People accomplish a lot even after they get tuberculosis, and I'm determined to do just that."

"How do you feel now?" asked Sankichi lightly, not wanting to treat Shota as an invalid.

"I feel very serious."

"That's interesting. Well, Shota, forget about everything in the past. Forget about the responsibility you've inherited. Do what you can for yourself. That's enough."

"Yes, I mean to. Even the bank people at home say 'Why doesn't your father forget the past and come home?' "

"When I stopped over at your home, we did a lot of talking. I hardly slept for three nights. I was quite frank with your mother, and we even talked about prison. I didn't mention it to her, but when Tatsuo left, why didn't he say that he would take the blame for what he had done and go to prison? Why didn't he say, 'But leave my wife and children'? The suffering he had to go through leaving his home —that was all for nothing because he made others suffer."

"That's right. If he had said he would assume responsibility, they wouldn't have sent him to prison anyway. But he thought differently. The only thing he had in mind was to escape going to jail. That's all. When I heard about it, I thought we were through."

They talked about Tatsuo in that manner, yet they felt a sense of awe at the thought of him. The respect due the head of an old family was still strong in them, though they knew that he was completely in the wrong.

Toyose brought out tray-tables. Shota coughed weakly as he ate, while Sankichi told him sympathetically about Otane's sad life. "I really scolded your mother this time. She got angry and bawled me out."

"Of course! At home mother was sacred and not to be criticized. Of all Koizumi Tadahiro's children, she resembles him most."

Shota seemed to long for his mother, Kosaku and his wife, and even the father who had deserted them.

"Let's visit Uncle Morihiko," Shota suggested the next day. "I haven't told anyone about being sick, not him either. And certainly not a word to mother. You're the only one I've told besides Toyose. She knows because . . . well, because she'll have to take care of me." He occasionally spoke with a cheerfulness incongruous in someone stricken with tuberculosis. Sankichi was relieved to see his nephew so sprightly, and he decided to go to see Morihiko.

"He's putting up a good fight too," Shota said as they went down the steps.

Returning home in the afternoon, Shota told Sankichi about Nagoya women and the music and architecture of the city. When they entered the house, they heard the adopted son reciting a sutra in the quiet room. They went up to Shota's room. Toyose, concerned about her own future, joined them.

"Toyose, what are you going to do?" Sankichi asked. "Will you stay here?"

"I don't know. I hate to leave him alone, but he doesn't want to give up the place in Tokyo either."

"You are nothing when you are a weak man." Shota sighed sarcastically as he looked at his wife. "She sounds so hostile these days, but I guess I can't blame her, I can't even support a wife at my age."

Toyose could find no word of answer.

"We should ask Morihiko for advice," Sankichi said, and changed his tone. "That old maid in Tokyo's very serious about looking after the house. I drop in occasionally, and she tells me she's got to keep the plants alive because the 'master' left them in her care. She's very devoted."

Shota laughed. "Uncle Sankichi, remember when I went to Gifu last summer? I sent you a post card about cormorant fishing. I still have your answer."

"What did I say?"

" 'Remember when I told you that I went down the Nagara River fifteen, seventeen miles in the midst of all the heat . . . with the fragrance of the summer grass?' "

"Oh yes, you said something to the effect that it was like traveling the Kiso Road. I could imagine how hot it was."

Shota heaved a deep sigh.

Sankichi decided to take the night train to Tokyo. Shota went to see his uncle off; they caught the streetcar to Nagoya Station, where they arrived too early for the train. Shota paced the well-lit station for a while and then suddenly said, "Aunt Oyuki, and Toyose too, are in the prime of life." His tone revealed the measure of pressure he felt from everything healthy.

Sankichi boarded the car bound for Tokyo. Shota stood at the window, holding his platform ticket. He seemed to feel the sharp edges of everything around him. The conductor dashed back and forth blowing his whistle. Shota, hunched over, stared intently at his uncle, who stood alone at the window. Sankichi, drenched in perspiration, looked like a wet bird.

"Remember me to Aunt Oyuki," Shota called as the train began to pull out.

The lights of the station and the dusky faces of people reflected fleetingly in the windowpane. Sankichi thought about Shota trudging back to his lodgings. When he suggested to Shota on the way home from Morihiko's inn that he go back to the country to recuperate, Shota shook his head, determined to carry on. He thought of the family, who knew nothing of Shota's failure, much less of his sickness. They had placed all their hope in him.

"What an unlucky man," he murmured. He stood at the window for a long time.

Chapter 20

I t was spring. Toyose and the old maid had lived alone in the house
by the river for more than four months, talking about Shota in
Nagoya. Toyose returned to Tokyo at the end of November and
spent a lonely New Year with the maid. It snowed often outside the
glass sliding doors facing the river. Each time, the Izu stones at the
pier and the house tops across the street turned all white. The singing
instructor upstairs lived with a man she called her younger brother.
There were rumors that they were moving, or rather that the owner
of the house was going to force them out. But while they were occupied with all these annoying matters, the season for the grass to
sprout around the house came again.

Soon Toyose was forced to give up the house. She was constantly
hounded by maids from teahouses and by owners of private hotels
in the gay quarters coming to collect the debts Shota had left unpaid.
She was weary of fending off the demands with excuses. And to top
off all her other problems, money almost completely stopped coming
from Nagoya. The rent had not been paid for several months, and
she had not given the maid her salary for quite some time. As she
paced the rooms, she decided to sell the furniture and close up the
house for good. But she was reluctant to strip the house down to
nothing, for she had doubts about being able to furnish another such
home.

The maid crouched by the sink and moved her hands slowly. Toyose stood on the wooden floor looking at her, thinking she would
give her all the small kitchen utensils.

"It wasn't easy to furnish and decorate the house like this," she
mumbled, as if to herself.

"Mrs. Hashimoto, I hope you will soon get together with your
husband," the maid said standing up and stretching herself, continu-
ously rubbing her rheumatic hands. "I didn't come to work for you

expecting something from you. I'm very worried that you are still living alone. We've had enough of waiting for Mr. Hashimoto."

Toyose went to look at the sky above the water. As usual, the steamboats and barges were plying up and down the Sumida River. Shota had trained a honeysuckle and some roses to grow up the stone wall just beyond the glass door, and he used to enjoy looking at them. She thought of selling the glass doors along with all the other furnishings.

The long-neglected bushes and plants were now budding. The sight took Toyose back to a spring some years ago. She recalled as if in a dream how after going to bed every night, her mother-in-law used to tell her the ways to attract a man, and to hold him. Toyose had listened so naively. Over the last few years, she always dressed in the latest fashions, determined to live up to being the wife of a stockbroker. She did everything one could to satisfy her husband's desires. She obeyed his every whim, trying to capture his love. She was not sure whether his lung ailment resulted from his overworked mind as he claimed, or if it was the inevitable dividend of his dissipated living.

At the end of February, Shota made a trip to Tokyo. He was very pale and seemed to be pushing himself solely on nervous energy. The maid whispered to Toyose that he said he was going to live ten more years, but to her he could have no more than two or three. He was drenched with icy perspiration every night of his brief stay, as though his vital essence ebbed out through his pores. When Toyose gave him a sponge bath, he called her "nurse" and asked her to rub his feet. This memory came to her as she stood by the glass door, and grief overpowered her; she remembered that she herself was in the prime of life.

"I'm going to Uncle Sankichi's. Watch the house for a while," she called to the maid, who came from the kitchen to see her off. The old woman's surprised eyes seemed to say, "Good heavens, Mrs. Hashimoto, your clothes are stylish all right, but you look like a kept woman!" She knelt at the entrance steps and looked at Toyose disapprovingly. The old-fashioned woman seemed to feel responsible for the whole household during her master's absence.

Toyose brooded as she walked down the steps. Sometimes the

years of her married life seemed to her a complete waste. She had none of the patience of Otane, who considered absolute subservience essential in a woman. Should she set out for Nagoya, or should she leave once and for all and go back to her old home? She was still vacillating when she reached the gate of her uncle's house.

Sankichi and Oyuki just sent off Oyuki's second younger sister, who had come to Tokyo on a brief visit with her husband. Toyose entered the guest room.

"Toyose, you knew Oai, didn't you?" said Sankichi in greeting. "She was a beautiful bride. She came to call on us." He seated her at the brazier, and he and Oyuki continued to talk about the newly-weds.

Toyose looked at her uncle and aunt as she listened to their stories. She decided not to mention what had been on her mind and said only that she was about to give up the house. She asked if Oyuki wanted any of her furniture, since it would be sold to some second-hand dealer anyway. "It's really a shame. But there's nothing I can do."

"Does Otane know about Shota's illness?" asked Sankichi.

"I don't know," Toyose answered pensively. "He doesn't say anything about that in his letters. She probably knows now. Kosaku went to see him in Nagoya. Even Uncle Morihiko just found out about it."

"I told him myself," said Sankichi.

Toyose looked at him sadly. "My mother-in-law tells me to go to Nagoya as soon as possible. But mother tells me to come home. Every mother thinks of her own child first, but my mother probably feels sorry for me."

"We all feel sorry for Shota and for you, too," Sankichi said.

Toyose seemed to pity herself. "I'll go and take care of him. All these years I've stayed with him only for his sake."

"Toyose, how long have you been married?" Sankichi asked, tapping the ash off his cigarette.

"Exactly eleven years."

"Then you were married a year after we were."

"As I remember," said Oyuki, "the head clerk of the Hashimotos came with his medicine and told us about the new bride."

"And you wrote me a kind letter, Aunt Oyuki. I was really happy for only about a year. Then troubles started. Mother got sick and was always in and out of bed. Then my father-in-law ran away."

A faint sigh escaped Oyuki's lips.

"Anyway, Shota and I have enjoyed a long friendship," Sankichi said, taking over the conversation. "When I was about eight, I was sent to study in Tokyo, and we attended the same elementary school, but of course in different grades. In those days Turkish fezzes were very popular, and Shota wore one with a tassle. We were close even then."

"Yes, old, old friends," replied Toyose. "When you were in Sendai, you wrote Shota. The letter turned up last year. I gather he always worried everyone."

"Did I write a worried letter?"

"It seems he asked you for your advice about his future. So many people went out of their way to help him that you'd think he ought to be able to accomplish something worthwhile."

Then Toyose told about the time her father-in-law absconded, about the telegram that came from her home, about how when she visited her family they tried to stop her from going back and how she fled to rejoin Shota like a girl running away to meet her lover.

Toyose had a great need to pour her heart out to someone and told them about the prediction of a fortuneteller who once said, "You are a sweet woman, but you have one flaw in your character: a touch of masculinity. You must watch out for that."

"As Uncle Sankichi says, it probably means I have some of my father in me." Toyose managed a wan smile.

The two older children were at the playful age, and they kept running in and out. The third, still a toddler, tottered between his mother and the maid.

"Oh, who's the little baby still looking for Mommy's milk?" Toyose teased, and the boy pulled back his hand that had made its way to his mother's breast.

"All gone!" Oyuki said adjusting the collar of her kimono.

"Aunt Oyuki, you're expecting again, aren't you? The maid and I have been saying you might be."

Oyuki blushed a little and smiled.

"Oyuki, is there any of Toyose's furniture you might like?" Sankichi called.

"Well, let me see . . . maybe your cutting board for fabrics and the fulling boards," she answered hesitantly, feeling sorry for Toyose.

"Those fulling boards are cedar and we had them made specially when we were still on the other side of the river. We thought we'd live in Tokyo for a long time. Anyway, I'll show them to the auctioneer and see how much they could bring, and then let you know." Her voice quavered a little. No one had much to say.

Just before Toyose left for home, Sankichi went up to the second floor and stood at the north window. He could see the sky over Toyose's house through the welter of roofs with their laundry platforms and chimneys. Smoke and dust fouled the spring air. As he looked, his thoughts turned to Shota.

Oyuki came up the steps and told him Toyose said before leaving that if Shota stayed even a week in one place, there was always some kind of affair, that he had even tried to make love to Oshun. "As she was leaving, she said she was very envious of me."

"But you say you're unhappy with your life," Sankichi said reproachfully.

"No, no, I'm not unhappy!" she said emphatically. He gazed at her for some time.

"We have nothing Toyose should be envious of. The only thing we have is our health," he said, turning back to his work.

That night they talked about Shota and Toyose until late. When the children fell sound asleep, Oyuki turned to Sankichi in an unusually earnest tone. "Sankichi, believe me, please . . . . You do believe me don't you?" she sobbed, burying her face in her husband's arms.

Sankichi wanted to say reassuringly, "What are you talking about? There's no question about our faith in each other now, is there?" But he remained silent, accepting his wife's tears with muted joy and sorrow.

The day before Toyose's scheduled departure for Nagoya, several items were sent over from her home. Among them were braizers, paintings, and kitchenware. There was also a portable altar Shota designed; Oshun had painted autumn leaves on the two small sliding doors for him.

Toyose herself came to say goodbye. She looked over the familiar pieces of furniture that she had enjoyed using. The brief but happy chapter of her life by the Sumida River was now over.

"On my way over, I stopped to see some acquaintances, and they said I always stop only to say goodbye." She seemed to want to pour out her feelings about her insecure, unsettled life to Sankichi and O-yuki.

"You know, Toyose, Naoki's grandmother has an opinion about your move," Sankichi said. The seventy-year old woman had prophesied that Shota, alone, would live three more years, but only one if Toyose stayed with him. But Toyose shook her head sadly and said that her husband's illness was much more serious than people thought.

Oyuki was sorry to see her go. She urged her at least to stay overnight and to leave for Nagoya from their house. But Toyose answered she promised her maid that they would stay over at an inn so that they could leave in the morning from an auspicious direction. They would share the expenses and enjoy the last night together as mistress and servant. But she was grateful for Oyuki's offer. Much of the furniture had been sold at shamefully low prices, and she was unable to pay all that she owed the maid. She had promised to send the balance to her from Nagoya.

"I gave her all the rest of my kitchenware. It would have gone for practically nothing anyway," she added.

Oyuki brought the tea traditionally served on leave-taking. Toyose told them that she stopped at Naoki's house to say goodbye. They talked about their mutal acquaintances. Sankichi remembered Oharu among the many girls Shota had known when he was young.

"You remember her, Uncle Sankichi! That was before I married into the Hashimotos, wasn't it? She has many children now."

"By the way," he laughed, "there's something that might displease you, Toyose. You know Shota's landlady in Nagoya. You used to admire her and say she was very capable. Well, she's taking good care of Shota, clothing him with a quilted bathrobe and other things. Morihiko told me."

"I'm not jealous of an old woman like her," she laughed, treating the episode as a joke. But as she was about to leave, she asked, "Uncle Sankichi, may I tell Shota . . . what you've just told me?"

The couple could not help laughing. Toyose said that when she reached Nagoya, she planned to find a sunny rooming house and move Shota. She seemed much happier as she left.

At the end of May, Sankichi received word that Shota went into a hospital in Nagoya, and shortly afterward came a telegram from the hospital: "Must see you. Come immediately."

He couldn't believe that Shota's condition had taken such a sudden turn for the worse. He was deep in the midst of work he could not interrupt. Also it was not clear about Shota's condition. He sent a telegram to Morihiko asking about the patient. The answer came that he should somehow arrange to come to Nagoya. Sankichi called Oyuki and told her he decided to drop everything and go.

He had hundreds of errands on the eve of his journey, but he wanted at least to let Kokin know about Shota's illness. When he had his friend telephone Mukōjima to ask if there was any message she might like to send, he learned that both Kokin and her mother were sick in bed.

He caught the train for Nagoya and reached Morihiko's inn toward evening.

The brothers stood at a window that let in drafts of warm air and discussed Shota's condition. Sankichi learned that Otane was at the hospital and was surprisingly calm. Morihiko reported, as if putting away one task after another, that Kosaku had written, requesting that, should anything happen while he was away on a sales trip, the body be cremated in Nagoya and the ashes sent home.

"That's certainly catching the ball before it bounces. But the letter's well written," he said, laughing loudly, and showed the letter to Sankichi.

The next morning Morihiko took Sankichi to the hospital. A placard bearing Shota's name was on the door of a second-floor room on a long corridor. It was actually a suite of two rooms: the one with a window was for the patient; the other, closer to the entrance, was for the family. Otane and Toyose were already there.

Shota was sleeping, his dark, sallow face buried in the sheets. But he soon opened his large eyes and looked at Sankichi in surprise.

"Oh, you're awake." Otane went to his pillow and spoke in a quiet, mothering tone. "I'm glad you had some sleep. Uncle Sankichi is here."

Shota half rose, attempted to bow to his uncles, and then fell back on his pillow. He waved an emaciated hand at Toyose and pointed to his mouth. Toyose brought him some liquid medicine to help moisten his parched throat.

"I wanted to see you just once more. The telegram might have sounded exaggerated, but I wanted to impose on you to come." He told Toyose to bring chairs for his uncles.

Toyose placed them beside the bed, and Morihiko and Sankichi sat down. Otane tried to make Shota rest as much as possible by speaking for him.

"He's been waiting and waiting for you since yesterday. He has a friend in Nagoya who paints in oils. He says that all he wants is to look at his friend's paintings in this room and to see his Uncle Sankichi once more. We talked to the friend, and he said nothing could be easier; he would bring different ones from time to time so that Shota won't get tired of looking at the same painting. He was very kind and hung that picture over there." She pointed to a small framed landscape on the wall that Shota could see from the bed.

Morihiko gave some advice to the two women on caring for the sick and went back to his inn. Sankichi stayed at Shota's side until afternoon. From time to time Shota dozed off and Sankichi went out in the corridor and had a cigarette. There, as white-uniformed nurses constantly passed by, he watched the summer sky through the glass doors.

Morihiko worried about those who were attending Shota. The inn was quite empty now that the fair was over, and the rooms were thrown wide open for a thorough airing. Sankichi and Otane came from the hopsital.

"I hear you offered to treat me to a bath, so I came just for a short visit," Otane said to Morihiko.

"I know you're all taken up with looking after the patient, but you mustn't neglect your own health, either of you. Take a bath and rest awhile. Since Sankichi's here tonight, I'll treat you both to dinner."

He called for the maid and looked back at his brother. "What do you want, Sankichi? How about some chicken?"

After their bath, the brothers joined their sister in the room for tea.

"This time you get a very high mark," Morihiko said to Otane. "I'm impressed."

Sankichi agreed that Otane was a completely different woman from the one he had known in the Hashimoto house some time ago. In her old age, in which everyone feared that she might go insane, to see such calmness was a completely pleasant surprise for the brothers.

They discussed the latest news from their other brothers. Otane told them about Minoru's letter that said that he finally won the confidence of others and was now able to send monthly living expenses for his wife in Tokyo.

"I wanted to show you the letter, Sankichi, but I forgot all about it when I left home," she said.

They talked about Sozo too. "A man manages to live somehow when he gives up everything. He goes on eating." Morihiko laughed as he made a typical remark for him.

The maid brought in the chicken on a large platter. They sat in front of the hot iron pan sizzling with hot fat and food over red charcoal embers. When they took up their chopsticks and began eating, it was still light outside.

"The dinner's too hot for this weather, but help yourselves," Morihiko said, tucking up his sleeves.

The chicken sizzled, and the scallions cooked soft in a few minutes. As they ate, Otane and Sankichi blew on the food to cool it. They relished the meal despite their perspiration.

Morihiko opened his kimono at the neck and wiped away the sweat on his chest. "I should have invited Toyose too."

"She's busy taking care of her patient. I'll change places and send her over. Let her have a bath," Otane replied quietly.

She soon left, concerned about Shota, and Toyose arrived just as the lights came on. She appeared sad, preoccupied probably with thoughts about her future. Late that night her older brother and Kosaku arrived at the inn from their home villages. The following morning, the Koizumi brothers and the rest assembled in the room to make plans for after Shota's death.

"Ah, you can't go home without seeing the innkeeper's daughter dance," Morihiko said hospitably. He called the little girl and asked her to perform for the guests; the grandmother accompanied her on the samisen.

Meanwhile, Shota grew steadily worse. In the afternoon, when the family gathered at the hospital, he had Toyose wash his arms and legs. His thighs were skin and bone. He was constantly nauseated and could keep nothing in his stomach. He was unusually excited and asked Toyose's brother and Sankichi to come to his side, and begged them in front of his mother and wife to take care of the family after his death. He said that some people might appreciate his efforts on his family's behalf after his death. He told Toyose he was sorry that he could not give her any happiness, but he asked her to remain and help her mother-in-law and Kosaku. At times his tone grew uncontrollably emotional, sounding almost theatrical. Toyose covered her face with her hands as she listened. From time to time, she moistened his lips with the liquid medicine.

"How do you feel, Shota?" Sankichi asked, standing by his nephew's bed. It was the third morning for him in Nagoya.

"I don't feel anything now." The sick man rested his hands on the white coverlet and looked up at Sankichi with his huge eyes. He seemed to realize how little time was left to him. That day he was calm, and his tone was the same as usual. "Sometimes I feel how frail and fragile the human being is."

The summer light brightened up the oil painting on the wall. A faint breeze came through the window, and summer clouds could be seen in the distance. Sankichi walked over, looked down on the quiet garden, and then returned to the sickbed.

"Shota, shall I write about you? I feel like writing about your life."

"Go ahead. By all means, please write, whether it's about the good or the bad," he answered emphatically, with a faint smile on his lips.

It was a rare opportunity for Sankichi to be alone with Shota.

Toyose was out laundering, and Kosaku was away. As Sankichi began to tell about the message from Mukōjima and the phone call, Otane came in from the corridor.

"Would you leave us alone for just a minute? I've something to tell Shota," Sankichi said. Otane went out grinning.

"I haven't heard a word from her for quite awhile," Shota replied when his uncle had told him of Kokin's illness. "We kept in touch until last spring, then she stopped writing."

"Toyose sent us three paintings from your house in Komagata. When I get home, I'll send one of them to her as a memento."

"Thank you, that will be nice."

Sankichi casually strolled out to the corridor and saw Toyose and Kosaku. He told them how delighted he was with Otane's condition.

"Mother is highly keyed up. I'm the one who gets encouraged by her," Toyose said. "Actually, she's completely broken up inside."

Kosaku led Sankichi to the stair landing where no one would hear him.

"Should we send word to Manchuria and let father know?" he asked.

"When the time comes, we'll send the news."

"All right; I thought so too."

They talked leaning against the balustrade. Kosaku said he was at a loss over Toyose's future. She was taking excellent care of Shota but seemed to have no intention of remaining in the Hashimoto family afterward.

Sankichi could not stay any longer in Nagoya, but he remained at Shota's side until afternoon. Shota's condition did not yet seem critical. So, he decided to leave for Tokyo, leaving Shota to the care of the rest of the family.

Sankichi made one last visit before leaving. "Shota, I must go now," he said, holding out a moist hand.

The uncle and the nephew clasped each other's hand for a long time. When Sankichi was ready to leave, Shota hurriedly looked for his hand once again and hung on tightly. "I'll keep my courage up, and I will see you once again," he said bravely as the tears gushed out and flowed down his dark cheeks.

"Of course you will," Otane said encouragingly, but she covered her face with both hands. Kosaku was in the next room, his head bent low.

A sterilizing lavatory was located at the end of the hall, and there Sankichi scrubbed his hands and took leave of his sister, while Shota tried to catch a last glimpse of him from his bed. Toyose was not in the room at the moment. Kosaku walked him to the hospital gate, and when he was alone, Sankichi could no longer hold his tears. He sobbed loudly.

"Oh, no, Shota has more than ten or twenty days yet. He knows it himself, and he's smart enough not to leave a will." Morihiko was talking to the visitors at the inn.

That night Sankichi took the train from Nagoya. The windows faced the dark night, and from across the distant sky, lightning flashed intermittently in the glass panes.

He returned home with the voice of his nephew still in his ears calling to him as they parted. It was already the beginning of June. Oyuki and Sankichi's nieces gathered to hear the news from Nagoya.

On the evening of the ninth, a telegram arrived announcing Shota's death. It also said that his body would be cremated that night. Sankichi handed the wire to his wife, and they looked at each other.

"I'm thirty-three this year, an unlucky age. I may well follow Shota when this baby is born," Oyuki said forlornly as she took out a snapshot of her dead nephew from a box in the upstairs cupboard. The photograph was from the Kabuto-chō days, showing his profile. She placed it in front of the name tablets of her three daughters and lit a candle on the altar.

"It feels lonely here somehow," Sankichi said, glancing around. The memory of Shota and Toyose coming to talk to him by the charcoal brazier suddenly seemed a long time ago. Over the past several years, young couples were formed and they came to visit, including Oshun and Oai with their husbands. Ofuku arrived with Tsutomu and their children to take up residence in Tokyo.

The night was hot and humid, without a breath of air. The heat was hard for Oyuki, who was near the end of her seventh pregnancy. With the sultriness and his steaming body, Sankichi could not sleep either, and the couple lay awake beside their three boys, discussing

Shota. They talked about Tsutomu, Ofuku, and about their own youth.

"Sometimes I feel as though I were three individuals," said Oyuki as she lay in the bed. "One was when I was very small, the other during my school days, and the third after I married you. Each one of me is a very clear-cut, isolated person. I was such a crybaby as a child." She spoke with deep feelings.

They dozed off for a while, only to waken again.

"I wonder what time it is, Oyuki. Isn't the sun coming up? They'll be cremating Shota now," Sankichi said as he opened one of the storm doors. He thought of Shota's body transported from the hospital to the crematorium before daybreak.

Outside it was still dark.